DESTINY'S STAR

The Road of the Faithful (Series)

RITA GIORDANO

To order additional copies of this book, contact:
Bookwhip
1-855-339-3589
https://www.bookwhip.com

Acknowledgments

I must thank my husband, who worked helping me. And thank you to all my students who over the years have inspired me to write this book.

DISCLAIMER

I must clarify for the sake of the reader. While the stories are taken from the Bible, and there are many direct quotes from the Scriptures, as a storyteller I have taken creative license in an effort to bring these stories to life. The detailed explanations of events as they took place include my opinion of the thoughts and emotions of the individuals involved. This book is a work of fiction, based on true Biblical events, and is in no way meant to add to or replace the Holy Scriptures. I pray they will speak to your heart and create in you a deeper love for the beautiful Word of God. May the Lord bless you in your walk with Him.

CONTENTS

PREFACE

The Bible speaks of the land of Canaan. This is a place of history, war, peace, and destiny—the land of Christ. This is where it all happens. God Himself chose and brought up a nation of people to take dominion over this land. He fought for them, and through their faith in Him, they became the nation of Israel.

This is the story of Abraham, then known as Abram, and the generations who followed him. The people, chosen of God, became a blessed nation. The Word of the Lord to Abraham was, "And I will make of thee a great nation, and I will bless thee, and make thy name great; and thou shalt be a blessing: And I will bless them that bless thee, and curse him that curseth thee: and in thee shall all families of the earth be blessed" (Gen. 12:2–3, KJV). And so we have been. The Hebrew people carried the Word of God to us. They have given us the Messiah, Jesus. We owe them our love and respect.

Abraham, the father of many nations, walked out of his tent and looked toward the heavens. In that moment of time, God the Father spoke to him. God told him if he could count the stars in the sky, then he would be able to count his descendants.

ABRAHAM, THE FATHER OF MANY NATIONS

By faith Abraham, when he was called to go out into a place which he should after receive for an inheritance, obeyed; and he went out, not knowing whither he went. (Heb. 11:8, KJV)

"Abraham." His name was spoken on the wings of eternity. Its sound, something like a whisper, was carried through the starlit night air. The sand stirred and whirled around him. The man listened, caught by the overwhelming realization that God Himself was beckoning to him. "You shall be the father of many."

Who has not heard the name of Abraham? The Bible refers to him as a friend of God, and a friend he was. The Lord actually revealed to him many specific events that would happen. His story, found in the book of Genesis, is the beginning of the nation of Israel and the beginning of the Christian faith. The Bible first tells us about him before he was Abraham. Then he was called Abram.

> Now the LORD had said unto Abram, Get thee out of thy country, and from thy kindred, and from thy father's house, unto a land that I will shew thee: And I will make of thee a great nation, and I will bless thee, and make thy name great; and thou shalt be a blessing: And I will bless them that bless thee, and curse him that curseth thee: and in thee shall all families of the earth be blessed. So Abram departed, as the Lord had spoken unto him; and Lot went with him: and Abram was seventy and five years old when he departed out of Haran. And Abram took Sarai his wife, and Lot his brother's son, and all their substance that they had gathered, and the souls that they had gotten in Haran; and they went forth to go into the land of Canaan; and into the land of Canaan they came. And Abram passed through the land unto the place of Sichem, unto the plain of Moreh. And the Canaanite was then in the land. And the Lord appeared unto Abram, and said, Unto thy seed will I give this land: and there builded he an altar unto the Lord, who appeared unto him. (Gen. 12:1–7, KJV)

Obediently Abram followed the Lord. He moved his little caravan of people and flocks from place to place. The Lord personally escorted him through the land of Canaan. God promised, "This land will be the inheritance of your descendants."

A drought took its toll. Abram made a regretful mistake. He moved his caravan to Egypt. Now he panicked; Pharaoh had taken his wife! He paced the floor of his tent. "I have to get her back," he said to his servant, Eliezer of Damascus, and his nephew, Lot. "I must speak to Pharaoh myself. There must be a way."

"You can't, Uncle! Sarai would not want you to place yourself or any of us in danger. What if he refuses to return her? He could kill all of us in a matter of minutes. We can't fight him. We are no match for the king of Egypt's military force. Sarai knows you would be risking us all. She understands what is at stake."

Abram looked at his friend and trusted servant. Eliezer held Abram's gaze. His eyes were fixed on his master as he calmly said, "Lot is right, Master. If you expose yourself, you may even place the mistress in danger. Your death would not help her. You must trust the Lord! He will deliver her."

Abram looked out into the distance; he could see the palace. It could easily be seen for miles. It had been a miserable year. Famine had spread throughout the land of Canaan. They journeyed into Egypt, hoping to find food and water for themselves and their flocks. Abram considered their precarious situation.

That day Sarai was forced into Pharaoh's harem by Pharaoh's servants. She was breathtakingly beautiful. Everywhere they traveled, her beauty was the main topic of conversation. Abram had more than once fought for his wife. It was an ongoing problem throughout their marriage. The moment a man of power saw her, Abram was in trouble. He was not proud of it; but he often passed her off as his sister. His plan should have worked. Usually the admirer would just pursue her. Whoever desired her would begin giving gifts to Abram, trying to woo the affections of Sarai as well as the favor of her "brother." Abram found that trick to work without a snag. It should have worked this time; but this time was different.

Pharaoh looked up as his enthusiastic, overzealous servant came bowing, "Please, Pharaoh, I must speak with you." He started again. "Sire, she has just crossed our borders." His hands were raised in excitement, a habit this particular servant had whenever speaking. His wide frame was covered by an ornately jeweled robe of white and gold that billowed around him as he rushed to deliver his message. "She is a dream beyond imagination, a beauty to which there is no parallel! Her eyes are green as emeralds. Her skin is soft as silk. Surely she will bring Pharaoh much pleasure."

The servant watched Pharaoh with hawkeyed perception. He hoped his discovery of such a ravishing beauty would serve to butter up his master. His eyes gleamed with self-satisfaction. Pharaoh listened with interest as his servant began to wax poetic, carrying on about the wave of her brow when he inspected her. "And spirit, sire, she is as spirited as an untamed stallion." The man finally ended his rather lengthy dialogue. At that moment, the princes of Pharaoh who had been there to greet Abram arrived. "Sire, the woman is beyond description." They each began to agree with the servant. "She is a rare beauty indeed!"

Pharaoh's brow shifted up as he added, "And? Did you detain her?"

"Yes, sire, she and her brother have been detained. We have them in the outer court. Would you like to interview them personally?"

Pharaoh shrugged. He had a full day, and there simply wasn't time to speak to this beauty now. "Speak to her brother, uh, what is his name?" He stopped, waiting for the answer.

"Abram, sire. He is a very well-to-do person. He has come here seeking refuge from the famine in Canaan. He has many servants and cattle."

"I see. Tell this man Abram his sister has been chosen to be blessed by the company of Pharaoh. Apologize for my absence, and escort her to her personal chambers. Be sure and reward this man on my behalf. I will speak to the woman later."

Abram sorrowed as he remembered that Pharaoh wasted no time. The moment he was told of her beauty, Pharaoh reached out and took her.

Sarai spoke as though she was used to being courted by kings. "Pharaoh, you do me great honor. However, I would like to return to my brother. He will be concerned for my safety." She sat regally, her head held high. Her long dark hair was looped, twisted, and then woven with jewels and placed high on her head. Her deep green eyes stared serenely into the dark eyes of Pharaoh. She was fearless. Pharaoh could not guess her age. Her flawless skin looked young and supple, but something in her eyes showed wisdom that was acquired over time.

The king leered at Sarai. "But you are here now, Sarai. You are my guest. I have already given Abram many gifts because of you. My servants have presented him with gold, delicacies from my own table, and camels. Is there anything you desire? You only have to ask."

She looked over at the king. This was not the first time she had been forced to deal with an overly exuberant suitor. She found it all quite annoying. She studied the deepset eyes of her captor. He reached over, running a lecherous finger down her arm. She shifted her weight away from him. He leaned a little closer.

She smiled condescendingly. "Your kindness is overwhelming, sire; but as you can imagine, I am very tired from all the day's events."

Pharaoh moved away, disappointed. "Of course."

Sarai stood, tipped her head gracefully, and followed a servant to her private quarters in the palace. Pharaoh was not used to being told no. He found the idea of pursuing Sarai invigorating. He was completely amused by the way she tilted her head as though he were no more than a flea. She was fascinating. Sarai was a woman worth courting. He watched her leave, holding her head high as though she were a queen. His servants had not exaggerated; she was the most beautiful woman he had ever seen.

Sarai stepped out of the door of her suite. The desert lay beautiful and dangerously barren before her. She was trapped in the palace. The veranda was too high for her to escape. Even if she could, she knew they would just look for her at the camp. That would endanger Abram. She could not take that chance. She would just have to outwit the old windbag. She looked off in the direction of the camp. She missed her husband. She spoke into the darkness. "Oh God, Abram must be frantic. Keep him from trying to rescue me. Please remind him You are able to deliver me. I know that in your time, You will. God, I trust You."

Peace filled the air. The night breeze lifted the dark silk of her long hair as she looked out into the starfilled sky. She unconsciously rubbed her shoulders as the cool air touched her beautiful, soft skin. Finally, the cold forced her to go inside.

She studied the oversized bed as though it were a beautiful trap. After inspecting it, she crawled in. She lay down and prayed through the night. She was comforted by the presence of God. She could not see Him, but she knew beyond a doubt He was there. The sun was beginning to rise. She could see its light filtering through the many windows of her lavishly decorated cage. Finally exhausted, she fell asleep comforted by her Creator.

Abram had also been praying. The Lord had given him peace. He would trust the Lord. Sarai would not be a captive for long.

It was almost noon. The gifts had been coming for hours. He was still receiving guests, who were sent to extend the pharaoh's respect. Abram grew weary. He could barely contain his anger. This whole situation was unnerving.

Again, he asked, "When will my sister be returned to us? She is greatly missed." The servant was quite perplexed as he once more tried to explain that Sarai was not coming back.

Abram was furious. "You tell Pharaoh to return my sister at once!" he said through clenched teeth.

Pharaoh's servant squirmed. Finally, pressured by Abram, he agreed to mention it to the king.

Days went by. Sarai had no choice but to indulge in the many beauty treatments. She was given a routine of oils and herbs to soften her skin. At the moment, she sat comfortably in a bath of oils. Her hair was tied up off her face and neck. It had also been treated with some concoction. She sank down, allowing the warm water to soothe her.

After this she would be given her daily rubdown, which she had decided was heavenly. It wasn't so bad being here in the palace. It would take months before she would be expected to actually entertain Pharaoh. She leaned back. The young servant girl who had been heating the water for her placed a warm compress over her brow. No, in reality there were worse things than being an unwilling guest of Pharaoh. She ran a hand over her freshly pampered skin. It was soft. Every imperfection had been found and removed by the resident aesthetician.

She refused to wear the hot wig, opting instead for her real hair to be twisted into many tiny braids. They were bundled together and held captive by ropes of gold. When she was not being pampered, she wore the makeup of the land. The eyeliner accented her green eyes to perfection.

The servant girl motioned for her to step out of the bath. She led her to a table where she was given her daily massage of oils that smelled of perfume. Her body, head to toe, was taking on this beautiful fragrance. She had never in all her life smelled so delicious. After her rubdown, she was expected to sit and rest while the oils soaked into her skin. The young servant girls wrapped her in a soft white fabric that was loose fitting and cool. While she waited for the oil to work its magic, she was served fresh fruit with this delightfully refreshing tea. Yes, it was true; there really were worse things than being an unwilling guest of Pharaoh.

CREATOR

> In the beginning God created the heaven and the
> earth. (Gen. 1:1, KJV)

Sarai had been summoned to sit with the king several times. She often entertained the ladies of the harem with her storytelling. They had in turn reported her to the pharaoh. He was intrigued and wanted her to share some of her stories with him. He often took advantage of the opportunity to impress her. She was very good at avoiding his advances. She continued to remind him that she wanted to return to her brother's camp. He was indulgent toward her. Once again she joined him.

"Sire." Sarai spoke with passion. "The God I serve cannot be contained in the shape of an animal or dreamed up by the imagination of man. He is omnipresent."

Pharaoh looked confused. "But how is it possible for Him to be present everywhere? That doesn't make sense."

"He is omnipotent," Sarai explained. "He is almighty and infinite in power. There is none like him in all the earth! He knows all things. Before any of these creatures were"—she waved a beautiful hand around the room, referring to the many images before her—"He was! He has created all things. He cannot be understood by the intellect of mere man. He is God of all, and His ways far surpass the hearts and minds of man."

An indulgent smile tugged at the corners of Pharaoh's mouth. "You realize, Sarai, I am no ordinary man. In fact, I am known as god on earth by my people." She was not impressed. He was finding Sarai to be exhausting. She had been blathering on for hours. His day of courting was going up in smoke as she went on and on about this God of hers. She was intelligent and more confrontational than he was used to in his women. She challenged everything he said, insisting on answers, as though he could explain why he believed his gods were so powerful. He groaned as he realized she was starting to explain the beginning of creation.

> In the beginning God created the heaven and the earth. And the earth was without form, and void; and darkness was upon the face of the deep. And the Spirit of God moved upon the face of the waters. And God said, Let there be light: and there was light. And God saw the light, that it was good: and God divided the light from the darkness. And God called the light Day, and the darkness he called Night. And the evening and the morning were the first day. (Gen. 1:1–5, KJV)

Her efforts were not in vain. She watched as her audience's attention turned from boredom to intrigue. She noted Pharaoh leaned forward as she quoted Scripture. She wanted to speak to all who were listening. Perhaps this was why she was here.

Pharaoh became engrossed as she spoke with passion. His servants listened, amazed that Pharaoh would allow a woman so much freedom. She rose to her feet. Her long hair now free of braids dropped thick down her back. She stepped to the middle of the room. Her eyes blazed with emotion as she continued to speak, acting out each scene for her audience. "God, the great eternal one, was lonely. He looked out over the earth and started to speak. His word was life. He spoke to the solar system, and it obeyed. He moved across the waters, looked up toward the heavens, and with a wave of His massive hand, said, 'Separate!' And God divided the waters from the sky. And God smiled. He looked at the body of blue above Him. He saw past the sky through the atmosphere, past the stratosphere, into the galaxies He had created and the ones He would create. His smile widened. Pleased, He cried out, 'This is good!' So looking up at the vast creation of the universe, He named it *heaven*. That was the second day."

"Surely, you don't believe one being created all this!" Pharaoh looked around the great room, noticing his images of the sun, moon, stars, and his god who ruled the waters.

Sarai smiled kindly. "Yes, sire, I do." She followed his eyes to the image of the god that ruled the water and said, "The next day my God spoke and said, 'All the waters come together. I want to see dry land.' The waters obeyed His word and rolled and moved and gathered together, forming oceans, lakes, rivers above ground and underground."

"You actually believe He created the Nile?" Pharaoh was speechless.

Her voice rang out gentle but firm. "The dry ground He named earth, and the bodies of water he called seas. Then God commanded the land to produce grass, herbs, and fruit with their seeds. And God liked it, and He pronounced it good. That was the third day."

She walked over and stroked his images of the stars, moon, and sun, studying them as one might study a work of art. Then she started to speak again. Pharaoh strained to listen. Her voice was soft; it was as if she were telling the story to herself. Suddenly, with enthusiasm, she walked toward Pharaoh, saying, "And God said, 'I want lights to fill the heavens to give light to earth.' He then created two great lights—the sun for the day and the moon for the night. He placed them in their places in heaven." As she spoke, she acted out the scene. Holding her hand as if it held a globe, she placed the sun in the sky. Then she reached out, picking up an imaginary moon and set it across from the sun. With one sweeping motion of her hand, she scattered the stars throughout the heavens. She looked into the eyes of Pharaoh. "That was the fourth day."

She moved back to the middle of the great hall, shouting, "Then God commanded, 'Waters bring forth in abundance life! Creatures that move come forth. Birds fly, soar into the sky and live. Whales come forth and inhabit the seas.' The great God saw that it was good. He commanded his creation to be fruitful and fill the waters and the sky with life. He blessed them, saying, 'Multiply and bring forth life!'" She stood in the middle of the hall with her hands stretched toward the sky. She stopped, lowered her arms, looked at her audience and said, "That, my friends, was the fifth day."

"Then God spoke to the earth and blessed it, saying, 'Let living creatures fill the earth: cattle, things that creep and great beasts.' And He smiled, and again He said, 'This is good.'"

She folded one arm across her middle, resting her elbow on it. Then she cupped her chin in her hand as if to ponder something and said, "God thought for a moment. He was still lonely. Then he said, 'Let us make man. He will look like us and have authority over the fish, over the birds of the sky, over the cattle and over creeping things that creep about the earth.'" Sarai knelt on the floor. "God took clay mixed with water and fashioned a man in his image. Then He"—she knelt close to her imaginary man and blew—"breathed into his nostrils God's life-giving breath. And man was created to be a living soul."

"Your God created man? If this is true, then why have I never heard of him?"

"Oh, Pharaoh, the truth is very sad. The man did evil. He was driven away from the presence of God." Her joyous demeanor of only a moment ago became serious, even sorrowful.

"Tell me, Sarai, what happened?" Pharaoh asked.

"At first things were good. God planted a beautiful garden." She extended her hand, pointing toward the water. "Three magnificent rivers ran through it—Pison, Gihon, and Euphrates. He brought the man into the garden and let him tend to it. But God told the man, 'Adam, you can eat of every plant that pleases you, only do not eat of the tree of understanding good and evil. The day you eat of that tree you will die.'"

"God walked every evening in the garden and talked to Adam. He brought the animals to Adam and let him name them. But Adam grew lonely. He needed a wife. So God caused him to fall asleep. God removed a rib from his side and used it to create woman. When Adam awoke, God presented her to the man. He was thrilled. He said, 'She has come from me. She is of my bone and flesh.' Adam named her Eve. God married them. Then He blessed them and said, 'Fill the earth.' They were happy."

"Then evil entered God's garden. The serpent spoke to Eve. He said, 'Did God really say not to eat this fruit?'"

"Eve answered, 'Yes, God has told us that the day we eat from this tree we will die.'"

"The serpent lied. He told her, 'You won't die. God knows that at the time you eat this fruit you will be as gods and you will know good from evil, right from wrong.' He appealed to the desire of every woman to be adored. That desire caused her downfall."

"She may have spoken only once to the serpent. He may have talked to her many times, we don't know, but she disobeyed God and ate from that tree. Then she gave some of the fruit to her husband. Adam and Eve understood what was right and what was wrong. They were no longer as innocent children. Their eyes were opened. The serpent had done his evil job."

"Then God returned to walk in His garden and talk to them as before. But they hid from Him. They knew they were uncovered, and they were ashamed. They tried to cover themselves. They made clothes from leaves. The voice of the Lord rang through the garden: 'Adam, Eve, where are you?'"

"Ashamed and fearful, Adam said, 'We are here. We hid because we are uncovered and ashamed.'"

"God said, 'How do you know you are uncovered? Did you eat fruit from the tree of understanding good and evil?'"

Sarai raised her arm. Extending her finger, she pointed at an imaginary person. "Adam said, 'This woman you gave me, she gave the fruit to me, and I ate.'"

"Eve rushed to explain what had happened. 'It was the serpent. He tricked me, and I ate.'"

"The serpent sank low to the ground. He ducked his head as he looked for a place to hide. He tried not to be seen."

"God was not happy. He told the man, 'Now the ground is cursed because of you. You will work, but it will not produce. Thorns and weeds will fill it. Only by sweat and hard labor will it grow food.' To Eve He said, 'You will have trouble in childbirth. Your desire will be toward your husband, but he will rule over you.' Then to the serpent He said, 'You will crawl across the ground on your belly. You will eat dust from now on.' The serpent shrank to the earth. 'I will bring dissention between you and the woman's seed. He will crush your head. You will strike his heel.'"

"Then God chased them from the garden. He placed angels to guard it. Man could never enter it again. They were no longer able to walk and talk with God. A great gulf of sin separates man from His presence. Only by His mercy can we ever be saved. That is why man started sacrificing perfect little animals. They are a reminder to God that one day man will be redeemed by God's sacrifice."

Pharaoh sighed deeply. He leaned back against his ornately decorated throne. A look of sorrow covered his face. She watched as he absorbed the news. A moment later, he leaned forward. His eyes locked on hers. "So what happened then? What happened when they left the garden?"

She shook her head sadly. "They had two sons. The first was Cain. The second was Abel. Cain was a farmer. Abel was a shepherd. At the appropriate time, they brought their sacrifices to God. Cain's gift was not good. He offered God his leftovers. But Abel's gift was wonderful. He offered the best he had from his flock. The Lord blessed Abel and honored his gift. But Cain's offering God did not honor. Cain became jealous of Abel. God spoke to him. 'Why are you upset? If you change and give a better gift, I will bless you and show you honor.' But Cain grew angrier daily. One day he rose up in anger and violently killed Abel."

"Then God said to him, 'Where is Abel?'"

"Cain pretended he had done nothing. 'How should I know? Do I take care of my brother?'"

"God said, 'What have you done? Don't you know that your brother's blood calls out to me from the ground? You are cursed. The earth will not produce crops for you. You are a fugitive. You will wander the earth.'"

"Cain's heart broke. He said, 'But God that is too much. I won't survive. If someone finds me, they will kill me. This punishment is too great to bear.'"

"God answered him, 'I will mark you. When people see your mark, they will know if they harm you I will punish them.' Then he left the presence of the Lord." Pharaoh sat stone-cold.

She continued, "God gave Adam and Eve another son to soothe their pain over Abel. His name was Seth. They had many children. Those children grew up, and then they had children. But man became more evil. One man whose name was Enoch pleased God. He walked with God. One day God took him."

"Mankind grew wicked. They did not think of God. They forgot why He had created them. God looked on man and became very sad. You see, God is holy. He is not like us. He does not look at evil. And men were very evil. God was sorry He had created man. So He purposed in His heart to destroy man from the face of the earth."

"But there was a man called Noah. He was kind. He loved God, and his ways pleased God. So the Lord spoke to him and told him, 'Noah, I am going to destroy man from the face of the earth, but you have found favor in my sight. Build a large ark of gopher wood. You will pitch the inside and the outside of it. When the time comes, I will flood the entire world.'"

"Noah began to work on the ark. Until the time of the flood, the earth had no rain. It was watered by a mist from the ground. The people around him laughed at him. He tried to explain, 'God is going to flood the earth. Join with me and save yourselves.' But the people did not believe. Only his wife, their three sons, and their wives believed."

"When Noah was finished with the ark, God commanded the animals to go into the ark for safety. They entered it in pairs, male and female. Noah and his family also went in. Then God shut the door to the ark and locked it."

"The flood was devastating. Noah and his family could hear the screams of the foolish people who had refused to listen. But they could not help them. The door to the ark was shut tight."

"All the fountains of the deep gushed forth. The heavens opened up and released the floodgates. God was through with the wickedness of man. The rain poured out of heaven forty days and forty nights. The mountains of the earth were covered. The ark rocked back and forth. Noah and his family prayed and grieved over the loss of life. Then God sent a great wind. He stopped the rain, and the ark rested on the mountain of Ararat."

"When the rain stopped, Noah sent a raven to seek out land. She flew all around. Then he sent a dove, but alas, she returned exhausted. There was nowhere for her to rest. So he waited then sent her out again. The second time she returned with an olive twig. When he sent her out the third time, she did not return. After many days, the land dried up, and the family of Noah left the ark. Noah and his three sons are the fathers of all the nations of the earth. At that time, God promised them He would never flood the earth again. Then God placed a rainbow in the sky to remind them of His promise."

Pharaoh listened as she spoke all the things in her heart. She told him of her God who was so vast He could only be described as "I am." Every day she told him of her God and of the faith He required from those who served Him. He was not certain when it happened; but one day, Pharaoh realized that he had begun to look forward to their visits, as much for her stories as seeing her. He had everything his heart could desire. But not one moment of his life had he lived with the unbridled joy of this woman as she spoke of her awesome God. She was amazing in every way. But as Sarai remained in the palace of Pharaoh, great plagues came upon Pharaoh and his household.

"Pharaoh," a voice spoke from out of the night. "You and your household are as good as dead! Return Sarai to Abram. He is her husband."

"Ahh!" Pharaoh awoke from a terrifying dream. His heart pounded. He was barely able to catch his breath. Sweat poured off his body. He felt as if he were on fire. He cried out into the night, but his servants did not come. He climbed out of bed, his body trembling. His legs felt weak. He could barely drag himself to the door of the veranda. He threw open the door and breathed in the fresh night air. From here he could see the light of Sarai's rooms. She was awake. He managed to call out again. Finally, one of his servants arrived. The man was not his usual steward.

"Where is Omar?" the king bellowed.

"Sire, he has fallen sick. I am afraid he is gravely ill." The servant speaking looked unsteady. His face was flushed. He seemed to barely be standing.

"And you?" the king inquired. "Are you also ill?" "Yes, sire," the young man said.

Worry lines creased the brow of Pharaoh. "Are there any others?"

"Sire, it seems the entire household has been stricken by some mysterious illness. We have sent for the doctors. If I might ask, sire, how are you feeling?" The young man watched the king with great concern.

"I am also ill. This is a plague. Send for Abram, Sarai's brother, immediately."

"Now, sire?" The servant looked confused.

"Of course, now, isn't that what I just said? And get my doctors." "Right away, sire." The young servant bowed and left.

The king slipped back into bed. He was not at all happy with his would-be brother-in-law.

Abram arrived within the hour. The king was barely able to raise himself up long enough to speak to Abram. "What have you done? All my servants and myself, we are all ill because of Sarai. Why didn't you tell me she is your wife?" Pharaoh confronted Abram.

"I was afraid you would kill me and take her."

Pharaoh snarled at Abram. "You were willing to let me take her for my wife? My entire household is sick. If I had touched her, I and all my servants would be dead."

"This way, mistress."

Sarai followed the young woman who had been assigned to care for her. The servant girl nodded at the guard as they walked toward a large door. The young man was all business. Quickly Sarai was escorted into the king's presence.

The king snarled at Abram. "Here is your wife. Now go, leave Egypt! Take everything you have with you. I don't want you here." Abram's heart beat rapidly. He glanced at his wife. If it were possible, Sarai had become even more beautiful in captivity. He didn't care how she was returned to him. He was thrilled to see her. "We'll leave immediately, sire." He smiled as he exited the presence of the king of Egypt. Outside the great hall, he took his wife's hand. They rushed from the palace as quickly as possible. The king looked at the young servant. "Tell the captain of the guard to see to it they leave Egypt. They are to be escorted out of this country tonight."

"Yes, Pharaoh." The young servant now understood. They were sick because of Sarai. He was more than happy to execute his master's instructions.

Back at the camp, the people were already making plans to leave. When Abram heard he was to be ushered into the presence of the king, he instructed them to be ready to leave immediately.

They watched for any sign of Abram. Lot scanned the horizon, pacing the ground, as if that activity would speed Abram and Sarai's safe return.

"They're coming!" was the cry from a lookout. "Both of them are coming." Lot rushed to the front. The caravan had done their best to be prepared for a quick exit. It was packed up and ready to go. Abram smiled at his friends and family. Pleased, he said, "Praise God! He has returned our beautiful Sarai to us!" Cheers rang out as the caravan rejoiced. He quieted the crowd. "And now, my friends, we must leave immediately. It seems that Pharaoh and his household have become mysteriously ill." Again the people shouted.

It was very early morning. The sun was just beginning to rise. The armed guards kept a distance but made sure their presence was known. He called out to his people, and they all began to leave Egypt. The little caravan of wanderers slowly made their way with their flocks, cattle, and all their possessions to the border of this beautiful and mysterious country. The guards did not leave them until they were completely out of Egypt.

Sarai and Abram flirted and played all the way back to Canaan, happy just to be together. They returned to Bethel, where Abram had built an altar. There they settled. Sarai and Abram watched the sunset. The many colors of gold, orange, and red played across the sky. They were so beautiful. It was as though God had painted the colors onto the blue canvas with a swipe of His massive hand. Breathless, she said to him, "We will be happy here."

Abram turned his gaze toward the horizon. "Yes, my love, we will."

Lot Takes Another Direction

And when Abram heard that his brother was
taken captive, he armed his trained servants, born
in his own house, three hundred and eighteen,
and pursued them unto Dan. (Gen. 14:14, KJV)

But happiness is often troubled by the realities of life. Only a short
while later, the peace in the camp was ended. "Your flocks are
eating all the grass!" Abram and Lot's servants accused each other
daily. Suddenly a fight broke out. Hastily they ran to the men
who were fighting. Abram pulled his shepherd off Lot's man. Lot
grabbed his servant, restraining him. This was becoming a daily
event. Abram ordered both of the men to go back to work. There
was not enough grass or water for their flocks. They also shared
the land with the inhabitants of Canaan. They had accumulated
sheep, cattle, and goats. The land was not able to feed all their
animals.

He looked at Lot and then shook his head. "We can't keep
breaking up these fights. We are brothers. Let's not argue with

each other. We should separate. You choose any place you like. I will go in the opposite direction."

Lot gazed out toward the Jordan Valley, near Sodom and Gomorrah. It was lush and green with plenty of water. The valley was like the garden of Eden. He chose to go there. He decided to settle near Sodom. He stayed near the cities of the plain.

> And the LORD said unto Abram, after that Lot was separated from him, Lift up now thine eyes, and look from the place where thou art northward, and southward, and eastward, and westward: For all the land which thou seest, to thee will I give it, and to thy seed for ever. And I will make thy seed as the dust of the earth: so that if a man can number the dust of the earth, then shall thy seed also be numbered. Arise, walk through the land in the length of it and in the breadth of it; for I will give it unto thee. Then Abram removed his tent, and came and dwelt in the plain of Mamre, which is in Hebron, and built there an altar unto the Lord. (Gen. 13:14–18, KJV)

Meanwhile, the king of Sodom and the king of Gomorrah formed an alliance against their enemies with three other kings. They revolted against the king of Babylonia, Chedorlaomer, the king of Elam, and their two allies. Five kings went to battle against four kings. The five had been subject to the king of Elam. The kings of Sodom, Gomorrah, and their allies were determined to get out from under the hand of the king of Elam. The battle was fierce. King Chedorlaomer of Elam and his allies were victorious over the kings of Sodom and Gomorrah and their soldiers. He took as prisoners Lot, along with all of Lot's wealth, as well as many of the people and all the wealth of Sodom and Gomorrah.

One of Lot's servants escaped. He ran to Abram and told him of the trouble. The man arrived exhausted from his ordeal. He fell into the arms of one of Abram's herdsmen. "I must speak to Abram, please, I must…" His words became unintelligible as he passed out.

Abram knelt over Lot's servant as he poured water into his parched mouth. The man was injured, but nothing serious. It seemed he was mostly dehydrated and suffering from exhaustion. Abram's men carried him to the camp.

Frantically Abram asked, "What has happened? Is Lot well? Where is your master?"

The servant labored to speak. "He has been captured. They have all been carried away! Everything is gone. The four kings have taken Sodom and Gomorrah. They raided them and took the wealth of the cities." The servant stopped, trying to catch his breath. An expression of sympathy for Abram crossed his face. "Lot was raided also. Everyone was taken."

His report sent shivers down the spine of Abram. "Is he alive?" The servant nodded. "He was alive when I escaped. I came directly here. We have to help them." The man tried to raise himself, but he couldn't. Exhausted, he fell back, unable to go any further.

Abram squeezed his shoulder. "You rest. You have done your part. We will go after them."

The servant smiled. "Thank you," he whispered as he fell into a deep sleep.

Abram wasted no time. "Call together all my men."

"Yes, sir." His faithful servant gathered everyone—318 men who were born in Abram's house. They prepared for battle. Abram was also joined by his friends and allies Aner, Eshcol, and Mamre.

Abram spoke to his faithful servants and friends. "Lot, his family, the men, women, and children of Sodom and Gomorrah have been captured by an army of four raiding kings. We will pursue them, and with God's help, we will bring back everyone and everything they have taken." The men of his company began to cheer their agreement. Slowly they quieted. Abram added humbly, "I thank you for your help."

Abram's small army rode hard after the army of King Chedorlaomer. They caught up with them late in the day. He made plans to attack that night. He divided his men into several different groups and placed them in strategic locations. The Lord fought for Abram and his men. The army of Chedorlaomer tried to escape, but Abram went after them. He caught up with them and rescued Lot, the other captives, and all the goods the raiding army had taken from Sodom and Gomorrah.

Mystery surrounded a man as He journeyed toward His destination. He had appeared from out of nowhere. He just was. He was Melchizedek the King of Salem, the city of peace. This King was as no other. He did not have a beginning or an end. He was to meet with Abram, the friend of God. He had a divine mission to bless Abram. The wind stirred softly as He walked. His royal robes moved in the breeze. His crown was one of splendor. His staff was in His right hand. The long robes of this mighty king blew in the breeze. Abram watched as the man approached him. He bowed himself to the ground, greeting the Great King, the High Priest of Salem. The divine King smiled at Abram.

> And he blessed him, and said, Blessed be Abram
> of the most high God, possessor of heaven and
> earth: And blessed be the most high God, which
> hath delivered thine enemies into thy hand. And
> he gave him tithes of all. (Gen. 14:19–20, KJV)

Abram shared 10 percent of all he had with the priest. Just as mysteriously as He had appeared, the great King of Salem disappeared. The elements of earth bowed before His almighty power in splendid unison. His robes flowed as he faded from sight (see Heb. 7:1–4).

The king of Sodom wanted to show his appreciation. He turned to Abram and said, "Thank you, my friend. You have returned our family members and friends. We need nothing more. I want to reward you. Please take all the wealth you have brought back as my gift to you."

Abram shook his head. "No. You are very generous, but I have already promised my God, the Most High, Creator of heaven and earth, that I will not take even a strap from someone's shoe. I don't want anyone to say, 'I made Abram rich.' It was my God who protected me, and He is the one who gives me my possessions." Abram looked at his three friends, Aner, Eshcol, and Mamre. "These are my friends. They went with me. Perhaps you could give them each a share."

The king of Sodom smiled. "You are all very brave. My city and I owe you a great debt. I will be happy to reward you."

The trip home was long but happily uneventful. Abram walked through the camp watching the men, who had ridden with him, play and interact with their children.

The Lord spoke to Abram in a vision. "Abram, do not be afraid. I will protect you and cause you to be very rich."

He asked, "Lord, why make me rich? What is the point? There is no one to inherit it. I have no sons. My servant Eliezer, from Damascus, is my heir. Why make me rich?"

The breeze stirred as he listened to the words of the Lord. The night sky of midnight blue was filled with twinkling lights. He sighed as he looked at them, amazed by the beauty of creation.

The Lord said, "You will have heirs. Your descendants will be like the stars of the sky in number, too many to count." Faith filled the man of God. He did not know how, but he knew God would do it. As he gazed at the stars, he knew without a doubt if God could create all this, He could cause one man to become a nation.

Abram believed God, and God called him righteous because of his faith.

A WIFE'S ERROR

> Now Sarai Abram's wife bare him no children:
> and she had an handmaid, an Egyptian, whose
> name was Hagar. (Gen. 16:1, KJV)

Sarai was filled with despair. Her heart broke daily as she continued to watch child after child be born of their servants into their household, while she remained childless. Slowly she lost faith. She knew Abram was destined to be the father of many people. She no longer believed she would be their mother. She observed her servants. One young woman, Hagar, stood out; she was a beautiful young Egyptian girl. She had proved to be a great comfort to Sarai. Hagar was always respectful and seemed to have a genuine affection for Abram. Sarai decided to speak to Abram.

"You want me to what?" Abram looked at his wife as if she had lost her senses.

"Abram, it is the only way. She is a good girl. She is healthy. She will give you a son."

"I won't do it." Abram shook his head. "I will not betray you." Sarai reasoned with her husband. "This time you must. How else can this great promise be fulfilled? I have spoken with her.

She is willing. Abram, I must hold a child of yours in my arms. I can't go on hoping, only to be disappointed. I can't face another year without your son to love." Sarai began to weep. The years of trying to have a child had been cruel.

"I can't bear it any longer. Children who were born to our servants are now having children. The women talk about me behind my back. I know they do. I have heard them. They think I am deaf. Before I can even walk away, they start to speak. They say I am the one who keeps you from having an heir." She looked into the face of the man she loved. "They are right. I can't do it any longer. I can't be that selfish."

Abram studied his wife. She was a woman of profound determination. But she looked tired. He could see the years of barrenness written in every line of her face. In her eyes, he saw the heartache of a childless life. She turned away, not wanting him to see her face as she cried. "Perhaps if she gives you a son, I can mother him. This may be our last chance." She tried to hide the river of tears flowing down her face. The feelings of despair that had driven her to this decision were ever present. God had rejected her as a mother. Perhaps He would be merciful to someone else. The overwhelming pain of rejection would not go away. It lay in her heart, threatening to crush her with its weight.

Abram listened to Sarai, pondering her words. "Are you sure?" The question hung in the air between them. Their eyes locked on each other. The pain that passed between them was born of total desperation.

Sarai nodded yes. The word simply would not come through her lips. The truth was, in her heart she was screaming *no!*

But she couldn't allow Abram to hear that word. She must never say it out loud. He needed an heir. She was giving him one, even if her heart shattered into a thousand tiny little pieces. She was not going to deny him a son.

Hagar was a servant. She had been offered the chance to be more. She knew her mistress was desperate for a child. She agreed, but she was not happy. She considered the conversation she had with Sarai. Her mistress acted so kind, trying to be delicate about the whole thing. Hagar felt trapped. *What can I do? I am only Sarai's servant. I am her property. I was given to Sarai, and now Sarai is giving me to Abram.* She decided to cooperate. She would become his concubine, a wife with neither rights nor position. But even that was better than being a servant.

Abram was kind to her from the day she came to live with them. Another man might not have been so considerate. She had learned to appreciate him. He was something like a kind old uncle. She thought of him touching her. The thought made her shiver. *But isn't it better if I do at least like him?* All she knew was this seemed to be an opportunity.

Hagar waited for Abram. As she thought about it, the more certain she was that this was the chance of her lifetime. It is unlikely that a servant would become a wife to her master. She had spent her life waiting for the promise of freedom. She would do whatever was necessary. Her son would be the heir to all this.

"Abram," she said as he entered the tent. "I have prepared dinner for you." She motioned to the cushions on the floor. "Please sit." She knew all his favorite foods. She moved over next to him. Her long, thick hair rested on the floor as she knelt to serve him. Smiling she said, "I am a little nervous. I hope you won't be offended." The slight tremble of her lips touched his heart.

"What are we doing to you? You are so young. Are you sure you want to go through with this?"

"I am a servant. My mistress is very kind to me. I hope to be of service to you both." She looked him in the face. "I want to be more than just a servant. I want to be the mother of your heir. This is a great opportunity for me."

Hagar was young and beautiful. Abram found her to be as charming as Sarai had predicted. The young woman seemed to cling to him. She had been around him long enough to know he was God's anointed. She admired him. She wished to please him.

His kindness touched her. She wanted him to be happy. She made sure he had anything his heart desired. Soon she was pregnant.

Hagar woke with a start. She was sick and convinced she was pregnant but decided not to tell anyone. She wanted to be sure. She dropped her hand to her stomach. She had awakened sick for the last week. She would tell them soon.

Hagar's thoughts went to Sarai. So it was true. The problem had been with her mistress all along. She smiled a cruel smile. Her mistress, the definition of beauty, the woman all men desired, the woman stolen by kings, was nothing. She couldn't even do the one thing women were created to do. She leaned back thinking of Sarai. *My mistress is so full of herself, always demanding, 'Do this, do that.' I am Abram's concubine. I did in just a matter of weeks what Sarai was unable to do in decades.*

As the days went by and she became larger, filled with the child her mistress wasn't woman enough to conceive, she hated Sarai. *How did I ever love her?* she wondered. Also, Hagar was confused. Her position had not improved. She was still the servant of Sarai. Abram seemed to be fond of her, but he did nothing to upset Sarai. She wanted to take Sarai's place. She was the one who was the mother of the heir of Abram. Why did she have to continue as nothing more than Sarai's servant?

Fire flashed between the two women as they looked at each other with contempt. "You don't understand." Hagar stood her ground. "You can't order me around anymore." She lifted her hand, touching her chest. "I am the one who is carrying his child. Every day he becomes more excited. He has waited too long to be a father. I am pregnant with his child. One day he will stop you from acting so high and mighty."

Sarai's eyes narrowed. She fought to control her anger. "Be careful, Hagar. No matter what you think, he is my husband. He will always side with me." She walked away angry. From the door of her tent, she looked back at the young woman. That gnawing question surfaced. *Why her, God? Why not me? Why?* Her heart sank. She was tired. She would deal with Hagar another day.

The days passed, but Hagar did not improve. Sarai tried to be kind; the girl simply became more arrogant. As she watched Hagar's belly grow, she was filled with jealousy. Abram was much more attentive toward the girl than necessary. For the first time in her marriage, Sarai began to take a back seat to someone else. She knew, of course, it was her own fault. But Hagar didn't have to always act so helpless. Hagar actually demanded that Abram stay with her through this pregnancy. She wanted his undivided attention. Envy welled up inside Sarai. She felt helpless as Hagar tried to advance her position with Abram.

Hagar watched her mistress play the pitiful wife. She decided it was time to be the one Abram wanted. This was the perfect opportunity to become the rich wife of Abram. She settled back against the cushion Abram had placed at her back. She took his hand, holding it tenderly in her own. "Abram, I love you. You know that, don't you?"

Abram was uncomfortable with this conversation. His heart was dedicated to Sarai, but he had come to feel very tenderly toward Hagar. He tried to explain. "Hagar, you are carrying my child. I have enjoyed our times together, but Sarai is my wife. She will remain my wife."

"Yes, of course, but you do love me just a little, don't you?" Her eyes pleaded with him for an answer.

He reached out and took her face in his hand and said, "Of course, I do."

She smiled up at him much like a cat with a mouse. She had won. She was still young and beautiful. Abram was falling for her. She would push Sarai completely out of the picture someday soon.

Sarai reached her limit. "Abram, Hagar's haughtiness is despicable. The girl will not work. She is insubordinate and condescending." Sarai watched her husband as she continued, "She is hateful. I gave her the opportunity to be the mother of your son, and now she is rude to me. It's your fault. You are the one who has spoiled her. You cater to her every whim. She now thinks she is superior to me." Abram did not want to be in the middle of this catfight. He did what any self-respecting man would do. He squirmed out of it. "She's your servant. You have the right to treat her any way you want."

Sarai decided to remind Hagar who the woman of the house really was. She treated Hagar badly. Sarai did not care if the girl was pregnant. She was going to learn once and for all that she was still a servant. Sarai forced Hagar to obey her. Hagar was hurt and humiliated. She left Sarai. She was upset and crying.

That night she could not sleep. *I've had enough. I'll show her.* Quickly she packed her things. She wiped her eyes, picked up her few belongings, and then slipped through the night undetected. *How dare she treat me like this? I won't wait on that cow anymore. I am the one who is pregnant. I am the one who should be treated like a queen. I am not coming back!*

The blanket of darkness quickly faded as the day dawned. The sun beat down on the young woman. She hadn't realized how foolish it was of her to leave until it was too late. At last she found a place to stop. There was a little spring. Hagar dipped her hand into the cool water and drank. She filled her water container. Then she wet a cloth and wiped her face, arms, and neck with it. She soaked it again and squeezed the water onto her head. There was a little shade nearby, so she lay down to rest. She decided to spend some time there until she could figure out what she should do.

She awoke. Someone was standing over her. The handsome young man seemed to know her. She sat up, startled by her visitor.

He smiled kindly then bent down to her level. He looked right into her eyes. "Hagar what are you doing?"

"I am running away from my mistress, Sarai." She studied the young man. His eyes were the kindest she had ever seen. Something in her told her he was an angel of the Lord.

His eyes danced with joy as he spoke. "Go back to Sarai and do what she tells you. You are pregnant with a son. You will name him Ishmael. I will greatly multiply your descendants. The Lord knows about your unhappiness. Your son will be wild and untamed, like a young donkey. He will be against his brothers" (see Gen. 16:12).

Hagar's heart changed. Something in his words made her feel loved. Just as unexpectedly as he had appeared, the man disappeared. But in her heart, she knew she had encountered the Lord. She called the Lord "the God who sees me." To Hagar, it seemed, no one had ever before really seen her. She had always just been the servant girl. When she was with Abram, she was simply a means to an end, even though he had treated her kindly. To her mistress she was an incubator. But God had singled her out. He knew her. He had spoken to her. She felt truly validated for the first time in her life.

The child kicked. She looked down at her belly. Lovingly she ran her hands over her abdomen. The large oversized protrusion was much more to her now than it had been the day before. She was not just someone's servant or mistress-wife; she was going to be a mother. The child was no longer a tool she could use to obtain favor from Abram or use to torment Sarai. He was hers. They couldn't get rid of her and just pretend she had never been there. The Lord had seen her sorrow, and He had pity on her. He was giving her His blessing.

She stood to her feet. Her strength was restored. She walked toward her mistress. She would obey the angel of the Lord. She would return.

Abram searched all morning for Hagar. He was sick with worry. No one knew how long she had been gone. He had stopped by to check on the girl. When he did, he discovered she was missing. His head hurt. He was heartsick. *Why didn't I stand up to Sarai? I should have defended Hagar. I should have reminded Sarai that she had started this whole thing.* As he waited for word of the young woman, he looked up. Hagar was coming back. "Where have you been, Hagar?" he asked. Abram was clearly upset. "You can't just go off like that. Something could have happened to you or the child."

"I went to find God," she answered. "I didn't know it, but He was what I was looking for."

Abram studied her. His kind eyes touched her heart. "And?" he had to know more.

"I found Him." Her face was calm, her voice steady. She continued, "We will have a son. His name will be Ishmael. God has seen my circumstance. He visited me and told me about the child. The Lord told me He would give me many descendants. Our son, Abram, will be wild and free, the father of many!" She stepped into Abram's arms.

Sarai stood in the door of the tent. She had heard everything. They did not know she was watching. Abram embraced Hagar. It was clear he cared for her. Sarai quietly left them.

In her own tent, Sarai cried out to the Lord. She had often known the hopelessness of being childless. Now she understood the torment of sharing her husband's affections with another woman. She was heartbroken.

Hagar gave birth to Ishmael. Abram was eighty-six. Hagar loved the child. Abram was a doting father. He was completely satisfied with his son. Sarai held the child, but the love she thought she would find was not there. She was happy for Abram, but Hagar was Ishmael's mother. She was just a bystander.

GOD'S PROMISES NEVER FAIL

And when Abram was ninety years old and nine, the Lord appeared to Abram, and said unto him, I am the Almighty God; walk before me, and be thou perfect. And I will make my covenant between me and thee, and will multiply thee exceedingly. And Abram fell on his face: and God talked with him, saying, As for me, behold, my covenant is with thee, and thou shalt be a father of many nations. Neither shall thy name anymore be called Abram, but thy name shall be Abraham; for a father of many nations have I made thee. And I will make thee exceeding fruitful, and I will make nations of thee, and kings shall come out of thee. And I will establish my covenant between me and thee and thy seed after thee in their generations for an everlasting covenant, to be a God unto thee, and to thy seed after thee. And I will give unto thee, and to thy seed after thee, the land wherein thou art a stranger, all the land of Canaan, for an

everlasting possession; and I will be their God.
(Gen. 17:1–8, KJV)

∞⧉∞

And God said unto Abraham, As for Sarai thy
wife, thou shalt not call her name Sarai, but Sarah
shall her name be. And I will bless her, and give
thee a son also of her: yea, I will bless her, and she
shall be a mother of nations; kings of people shall
be of her. (Gen. 17:15–16, KJV)

Abraham bowed himself before the Lord and began to laugh.
Why, the very thought of it was hilarious. He didn't want to be
disrespectful, but how could a hundred-year-old man father a
child? Then he remembered Sarah. She was ninety. He knew
she was well past being able to bear children. He tried to control
himself, but he couldn't stop laughing, "Oh Lord, let my son
Ishmael receive your blessing."

The Lord insisted, "In about a year, Sarah will give you a son.
You will call him Isaac. I will establish my covenant with him.
Ishmael will also be blessed. But Isaac is the child of this promise."

"Abraham, what is going on?" Sarah was concerned. Abraham
tried to speak. Joy overwhelmed him. He smiled at his wife. "The
Lord spoke to me. Once again he promised to make me the father
of many nations. I asked him to favor Ishmael with His promise,
but he refused. He said that you were no longer Sarai, but from
now on you will be called Sarah. He also said that you are the
mother of the chosen child and that you would bear me a son in
my old age." When Abraham reached the part of them having
a child, he started to laugh. He laughed so hard he could barely
speak.

"He actually said I would have a son?" She was shocked. They
both laughed at the thought.

Abraham smiled at his still-lovely wife. "You are still my
treasure."

"Abraham, wouldn't it be wonderful?" she asked.

One day, Abraham looked up and saw three men. They were obviously angels of the Lord. He went to them, bowed and said, "If you will allow me, I will prepare food for you." The men smiled at their friend. They had a long day ahead of them. But meeting with Abraham was a priority. They graciously agreed.

Abraham ran to Sarah. "Quick, bake bread for our guests." "Who are they?" she asked.

"They are messengers from the Lord." He looked at Sarah. She could see how serious he was.

Hurriedly, she said, "You go and talk to them. I'll take care of this."

Abraham chose out his prize calf and handed it to a servant. Then he returned to the angels. When the food was ready, he served them a delicious meal of savory meat, cheese, and milk. They all enjoyed the food, laughing together and talking.

"Where is Sarah?" the angel of the Lord asked. Abraham motioned toward the tent. "She is inside."

The angel of the Lord looked in her direction and said, "When I return next year, she will have a son."

Sarah listened from the door of the tent. She giggled out loud. *Sure I will*, she thought. *I'm an old woman. How can an old woman like me have a baby?* She snickered. She thought of Abraham. *He would be one hundred years old!* She bit her lip, as she tried not to be overheard laughing.

> And the Lord said unto Abraham, Wherefore did Sarah laugh, saying, Shall I of a surety bear a child, which am old? Is any thing too hard for the Lord? At the time appointed I will return unto thee, according to the time of life, and Sarah shall have a son. (Gen. 18:13–14, KJV)

Sarah peeked out of the door. She was amazed.

The angel of the Lord watched her. His eyes pierced her through as though they were swords flaying her and leaving her private thoughts open for inspection. Sarah was afraid. "I didn't laugh," she said.

The man with the piercing eyes looked into her soul and said, "You're lying. You did laugh."

The three men got up from their meal. They were refreshed. They looked out toward Sodom. Their expressions were somber. The Lord spoke to Abraham. "Should I keep a secret from Abraham?" His mysterious question hung in the air. Abraham watched him waiting for him to continue. "I will make you the father of many. I know you will teach your children of me. I will tell you what I am doing. I know about the evil of Sodom and Gomorrah." Abraham held his breath. For a long time he had been concerned about the people in the area. He had heard many reports from Lot's men. He watched as the angel of the Lord continued, "I have heard the people are very wicked. I am going to Sodom and Gomorrah to see for myself. If they are as wicked as I have heard, I will destroy them." The three men looked off into the distance. There was a look of purpose on their faces.

Abraham followed their gaze toward the valley of Jordan. The lush green land lay as an oasis before them. He thought of the people of Sodom. "Lord, will you destroy good people with bad? You won't do such a thing. What if you find fifty good men? Will you destroy the city then?"

The Lord answered, "No, Abraham. If I find fifty good men, I will not destroy the city."

Abraham continued, "What if you can't find fifty? Lord, what if only five are missing? Will you destroy the city if there are only forty-five?"

"No," the Lord answered. "I will not destroy the city if I find forty-five."

"What if there are only forty?" Abraham asked.

The Lord answered, "I will not destroy it if there are forty." Abraham was afraid, but persisted. "Please don't be offended, my Lord. What if you only find thirty good men?"

The Lord said, "If I find thirty good men, I will not destroy it."

Abraham said, "Since I have dared to speak, please allow me to continue. What if there are only twenty?"

The Lord answered, "I will not destroy it for the sake of twenty." Then Abraham pushed the Lord one more time. "Please, Lord, don't be angry. What if you can only find ten men?"

The Lord said, "I will not destroy it for the sake of ten men." Then the Lord left, and Abraham went back to his tent.

Two of the men who had spent the day with Abraham walked into the city of Sodom. The angels had already searched out Gomorrah. They were followed. The people of the city were in a drunken state. They had been partying for hours. They watched the two perfect young men as they walked the length and breadth of Sodom. These angels had eyes that pierced the hearts of anyone they looked on. They were not pleased. They looked for ten good men. They knew Abraham had bargained with the Lord for the lives of the men and women of the two cities. They searched everywhere, but they found only one good man.

Lot saw them as they approached the city. He was very concerned for their safety. His neighbors tended to become rough when they were partying. He went to the angels and bowed. "Sirs, would you please do me the honor of being my guests for the night?"

The angels answered, "No, thank you. We will stay out here in the city streets. We will be fine."

Their shocking good looks frightened Lot for their safety. They were taller than most men. Their faces were picture-perfect. They were handsome in every way. Lot panicked. "Please indulge me. It would be a great honor if you would allow me the privilege of being your host."

The men of the city were cruel. Rape was a common occurrence. They were violent, vicious men. The angels observed the men of the city warily. Pride mingled itself with violent lust as they made plans to rape the angels of the Lord. They followed Lot and the two angels to Lot's home.

The night sky became oddly different. A cloud moved in front of the moon, casting a strange light. A brutish man with a scar above his eye watched them enter the home. A cruel smile crossed his ugly face. "So, Lot thinks he can protect them." His companions laughed; the sound was hollow and without mirth. "We'll just see about that." Again laughter rang out.

The angels hearing them looked at each other. They looked at their companion also, the man no one saw. He had spent the day with them. He spoke face-to-face with Abraham. He had promised to be merciful. But He was an individual of justice. He could not allow sin to run rampant. He could not allow men to openly rape and brutalize people with no consequence. We often forget about Him. We forget He is watching us, looking into the part of our souls that we hide. We forget He sees who we really are inside. He watched these men of Sodom also. He had seen enough. He nodded to the two angels.

Outside Lot's house, the men of the city were forming a mob. They decided to take Lot's home by force. They would break down the door.

"Lot!" they called to him. "Send out the men who are visiting you. We want to rape them." The men were literally storming the house. They flanked all sides and were preparing to break in.

Lot tried to reason with them. He stepped out of his home. "Brothers, these men are here under my roof. They have my protection. Please, don't do this wicked thing. I have two young daughters. Take them instead."

Lot's daughters looked at each other. Their eyes grew larger as fear gripped them. They looked over at the angels, horror showing on their faces. One of the angels smiled reassuringly. Raising his hand, he placed it on the shoulder of the younger girl. Her lower lip trembled slightly. She tried to be brave, but her heart was pounding hard. She felt like a trapped animal unable to move.

"Who are you to lecture us?" The men of the city grew angrier. "We have accepted you, and this is how you repay us—by judging us. We will make you sorry!" The men started to grab Lot, but the angels reached out of the door and pulled him in.

Lightning flashed. A bright light from heaven shot out at the demon-driven men of the city. "My eyes! I can't see!" Some of the men grabbed their eyes and started wiping them. Others kept groping for the door. "Where is the door?" They couldn't find it. They felt for the handle—nothing. They couldn't see. The angels had blinded them.

The angels were no longer interested in waiting. "Do you have any family in this city? We have been sent here by the Lord to destroy this place. If there is anyone, go and speak to them now. The stink of the sin of this land has reached the nostrils of the Lord." In the end only Lot, his two daughters, and wife were rescued. Early the next morning, the angels rushed them, forcing them to leave. "The city will soon be consumed by flames. Escape to the mountains!" The angels warned them, "Do not look back on the city. The person who does will be destroyed."

The Lord rained fire and burning sulfur. Lot was terrified. His wife was in front of the little group of refugees. She started to slow down; she was so tired. She missed her beautiful home. She had to see what was happening. She glanced back at the life she was leaving. Something from the sky struck her. She was changed into a pillar of salt. Lot and his daughters stared at his wife. Horror filled them. They didn't dare look toward the city. They began to run as fast as they could.

The people of Sodom and Gomorrah ran for cover. Out of the sky fell fire from heaven. The blaze of it hit the earth. The fire was like rain. People screamed as they were consumed by the flames. The smell of sulfur rose up to heaven, replacing the stench of sin. Fire caught the trees, lapped up the water, worked its way up the walkways to the homes of the people. While it burned its way through the streets, the screams of the people could be heard.

Lot fought the impulse to turn and look. "Don't look!" His voice shook with fear. "Run! Just keep running!"

Hell visited earth, claiming its prey, the lost souls of the men and women of those cities. The earth was cleansed by the intense heat. The smoke rose. It lapped up the sky, billowing toward heaven in huge, dark clouds.

Abraham passed the night in prayer. He was concerned for Lot, his family, and their neighbors. He rose from his place of prayer just as day was breaking. He ran up the hill to the vista point, where he had talked to the Lord. He looked out toward Sodom and Gomorrah. The devastation was unbelievable. The smoke rose toward heaven in two pillars. "Oh God," he breathed out as he watched the burning cities. His strength left his body. He sank to his knees.

Sarah could see her husband's sorrow from the distance. "Oh Lord, help him!" She pleaded. She ran toward Abraham. When she reached him, he was mourning. She looked out to see the pillars of smoke. "Oh God," she moaned. Her hand reached for Abraham. He held it tightly.

The men and women of the camp were struck by the sounds of grief coming from the hill. Eliezer ran to his master. "Abraham, what is it?" Abraham pointed.

Many of the other servants came to check on them. They all watched in devastated horror as the smoke billowed its way toward heaven. "What is it?" they asked.

Abraham shook his head. It is the judgment of God.

Slowly Sarah spoke. "How sad the Lord must be today. If we are hurt by this great loss of life, He must be very sad. God who loves all men and created them to live abundant, happy lives must be heartbroken. Sin is a great sorrow to the heart of God. He is too holy to look on evil."

Abraham nodded. "Sarah is right. God is just. Blessed be His name. He desires that no one should perish. But man continues to sin against Him and against each other. He destroyed the earth once with a flood. But He has promised never to do that again.

However, when sinfulness takes over, God will bring justice. How many of the victims of those cities have cried out to God for justice?"

Lot and his daughters went to the nearby town of Zoar. But because he was afraid for their safety, he decided to take his daughters and move into the mountains. He found a cave. They were at least protected from the elements.

Lot's daughters had lived many years with the immorality of Sodom. They had come to accept things their father would not think of. His daughters looked out from their perch on the mountain. They were afraid to go back to Zoar. They felt like they were the last people on earth. They couldn't live without children. In their desperation, they did the unthinkable…

Today, we as a culture spend our time familiarizing ourselves with sin. We have become immune to its effects. These lovely young women lost themselves in the sins they were exposed to. They misplaced their compass of right from wrong. They were raised by an amazing man who loved God, and they were delivered by God from certain death. But they were corrupted by the atmosphere they grew up in. They plotted to get Lot drunk; then they each slept with him so they could have children. We must remember the daughters of Lot and pray for our children. We as a nation have lost our moral compass and are wandering around in a land of immorality.

ISAAC, THE CHILD OF PROMISE

Through faith also Sara herself received strength
to conceive seed, and was delivered of a child
when she was past age, because she judged him
faithful who had promised. (Heb. 11:11, KJV)

Sarah was pregnant! She could not believe it. She was elated. She knew she should stay inside and modestly hide that fact, but she didn't want to. She had prayed for this baby for the last seventy years. She was going to flaunt it. She walked in and out, all around the camp, proudly displaying her belly. This was her miracle! No one knew better than her and Abraham how much of a miracle this child was. She had given up completely. She was just waiting to die when the men came to visit.

She thought back. Something happened to her when the angel of the Lord looked into her eyes and confronted her doubt, as he continued speaking with Abraham, asking, "Is any thing too hard for the Lord? At the time appointed I will return unto thee, according to the time of life, and Sarah shall have a son" (Gen. 18:14, KJV). Ever since those words were spoken, life was renewed in her. Until that moment, her faith had died. She could believe

God would move for her husband. She could not believe for herself.

As she considered it, she realized she had been changing for a while. Since God had given her a new name, every time someone spoke to her, calling her Sarah instead of Sarai, she felt singled out. Then when the angel of the Lord announced she would have a child, something in her heart came to life! Faith rose up inside her on the wings of hope. She became a woman of destiny. She was part of the promise.

She thought, with delight, of the changes in Abraham. He was different too. Suddenly he behaved as if he were a young man. He had brought her flowers, sung to her, and quoted poems. She couldn't remember the last time he behaved so romantically. He looked at her as if she were the most beautiful woman in the world. When he did, he was so serious she became embarrassed. He still remembered the girl she once was. It was as if he didn't see the wear and tear life had marked into her features. His love was so vital to her very breath! She could hardly think of taking a breath without him. Now, thanks to the Lord, she carried his child. She couldn't imagine being happier.

Hagar was her only problem. The younger woman often threw it up to her that Ishmael was the oldest. She was a threat to the very promise of God. Sarah new it was her fault. She would have to face her mistake, or Isaac would pay the price. But for now, she just allowed herself to enjoy her condition.

"Have you heard?" the women asked each other as Sarah walked past them. She could hear the hushed tones as they observed her present conditions. The speaker continued to speak. "The Lord visited them. He told Sarah and Abraham she would have the child of the promise. Look at her. She is pregnant. It is a miracle!"

Sarah smiled to herself as she moved in and out of the camp. She had many times been the topic of gossip. But this was one time she enjoyed, knowing that everyone was talking. She was chosen also. God had vindicated her. She was not the outcast daughter of God as everyone had supposed. She was claimed by God. Until now it was as though God Himself had rejected her. In her culture, not being able to bear children was the mark of a woman who had no value. But God had stamped His approval on her. She laughed to herself as she considered it. The Lord called the child Isaac. *His name means laughter*, Sarah thought. She was the happiest she had ever been.

—∞◦◦◦✦◦◦◦∞—

"It is time!" The message rang out throughout the camp.

The ladies had been watching Sarah as if she might explode for days. Isaac was welcomed into the world. He was the beautiful son of Abraham and Sarah. The midwife placed the child on her stomach. She looked into his eyes for the first time and said, "Yes, little one, you will bring me laughter." Then from somewhere deep inside her being, she began to laugh!

Abraham walked into the tent. He was crying. He had been so afraid. He knew the child would be fine, but what about Sarah? How could he face life without her? He looked into the face of the woman he loved.

She laughed from pure joy. "Abraham, here is your son. I am laughing, and everyone who hears my story will laugh with me. I have given you a son in your old age."

Unfortunately, Hagar was not laughing. She tightened the grip on her son's shoulders. He escaped from her and ran to see his new brother.

"Father," he called out. Rings of dark curls covered his head and spilled onto his smiling face.

Abraham reached out to the boy, embracing him, "Ishmael, I want you to meet your brother Isaac." The young man was fascinated with the tiny child.

But poison has a way of corrupting even our innocent children. When Isaac was old enough to eat solid food, his father gave a party for him. It was a wonderful day. There were lots of people who came just to enjoy the blessing of Abraham and Sarah.

Sarah looked up and noticed Ishmael's behavior toward Isaac. The older boys were making fun of Isaac, and Ishmael was the leader. It was time. She knew from the beginning she would have to do something. Now, as she watched the youth boldly harassing her son, she knew she had to act.

Isaac fell backward. His tiny frame hit hard on the ground. He did not understand. Crying, his little fist came up to rub his eyes. The bigger boys continued to torment him.

Her heart broke for her son as she considered the future. What future? If Hagar had anything to say about it, Ishmael would be the only heir. Hagar was right. He was the oldest. The birthright was lawfully his. No, she would not allow that. "I want him out of here!" Sarah stood her ground. She was, at that moment, exactly what every woman who sees her child threatened is. She was a lioness protecting her son. "There is no way that boy is going to inherit with my son. If we allow him to stay, what will happen to Isaac? He is the oldest. And he is already making fun of Isaac. Isaac is the child of the promise. He is the son of a servant. Hagar's son will not inherit with Isaac. Get rid of them both!"

Abraham's heart shattered. "Sarah, what are you saying? I can't throw one son away for another. How could I do such a thing?" "Abraham, you will do it now. I will not allow that child to inherit with my son!"

Abraham had to be alone. He went outside to pray and think. He sat overlooking the wilderness in his favorite spot. He often took refuge here, seated in the shade of the oak he loved. The day had been warm. Sarah wasted no time. As soon as the party ended, he was hit with this. "Oh God." The moan was one of hopelessness as he cried out to the only one he knew would listen. "What shall I do?" He spoke to the Lord, telling him everything—all his pain, all his joys. How could he choose one son over another? He was alone. Grief shook him as he thought on Hagar and Ishmael.

The Lord spoke to Abraham. "Sarah is right. Do as she has said. Send the boy and his mother away. I will take care of him.

And I will make of him a great nation because he is your son." The desert air blew. The sand swirled around him. He could hear the voice of the eternal ages. There was a certainty in God's words.

Abraham rose early. He kissed Ishmael goodbye. "The Lord be with you, my son." Abraham had packed food for their journey. He placed the pack on Hagar's back and sent them away. They wandered into the wilderness.

Hagar felt the heat of the desert scorching her body. She became disoriented. *Which way do I go?* She couldn't think; her brain was foggy. She looked over at the child. Ishmael was suffering. He did not speak; he just followed her. She was desperate. The food had run out. The water also was gone. Hagar knew they were close to death.

She came to a small growth of brush. "Ishmael, you stay here in the shade." She went on a little farther. She fell to her knees. Cupping her face in her hands, she pleaded, "Oh God, don't let me see the child die." Tears filled her eyes, spilling over onto her cheeks as she prayed. "You once heard me. You said this child would be the father of a great nation. We are dying. We are hopeless in this desert." The sun beat down on her head. She hurt everywhere. Her face was covered by particles of sand. Sweat ran down the back of her spine. She waited for the end.

Ishmael sat alone, his spirit barely clinging to life. In desperation, he cried out to the Lord, "Lord God of my father Abraham, save us. Don't let us die." The youth had many times prayed with his father. He knew the God of Abraham. He was the one true God, the only one who could rescue them. The teaching of his father raced to his memory as he prayed. The desert heat ceased to exist as the prayer poured out of the heart of a desperate young man.

> And God heard the voice of the lad; and the angel
> of God called to Hagar out of heaven, and said

unto her, What aileth thee, Hagar? fear not; for God hath heard the voice of the lad where he is. Arise, lift up the lad, and hold him in thine hand; for I will make him a great nation. And God opened her eyes, and she saw a well of water; and she went, and filled the bottle with water, and gave the lad drink. And God was with the lad; and he grew, and dwelt in the wilderness, and became an archer. And he dwelt in the wilderness of Paran: and his mother took him a wife out of the land of Egypt. (Gen. 21:17–21, KJV)

Isaac grew and flourished. He was handsome and intelligent. His mother's life was wrapped up in the boy. His father loved Isaac as if he were his only son.

Isaac played trustingly in the distance. Abraham spoke with the Lord. "Abraham," the Lord said. "Take your only son, Isaac, to Moriah and sacrifice him there as a burnt offering to me."

The old man fell over with pain. His heart felt as though it were beating out of his chest. He leaned heavily on the staff. His eyes filled with tears as he searched the distance for Isaac. He heard the boy laughing with his friends. Unconsciously he rubbed at the pain in his chest. Slowly he regained his composure. His features echoed determination. A small nod of agreement bobbed his head. Slowly he walked back toward the tent. He would pass this night fasting.

Abraham got up early the next day. He took two servants and Isaac. He gathered wood and brought a torch for fire. They traveled for a few days. "Wait here," Abraham instructed his servants. He and Isaac went on. Isaac carried the wood up the mountain. Abraham carried the knife and the fire.

Something was wrong. Isaac knew his father was on a mission from God. He could sense it in the look of resolve on his father's face. Sarah felt it too. She had hugged him so tightly before they left he could barely breathe. She watched them go. She looked sad when she said goodbye.

He watched as his father purposefully climbed the mountain. The rough terrain was hard to navigate. Isaac caught his father and steadied him as Abraham started to stumble. "Be careful, Father," the boy warned. Abraham was in front of him. His father was sure-footed, but on this slope, anyone would have difficulty. They kept climbing.

Isaac wondered, "Father, we have the wood and the fire. Where is the lamb?"

Abraham cringed as his innocent son asked the question. "The Lord will provide the lamb for Himself," was all he said.

By the time they reached the top of the mountain, Isaac realized what was going to happen. He looked into the sad eyes of his father. The young man held out his wrists as his father tied them. Abraham also tied his ankles. He placed the wood on the altar. He picked up his son, placing him on the wood. Isaac did not try to fight back. He was willing to be sacrificed. Tears rolled down his face as the young man waited for his father to kill him. Abraham prayed. Then raising the knife over Isaac, he aimed it at the boy's heart. He had to be quick. The child could not suffer any more than necessary.

Out of heaven came a voice. "Abraham! Abraham! Do not hurt the child! I know now, you truly fear God. I know now you love me. And you are willing to do anything for me." Then Abraham looked up and saw a ram caught by its horns in the brush. He sacrificed the ram, instead, as a burnt offering. "And Abraham called the name of that place Jehovah-jireh: as it is said to this day, In the mount of the Lord it shall be seen" (Gen. 22:14, KJV; *Jehovah-jireh* is "the Lord my provider"). The Lord received the sacrifice. He was pleased with Abraham. Abraham knew that the Lord would do all he had promised even if he had to raise Isaac from the dead (see Hebrews 11:17–19).

> And the angel of the Lord called unto Abraham
> out of heaven the second time, And said, By myself
> have I sworn, saith the Lord, for because thou
> hast done this thing, and hast not withheld thy
> son, thine only son: That in blessing I will bless
> thee, and in multiplying I will multiply thy seed
> as the stars of the heaven, and as the sand which is
> upon the sea shore; and thy seed shall possess the
> gate of his enemies; And in thy seed shall all the
> nations of the earth be blessed; because thou hast
> obeyed my voice. (Gen. 22:15–18, KJV)

Isaac and his father walked down the mountain together. Their lives were forever changed. A son, as good as dead, was brought back to life, resurrected! A father had proven his love for God, not just to God but also to himself. The one person Abraham believed he could not do without, he was willing to give up. His love for Isaac was not greater than his love for God. He was willing to give his only son!

Many times in the Old Testament God provides word pictures of Christ. We find these illustrated sermons in many places. This is one of them.

God understood what that sacrifice meant. You see, God the Father did not ask for the life of Isaac on a whim. In fact, the customs of the time were that many children were sacrificed to different pagan gods. This practice God hates. He was testing the one man He believed He could trust with His deepest sorrow. God knew one day He would allow His own son to be led up a rugged hill. He would allow nails to be driven into His hands. And there in the presence of humanity would hang the ultimate sacrifice for the sins of mankind, God veiled in the flesh, Jesus Christ the Messiah. He too carried the wood that He would be crucified on. He too would willingly be sacrificed. God shared His greatest heartache that day with Abraham, his friend. But because of God's love, Isaac was saved.

Isaac also experienced something he was not able to understand. He had been willing. He could have run away. He could have escaped the brutality of an old man. But he chose to do the will of his father. He chose to show his love for his father and for God by willingly laying down his life. He chose to believe God's faithfulness rather than to fear death. He knew God could raise him from the dead! And God did prove that He was faithful. There, on a hilltop, a father and son were transformed. Even though they could not truly understand what their sacrifice had meant, God took comfort in knowing that they were willing to give their all because they loved him completely, just as God the Father and His son, Jesus, were willing to give their all because they loved mankind completely!

As for Sarah, she watched as her husband walked away with her son, the one who was chosen, and the heir of the promise. She stood by quietly as her husband offered to God her greatest joy.

Mary also watched as her son was taken from her care. He was led away. She did not know why her son, her promised son, had to die.

Sarah lived to be 127 years old. She died in the land of Canaan. Abraham purchased a piece of land there, in Heron, where he buried her.

A Bride for Isaac

And Rebekah arose, and her damsels, and they
rode upon the camels, and followed the man:
and the servant took Rebekah, and went his way.
(Gen. 24:61, KJV)

When Abraham was very old, he spoke with his most trusted servant, Eliezer. His beloved servant watched him carefully. Eliezer was concerned for his friend and master. This man had never treated him as a servant. Abraham had dealt with him respectfully to the point of giving him the inheritance of a son. Of course, that was before Isaac. He smiled when he thought of the years that had passed. Abraham was still his most valued friend.

Eliezer's granddaughter finished fluffing a large stack of oversize pillows, making them as comfortable as possible for Abraham, then silently left. Abraham sat leaning against the stack of pillows. Eliezer dragged his attention back to what Abraham was saying.

"My son Isaac needs a wife. He has been unhappy since the death of his mother. I want you to choose a young lady for him. Don't introduce him to any of these local girls. They won't be able to make him happy. He needs a wife who will understand him, someone who will serve the Lord. Promise me, in the presence of the Lord God of heaven and earth, that you will not allow him to marry any of our neighbor's daughters. Return to the land where I was born and bring back a bride from my father's household." Eliezer studied Abraham. He was used to following instructions, but he did have one concern. "What if I cannot find a young lady who is willing to leave her family and come here? Should I take Isaac to her?"

"No, absolutely not. Beware that you never take him back there. God has promised my descendants this land of Canaan. He must remain here. God will lead you to the young woman." Eliezer nodded. "I promise. I will do as you have asked."

The next morning, Eliezer rose early. He called some of the eager young men together. "I have been instructed to return to our homeland. Who would like to take this journey with me? It will not be easy. We leave today. You must be willing to work hard and travel all day." Several men raised their hands. "Thank you. I expect to leave immediately. Come with me. We have some loading to do." Soon they were saddling and preparing their camels. They placed the most elaborate decorations they had for the camels on them. The bells rang softly as they added decorative ornaments all along the reins.

"Are we going to visit a king?" Seth asked his friends as they loaded the camels down with chests of goods.

One of the boxes shifted. "Be careful," Eliezer cautioned the young men. "This cargo is very delicate. Remember, Seth, these gifts are for a young lady. Your mother has gone to great lengths to pack these items carefully. We must honor her work by treating them with respect."

"Yes, sir." Seth smiled back at his friend. Eliezer was older, but he had always been kind to Seth.

The caravan set off for the far and mysterious land of Mesopotamia. Seth and the other young men were excited. This was a chance to see a land they had only heard about from their parents and grandparents. They played, laughed, and talked most of the way.

"I hear it is beautiful," Saul said. "The land is filled with wonders."

"They worship other gods," Seth observed. "I wonder, will she be very beautiful, this bride of Isaac's?"

Eliezer listened to their young questions. They were as all young men full of zest for life. This journey was just what they had needed. These weeks of travel would calm some of their longing for adventure.

The camel rocked back and forth. Eliezer was used to the slow gate of the animals. He sat comfortably under a shade provided by a small awning attached to the camel's saddle, but it did nothing for the pain in his old joints. The journey was very difficult. The heat was oppressive. The precious servant was an elderly man himself, but he would not have understood someone else being asked to go in his place. He took his job of caring for this chosen family very seriously. To him it was his calling. He had been Abraham's right arm for many years. It was a privilege to serve his master. Abraham was a man of purpose. Eliezer had purpose because of the value the Great God placed on Abraham. He served God by serving his master.

Travel was slow, but the tiny caravan moved at a steady pace. The desert gave its own familiar beauty. Eliezer gazed out at the wondrous landscape. His heart was full. This was an important mission. God willing, he would complete it. He had been praying for one last important job, something he could do to further the promise of the Great God. As his camel moved along, he knew this was the answer to his heart's desire.

It was late in the day when he finally arrived at his destination. He had ten camels loaded with gifts from his master to the bride and her family. He made sure to bring all the best Abraham had to offer.

The caravan stopped in front of the city. Outside the city gate was a well. "We will rest here," he said to his companions.

The women began to gather around the well for water. He chose his spot. Then he prayed, "Oh God of my master Abraham, show my master favor by having the young woman of Your choice come here. I will ask her for a drink. If she agrees and says, 'I will bring water for your camels also,' let her be the bride you have chosen for Isaac."

As he finished praying, he looked up. There was a very beautiful young woman coming to the well carrying a water pot. She filled it. Eliezer asked her, "May I have a drink?"

Rebekah looked at the kind gentleman who was speaking. She instantly felt compassion. He looked very tired. She noticed his camels had not been watered. She smiled. "Yes, here, and I'll get more for your camels." She poured the water into a trough for the camels. Then she made several more trips to the well. Finally, they were all watered.

Eliezer watched, wondering if she was the woman God had chosen for Isaac. After she was done watering the camels, he gave her a golden nose ring and two large bracelets. "Whose child are you? Does your family have room to let us stay the night?"

Rebekah smiled at her new friend. "My father's name is Bethuel. My grandparents are Nahor and Milcah."

Joy leaped into the heart of Eliezer. Nahor and Milcah were the parents of Abraham. Eliezer bowed himself and worshipped the Lord. "Praise You, oh God, for all Your kindness to my master Abraham. Thank You for bringing me directly to his family."

Rebekah ran and told Laban, her brother, that a man from the house of Abraham was in the area, visiting. "Laban, he has many camels and needs a place for himself, the camel drivers, and the camels to stay."

"Where is he?" Laban asked, excited. "I will go and meet the man." As he hurried to meet the caravan from Abraham's camp, he noticed a stranger walking toward him. "Eliezer?" he asked.

The man nodded. "Yes, sir."

Laban laughed. Joyfully he greeted the visitor. "I will show you where you and your men can sleep. We also have a place for your camels and plenty of food for them as well." He tended to the men who had accompanied Eliezer. He gave them water to wash their feet and showed them where they could rest. He gave them feed for their camels and more water for the evening. Then Laban sat down to dinner with Eliezer.

Eliezer was too excited to eat. "I cannot rest until I have accomplished my mission. You see, I was sent here by my master, Abraham, to find a wife for his son, Isaac. My master is very rich. He has cattle, sheep, gold, and silver. He is a very great man. His son, Isaac, is his only heir. My master made me swear to him that I would not take a bride for Isaac from the women of Canaan but that I would return here and bring back a bride from his father's house. When we arrived, I sat down to watch the ladies come for water. I prayed that God would show me who the young lady was by giving me a sign. I said, 'If I ask her to give me a drink then have her agree and also draw water for the camels.' Immediately Rebekah came to draw water. She did just as I asked God. So you see, God has prospered my journey and chosen your Rebekah as the bride of Isaac. Now if this is good with you, let me know if she will marry my master's son."

Laban, his mother, and Rebekah listened closely. When Eliezer reached the part about Rebekah returning with him to marry Isaac, she was stunned. God had chosen her.

Laban studied the stranger. It was just like Abraham to send someone here to find a bride for Isaac. His eyes caught his mother's. They did not have to speak. They knew what the other one was thinking. His mother looked at her beautiful Rebekah. "It is right that she follow the Lord. God has chosen her. She must go." Laban nodded his approval.

"I have brought many gifts from my master Abraham for both of you and Rebekah." Eliezer motioned to Seth. The young man disappeared. In a few minutes, he returned with his friends, the other camel drivers. Rebekah's mouth flew open. They were loaded with packages. "A blessing from the house of Abraham," Eliezer said. They laid them out in front of her brother and mother. "And for you, mistress." Eliezer watched as they showered her with the gifts. He had handpicked everything. For Rebekah, among the gifts were jewelry, perfumes, and a new wardrobe.

That night Rebekah could not sleep. She decided to take a walk. She needed to think. Out in the open, things seemed clearer to her. *Isaac is the child of the promise. His very birth was a miracle! God*, she said in her heart. *I don't understand why you have chosen me. But I will go. Show me how you want me to live. Teach me to be a good wife to this man of destiny. I place my life in your hands. Please give me love for him, and help him to love me too.*

She considered her prayer. *As the wife of Isaac, I will have everything I could ever want*. The gifts were wonderful. Laban was thrilled by the monetary blessing. But they were not the reasons she had said yes. God had singled her out. For the first time in her life, she felt called. *I will be the mother of God's chosen heir. From my descendants, kings will be born!* She sat down. Thoughtfully she considered the stars. God had spoken to Abraham, telling him that he would be the father of nations. Excitement coursed through her veins. *Now, because of God's divine purpose, I will be counted among the mothers of the promises of God. What a difference a day makes!*

Yesterday she was looking at the pool of local men for potential husbands. Laban had rebuked her for being too picky. *Today*, she thought, *I am a woman of destiny.* "Thank you, God." She prayed, closing her eyes and smiling up at the sky. She breathed in the cool night air. She opened her eyes, batting her long, dark lashes at the stars that twinkled high above her head like a million diamonds filling the sky. *Today my life begins!*

The next morning, Eliezer wanted to leave immediately. Laban was disappointed. "My mother and I were hoping that Rebekah could spend at least a couple of weeks with us before leaving."

Eliezer was adamant. "Please, do not delay me. The Lord has blessed my trip. Now let me return to my master."

They called Rebekah and asked her if she was willing to leave so soon. Rebekah weighed the words of the elderly man standing in front of her. "You say Isaac's mother, Sarah, has passed away?" She watched as he confirmed with a nod. "All right, I will go with you now. The Lord led you here with haste. Perhaps Isaac needs me."

She packed up everything she owned. The camel drivers secured her things for her. Her mother cried quietly. She reached over and gave her a hug. Her brother looked completely heartbroken. She reached out to him also. "I will send word whenever there is a caravan coming this way." Then she hugged him. "Take care of Mother," she whispered. "I love you both very much." And with that, their Rebekah left.

Isaac had been unhappy since the death of his mother. He did not complain to his father, but he was very lonely. He knew better than to marry one of the local women. He knew his mom and dad would never have approved. But lately his loneliness was unbearable.

He was walking in the field. He often got alone to talk to God and think. His father had sent Eliezer to bring him back a bride. He was on pins and needles. He wondered what she would look like. Would she ever agree to just come here? They were complete strangers. Questions bombarded his mind as he waited for Eliezer to return. He looked out into the distance. He could see the camels Eliezer had taken with him. They were back. He walked toward the caravan.

Rebekah saw a young man coming their way, "Eliezer, is that Isaac?"

"Yes, mistress," he replied.

She had allowed her veil to fall as they were traveling. Quickly she placed it over her face and secured it. Almost immediately Isaac was with them. His men greeted him, but he never took his gaze off Rebekah.

Her camel snorted, lumbered, and slowly knelt. She cautiously dismounted. Isaac stood before her. This is the moment they had both been anticipating. She wondered, *Will he love me? Will he even like me?* Gracefully she bowed to him. He extended his hand, pulling her up. He was strong and tall. She had to look up at Isaac. Her eyes searched his face. To her delight, he was very handsome. As he smiled, his whole face lit up. Even his eyes smiled back at her. She liked him.

Eliezer's story was very entertaining. Isaac took Rebekah for his bride. She was more beautiful than he had imagined. He fell in love with her the moment he saw her. His heart sang with joy as he praised God for ending his loneliness.

"Rebekah, this is my mother's tent."

Rebekah took in the beautiful furnishings with their luxurious textiles. This tent was like no other.

"Will it do?" He looked at her, wanting her approval. "Yes, Isaac. I have never been surrounded by such luxury." "Anything you want is yours, my darling. All you have to do is ask. If I can get it for you, I will."

She looked into the kind eyes of the most beautiful man she had ever seen. "I have everything I need, my husband," was her reply.

The long days of sorrow dissolved into his past as Isaac started his life with his bride.

After Sarah's death, Abraham married Keturah. They had six sons. He died at 170 years of age. He gave gifts to his other sons, but Isaac was his heir. Isaac and Ishmael buried their father in the field Abraham had purchased to bury Sarah.

After the death of his father, Isaac prospered. God poured out blessings on him.

TWINS

> And they blessed Rebekah, and said unto her,
> Thou art our sister, be thou the mother of
> thousands of millions, and let thy seed possess the
> gate of those which hate them. (Gen. 24:60, KJV)

The newlyweds enjoyed all life had to offer. They were in love and very rich. There was only one problem. The years went by, but Rebekah did not become pregnant. Isaac tried to comfort her. "Rebekah you are my wife. I love you more than I could ever imagine loving anyone. My mother waited until she was ninety before I was born."

"Ninety," his wife bawled. "I can't wait until I'm ninety! What's wrong with you? I want to have children while I am young. I grow older every year. Isaac, what will I do? You have given me everything. We have all the wealth two people could want, but we have no heirs."

He tried to encourage her with statements like "You are all I need." But deep down inside, he knew it wasn't enough. Rebekah was one of those women who had to have children. She was born to be a mother. Her heart broke more every day. At first she was content to wait on the Lord, but now she was heartsick.

Isaac was used to talking to God. He pleaded with the Lord for children. "God, you know my wife. You created her. She is heartbroken." He prayed fervently, and God heard him.

Rebekah was sick. Her stomach would not settle. She tried to think of what she had eaten to upset her stomach, but nothing came to mind. She tried different things but could barely get any relief. Then she noticed something else…

Isaac watched his wife grow. She devoured everything the cook put in front of her. It seemed to Isaac there was never a time she wasn't hungry. One thing for sure, Rebekah was beautiful pregnant. She, of course, complained about everything. She seemed to grow overnight. It was impossible for her to get comfortable. When she finally was, he was loath to do anything to cause her to have to move.

"The child moves all the time." Her large eyes watched Isaac. "I don't understand. It's as if he's beating me up. See?" She pointed to her belly as a protrusion bounced. "What is going on with this child?"

She went to the Lord. She needed to know what was happening with her son. The Lord answered her, "You will deliver twins. You are carrying two nations. One nation will be stronger than the other. The oldest son will serve the younger."

Rebekah woke in great pain. The midwife was called. The boys were born. The older was very red. He was also hairy, so they named him Esau. The younger entered the world holding onto his older brother's heel. They named him Jacob.

The twins were always at odds with each other. Even as babies they wrestled constantly. The nurse watched as the two played on the floor. Jacob saw Esau with a toy he wanted. He watched until his brother wasn't looking. Slowly he slipped it away from Esau. Then triumphantly Jacob held it up for Esau to see. Esau also watched Jacob. Innocently Jacob crawled around on the blanket, ignoring his stolen toy. Esau moved into position. When Jacob least expected, Esau used his toy to pound Jacob on the head. Rebekah ran to answer Jacob's cry. She reached down and lovingly picked up Jacob. "Esau hit him, Isaac. He was just crawling across the floor."

Isaac smiled tolerantly at Esau. "They are boys, Rebekah." He picked up Esau and cuddled his chunky little man.

The boys had almost nothing in common. Jacob loved to tend his father's sheep. He had a gentle way about him. He was Rebekah's favorite. Esau was a hunter. He was born to be out in the open field. He could not be kept inside. He was Isaac's favorite.

Isaac was forty years old when he married their mother. Rebekah and Isaac were married twenty years before the boys were born. At last Rebekah had her family. Isaac had his heir. He, of course, intended to pass the inheritance on to the older son. Rebekah knew God had other plans. She remembered the Lord telling her the older son would serve the younger. She watched her sons as they struggled over everything. Jacob was not satisfied to be the younger brother. He wanted the promise his brother had. Rebekah watched as Jacob hungered for Esau's birthright. She tried to explain to Isaac, but Isaac did not listen. "Esau is the oldest. He is the rightful heir."

Esau came in from hunting. He was famished. He had been hunting for days. "What is that smell?" He looked over at Jacob. "You are cooking again." He laughed at Jacob as he reminded him, "That's women's work." The pain in his stomach screamed at him. He couldn't go any longer without nourishment. He reached into the pot. Jacob soundly smacked him with a spoon. "Get your own food. I have work to do. I can't be cooking for myself and you."

Esau bawled, "I am starving. Give me some of your dinner." Jacob dished up the food. He smelled it and tasted the wonderful stew. "That is good." He watched Esau. "I could be persuaded, that is, if you make it worth my while."

Esau leaned back. "Of course, everything has a price with you, doesn't it? What do you want?"

"Sell me your birthright." Jacob watched his brother with the intensity of a cat watching his prey.

Esau growled at Jacob. "What, are you crazy? What are you talking about?"

Jacob reasoned with his brother. "You don't want it. You never have. All you care about is hunting and fishing. Sell me your birthright. I have always wanted it. It should be mine. At least I appreciate it."

Esau looked at his younger brother. He never could understand why Jacob put so much importance into it. Jacob was right; he had never been interested in the responsibility it represented. "What good will it do me if I'm dead? It's yours. Now give me something to eat." Jacob handed him a bowl of stew. He offered him some bread and wine to wash it down. Jacob could not believe his luck.

The years went by. Rebekah overheard Isaac speaking to Esau, "I am old, my son. It is time for me to bless you before I die."

"Father, don't say such a thing." Esau loved Isaac. To him his father was what the promises were about. The old man had lived a full life. Isaac had spent his days and nights serving the Lord God Almighty. How could he ever be the man his father and grandfather were?

Isaac leaned back onto his cushions. He arranged them the way he liked them. Finally, he sat comfortably. Esau had just brought his father in from the outside. Every day Esau came to visit his father. He always took Isaac for a walk. Isaac was blind. Esau made a point of talking to his father of the sky, describing the clouds. He would tell his father of the herds. Esau took time to see and tell his father what he was looking at. Isaac enjoyed his son so much every day. He depended on Esau to visit him and take him outside. Today his father had walked farther than usual. Esau noticed the slowness of his steps but disregarded it as old age. Isaac, however, saw it as a sign. He spent time breathing in the day. He believed he did not have many more to go. Isaac was ready to join his father. He had peace.

"We must face it, my son. I will not live much longer. But you are in your prime. Now this is what I want you to do. Go hunting and bring me back your venison I love so much. I will eat my favorite meal then I will bless you."

Esau embraced his father. "As you wish, Father. I will return with your dinner."

Rebekah had an idea. She ran to the field where Jacob was tending his flock. "Jacob, your father is planning to bless Esau. Kill me a lamb, and I will prepare it the way he likes. You will receive the blessing. Esau must not receive the blessing. The Lord told me you are the child of the promise. I have not been able to make your father understand. We must deceive him."

Jacob stopped dead in his tracks. "I cannot!" he protested. "Father will know it's me. He will curse me." Terror marked his face.

"No, my son, the curse will fall on me if your father finds you out. Now hurry. I cannot allow one of these local women Esau has married to become the mother of the promise. They are cruel, uncouth women who grieve me every day. I don't know how your brother puts up with them."

Jacob obeyed his mother. He stole the blessing from his brother and slipped out of his father's tent undetected. His heart raced. His hands shook. He squeezed them into a fist. He was still laboring to breathe even after he left Isaac.

He heard the voice of Esau. "Jacob!" The scream could be heard by everyone in the camp. His brother was on the warpath. Jacob knew he would have to run for his life. Esau was not going to forgive this betrayal.

Esau planned to kill Jacob. He knew brothers should not hate each other, but he hated Jacob. Hadn't he sold his birthright to Jacob? Wasn't that fair? He thought about that scheming brother of his. *Jacob has never been happy.* Esau wanted none of the lavish things. Esau was satisfied with the simple things of life. But not Jacob—he had never been satisfied. Even when they were born, Jacob had his hand around Esau's heel. He always wrestled with Esau. Isaac was not well after Jacob had pulled his little charade. Isaac became sick. Esau plotted Jacob's death. *Father is old. His health is failing. I will wait for now. When he is buried, I will kill Jacob.* He smiled. He had plenty of time for revenge. His place was with his father.

Jacob realized he had to escape. His father and mother said goodbye to him. It was one of the most difficult things Jacob had ever done. It hurt to leave his father, but his mother insisted. "You must go, my son." Isaac blessed him again before he left. Now he was on the adventure of his lifetime.

He finally stopped to rest. He found a terrific rock. He decided to use it for a pillow. As Jacob slept, a marvelous thing happened. He saw a ladder. It reached up to the very throne of God. He looked, and angels were using it to go up and come down. As he watched this sight, the Lord spoke to him and said, "I am the God of your grandfather Abraham and father Isaac. I will give this land you are sleeping on to you and your children. You will have many children. They will be like the dust of the earth in multitude. Because of your children, all the families of the earth will be blessed." When Jacob woke up, he was afraid. He thought that place was a gate to heaven. He placed the rocks he had laid on as a memorial then poured oil on them. He said to the Lord, "If you will keep me safe and bring me back again, I will serve you, and I will give you one-tenth of everything I own" (see Gen. 28:11–22).

Jacob journeyed to the homeland of his mother's brother Laban. He came to a place where there was a well. Shepherds stopped and were waiting for the rest of the people who watered their flocks to come. There was a large stone over the well. The men of the area would all move the stone at a certain time of day, water their flocks, and then move it back. Jacob asked these men about his uncle Laban, "Do you know him? Is he in good health?"

"Yes, we know him, he is well. Here comes his daughter Rachel now." Jacob looked up and saw Rachel for the first time. He moved the stone and let her water her flock. Then, with tears in his eyes, he kissed her and told her who he was. At that moment, he fell in love with Rachel.

JACOB, RACHEL, AND LEAH
THE WRONG BRIDE

And Jacob served seven years for Rachel; and they
seemed unto him but a few days, for the love he
had to her. (Gen. 29:20, KJV)

Leah looked at herself realistically. She was not exactly unattractive. In fact, by most standards, she would have been considered quite lovely. She was shy, and her eyes, though soft and appealing, were weak; but she was still beautiful. Her long, dark hair was soft and healthy. She had a beautiful smile; her teeth were straight and white. She had a lovely figure and stood her full height carrying herself with grace and poise. No, she was not Rachel; she was only Leah.

All her life she had been haunted by Rachel's beauty. Now, she thought with considerable pain, of the man she loved. He too was totally captivated by Rachel. It wasn't that she did not love Rachel; she herself could understand why everyone found Rachel to be so lovely. Rachel was, in fact, the most beautiful woman Leah had ever seen. She sighed. How could she possibly compete with someone like that? Rachel was the one everyone loved, and Leah knew it. She had been blessed and cursed to be the older sister of someone like Rachel.

All the women in Leah's family were famous beauties. Rebekah, her aunt and father's sister, was often spoken of by the locals who remembered her beauty. Sarah, who had married Abraham, was renowned for her beauty. She was so beautiful that Abraham, Sarah's husband, was often afraid to travel with Sarah as his wife. He had more than once passed her off as his sister. Leah remembered the stories. Sarah was actually taken by kings of the area for their harems, until God rebuked them for Abraham's sake. Leah sighed again. She had not inherited that beauty. Rachel had.

She looked out of her window and saw Rachel playing with the little lambs she loved so much. She was breathtaking even to Leah. Her hair fell around her face and down her back in little ringlets. The laughter on Rachel's face showed her smile and warm personality. Jacob watched Rachel, taking in everything about her. He just stood there looking at her as though she was all he ever needed or wanted.

Jealousy crept up. All the love she felt for her sister paled compared to the love she had for Jacob. She knew she could never have him, but her heart refused to understand. Why had she been born into a home with someone so perfect and beautiful? Rachel had virtually stolen the love of everyone Leah cared about, but the adoration of Jacob—it was more than Leah could stand.

She went to work and started to prepare breakfast. Even now she was the one cooking and caring for everyone, while Rachel, the precious one, was outside playing with her lambs and talking to Jacob.

Leah and Rachel's father, Laban, walked into the kitchen and noticed Leah slamming the food and dishes onto the table. "Why are you moping about?" he asked.

She looked at him, her dark eyes blazed with anger. "Rachel never helps me. She is outside right now, just laughing and having a good time entertaining Jacob."

Her father looked at her and said, "She is promised to him. He will soon be able to marry her. He has fulfilled his contract with me for her hand."

Tears immediately filled Leah's eyes and started to fall down her cheeks. Laban looked at his daughter and knew her pain. He took her in his arms and held her for a moment. "There is a way, you know. I know of a way to make him marry you."

"How"—Leah looked at him blankly—"how could you do that, Father?"

Laban patted her hand. "You leave it to me. When the time comes, you must obey me completely. Are you sure you are willing to do whatever you must to marry him?"

Nodding, she said, "Yes." Then a pang of guilt struck her. "What about Rachel?"

Laban wiped her eyes. "Is it not the responsibility of a father to take care of both of his daughters? I will also see to Rachel's future. Now run along. I will take care of this for you and Rachel." Leah left her father. She felt guilty, but the guilt was not as hard to bear as losing Jacob. Maybe, in time, he would come to love her as she loved him. She remembered the way he looked at Rachel. Her heart sank as she recalled his smile when Rachel walked into the room. *No, he could never love me like that.* As she looked out into the field, she noticed the sheep. All she saw were odd, misshaped forms. She sat down and watched them, thinking and knowing what she and her father were planning was wrong. Rachel looked radiant. Her eyes shone bright with anticipation. She looked into Jacob's eyes. He was happy. They sat talking about their future, their marriage, and their children.

Jacob had plans to build his own flock. He was ambitious and a natural-born herdsman. He loved the out of doors and thought of new ways to graze the herd he kept for Laban. Everything Jacob did prospered Laban.

God's blessing was so mighty on Jacob; Laban did not see how he could do without him. He was not ready to let Jacob go. While Jacob served him faithfully for Rachel's hand in marriage, Laban prospered beyond his imagination. He was not about to allow Jacob to start his own heard, leaving him to just barely survive, as he had before. Laban devised a plan that was so beautiful, he could not help but laugh as he thought on it. Joy virtually reeked from him as he walked out to speak to Jacob.

"My son," he greeted Jacob warmly. "I see you and Rachel are making plans again. When is the happy day?"

Jacob smiled boyishly as he said, "As soon as you agree."

"Well then, since I agree, why not this week? I will make all the plans. We have guests to invite, and I will throw the biggest wedding celebration this place has ever seen. How could I not? You are marrying my daughter. We will eat, drink, and dance. I will take care of everything."

Jacob was speechless. Everything he had ever wanted was now his. Rachel was all he thought of. To him, it seemed as though the seven years were nothing. He served Laban joyously. Just knowing she would be his wife was all he needed.

The wedding day arrived. Laban was fluttering around, seeing to last-minute details, like a concerned father of the bride should do.

"No, Father!" Leah said with an air of desperation. "We cannot do this."

Laban reminded her, "You said you would do anything."

She felt sick as she tried to convince him. "Yes, but I didn't know you would ask me to marry him in the place of Rachel. If we trick him, he will hate me. I will never be able to win his love." Laban reasoned with her. "You are the oldest. It is the custom of our people that the younger not marry before the older. This is the proper way it should be done—"

She interrupted him. "But you are tricking him! He will never understand!"

Laban continued, "Listen to me, you are both my daughters, and you both love him. How can I break one of your hearts to make the other happy? At first he will be offended, but I will give Rachel to him also. She is your sister. They will both forgive you with time. This way he provides for you and Rachel. He is a good man. He is the heir of Isaac. There is a promise from God Himself on that family: He will bless Abraham and his descendants. Don't you understand? You love him for a reason? You are a part of God's plan. Your children will be great and the descendants of Abraham. They will be heirs to God. They will grow to understand."

She looked at Laban. Her father was good at this sort of thing. He always managed to have his way. No matter how wrong a thing might be, he had a way of turning it to his good.

Leah dressed for the wedding. Her father hid Rachel somewhere; Leah did not know where. She was careful to hide her face. She wrapped the veil around herself and prayed for God's help to change the heart of Jacob.

Rachel was frantic. "You can't do this, Father!" she cried out. "Jacob is promised to me!"

"Yes," he said, "and you will have him, just not now."

She screamed and cried and threw her best tantrum. It did her no good.

"Here, my son." Laban grabbed a bottle of wine from the servants as they passed by. "We must celebrate." Everything was going along according to plan. Jacob was almost drunk enough. Just a few more cups of wine should do it. Laban looked into the eyes of his young pigeon. *What a terrific son-in-law you will be,* he thought as he continued with his plan to get his hands on the family inheritance of Abraham and Isaac. He knew how wealthy Jacob's family was. Even kings were not as rich.

The wedding went off as planned. No one was the wiser. Leah walked up to her husband-to-be, fear causing her hands to tremble. She wore Rachel's clothes. She had applied Rachel's scent. But still, she was concerned that he might recognize her and make a scene. She could not bear the public humiliation. She was hardly able to make her legs work. She looked up and saw her older brother. He looked directly into her eyes, the only part of her that was not covered, and gasped. She looked at him, silently pleading with him not to expose her. He stepped back, swallowed, and let her pass. Being careful to look down, she approached Jacob. He was smiling, warmed by the glow of all the wine her father had been pouring down him. The ceremony was done. They were man and wife. The partying was now underway.

The flurry of activity kept Leah from being able to think. What had she just done? She was trapped. There was no escape. She felt the room spinning around and almost fainted, falling back against Jacob. He caught her and held her tightly. "We should retire," he whispered into her ear. "It is late, and you are tired." She tried to speak, but words would not form. The pulse in her neck pounded so hard she ached from it. What she felt was far beyond fear. Leah was terrified!

Jacob swept her off and away from the protection of the people. He looked forward to being alone with his bride. He kept calling her Rachel. Every time she heard him speak that name, she wanted to cry out, "I'm not Rachel!" But she didn't. She let her father trick him. She was just as guilty. Tomorrow she would be found out, but tonight, she was his wife, the woman he loved. She would take what she could get.

Jacob woke up. Beside him was the woman of his dreams. He couldn't believe his luck. Not only did he love her, she loved him. He reached out to the beautiful woman next to him and turned her over. Her hair covered her face like a veil. He gently removed the strands. It was not Rachel!

"Leah! What are you doing here?"

She looked away. "You married me."

"No," he said. "I married Rachel. You and your father have tricked me. Where is Rachel?" he demanded.

She sobbed as she said, "I don't know." She reached for something to cover herself as she continued, "Father hid her somewhere."

Jacob looked at her as though she were something vile. "She had better be unharmed! Why didn't you cry out? How could you do this to me and Rachel, your own sister?"

Leah tried to comfort him. "She is all right. Father would not hurt her."

"Not hurt her?" he shouted. "How can you say that? She thought we were getting married, and now I'm married to you. Believe me, he has hurt her! You both have!"

She sank back into the pillows on the bed. Her heart was breaking. She could not answer Jacob. He was right. She had hurt Rachel. "Forgive me," she whispered. "Please, Jacob, forgive me."

"I cannot," he said coldly and left.

Leah sat alone in their room, crying. Her heart was truly broken. Jacob rushed up to Laban, grabbing him by the throat. His look was murderous. "Where is she?"

Laban spoke carefully. "She is fine, my boy. I will get her for you. Just let go of me."

Jacob walked closely behind the old fox. He was not going to trust him again. Laban opened a locked door, and there in the corner of the room was Rachel. Jacob could see she had been crying. "I should kill you for this!"

Laban looked at his son-in-law. "You can have them both. You know our customs. It is not proper for me to give you Rachel before Leah has married. I will give you Rachel too."

"What's the catch, old man?" Jacob spoke through gritted teeth.

Laban smiled. "Well, naturally, I value both of my daughters equally." Laban felt Jacob tightening his grip on his arm. His smile faded as he added, "But since it's you, of course, you can marry her right away. Just spend the week with Leah. Afterward, you can have Rachel also. I won't make you wait the seven years. This time you can work it off after you marry her." Jacob tightened his grip. "If you kill me, she will not forget it. You want her to come to you willingly, don't you?"

For the first time, Jacob saw Laban for what he was. He shoved Laban away. "All right, you have a deal. If you cross me again, I will not be responsible for my actions."

Laban nodded. The deal was set. He would have the labor and blessing of Jacob seven more years.

Jacob turned to Rachel. She ran to him, and they embraced. "I am sorry, my love. He tricked me. I thought Leah was you. I have married your sister." The words left his mouth painfully.

Rachel looked at her father. "How could you do this?" Laban tilted his head and asked, "And you, Jacob? What did you do to your own father, Isaac? Did you not trick him and betray your own brother to get what you wanted? You are my nephew, the son of my sister. It would seem the fruit does not fall far from the tree. You see, children, we are all family, and as family we are all alike." Laban's words, spoken for effect, hit their mark. Jacob looked stricken. All the blood drained from his face. He was ashamed. Laban was right. Jacob walked away. Even Rachel could not comfort him.

Out into the field he wandered. How far, he wasn't sure. There he cried for Esau, his brother. His conscience had often pricked him, but now it was screaming relentlessly. *You did this! You started this whole thing! You deceived your own father! Now God has allowed you to be deceived!* There, under the shade of a tree, he wept and repented. "God, forgive me!" His remorse seemed unbearable. He suddenly thought of Leah. He realized he had been cruel. Somehow, he would forgive her.

Rachel looked at her sister with disgust. "How could you marry him? He will never love you! You have betrayed me! I will never forgive you! You wait. When he is my husband, I will keep him from you."

Leah walked away dejected. She had made a huge mistake. This would follow her forever.

Jacob finally returned, long after dark. Leah stood in the corner of their room, waiting for him. She did not dare to go near him after all she had done. She only wanted him to forgive her. He looked her way. He was tired, and his eyes were swollen from crying. He breathed out the words, "I am sorry. I was cruel. You know I care about you. I don't want to cause you pain."

She felt hope for the first time that day. "I am the one who was cruel. Your forgiveness is everything to me. Are you hungry?" "No." He said the word with a final tone. She knew he was not prepared to speak to her more than that. He picked up some of his things and left. Leah stood alone in the dark, watching the shadows on the wall. She knew he would not offer more than what he honestly felt. At that moment, she was comforted just to know he did not hate her.

FAMILY LIFE

> And Leah conceived, and bare a son, and she called his name Reuben: for she said, Surely the Lord hath looked upon my affliction; now therefore my husband will love me. (Gen. 29:32, KJV)

Time passed quickly. Jacob stayed out in the fields with the sheep. Rachel prepared for her marriage to Jacob. Laban made another big feast, and he saw to it there was wine and dancing. Rachel almost forgot the pain of Leah's betrayal. Then in the shadows, she saw Leah.

Leah watched her sister from a solitary place. She wanted to enjoy this day with Rachel. They often as children giggled about their wedding days; always, they were at each other's side. They planned to help prepare the bride for her groom. How could they have known how different it would be from their childhood fantasies? She missed Rachel. She watched her and hoped they would be close again.

This time Jacob did not trust Laban. He remained sober. Before marrying Rachel, he removed her veil, just for his own peace of mind. He watched everything she did and did not let her leave his side. He was afraid Laban would take her from him.

He said his goodbyes and left, to be alone with his bride. Leah noticed they never looked her way. Leah's father walked up to her, smiling. His plan had worked to perfection. "You see everything will be fine."

"No, Father, you are wrong, and I was wrong to listen to you! He loves her. Now I have not only lost the man I love, I have also lost my sister." Tears ran down her face. "She hates me!"

He looked at her tenderly. "Leah, you have always been the sensitive one. She will need you someday, and she will forgive you. Rachel is like a child. I spoiled her too much. She wants everything her way. And just as a little girl who wakes up to find her life is not perfect, she has awakened from a beautiful dream. She will come to her senses some day." Leah dropped her head. Laban held her and said, "You will see, my dear. She is your sister. It will be fine."

Weeks went by, and Leah did not see Jacob. He had taken Rachel somewhere private. She waited for their return.

Leah was unloved. The Lord felt her pain and had mercy on her. She was sick often and felt sick now. She lay in the cool, trying to rest. Her servant, Zilpah, cared for her. She watched over Leah as Leah cried and worried over Jacob and Rachel. Leah was pregnant.

Her fear of the unknown changed as she started to show. Her heart was full; she would be a mother. She had always dreamed of being a mom. She openly praised God: "I know God has shown me mercy. He knows my husband does not love me." For the first time since she married Jacob, she felt she would have love. The child's name was Reuben. He was a beautiful boy. His father was there for his birth. Jacob had been spending more and more time with her as the birth drew near.

Each woman now had her own place, away from the other. Jacob could not take the bickering. He moved Rachel to a private tent away from Leah.

Rachel was not happy. Leah had given birth to Jacob's first-born son. How could she not be miserable? She went to see her sister and the child. He was so small and perfect. Leah held the child as though he were breakable. Leah was glowing. Rachel could not help but notice how completely beautiful Leah was. She also noticed the closeness that had somehow started to form between Jacob and Leah. Jacob leaned over Leah as she held their child. Rachel grew more familiar with jealousy. She was not able to compete with this. Her husband could not be kept from his own son, or could he?

She threw a tantrum when they returned home and let Jacob know she would not allow him to visit her sister anymore. Jacob left and went to Leah. Leah became pregnant again. Rachel was beside herself. She did her best to convince Jacob to come back to her. She had no choice but to let him go to Leah's.

He talked about Reuben daily—the child this, the child that. She was weary with it all. "I want a son too!" she demanded. She was completely overcome with jealousy of Leah. She insisted, "Jacob, either you give me children, or I will die!"

Jacob was unable to reason with her. "Am I God? How can I give you a son? Have I kept you from becoming pregnant?" He was angry with Rachel. "I am not the one who has kept you from having children!"

Meanwhile, Leah gave birth to Simeon. Rachel recalled Leah saying to her, "The Lord knows how unhappy I have been. Now Jacob will love me!" Her heart sank as he lovingly returned to Leah's side, caring for Reuben and for Leah, as the pregnancy was so difficult. Rachel wanted to scream. She wanted Jacob's undivided attention. Now she had to share the love of Jacob with, if not Leah, at least Leah's children.

After the birth of Simeon, Rachel tried to be, at least, polite. Wasn't it better if she shared the lives of Jacob's children with him, even if they were not hers? Then she found out Leah was pregnant again!

She was jealous beyond reason. "Give me children!" she demanded of Jacob. He was angry. Jacob flew into a rage. "Am I God?" he asked her again. "He is the only one who can give you children!"

Then Rachel told him, "If you love me, you will marry Bilhah, my servant." She was desperate. "I have to have a son. She can have children for me. How can I go on without children?' Rachel's heart seemed to be breaking. She was completely irrational. Jacob could not make her understand that he loved her, even if she never had a child. It was an acceptable custom at the time: if the husband and wife agreed, he could take another woman who would have children on behalf of his wife. So Rachel gave him Bilhah.

Bilhah was perky and very talkative. She was not in love with Jacob. She did not see him as the beginning and ending of her happiness. She was laidback and easygoing, unlike Rachel or Leah. She was petite, with large almond-shaped eyes. A curtain of long, dark lashes surrounded them. Jacob liked the look of mischief they often got. He had many times watched her as he and Rachel were involved in their conflicts. She would look at him as if she had a secret joke he was not aware of. Her long hair was always pulled up and out of her way. She laughed easily, something Jacob needed. Jacob found her to be a welcome distraction from his other wives. To his surprise, Bilhah made him laugh.

She understood Rachel's need for children. "You have to understand, Jacob. If a woman does not have children, she is good for nothing. We are told from birth that our only value is in being mothers. Poor Rachel, she loves you so much. Her heart is breaking while she prays and hopes to become pregnant. Leah seems to produce children by thinking them into existence."

He liked Bilhah. They both understood each other. She was willing to do what she could to help Rachel. She loved Rachel, and she made his being with her a delight. There was no pressure. She was willing to let nature take its course.

Bilhah became pregnant very quickly. Rachel was thrilled. They planned for the baby as though it were royalty on the way.

When the child arrived, to Rachel's delight, it was a boy. Rachel named him Dan, She said, "God has shown everyone around me I have value. He has heard my prayer. He has given me a son."

Bilhah was thrilled for her mistress. Then Bilhah became pregnant again and gave Jacob a second son. She presented the baby to Rachel. Rachel named him Naphtali. Rachel told her, "I have had a difficult struggle with Leah, but now I am winning!" Leah sat in the shade of a tree. She watched her sons play. Jacob was spending much of his time with Rachel and Bilhah. She was not happy. It was hard enough to keep his attention when there was only Rachel. But now he had Bilhah! She could tell, by the way he spoke of her and her sons, that he was not exactly unhappy with their new arrangement.

She seethed as she thought on Rachel's last barb. Rachel had said, as though she were the boys' real mother, "Their father is so happy with the boys that he can't wait to come home and play with them." Rachel had looked at her as though she were a cat with milk.

Leah began to panic. "What if he doesn't ever come back to me? What if he just stays with Rachel, pretending these are her sons?" Her mind raced as she mentally tortured herself. That afternoon she was having one of her headaches. She started to become very sick.

Zilpah tried to comfort her. "Mistress, please, I beg of you. You must not think like this. I have sent for the master. He is coming. You must not let him see you like this. He cares very deeply for you. This will upset him very much."

Jacob finally arrived. He spent that evening and all the next week with Leah. He held her and comforted her. He tried to make her understand she was the mother of his children and he cared for her.

Leah used every trick in the book to keep Jacob around. She was determined to give him more children. Every excuse she could think of, she used to keep him coming back. After a while, she realized that she wasn't getting pregnant.

Jacob was to the point of hopelessness. Leah had been crying for days. He begged her to stop. She said over and over again, "But you love Rachel. No matter how many sons I have given you, you still love her!" She was pitiful as she said, "I love you, the way you love Rachel. I can't compete with her beauty. Now she has these sons. She throws them up to me all the time, Jacob." Leah threw herself down on the bed and buried her face into the pillows. "I have tried. I just can't get pregnant."

Jacob knelt down beside this woman he had learned to care for. "It is all right, Leah. You know I am more than happy with the sons we have. Why can't you understand it's not a contest? Sure, I love Rachel, I always have. But that doesn't mean I don't care for you very deeply. Your love for me has forced me to love you back. That is why Rachel has been so hurt. She knew I could not help myself."

Leah rolled over so she could see him. "But what if you stop loving me? You love me just a little compared to Rachel, I know that. What if you stop loving me altogether? I can't live like that, Jacob. I have to have your love. I know what I did was wrong. Every day I pay for it. But I would do it all over again. I love you the way you love Rachel. I can't help myself." She buried her face back into the pillow, unable to face him.

He was hurt for her. No matter what he did, someone was always hurting. She and Rachel could never be happy.

She stopped crying. Her face looked like a little girl's as she announced, "You have to marry Zilpah. I don't know why I didn't think of it before. She is young and strong. She can have lots of sons for you. Just because I've stopped getting pregnant doesn't mean Zilpah can't."

Jacob shook his head no. Panic rose quickly as he declared, "This is ridiculous! You and I have children. This whole thing with Bilhah, it is just for Rachel's sake. Leah, I don't need any more wives!"

Leah burst into tears again. "See, you only love Rachel!" Her heart was broken.

Jacob was desperate to comfort her. "Please, Leah, this isn't good for you. You can't allow yourself to be hurt like this." She did not stop. After a few days, Jacob gave in and agreed to marry Zilpah.

Zilpah was quiet. Her loyalty to Leah was unwavering. Jacob marveled at the love these servants had for Rachel and Leah. He could not understand how they could be willing to go along with his wives, just accepting their decisions. "Don't you have any objections?" he asked Zilpah. "I mean you are willing to do anything for Leah."

Zilpah spoke very carefully. Jacob noticed she always thought before she said anything. "I don't have the luxury of decisions. I am her servant. But she is good to me. I have served others who were cruel. Leah doesn't know how to be cruel. She only knows how to love."

Zilpah turned out to be as fertile as her mistress. It seemed to Jacob that he had just looked at the woman when she became pregnant. She gave birth to a handsome baby boy. Leah named him Gad.

Jacob smiled as Leah danced around the room. It was good to see her happy. Smiling, she said, "Oh, Jacob, I am so lucky!"

It didn't take long before Zilpah became pregnant again! Leah was thrilled. She praised the Lord singing. She began to announce, "Other women will look at me and know God's blessing is on me. They will know I am happy when they see all my sons!" She rejoiced and named him Asher.

Rachel was tormented. Her heart melted when she thought of Leah's sons. She immediately decided to stop Leah and Zilpah from getting pregnant. She managed to keep Jacob occupied with her and away from them!

Reuben was out exploring when he found some mandrake roots. He took them to his mother. Rachel wanted them. She asked Leah to share them with her. Leah was angry. She had not been allowed to be with Jacob for a very long time. Rachel was so spiteful after the birth of Zilpah's two sons. Rachel put so much pressure on Jacob that he would not stay with her or Zilpah.

She asked Rachel, "Haven't you done enough? When will you be satisfied? You know he loves you. He won't even come near me. He doesn't want you upset. Now you even want my son's man-drakes. They are a gift from Reuben. Why should I share them with you?"

Rachel felt a pang of conscience. She had been keeping Jacob away from Leah and Zilpah. She did not want to take any chances with them becoming pregnant. She knew better than to punish him for going to them. She had finally gotten smart. Every time he wanted to see Leah and her children, she would agree with him. "Yes, Jacob, your children do need you." Then she would distract him. It was so easy to keep him away from Leah and Zilpah. She was the one he loved. She was the one he actually wanted. She just had to make him feel completely loved. He didn't go anywhere when she turned on the charm.

She decided to be generous. "All right," she sighed. "You can spend time with him if you'll give me your mandrakes."

Leah was quick to agree. She was happy. She had made a good deal. She would be with Jacob. Perhaps the Lord would allow her to become pregnant again. She bathed and perfumed herself.

Jacob tended the sheep all day. He wiped the sweat from his face. His staff was in his hand. He had just turned the flock over to his friend to watch while he was away. He looked up, and Leah was coming toward him. He felt sick. He did not want to be in the middle of his wives' squabbles.

"You have to come with me," she said. Jacob listened to her story about the mandrakes. He had lost the ability to argue with these two women. They each looked on him as the answer to their unhappiness. He worked all the time and came home to bickering; it was exhausting.

God answered Leah's prayer; she became pregnant with her fifth son, Issacar. Rachel watched once again as Jacob, the everloving father, cared for her sister, leaving her alone while he waited on and tended to Leah!

Then Leah became pregnant again and had a sixth son. She named him Zebulun. Leah felt fulfilled; she had given Jacob six sons. She knew he would respect her now. In his way, Jacob did love Leah. Their closeness unnerved Rachel.

Leah became pregnant and gave him a daughter, Dinah. Jacob was totally enchanted with the little doll. She wasn't anything like the boys. She held his heart the first day he held her in his arms. Jacob loved being with Leah. Her children were a joy. Leah was a wonderful wife. She thought only of him and the children. But even with all that, his one true love was still Rachel. Sometimes when he was with Leah, he longed for Rachel.

Rachel was not happy over the new baby. Leah had managed to capture Jacob's attention again. Whenever she gave him another child, Rachel lost a little bit of him. She was obsessed with Jacob. She wanted all of him, not just pieces of his heart. He continued to daily remind her she was his one true love. But Rachel knew Leah had made an impact. If only her father had not given Leah to Jacob, she would have a much better life.

She watched as the new baby girl played. Her heart was broken in two. She did everything she could think of to ensure Jacob continued to love her most, but it did not fill her need for a child. She longed to hold her own son in her arms. "God, why have you forgotten me? You know how much I love Jacob. How can I go on if I never touch the face of my own child? If you will not give me a son, then take my life. I cannot bear this any longer. Leah steals the love of my husband, one child at a time, while you deny me motherhood."

Alone in her room, she knelt on the floor with her face in her hands. Sobs racked her body as she begged God for a son. This time she did not ask Jacob to give her a child. She talked to God. She poured out her soul to the Almighty. Her heart was broken before the Lord. She could not go on childless. God heard her prayer. He had mercy on her. She was His. He loved her. God wanted her to understand just how important she was to Him. She gave birth to Joseph. She looked at her bundle of love. "God has taken away my shame." She smiled angelically as she said, "May God give me another son."

Leah was fully prepared to resent the child, but the moment she looked at Rachel's face, her love for her sister took over. She was happy for Rachel! The child was perfect. She instantly loved him. She sat near Rachel, watching her suckle the child. Leah could barely speak. "Rachel, I am sorry for my part in your unhappiness. I know you love Jacob. I have been a terrible sister to you. I promise not to be hateful to this child. Seeing you with him today makes me very happy for you. Please, can't we find a way to be sisters again?"

"Tears rolled down Rachel's face. She had not expected this from Leah. She knew she could not stop resenting her just yet, but she wanted to. She nodded and said, "I promise, Leah, I will try. But it may take time."

Leah nodded. "I understand. I have always loved you."

Jacob was so proud of Joseph. He could not help himself. He loved all his sons, but Joseph was different. The child was beautiful like his mother. Every day Jacob awakened just to see his sweet boy. Joseph brought him so much pleasure. For a long time, Jacob watched Leah and Rachel suffer from jealousy and envy. Now here, with Rachel and this child, Jacob found comfort. This is what they had planned so long ago. He felt sorry for Leah. He loved their children, but his heart was bound to Rachel. She was his one true love, and now she had given him a son.

Joseph grew quickly, learning something new every day. The older children could not help but notice the love Jacob lavished on Joseph. The demon of jealousy that had plagued their mother and Aunt Rachel now burrowed into their souls. They watched their father play with and teach Joseph, and they waited for their turn. Their turn did not come, and when it did, it was as tepid as the love he showed their mother.

Jacob learned of the jealousy of his brothers-in-law, the brothers of his wives. For some time now, he worked for Laban with an understanding. He was to receive all the animals with color or markings. Starting from the day they made the agreement, Jacob was supposed to be able to go through Laban's herd and gather all the colored or marked animals. But Laban deceived him once again. Laban went through the herd himself. He chose out all the colored and marked animals. Then he gave them to his sons to care for. They moved them a few days journey away from Jacob and Laban's herd.

Jacob was as cunning as his uncle. He chose out different trees. Some of them were almond, poplar, and finally plane trees. He cut some of their branches, and he peeled off strips of bark. His plan was to place them where the females who were the strongest were watering. When they came to drink, they mated. He was careful to watch for the prize animals. He only placed them there when the healthiest animals were drinking. He removed them when the sick or weak animals were at the water. God showed him in a vision that all the babies being born were streaked, grizzled, spotted, or colored. When the lambs were born, it was as in the dream. He received the marked animals for his wages.

Laban was very unhappy. His prize animals only gave birth to stock for Jacob. His own herds did not increase; in fact they grew smaller and weaker. While Laban's sheep, goats, camels, and cattle, decreased, Jacob became very rich, leaving Laban poorer all the time.

Laban looked out at Jacob's herds with contempt. He had tried everything. If he told Jacob he could have all the streaked animals born, all of them were streaked. If he changed it and said only the spotted, then all at once the animals born were spotted. He could hardly contain his animosity. Every day he grew angrier. Now Laban's sons accused Jacob of stealing from their father. Laban no longer seemed to like Jacob. He resented the younger man's ability to outfox him. He had used Jacob for fourteen years, forcing him to work for his daughters. When he finally started to pay Jacob for his management of the herds, he tried to cheat him. Jacob had not argued or fought against him. He simply trusted the Lord to help him by giving him colored and marked animals.

Laban resented the loss of what he considered his. He thought all that Jacob owned really belonged to him. These were his daughters, their children were his children, and the flocks were his flocks.

> And the Lord said unto Jacob, Return unto the
> land of thy fathers, and to thy kindred; and I will
> be with thee. (Gen. 31:3, KJV)

Rachel and Leah walked into the field where Jacob was tending his heard. They had been summoned. Jacob usually did not ask to see both of them together. It had to be important. They followed the servant Jacob sent to fetch them. He was a sweet young man. They looked at each other apprehensively. Leah came right out and asked, "Rachel, do you know why Jacob wants to see us?"

Rachel shook her head. She had no idea. She only knew it had to be important. They quickly arrived at their destination. Jacob sent the boy on ahead after giving him instructions about the flock.

When the young man was out of hearing, he explained, "Your father is not happy with me. I am always under suspicion. He has turned against me. I know your brothers are talking about me. They talk to the servants. The servants tell me what they say."

"What do they say, Jacob?" Rachel asked.

"They say I have stolen your father's livestock. They say I tricked him into paying me too much for my work. It becomes more difficult all the time. Some of the servants won't work for me as they should. They don't respect me. I have been praying about it. The God of my father has spoken to me. He has told me to return to my homeland. I asked you to come here to discuss this with me. I want to know what you both think."

Leah was alarmed. "But what about Esau? What if he still wants to kill you?"

Jacob answered, "If God is with me, I will be fine."

Rachel looked at her husband. "You have to do it. If God has told you to return home, you must go. Jacob, God is in everything you do."

Leah looked at Jacob and Rachel. "Rachel is right. You must obey the Lord. We are your wives. Our place is with you."

Jacob loved these women. "I don't want to force you to go. You may never see your family again. My mother never saw her family after she married my father."

Rachel studied him. "We always knew you would return home. That is the land the Lord promised to Abraham and Isaac. How can you take your place as their heir if you do not return?"

Then the girls became very serious. "Our father sold us. He forced you to work for us as his slave. Then when he finally started paying you, he has done everything he could think of to try to keep you from having anything. What he owns should be ours anyway. We are his children. But he sold us, and now he's angry because you are finally accumulating wealth. We will go with you."

Jacob was relieved. "Thank you," he said. "I need to know I can depend on you. I want to move out while your father is away. If we leave immediately, we should be able to travel at least three days before he knows we're gone. If he catches us trying to leave, I am afraid he will force you and the children to stay. We must leave now. This is God's timing."

Rachel and Leah agreed. "He would use us to make you stay and serve him. We will be ready to leave as soon as you want. We will go back to camp and take what we can carry now. Everything else we will leave."

Rachel cradled Jacob's face in her hand. "Don't worry. We will go with you. There is nothing here for us."

So Jacob traveled back to Canaan with his wives, his children, and their flocks. Laban was some distance away shearing sheep. Jacob left without saying goodbye. He did not want to have to fight Laban for his family and flocks. He left quickly.

Rachel was concerned that Jacob's brother, Esau, might not welcome them. She decided to steal her father's gods. They were valuable. As she thought how he had just sold her, she felt justified. They might need to sell them later. She hid them carefully in her things.

Laban received the news of Jacob and his daughters. He was livid. "How dare he take my daughters and my grandchildren?" His temper exploded as he thought how Jacob had stolen his flock and now his children. He gathered together all his relatives and as many men as he could.

Jacob traveled three days' journey. The flock, cattle, goats, and his family were exhausted. Their journey was slow. Laban was sure he could catch him. *I will make him sorry*, he promised himself. The night before he caught up with Jacob, the Lord visited him in a dream and warned him not to mistreat Jacob.

Jacob looked up. He had been watching the dust in the distance. He knew it was Laban. He braced himself.

Laban rode into the camp. He stepped down from his horse and said, "What have you done? Why did you leave without saying goodbye? I would have liked to kiss my daughters and grandchildren goodbye before you left. What was your hurry? I know you are anxious to return to your homeland, but I would have given you a farewell party." He was surprisingly calm.

Jacob spoke with caution. "I was afraid. I thought you would take your daughters away from me. I didn't think you would let me go."

Laban fought to control his temper. He said, "These are my daughters, and their children are my grandchildren. Your flocks are mine. Everything you have is mine." Jacob could see Laban was fighting to stay calm. Laban continued, "If it were not for your God, I would have forced you to give me my children back. You have been very foolish to leave like this. Your God spoke to me in a dream and told me not to harm you. These are my children and grandchildren. What harm would I do them?" He suddenly remembered his idols. He placed his finger in Jacob's chest. "Why have you stolen my gods?"

Jacob was more angry than afraid. He looked into the face of this deceptive little man. Twenty years of working in the freezing desert—cold at night and bitter heat of the day—came rushing back. Jacob looked at his wives and kids. He had had enough. He shoved Laban's finger away from his chest as if he were swatting a fly. "No one has taken your gods. Look around, see for yourself. I had to leave quickly. I was afraid you would take your daughters from me. I knew you and your men could overpower me. But no one has stolen your idols. Let the person who has stolen your gods die!"

Laban scowled. He nodded to his sons who immediately started searching the camp. He paced throughout Jacob's tent, looking everywhere. He went through all the luggage. Then he checked in the children's things. He was getting tired and just a little embarrassed. He looked over at Jacob, who was watching his every move. He finally ended up in Rachel's tent, the only place he hadn't looked.

She sat quietly on her camel's saddle. "Daddy!" she squealed. "I'm so glad you came to say goodbye. I'm sorry I can't get up." She lowered her voice. "This is a time of inconvenience." She looked enchanting. Her beautiful face was covered by a thin scarf. She was his angel. He looked into her eyes and melted.

Jacob stepped to the door of the tent, blustering, "Well, where are these gods of yours? You know I have never worshipped any god but the Lord. And still you come here as though I am a thief to confront me. Where are they? Why haven't you been able to find them?" Jacob looked exasperated. "I have worked faithfully for you for twenty years. I labored fourteen years for your two daughters. Not one time did you pay for any of the sheep or any of the herds that were damaged or killed. I paid for them! I had to! You forced me!"

Jacob turned and paced the ground. He reached up, dragging a shaky hand through his hair. He glared in the direction of his brothers-in-law, daring them to speak. He turned back to Laban and continued, "I have tried to get along with you, but you have continued to cheat me. If you said my wages would be the grizzled lambs, then all the lambs were born grizzled. If you decided they should be the streaked, then all of them were streaked. I have not cheated you. It is the Lord who has blessed me. He is the one who caused my flock to be established out of yours."

Laban was speechless. Jacob pointed his finger and poked it into Laban's chest. His brothers-in-law moved toward him. He shot them a look that stopped them in their tracks. "I worked for you through the heat of the day. Then I stayed with the flocks all night as the temperature dropped. I was cold watching and caring for your herds. When you started paying me wages, you changed the wages. But God knows your cruel heart. He knows how hard I have labored. He would not let you cheat me!

"I know if my God had not warned you in that dream not to harm me that you would now leave me penniless. But my God, the awesome Almighty, the God of my father Isaac and grandfather Abraham, has not allowed you to harm me."

Laban was purple. His blood pressure shot up. "How dare you talk to me like this? Everything you have, you have because of me. Your wives are my daughters. Your children are my grandchildren. Your herds, absolutely everything you own, is mine!" His sons shifted as if they were ready to fight. Laban recalled the dream. He licked his lips, smiled, and tried to calm the situation down. "But we are family. We should have peace between us?"

Jacob nodded his agreement. He wanted peace with Laban. "We will make an agreement between us. I will build up a memorial for us out of these stones. When we see them, we will remember we are family. I will not go past this to harm you, and you will not go past this place to harm me. These rocks will be our witness before the Lord."

Laban agreed. "We will remember when we see this memorial." Tears came into his eyes. He looked over at his daughters and grandchildren. He remembered the pain his daughters had suffered already. "I am concerned for my daughters. I will not be here to see if you mistreat them. Promise me before the Lord you will be kind to them. Also promise you will not marry again."

Jacob was happy to promise. He shook his head in agreement. "I promise. This memorial of rocks is a witness between us."

Jacob was beside himself with worry. He paced the floor of his tent. "Rachel, can't you understand this is serious?"

Rachel looked at her husband, confused. "Jacob, it is over. Father has left in peace."

"But it isn't over." Jacob looked into the eyes of his mischievous wife. "Your father was cursed because of these idols, and now the curse is on us."

"No," she laughed. "There is no curse. You are being superstitious. They are valuable. If we need to, we can sell them." She looked over at her newly acquired treasure.

Jacob followed her eyes. He watched as she admired them. "Can we?" Jacob asked. "Can you actually part with them? Don't you see they are an abomination to God? He is a jealous God. He will not allow people who worship any god other than Him to prosper. There is always a curse with anything we place before God. Blessings and curses are real. Just as my father blessed me and told me, 'God will bless you and make of you a great nation.' Look around you—I have eleven sons. The blessing is coming to pass. The same is true of a curse!"

"But don't you understand," she reasoned. "I will always serve God. I know He is the great God."

Jacob said very clearly, "He is the only God. These are gods of stone and wood. They have eyes, but they do not see. They have ears, but they do not hear. You cannot set Him on the shelf of your heart beside these things. He will not stay there!" Jacob could barely contain himself. He was red with anger. "He is a jealous God. You, of all people, should be able to understand jealousy. Isn't your jealousy for me the reason you and Leah can hardly speak to each other? You hate knowing I have even looked her way. If I dare to spend time with her, even to see your own niece and nephews, you are crazed with jealousy. If you are filled with such anger toward your own sister, whom I know you love deeply, how does God, who is love, who has created us and supplied our going out and coming in, feel about the betrayal you have just shown Him?"

Rachel grew pale. For the first time, she understood why Jacob would not look at or handle her father's idols. He often rebuked her and warned her about bowing down to them. She had not heeded his warnings. "Jacob, what will I do?"

He looked into the eyes of the woman he loved and said, "Repent. Ask God's forgiveness. That is all any of us can do."

"Will we still be cursed?" She looked numb. Jacob began to tremble. "I keep thinking about my telling your father the person who has stolen his idols would die." Jacob was pale. "The curse came from my lips. Just as my father spoke a blessing over me and it has come to pass, I have spoken a curse, and I cannot stop it. We have allowed this curse into our lives, and there will be consequences for it.

Alone in her tent, Rachel prayed, "God, forgive my sins, and give me a new heart. Protect my husband, Joseph, Leah, and her children. I am the one who sinned. Let this sin be on me alone and no one else. I am in your hands." Tears rolled down her face like water. She repented for years of anger toward her sister. She longed to have been a better aunt, and she prayed for her son. Somehow, in the midst of this whole problem, she began to feel really whole. She was not at peace since the day she swore to never forgive Leah.

"Poor Leah," she whispered to the Lord. "She always did what Father said." For the first time, she felt compassion for the sister she once loved so much, and that realization made her very ashamed. Jacob was right. She knew better than anyone how jealousy destroys love. Aren't we all made in God's image? He created us to be like Him. *If I have been so jealous of my sister, how must He feel when His people turn to other gods and not to Him?* Her mind reeled as she contemplated the thought. Oh, she had been foolish.

JACOB GOES HOME

And Jacob was left alone; and there wrestled a
man with him until the breaking of the day. And
he said, Thy name shall be called no more Jacob,
but Israel: for as a prince hast thou power with
God and with men, and hast prevailed. (Gen.
32:24 and 28, KJV)

Jacob walked away from Rachel. His heart was heavy. He was
moving his entire family to his homeland. It still pained him as
he thought about the way he had left.

Esau was the firstborn son; they were twins. Jacob missed
being the heir by only a moment. Esau was the legitimate heir
to the family fortune and the promise of God. The wealth had
never meant anything to Jacob. The truth was he had suffered
knowing that he was not the heir to the promise. His conscience
pained him as he remembered the way he tricked his father and
betrayed his brother.

Jacob recalled how he planned ahead. He waited for the right
opportunity. Esau came home from a hunt, exhausted and hungry.
He wanted Jacob to feed him some of the stew that Jacob was

making. Jacob took full advantage of the moment: "Sell me your birthright."

Esau looked at him as if he had lost his mind, then Esau actually agreed. He said, "What good is my birthright if I die?"

Even now, Jacob did not understand how Esau could have done it. Jacob lived for years with the one desire—to have that very birthright—and Esau sold it to him for a bowl of stew.

Jacob looked around at his cattle, his sheep, his rams, his camels, and his donkeys. His eyes fell on his children. They were God's promise to Abraham. God said to his grandfather, "I will make your seed to multiply in number as the sands of the sea." How could Esau sell a promise as great as this? These children were the fulfillment of God's very own word. Jacob treasured the promise of God. As a child, his heart was broken when he observed Esau treating that heritage with such disdain. Esau hated his birth-right. But Jacob could not excuse his own deceitful actions. No wonder he had married women who were obsessed with jealousy. He was one person who had no right to judge their behavior.

Thinking back now, he could still see his mother's face as she spoke to him: "Your Father has sent Esau to kill a deer and prepare it for him. He intends to bless Esau today. This is what you will do. Take a young goat and bring it to me. I will prepare it for your father the way he likes it."

Jacob refused: "He will know it isn't me; and instead of blessing me, he will curse me!"

Jacob's father, Isaac, was blind from old age; but he was very alert.

"No, my son," she said. "Do as I tell you. If your father realizes it's you, and not Esau, the curse will be on me." He obeyed his mother. He could still remember the smell of that dinner. No one cooked like his mother. She had an extra coat of Esau's, which she was mending. She dressed Jacob in it. She looked sad as she spoke: "My life is nothing but trouble because of these local Hittite women. Promise me that you will not marry here, as your brother has." Then she took some of the goat's skins and tied the skins to Jacob's arms and also around his neck. Esau was hairy, but Jacob's skin was smooth.

He went into the tent of Isaac and presented the dinner to his father. His father was suspicious. "Why were you so quick?"

Jacob tried to sound like his brother. "Your God gave me favor," he replied.

But Isaac was still suspicious. "You sound like Jacob." Jacob was unable to breathe. He panicked as Isaac caught him by the arm and felt the skins. The old man looked confused, "The voice is Jacob's, but the skin is Esau's." His father persisted. "Come here, my son, and kiss me." Then Jacob leaned over and kissed his father. Isaac held him and smelled his garment. "Yes, this is the smell of my son Esau. You smell like an open field."

Jacob listened as his father blessed him. He remembered every word, Isaac had spoken: "May God give you dew for good crops and harvests of grain and wine. May nations serve you. May you be the ruler of your brothers. May your mother's sons bow before you. Those who curse you are cursed, and those who bless you are blessed." Immediately after receiving the blessing, he left his father. Soon Esau arrived with the dinner he had prepared for Isaac.

Jacob's mother instructed him to go to her brother Laban. Jacob barely escaped with his life. Esau was determined to kill him. Jacob traveled to Laban's for refuge. He lived there for twenty years. Now he was coming back, back to the homeland and the brother he had left so long ago.

He moved his camp and herds slowly. He did not want to push them or the children. Jacob looked up, and angels were coming to meet him. As he saw them, he exclaimed, "This is the camp of God!"

God directed him to go home, but he was still concerned about Esau. His heart pounded as he considered his children and his wives. "Oh God, please give me wisdom to protect them. Help me to be reconciled to Esau." He decided to send messengers ahead to speak to his brother. He said, "Say this to my master Esau: 'Greetings from your servant Jacob! I have been living with our uncle Laban. I own much livestock and servants. I am sending these messengers to announce my return. I pray you will forgive me.'"

Jacob waited expectantly for news from his messengers. They returned riding hard. "Sir, Master Esau is coming to meet you with four hundred soldiers."

Jacob was beside himself with worry. "What did he say to you?"

They sat down to rest. "We rode here as quickly as we could. We told him everything you said. He did not strike us or act as if he would harm us. After a moment, he looked at his own men and ordered them to prepare to come and meet you. Then he said to us, 'My brother is finally coming home. We will ride out to meet him. Return to his camp and tell Jacob, "I am coming with four hundred of my soldiers."' After that we left."

Jacob walked away from the others. He could not let them see the fear in his face. He thought for a moment, and then he looked over at his servant and said, "We will divide the camp into two camps. If Esau attacks one, perhaps the other will be able to escape." The men worked quickly.

> And Jacob said, O God of my father Abraham, and God of my father Isaac, the Lord which saidst unto me, Return unto thy country, and to thy kindred, and I will deal well with thee: I am not worthy of the least of all the mercies, and of all the truth, which thou hast shewed unto thy servant; for with my staff I passed over this Jordan; and now I am become two bands. Deliver me, I pray thee, from the hand of my brother, from the hand of Esau: for I fear him, lest he will come and smite me, and the mother with the children. (Gen. 32:9–11, KJV)

That night Jacob prepared a present for Esau. He chose out of his herds two hundred female goats, twenty male goats, two hundred lambs, and twenty rams, thirty female camels with their young, forty cows, ten bulls, twenty female donkeys, and ten male donkeys. Jacob prayed softly to himself, "Lord, cause Esau to receive my gift with joy."

He looked over at his servant, who had helped him through the night. He looked tired. Jacob noticed the lines of concern on his trusted servant's face. "This is what you are to do. Go on ahead of us. We will follow you. Take each herd of animals separately. Keep a distance between each group. When Esau sees you, he will ask, 'Whose are these, and where are you going?' You are to tell him, 'They belong to your servant, Jacob. He is sending them ahead to you as a gift.' Perhaps if he receives these gifts, he will not be angry when he sees us."

His servants went on ahead. Jacob moved the rest of the camp across the river. He stayed behind. Jacob intended to spend the night seeking God. A man came into the camp and wrestled with Jacob. "Bless me!" Jacob demanded.

"Let me go," the man replied.

"No," Jacob answered. "Bless me." His heart was pounding as he continued to wrestle with this man. "Who are you?" Jacob asked. Jacob knew from the moment he first saw this man that he was no ordinary man. Jacob asked him again, "Who are you?" The stranger replied, "Why do you need to know?" When the angel realized Jacob would not give up, he reached over and hit Jacob in the hip. Jacob's hip went out of joint, but he continued to wrestle with the angel. "Bless me before you go." Jacob was tired, and he was hurt.

Finally, the other man asked him, "What is your name?" "I am Jacob," he replied.

"From now on, you will be called Israel because you have struggled with God and men and won."

Then Jacob released the man. He had looked into the face of God and lived. His struggle had come at a price; now he limped.

Rachel paced the floor of her tent. Joseph was sound asleep, but Rachel was wide awake. Her beautiful, long, flowing hair was caught by the night wind as she walked out of the tent for some fresh air. She could see Jacob's fire in the distance. He was always talking to God. She said a prayer herself as she watched his fire from the camp flicker in the night.

She reached down and stroked her tummy. "Easy now," she said to the child in her belly.

Her silhouette from the moonlight showed just how pregnant she was. She did not discuss traveling pregnant with Jacob. He had so much on his mind already. He knew her father would pursue them, and he did not know if his brother still wanted to kill him or possibly all of them. She kept the pregnancy a secret from her father. Now she was thankful. She knew her father would not have let her leave if he had known. Jacob would not have left her behind. God spoke to Jacob, telling him to return home. Jacob had to do what God asked of him.

Rachel was weak. The child was heavy for her to bear. Her servants waited on her as much as possible, but they could not remove the difficulty of this journey from her. She was trapped. She had to go forward. This child would be born in Jacob's homeland. He would inherit with his brothers in this land that God had promised to Abraham and his descendants.

She prayed, "Oh God, help me to have this child. Give me another son for my husband, Jacob. Strengthen me enough to give birth to my child." Her only concern was for her child as she prayed: "Don't let this child die!" The evening stars were a blanket above her head as she prayed for her husband and her sons. Rachel watched Jacob as he walked toward the camp. He was limping. "What happened?" Jacob was changed. His face glowed as he recounted to Rachel how he had struggled with God! She did not tell him of her own struggle with God, begging Him to spare their child.

The morning was beautiful. Jacob looked out into the distance. He saw Esau coming with his four hundred men. His heart sank. They were riding hard. He arranged his family into a column. Jacob placed his two concubines and their children in the front then Leah and her children. Last he placed Rachel and Joseph in the rear. Jacob rode on ahead of them all.

After all these years, he was finally face-to-face with Esau. He bowed himself before Esau seven times.

Esau watched him approach. He could not wait any longer. He ran to Jacob. "My brother! At last you have come home!" He was overjoyed. Jacob held Esau tightly. He had missed his brother. "I've been away too long. Seeing you is like looking into the face of an angel." He cried and embraced the neck of his brother. He was finally free from the guilt and the fear. Esau had forgiven him!

Esau looked confused. "Who are all these people?"

Jacob smiled proudly. "These are my children and my wives." Esau was speechless. "So many?" His eyes swept across the crowd. "These are all yours?"

Jacob laughed as he watched Esau take in his large family. He began to introduce them. Esau noticed the beautiful woman in the back with the young child. She looked into his eyes and held his gaze. As he watched her, he thought her eyes were the most beautiful he had ever seen. He looked back at Jacob. "And what were all the herds we passed?"

Jacob was still smiling. "They are my gift to you."

Shaking his head, Esau embraced his brother. "No, you keep them. I have more than enough already."

Jacob insisted, "Seeing your smile is like seeing the face of God! Please, keep them." Esau looked into the face of his younger brother. He could see the years had taken their toll on Jacob. Reluctantly he agreed to accept the gift. He spoke with love and excitement. "Come, I will escort you home."

Jacob looked at him, concerned. "I am sorry. The children are young, and the journey has already been difficult for them. There are also the flocks and herds to think of. They must be moved slowly. I will follow you and meet with you again at Seir."

Esau did not want to leave Jacob behind. He did not realize how much he had longed to see Jacob until he looked into his face. He loved Jacob much more than he had ever hated him. He shook his head and agreed, "If that is best for you." They agreed to meet again soon, and then Esau and his men left.

Rachel was not doing well. She finally had to tell Jacob. He stopped traveling, but she was still suffering.

"It's too soon!" he said to Leah.

She spoke with compassion. "I know, Jacob, but she is not strong enough to carry this baby any longer. She is going to have this child tonight."

He could hear the screams of his beloved wife. His heart was breaking as she cried out. Jacob ran to Rachel and watched in horror as she barely clung to life. He fell down beside her and prayed. She became weaker. The baby was finally born.

"He will live," the midwife told Jacob as she handed the child to Leah.

Jacob was crying as he held Rachel's hand, continuing to pray. Rachel looked at her husband. "Call the child Benoni." This means "son of sorrow." Then she died.

Jacob could not be comforted. Only when he looked at her sons could he take the pain of losing Rachel. Her sons were all he had left of her. Leah continued to try to help him, but he would not let her. He called the baby Benjamin, which meant "son of the right hand." Leah reached out to the children and tried to be a mother to Benjamin and Joseph. Her sons saw their father's grief as treason toward their love. They could not overlook his obsession with Rachel and her children.

Leah reasoned with them. "You don't understand. He loved her the moment they met."

"Why do you defend him?" Reuben asked. "He has all but abandoned all of us."

She acknowledged, "I know he has been distant, but he is your father, and I know he loves you."

"Yes, he loves us." Judah acknowledged. "It's just that he loves them more, much more."

Leah left her children grumbling about Jacob and went to care for Benjamin. He needed her. The poor boy will never know his mother. She cried as she thought of Rachel. A lump formed in her throat. She and Rachel had finally started to get along. She was too young. Why did she have to die? She could not escape the guilt that still plagued her. Rachel had forgiven her. But Leah could not forgive herself. Her children could not understand. She was to blame for the problem. "Here, little one," she reached for the child. Her arms encircled the precious gift Rachel had left them. "I will care for you. Don't worry, my darling, you are loved." In her heart, she was his mother. She looked into the beautiful face. This angelic face was the image of Rachel. Joseph watched as she talked to the child. "Would you like to hold him?" she asked. He smiled warmly at her as she handed him the darling bundle. "He is very delicate. You must be careful." She watched as Joseph held his brother, pride showing on his young face.

"I can't wait for him to get big. I will teach him everything," he said. As Leah watched Rachel's children, her grief was relieved. Rachel would never really be gone as long as her children were here.

Jacob felt alone. His heart was broken beyond repair. His sons had grown up to be cruel men. He sat in the shade of his tent, watching his older sons tend their flocks. They were fighting among themselves. He thought back to their most recent escapades in Shechem.

While camped near Shechem, the young prince sexually assaulted their sister, Dinah. This young man was in love with Dinah. He tried to make it right by marrying her. The sons of Jacob dealt deceitfully with the young prince and his father. They entered into a covenant with the men of Shechem to allow their sons and daughters to marry. The men of that land received their news joyfully. The only requirement the sons of Jacob had was that they become circumcised like Jacob and his sons. All the men of Shechem complied. While they were recovering, Levi and Simeon took their swords, went into the town, and killed the men of the city. The sons of Jacob took back their sister and carried off all the wealth of the town.

While he considered their behavior, Jacob watched as they joked and worked. The scuffles of a few minutes ago passed quickly. He thought now of the way he responded to their cruelty: "How could you do this?" he had asked. "You have caused me to stink among all the people of the land! They will come into our camp and kill us all! We are a small group. How can we stand up to the people in this area?"

Once again the Lord spoke to him and told him to move the camp to Bethel. Jacob instructed all his family and servants, "Turn from your idols and serve the Lord." The young men and women who stood by listening felt embarrassed. They knew they should not be bowing down to idols. God was constantly showing his faithfulness to Jacob. Conviction struck them; they repented. Then they gave their earrings and idols to Jacob, and he buried them. He built an altar in Bethel to the Lord. The Lord visited him there.

> And God said unto him, Thy name is Jacob: thy name shall not be called any more Jacob, but Israel shall be thy name: and he called his name Israel. And God said unto him, I am God Almighty: be fruitful and multiply; a nation and a company of nations shall be of thee, and kings shall come out of thy loins; And the land which I gave Abraham and Isaac, to thee I will give it, and to thy seed after thee will I give the land. (Gen. 35:10–12, KJV)

Jacob knelt before the Lord. There he worshipped God. After he regained his composure he decided he would mark the place where

God had visited with him. He looked around; nearby he found a large stone. He worked to move it into position. Then finally, after placing it where he wanted it, he offered a drink offering and anointed it with oil. He named the place where God visited him Bethel.

Jacob left Bethel and went to Ephrath near Bethlehem. That was where Rachel's pains with Benjamin had started. The pain in his heart was so great; just thinking of Rachel made him feel sick.

He watched as his sons and servants prepared to move the herds to better grazing. Slowly they disappeared into the horizon. Jacob wept as he prayed, "Oh Lord, my heart beats after Rachel." He prayed as the sun set onto another day in the desert.

Leah watched her husband retreat into a solitary place of pain. She moved to sit beside him. He reached out to her for the first time since Rachel's passing. He took her hand. Quietly they sat there and watched the sunset. The world would continue. No matter how much it hurt now, life would go on. She laid her head on his shoulder. Without speaking a word, they comforted each other.

"Joseph!" One of the young servant boys called out to him. They were great friends and spent many hours playing together. Joseph ran toward the child. "Watch, Joseph, I have been practicing." He laughed as he talked to Joseph about the game they often played. Now, taking his slingshot, he fired away at a tree. Joseph laughed and began to fire his own weapon. Jacob watched his son with excitement. He saw Rachel in every expression. His love for Joseph seemed to be boundless.

Reuben moved quietly to his destination. Bilhah was still young and attractive. She turned to him when Rachel passed away. Now they were close, closer than they should be.

"You shouldn't have come here. If Jacob ever finds out…" Her words hung in the air as Jacob walked up behind Reuben.

"If Jacob ever finds out what?" his face was livid as he spat the words back at her. Reuben turned around to find his father looming behind. Without warning, Jacob grabbed his son and threw him out of the tent. Jacob blustered, "They told me, but I did not believe it! I would never have believed it, never, if I had not seen this with my own eyes!"

Shame flooded Reuben's face. "She's a woman, Father, a human being. You treat her as if she were nothing. She is a wonderful person. I love her."

Jacob's eyes flashed. "Oh, you love her? Well, that makes this just fine, doesn't it? The only problem is she is my wife!"

Reuben shrank from his father's anger. His father was never this angry with him before. He looked at Bilhah.

She stood, stone still. "Go!' she said. Reuben watched as his father challenged him to defy him. He stood up to Jacob. "Father, all you ever think about is Rachel and her sons. We are all people. We all love you. But your only true love is for Rachel, Joseph, and now Benjamin. You can't seem to love all of us. We follow you, work for you, and wait for you to show us one-third the love you show Rachel's children. Why can't you love us like that? Why can't you love me like that?" Tears ran down Reuben's face as he poured out his heart to Jacob.

Jacob looked remorseful. "I have always loved you and all my children." The words seemed to come from the depth of his soul. "I can't deny my love for Rachel or her sons. But never in your life has one day gone by when I did not love you. I would give my life for each one of you." Jacob reached out to comfort his son. Shame got the best of Reuben. His tears ran wildly down his face. He turned and ran from Jacob.

Jacob looked at Bilhah. "I will care for you and your children, but I will never trust you again."

Bilhah had often feared this moment. Now that it was here, her heart was more broken than she had ever thought possible. She had never been given the position of Rachel or Leah, but in her own way, she loved Jacob. She had gambled big and lost. Jacob looked away from her and walked out.

THE COAT

> Now Israel loved Joseph more than all his children,
> because he was the son of his old age: and he made
> him a coat of many colours. (Gen. 37: 3, KJV)

Jacob had several problems. Reuben had proven himself untrustworthy. Simeon and Levi had shown themselves to be cruel. He searched his sons for one he could trust. The only one was Joseph. Joseph grew daily with the beauty of his mother and intelligence of Jacob. Everything he did prospered. He worked faithfully for his father. Jacob relied on him. And as time went by, he began to wonder more and more about the others. There were reports of his sons' bad behavior from the servants and neighbors nearby. Jacob's sons were making their mark. They were becoming known for their bad attitude toward others.

Joseph also kept his father's herds. When the sheep were with Joseph, they were safe. When he left them with Joseph's brothers, there was always a few unaccounted for. Jacob turned to Joseph more often. As Joseph grew, he pleased his father in every way.

One day Jacob presented Joseph with a gift. Joseph was excited. "Why, Father? This coat is so expensive." Joseph felt the extravagant fabric. "This is the nicest coat I have ever seen." His smile was from ear to ear.

Jacob said, "You have earned it. When your brothers watch the flocks, there are always some missing. When you watch the flocks, they are always accounted for."

Joseph positively strutted in his beautiful robe. He ran to Leah. "Look, Mother, look what Father has given me! Did you ever see such a beautiful coat in your life?"

Smiling, she said, "Joseph, you are so handsome in it. You look just like your mother."

Joseph looked serious. "Do I really?"

She nodded as she sat down. "Yes, I see her face in yours more every day." Then she looked at Jacob as Joseph ran to show his friends his beautiful coat. Her face was somber. "You will offend the others," she warned.

Jacob sighed. "Let them be offended. Joseph has earned it." Leah watched her husband walk away. He had just done something very foolish.

Joseph was going from friend to friend and servant to servant. "Look at my coat my father gave me." Everyone was properly impressed, everyone except his older brothers.

"Father continues to spoil that little brat!" Simeon looked at Joseph as if he were a viper. "Someday we should take care of him once and for all."

Levi looked at Reuben. "It's not enough that we know he's Father's favorite. Now he also has a coat to prove it."

All of Jacobs's sons looked on Joseph as a threat. Day after day they watched the young man become the son Jacob had longed for each of them to be. The demon of envy that had so long plagued their mothers rose up. They hated Joseph!

Jacob sent Joseph to watch his older brothers. He had received many reports of their behavior. "Keep an eye on them, and let me know when they do something wrong."

⸺ ∘∘❀❖❀∘∘ ⸺

Gad was angry. "So now you are here to spy on us?"

Joseph stood his ground. "The way you are treating people is being reported to Father. He simply wants you to be fair with our neighbors. All you have to do is try to be kinder to everyone and stop stealing sheep. He knows you are eating them regularly and giving them away. He is concerned you are not behaving responsibly."

Gad reached for him. His brothers restrained him. "You little brat! I'll kill you!" He snarled at Joseph. "I'm sick of you spying on us and reporting to Father. How dare you lecture me? You're just a child. You don't know anything."

Joseph shook his head. "I know enough to not steal from Father."

When he returned home, he told his father what he had seen his brothers doing. Israel was not happy. His brothers realized, once and for all, they would have to eliminate their father's spy.

Joseph had a dream. "Asher, Simeon, Gad," he called out to all his brothers. "Come and hear my dream. I dreamed we were all in the field, harvesting bundles of grain. I dreamed my bundle stood up, and all your bundles gathered around it and bowed low before it." His brothers looked at him with disgust. "Don't you have anything better to do than dream stupid dreams like that? It doesn't matter how much Father favors you. He is old, and when he is dead, you will not be giving us orders."

Judah looked out into the night air as if he were speaking of something completely unrelated and said, "Beware of yourself, little brother. No one is going to take our inheritance away from us. None of us is going to serve a sniveling little brat, no matter what Father thinks."

Joseph dreamed a second dream. Again he called to his brothers. "Come and hear my dream."

Jacob was nearby, so he and Leah also listened. Smiling tolerantly, he asked, "What was your dream, my son?"

Joseph took a deep breath and said, "I dreamed the sun, moon, and eleven stars bowed before me."

Jacob was not pleased. His voice reflected his lack of enthusiasm, "So, what are you saying? Will your mother and I and all your brothers bow down before you?" Jacob scolded Joseph, but in his heart he wondered what this meant. Joseph's brothers took the news with renewed anger. They hated Joseph as much as Jacob loved him.

One day Jacob sent Joseph on a journey to check on his brothers. They were pasturing the flocks near Shechem. Jacob became concerned about them. He looked at Joseph. "I am worried about your brothers. Will you go and check on them for me? They have been gone for some time."

Joseph agreed. "Of course, Father." He was glad to help Jacob anytime he needed him.

Joseph's brothers watched him coming from a distance. Their anger, never far from them, surfaced. "Here comes the dreamer. Let's kill him and tell Father a beast did it." They plotted Joseph's demise.

"Greetings, brothers." He smiled at them. They were not willing to listen to any more of his chatter.

One of them grabbed him from behind. "Let's kill him and be done with it."

Reuben tried to rescue him. "Let's not kill him. Why should his blood be on our hands? We can throw him into this pit and let him die without ever touching him." Reuben's brothers agreed.

Reuben planned to save Joseph, but he knew he couldn't fight all his brothers himself. He considered his options then decided to return when it was dark and save the boy for their father's sake. He thought, *For now, Joseph is safe.* He needed to tend to the sheep he had left behind so he went back to work. Meanwhile, Jacob's sons saw a caravan traveling toward them.

Judah said, "I have an idea. Reuben's right. Why should his blood be on our hands? We can sell him to this caravan and, at least, we will make a profit off him." His brothers nodded their agreement. They were satisfied.

They had tossed him into the dry well without any regard for how he would land. He was hurt and bleeding. Joseph sat alone in the dark, crying. He understood at last how much they really hated him. They would have killed him if Reuben hadn't intervened.

Someone called out to him. "Dreamer, are you in there? Here, take this rope." He almost laughed with relief. He could not wait to be released from his prison. He grabbed the rope, and they pulled him out. But before he could do anything, they tied a rope around his hands and gagged him.

"He likes to talk," Zebulun said.

A stranger took him and started to pull him forward. His eyes fell on his coat. His brothers had stripped him of it before throwing him into the well. He watched one of the strangers from the caravan count out twenty pieces of silver. Tears stung his eyes. He looked into the eyes of his brothers. They had no mercy. He thought of his father as he was dragged along behind the caravan and away from the life he knew.

Late that night, Reuben returned. He sneaked into the camp and lowered down a rope, whispering into the well, "Joseph, take the rope. Hurry before someone sees us." There was no answer. "Joseph, are you there?" Still there was no answer. He stopped caring if his brothers could hear him. "Joseph!" he shouted. "Answer me!" Nothing!

He rushed to his brothers. "Where is the boy?"

They laughed as they answered, "We got rid of him once and for all."

"How?" he asked. Desperately he pleaded with them. "What did you do to him?"

His brothers answered with some satisfaction, "We sold him."

"You did what?" Reuben was speechless.

"Not long after you left, a caravan passed by here, so we sold him."

Reuben was horrified by the news. He tore his robe. "What have you done? Don't you realize what your actions will mean to Father? He can't take this. Father will never stop mourning that child!"

"That is just the point," Simeon said. "We are tired of Father's constant concern for Joseph. Why do you care? You were more than happy to go along with us this afternoon."

"No, I wasn't!" he replied. "I just said that to stop you from killing him."

The sons of Jacob looked at each other. None of them except Reuben felt any remorse.

"Listen here," Levi said with menace in his voice. "You're not going to tell Father what happened. You're in this as far as we are. We have it all worked out. We will tell Father we found the boy's coat on our way home. We will tear it and drench it in blood. Father will think a wild animal has killed him. We will all stick together. If anyone betrays us, he will meet the same fate as Joseph." He looked at Reuben with murder in his eyes. The light from the fire reflected his resolve. Reuben could not help Joseph. He had no choice. He agreed to their plan. What good would it do for their father to know how low his sons had become?

———∘∘∘❖∘∘∘———

"My son! Oh, my son!" Jacob wailed. His screams were something unearthly. He sounded as though his soul was being ripped from him.

Reuben ordered the women, "Bring him some water. Get him a towel for his head. Father, you must try to calm yourself."

Israel's sons watched their father as he grieved in a way they had never imagined. They began to realize the depth of their betrayal as they watched their father dissolve into a grieving old man in front of their eyes. Jacob would not be comforted. He clung to Benjamin as though he were his only link with sanity.

"No harm must come to him. He is all I have left of his mother." If the sons of Jacob thought life was difficult before, they started to learn what true hardship was. Watching their father grieve day after day was unbearable. They became so eaten up with guilt it consumed them. Jacob's sons started to stay away from their father. Watching him grieve was indescribably painful! They were willing to go anywhere to not be where Jacob was. His grief was their reminder of their sin.

Judah moved away and established his own camp. He could not watch his father suffer. His guilt tormented him.

JOSEPH INTO CAPTIVITY

And Joseph was brought down to Egypt; and Potiphar, an officer of Pharaoh, captain of the guard, an Egyptian, bought him of the hands of the Ishmeelites, which had brought him down thither. (Gen. 39:1)

The journey was hard. Joseph was burned by the sun. Every muscle in his body ached. He looked at his captors and wondered what life held for him. They were Ishmeelites. From what Joseph was able to overhear, they were on their way to Egypt. He looked around for a way to escape but was held prisoner by the desert. Even if he could get away from these men, he would die in the desert without water. One of the men finally handed him a small piece of bread. That was the only food he had all day. Joseph was hungry, but the pain of his body in no way compared with the pain of his heart.

"God," he prayed into the night. "I am in Your hands. Lead me to a place where I am safe." As he considered the circumstances that had led him to be here, he realized to go home to his father would mean certain death. His brothers would not allow him to live. They couldn't allow anyone to know the truth. He thought of his father. *It is better for him to think I am dead than to know the truth about his sons.* Joseph decided to go on. God was with him. This could not have happened to him if God had not allowed it. God was taking him on this journey. He prayed on. "I place myself in Your hands." The heavens seemed to open up. The night was suddenly beautiful as he submitted himself to whatever God had for him. A soft breeze whispered through the air, and peace filled his heart. God was with him. He would be fine.

They finally arrived in Egypt. This metropolis was buzzing. It was incredibly interesting to a young man of seventeen. He looked around as he was ordered to stand here or there.

Joseph watched as a man of obvious influence approached the market. Already some of the men and women he was brought to market with had been sold. He looked at this man of affluence and decided to try to get his attention. Joseph spoke intelligently for himself when questions were asked concerning him. "I am seventeen," he said. "I believe, sir, I could be most helpful to you in many ways. I have been educated. I read, write, and do mathematics." His eyes held the gaze of Lord Potiphar, the captain of the palace guard. The older man studied Joseph. He was amused by the boldness of this young slave. "I assure you, sir, I will work faithfully. I serve the one true God. He it is who determines the future of us all. It would be a dishonor to Him if I showed you disrespect."

Potiphar laughed, amused with Joseph. He was convinced. "I will buy this young man."

Once again Joseph was sold. He went home with his new master. Joseph promised himself he would not dishonor God. "I will be the best slave this man has."

Joseph kept his promise. He worked harder than anyone. The long hours kept him from thinking about his home. He was so homesick at times life seemed unbearable. He missed his father and Benjamin so much it hurt. There were times when he would notice the children playing at the market, and one of them would remind him of Benjamin. At night he dreamed of home, of his father and mother. It hurt when Rachel died, but then he still had his father and brother. Now, he had no one. These thoughts were difficult and led to more heartache; so he worked.

The work was fun and brought him favor with his master, Potiphar. It was strange, but his master had become a friend to him. Potiphar trusted and respected Joseph. After only a few months, Joseph had handled the household finances well enough, Potiphar noticed financial increase. He happily turned over all the household responsibilities to Joseph.

"You are the best servant I have, Joseph. I can leave anything to your care and know you will handle it as though it were yours." Potiphar was often away on business for the pharaoh. Joseph's master was a very important man. He needed Joseph. His master's confidence in him became a badge of honor. He was determined to show himself a good representative of God Almighty. When his heart became heavy, he often went out into the garden and worked. The times he was in the garden were his favorite. That was when he talked to God. At those moments of quiet, he worked out his heartache with his only confidant. Every day he became closer to God. The earth and all of creation seemed to scream the deity and majesty of God Almighty.

He worked to improve his own pettiness. He often thought of the things he did to antagonize his brothers. He realized nothing excused their behavior, but he had often thrown his father's love for him up to them. It hurt that they did not love him as their own brother. Now he thought of all the things he said to get even with them for their rejection. "Father God, I am sorry for all my sins." Joseph spent hours in the sun working where he was most happy. The sun browned him, and the hard work toughened him up. Joseph added a watering system to the grounds. His gardens became the most lush and exotic of all the area. Potiphar was generous and allowed Joseph a free hand to purchase any plants he needed to make the landscape more dramatic.

The wife of Potiphar looked out of her garden window. There he was again. He worked all the time. Joseph was most attractive. She often watched him while he worked. She was tired of just watching. She walked down the corridor of her home and out into the garden. There was shade everywhere. Joseph had planted large trees and made structures for her to recline under as well as to keep her cool. Potiphar had not been home for days. He often left her while he tended to his so-called business. He was the captain of Pharaoh's guard. He could get someone else to tend to some of his responsibilities, but no, not him. She snarled her nose as she thought of his most recent neglect of her. He did not understand how lonely she really was. She was tired of waiting on him to notice her. She was, after all, his wife.

She spoke to Joseph as he walked by. He smiled shyly at her. He seemed afraid to even look her way. "Joseph," she called out. "Come and sit with me. I need someone to talk to."

He hurried to assist her. "Excuse me, mistress, how may I help you?"

She sat down on one of the many seats he had built for her and his master. She leaned back and propped up her legs. Stretching slightly, she patted the cushion next to her. "Sit. I am lonely."

His eyes took in her alluring smile. The way she compelled him to look at her caused him to flush. He was very uncomfortable around her and certainly did not want to sit and talk to her now. Reluctantly he sat across from her, keeping his distance. "Mistress, I should be working. What will my master think if he sees me sitting here talking to you?"

She looked at him, honey dripping from her lips. "He will think you work hard enough you should take a break. Besides, I am just as important as any silly job you are working on. Surely you won't deny my happiness is your first responsibility."

He watched her carefully. Joseph did not trust her. She was someone he feared. When she was near him, it became hard for him to concentrate. The fragrance of her lingered in the room after she left and played tricks on his mind. Her beauty was something he spent hours trying not to think of. He noticed the way she seemed to amuse herself with different servants. He made up his mind not to fall into the trap of being one of those men. Oh, she was beautiful. Joseph looked at her with the eyes of a man. She was perfect. Her skin and body were flawless. But something about her made his skin crawl. He watched the way she treated Potiphar. Sometimes he thought his master stayed away to avoid her scorn. She had a viper's tongue. Her huge, dark eyes were intoxicating. She looked at him longingly.

"Why don't you sit closer? I won't bite." He was nothing more than an afternoon's distraction for her, but she was a trap. She was perfectly designed to make men fall from God's grace. She reached for him. He looked away, pretending not to notice her positioning herself to embrace him. He was beginning to perspire. So what if he allowed himself a few moments of pleasure in her company? His master really didn't have to know. That thought shamed him. How could he deceive the one man who had befriended him? His master trusted him, and what about God? How could he hurt the Lord by spitting on his salvation with such a hateful sin? His conscience prevailed. He could not allow her to catch him off guard. "I am sorry, mistress. I really must attend to an urgent matter. I cannot put it off any longer. I will see you later." He jumped up and left as quickly as possible. He had to keep his distance. At that moment, Joseph was as much afraid of himself as he was his mistress.

She was a beautiful woman. He was only a man. He often thought of her and prayed for God's help. Every day it became more difficult. His heart sank as he thought of his master. He felt sorry for Potiphar. She was an embarrassment to her husband. He purposed in his heart not to let her seduce him.

The days went by quickly. Joseph stayed as far away from his mistress as possible. If she called for a servant, Joseph made sure one of the young ladies tended her. He tried to not only keep his distance but to protect the other male slaves as well. His decision was to keep her from the opportunity of bringing disgrace upon

Potiphar. She was very determined to have her way. The more he avoided her, the more she tried to trap him.

He worked late one day. He did not notice the time. He looked up, and there she was.

"Mistress." His voice carried an air of surprise. "I am sorry. I did not mean to disturb you. I thought you were still away on business."

She smiled sweetly. "Oh that, yes, I finished earlier than planned. I was tired so I left. Where is my husband?"

Joseph dropped his eyes and looked at the work he was doing. "He is still at the palace."

She moved closer. "So he's working late again?"

"Yes, mistress." His voice was barely above a whisper.

She laughed. "Look at you. It seems as if you are terrified of me. You know, Joseph, I could make your life much better? You really don't have to work. You could have everything your heart desires." She slowly moved closer, wrapping her arms around him. "I will be so good to you."

Joseph panicked. "No, mistress, I can't do this thing! My master trusts me. He has put everything he owns into my hands. I can't betray him in this way." He reached up and removed her hands. "What you want from me is a sin. It is a sin against God and my master. I cannot do this." He turned his back on her and started to leave.

She clung to him. "Joseph, you are safe with me. My husband will never know." She pulled at his clothes.

He continued to try to reason with her. "Please, I beg you, listen to me."

He was desperate. She held onto him, begging him to stay. His heart was pounding. He was trapped. He tried to remove her hands, but she had a death grip on his robe. He stepped out of the robe and ran out of the room.

His robe was in her hands. He heard her scream. "No!" He did not look back.

She was angry. "How dare he reject me? He will regret his decision." She still held his robe. "Help!" she screamed. "Someone help me!" she cried out, pleading for her servants to help her.

"What is wrong, mistress?" The men were there within seconds. She sobbed hysterically. "He tried to force me!"

The men were alarmed. They searched the room. "Who, mistress?"

She raised her hand, pointing. "That Hebrew my husband brought here to insult me! He tried to force me! I screamed! When I did, he ran away. See, I have the robe he was wearing." Another sob broke through her voice.

The servants looked at the robe questioningly. "Joseph tried to harm you?"

She was angry. "Didn't I just explain? Go after him! He will not mock me. My husband will take care of him."

The servants looked at each other. They knew Joseph. This did not make sense. They quickly made their way to Joseph's quarters. His friends looked at him apologetically. One of them tied his wrists behind his back.

"We have no choice. We have to lock you up, Joseph." The man speaking was a friend of Joseph's. "She is determined to punish you." He put Joseph in a storage room with no windows and closed the door, securing it from the outside.

Joseph waited for Potiphar to come home. He knew his master would believe his wife. She was very convincing when she wanted to be. He prayed, "God, please save me. My master will kill me." He waited desperately for help. None came.

It was late when Potiphar walked through the door of his home. He was tired. He had spent many hours with the pharaoh. He noticed the house was still bright with light. "What is going on?" he asked one of the servant girls.

"It is the mistress, sir. She is in distress."

Potiphar ran to his wife's room. "Darling, what is wrong?" She cried as she told her husband of the way Joseph had behaved. "I am so ashamed." She hid her face in the pillows. "I can't face anyone here! He just attacked me as if I were a common prostitute!" She was beside herself. "Here, this is his robe! He had already taken it off when I cried out for help."

Potiphar was beyond reason. "I will kill him for this!" he shouted. "How dare he come into my house and attack my wife?" He drew his sword. "Where is he?" he demanded.

"Sir." One of the servants spoke to him. "Sir, please think of the mistress. She is embarrassed already. If you kill Joseph, it will become well known. People will discuss it, and the mistress will be even more embarrassed. If you put him into prison, you can say he robbed you, and the mistress does not have to be mentioned. People will forget, and the mistress will not be humiliated."

Potiphar weighed the words of his servant. "Yes." He called out to his guards. "Take him and put him in prison!"

It was done. Joseph's friend and fellow servant had said the only thing he could think of to spare Joseph's life. The rest was up to Joseph's God.

JOSEPH IN PRISON

But the Lord was with Joseph, and shewed him mercy, and gave him favour in the sight of the keeper of the prison. (Gen. 39:21)

Joseph's life had been spared only to become a prisoner. His master had not killed him, but Potiphar had ordered him beaten and put in shackles. He was thrown unceremoniously into a cell. The stench was beyond imagination. He finally slept from pure exhaustion.

The next morning he awoke to the sound of a man bringing breakfast to the prisoners. "Here you go," he said as he opened the small door to slide the bowl of food into Joseph's cell. Joseph looked at the breakfast and immediately became sick. "What's your problem?" the man said as he watched Joseph. "Ah yes, I remember they beat you, didn't they."

Joseph spoke for the first time. "Sir, I am innocent of this crime." The prison rang out with laughter as one of the prisoners called out to Joseph, "Hey, thief, we are all innocent." Again there was laughter.

Joseph tried to explain. "I have been falsely accused. I was brought directly here without a trial."

The man spoke honestly. "You won't get a trial. You are a slave. You were sent here by Lord Potiphar. No one is going to hear your case. You are here now. You might as well accept it. Your only hope is for Potiphar to change his mind or the pharaoh to pardon you." Joseph looked at the man hopelessly. The head jailer continued to speak. "This is not the sort of place a man gets released from. I'm not a prisoner, but I am here working, doing pretty much everything that gets done. They don't give me enough help, and I barely get through with one task before I need to do something else. The missus is not happy either. She complains, says she never sees me. She's a fine wife. The kind of woman a man likes to go home to."

Joseph looked around. "Can't you get some of the prisoners to help you? If everyone did something, this place would run itself." The head jailer looked at Joseph in shock. "These are not people I can trust. They would just as soon kill me as look at me. What if they escape? Pharaoh would have my head. No, sir, I like my head right where it is."

Joseph reminded him. "I was sent here without a trial. I have done nothing to deserve this punishment. How many of these prisoners are like me?"

Again the jailer looked at Joseph, shocked. "Well," he started to think. "I do know of a few. Perhaps they could be trusted."

The next few days Joseph spent familiarizing himself with the way the place functioned. He became friends with the head jailer. "I think if you make a few modifications, you can run this place much more efficiently, with fewer complaints."

The jailer spent time talking to Joseph. He liked him and was quickly forming the opinion that Joseph was indeed innocent. "What would you do if you were me?"

Joseph made his suggestions as they walked along the corridor of the prison together. He allowed Joseph to move more freely than the others. Joseph volunteered to help him and was proving to be very intelligent. The head jailer made a decision. "I'll tell you what. Why don't you try making some of these changes yourself. You run this side of the prison. If things go well, I may get you to help me with all of it."

Joseph wasted no time. He was disgusted by the poor living conditions and often refused to eat the food. Annoyed, he asked, "Pharaoh sets aside a portion of food for this prison. Why are we always expected to eat spoiled food?" He consulted with the head jailer, obtaining permission to hire new cooks as well as people to deliver their supplies. He was sure their provisions were being sold or used for some other purpose. When he brought in people he chose personally, the food supplies improved drastically. The new cook took pride in serving goodtasting food.

The prisoners were very happy. Joseph spoke with them and convinced them to clean their own cells as well as themselves. He organized the guards who were sent to help, and they started cleaning outside the cells and even around the exterior. There was a courtyard. Joseph noticed it was unkempt. He set out to make it beautiful. He assigned prisoners to plant a garden. Soon they were growing their own vegetables. With Joseph's touch, their garden became lush, a thing of beauty in a place of darkness.

Before long the prison ran itself. The head jailer was complimented for his efficiency. Even in prison, Joseph was blessed, and he was a blessing to everyone around him.

The head jailer watched his young friend. Joseph stood looking out of the only window in the prison. "What is it, Joseph?" he asked.

Joseph studied the stars. "I am innocent. I have done nothing to be here. My only hope is for my God to have mercy on me and cause my master or Pharaoh to pardon me."

The head jailer had listened to Joseph speak of his God many times. He was intrigued. "Do you really believe your God can save you, Joseph?"

"Yes, I believe He can. I serve the one true God. His desire is that none should perish. He created all that is and has been.

He can deliver me. When He is ready, I will be set free." Joseph said the words with such conviction the head jailer believed him.

"Yes, I believe your God will save you, but what about me? Would your God save someone like me?"

Joseph looked into the eyes of his friend. "Yes, God is God of everything and everyone. My God asks only that you believe in Him. God's heart is opened to all of us. His mercy is from everlasting to everlasting. He is above all things. There is no other god. He is the only one."

The head jailer listened. "I have often prayed to my gods. They have never delivered me. If your God delivers you, I will know He is the one true God!"

There were two prisoners. One was Pharaoh's head baker, the other was Pharaoh's chief butler. The captain of the guard assigned Joseph to take care of these men. Joseph noticed they were both very unhappy. "What is wrong?" he asked.

They told him they both had a dream, and no one could interpret their dreams. Joseph sought to help them. "Dreams are from God. God is able to give the interpretation. What did you dream?"

The chief butler spoke first. "I saw a vine with three branches. It blossomed. Then there were ripe grapes. I held Pharaoh's cup in my hand. I took the grapes and squeezed the juice into it. Then I gave the cup to Pharaoh."

Joseph nodded his understanding. "The three branches are three days. Three days from now, you will be released from prison. Pharaoh will return you to your position as his chief butler. Please have mercy on me and remember I am here when you return to Pharaoh. Tell Pharaoh about me and ask him to let me out of here. I have done nothing wrong."

The chief baker saw the interpretation of the chief butler's dream was good. He also told his dream to Joseph. "I dreamed that I carried three baskets of pastries on my head. The top basket held different baked goods. But birds came and ate them."

"The baskets are days. In three days Pharaoh will cut off your head."

Pharaoh's birthday was three days later. He decided to give a banquet for all his officials and household staff. He sent for his chief butler and chief baker, and they were brought to him from the prison. He restored the chief butler. Then he sentenced the chief baker to be killed, as Joseph had predicted. Pharaoh's chief butler forgot Joseph.

Joseph waited to hear of news from the chief butler. None came.

JOSEPH BEFORE PHARAOH

And Pharaoh said unto his servants, Can we find
such a one as this is, a man in whom the Spirit of
God is? (Gen. 41:38, KJV)

Two long years later, Pharaoh had a dream. In his dream, he stood
on the bank of the Nile River. There he saw seven fat, healthy-
looking cows. These came out of the river and started grazing near
its bank. As he watched them, seven different cows came up from
the river. They were thin and sickly looking. They stood beside
the fat cows. The thin cows ate the fat ones! The dream ended.
Pharaoh woke up.

Then he dreamed another dream. He saw seven heads of grain
on one stalk; every kernel was well formed. Then seven ugly heads
appeared. They were shriveled and withered by the wind. The
thin heads consumed the seven beautiful heads! Again Pharaoh
woke up.

He was troubled. He awoke to the feeling of impending doom.
He was sweating and found it almost impossible to draw a breath.
Pharaoh was having a panic attack. His dream, he knew, had a
meaning—but what? He tried to ignore the fear that had swept

over him. He walked to the window of his palace and looked out. He had to get some air. He opened the door, stepping out onto the veranda. He took a deep breath. His eyes searched the city he loved. Everything was quiet, but still he felt uneasy. He continued to stare out into the distance. He often watched the city at night. Under the blanket of the stars, it seemed magical. Tonight the stars were especially magnificent. They sprinkled the night like a blanket over the earth. He watched them for a moment. His breathing was normal again. He made the decision not to ignore the dreams.

The morning did not change his mood. He listened to business for hours. "Stop! Just stop! I've heard all that I'm going to listen to today. I want to speak with my counselors. We will continue the business of state at another time." He dismissed his accountants to speak with his counselors. "I tell you I need to know the meaning of these dreams. I won't be able to rest until I have some answers." He called his magicians and wise men, but they could not interpret the meaning.

The chief butler's mouth flew open. "Oh, Pharaoh, I forgot. There is a young man who can interpret your dream."

"Who is he? Bring him to me at once."

The chief butler looked sadly at Pharaoh, "Sire, he is in prison. I met him when you were angry with the chief baker and me. We both had dreams. He was able to interpret them, and they happened exactly as he predicted. He told us what each of our dreams meant." The butler poured Pharaoh another drink. "Everything happened exactly as he said. I was returned to my position, and the baker was put to death."

Pharaoh spoke to his guards. "Bring him to me at once."

"Joseph!" The head jailer had been running. He leaned over as he tried to catch his breath. "Joseph, Pharaoh has called for you!"

Joseph's heart skipped. "The pharaoh? What does he want?"

The jailer's face was red from exertion. "I was just ordered to release you into the custody of the palace guards. This is it, Joseph! All this time you've been waiting. Now your God has provided you with an opportunity to speak with Pharaoh personally! I know this is the answer to all your prayers!" Joseph's friend laughed as he hurried him along.

Joseph was taken to the palace and immediately ushered into a side room. There he shaved and was given fresh new clothes. He picked up the garment as though it were golden. It reminded him of another time when he had been given a coat. Tears filled his eyes. "God," he prayed. "I know You are behind this. I need wisdom to speak to Pharaoh. I know You are the reason he has called for me. Grant me the words to speak. Help me to speak only what You want me to say."

The men who were guarding him spoke up. "Come, we cannot keep the pharaoh waiting."

Joseph was now thirty years old. His whole life had been leading up to this moment. He took in a deep breath and entered the presence of Pharaoh. Pharaoh spoke to Joseph. "I have heard that you can interpret dreams. I have had two dreams, and no one has been able to tell me what they mean."

Joseph looked into Pharaoh's eyes and said, "I do not have the ability to tell you the meaning of your dream. But God will give us understanding and bring you peace."

Pharaoh told him the dreams. "I told these dreams to my magicians and wise men, but they could not tell me what they mean." Joseph studied the tiles on the floor. He looked up into Pharaoh's eyes. His calm demeanor left no doubt he understood the dream. "Both dreams mean the same thing." Joseph spoke boldly to Pharaoh. "God is telling you what He is going to do. The fat cows and the well-formed ears of corn are seven years of blessing. God will bless the earth with abundance. The ugly cows and withered corn are seven lean years. God is warning Pharaoh that after seven years of abundance, there will be seven years of famine." The expression on Joseph's face held concern. "This famine will be so bad that the good years will seem as though they never happened. It will destroy the land. You dreamed the dream twice. God confirmed that it will happen soon.

"I suggest that you find the most intelligent man in Egypt and put him in charge of a food collection and storage program. Place men in charge who will collect one-fifth of the crops during each of the seven good years. They should save the excess of the crops in storehouses for the future. If you don't, famine will come, and people will die."

Pharaoh and his counselors listened carefully. After hearing the interpretation of the dream and Joseph's suggestion, they discussed who would be wise enough to take on this great responsibility. Pharaoh made a decision. "Who is wiser than Joseph?" Speaking to Joseph, he said, "Who is as wise as you? You are the wisest man in the country. The spirit of God is in you, and you are able to understand the dream. You will be over this project. I place you over my household. I am the king, but you are next to me. Nothing can happen in Egypt that you will not know about."

Pharaoh gave Joseph total control of all the land of Egypt. He gave Joseph his own signet ring and a new name. "You will be known as Zaphenath-paneah." He also gave Joseph a wife. Her name was Asenath. Joseph looked at the beautiful woman Pharaoh presented to him and was pleased. She comforted him and gave birth to two sons during the years of abundance. The oldest son was named Manasseh. The younger son was called Ephraim. He said, "God has made me fruitful in the land of my suffering."

During the time of abundance, Joseph directed his men to store a portion of all the crops grown in Egypt for the time of famine. There was so much stored up they could not count it. Then the seven years of famine started.

Joseph's Brothers

Now when Jacob saw that there was corn in Egypt, Jacob said unto his sons, Why do ye look one upon another? And he said, Behold, I have heard that there is corn in Egypt: get you down thither, and buy for us from thence; that we may live, and not die. And Joseph's ten brethren went down to buy corn in Egypt. (Gen. 42:1–3, KJV)

The old man leaned heavily on his staff. He reached down, scooping up a handful of dirt. He looked out over the dry, barren land. There was no rain. There were no crops. In the background he could hear the bleating of sheep. The last little bit of grass was quickly becoming depleted. The dry, hot wind picked up the dirt in his hand and carried it off into the desert. Jacob did not know what else to do. They would have to go to Egypt to buy food, or they would all starve. With every day that passed, the famine grew worse.

Jacob called a meeting with all his sons. "Why are you standing around looking at each other? Go to Egypt. They have food. We will die if you don't buy us something to eat."

Judah agreed with his father. "You are right, Father. I have heard the same report. Egypt has plenty of grain. They say Pharaoh was warned in a dream by God that famine was coming."

Asher asked, "Are they actually willing to sell to us, even if we are not from Egypt?"

Judah nodded. "Yes, I spoke with a caravan that had gone into Egypt to trade their supplies. There is one man appointed by Pharaoh who is in control of food distribution. Apparently he is the one we should talk to. I understand anyone with the money can buy food from him. They say he has already made Pharaoh much richer than before this famine started, since no one else has food."

Benjamin spoke up excitedly. "I will go with you."

Before he could say any more, Jacob intervened. "I am sorry, my son, but you cannot go."

Benjamin looked pleadingly at his older brothers. The curls of his head sprang out of control. The boy was handsome. He had his mother's eyes. He dropped his head in disappointment.

"Father," Reuben came to Benjamin's defense. "He is not a child. It is time he took on some of the responsibilities of a man. He wants to help us. You have to allow him to be a man."

Benjamin looked at his father hopefully. "Please, Father. It is only fair that I too contribute to the family."

Jacob looked at his son tenderly. "You do contribute. You are always the first to help. I need you here. I can't move like I used to. My hip has become more painful. Your help to me is more than enough contribution."

All he could say was, "Yes, Father."

The sons of Jacob decided to make the journey to Egypt. They looked out into the horizon. They dreaded the heat of the day. They carried plenty of gold to buy their provisions and donkeys to help bear the load. They did not take their younger brother Benjamin.

Simeon raised himself up from where he was seated. "Father is old. He is too afraid something will happen to the boy."

Reuben looked at the others sadly. "Yes, he is afraid." No one said any more. They each knew what the others were thinking.

The journey was long, but the sons of Jacob finally walked through the gates of the city of Pharaoh. They asked around and confirmed the information from the caravan was correct. There was one man they had to speak with before they could buy food.

Simeon spoke excitedly to the others. "This man, Zaphenath-paneah, is next to the pharaoh. Only with his permission can we buy anything." They waited all day long. The heat was exhausting. The line of people coming to buy bread seemed to be unending. Reuben took out his container of water and handed it to his brothers. They each drank sparingly of the precious fluid. Finally, they were next in line to speak to the man. He took the payment from the family in front of them, and they received food without any problem.

"That seemed easy enough." They agreed among themselves, whispering, "At least we'll be done soon. Then we can leave this place."

Joseph saw his brothers waiting to speak with him. They had been in the line for hours. His blood pressure rose slightly as he recalled the last time he was with them. He recognized them early that morning. He watched them approach. He knew he had the upper hand. He looked nothing like he did when he was young. Joseph was still very handsome. The face of Rachel was still evident, but he was no longer seventeen. The years in prison had hardened him slightly, giving him a rougher exterior. His eyes, so much like his mother's, had been carefully painted. Joseph recalled the way he looked when he first started dressing like his adopted people. He hardly recognized himself. He was adorned in the most extravagant fabric Pharaoh could obtain. Pharaoh enjoyed giving him gifts and often sent fabrics and clothiers to present Joseph with his expensive gifts. He was wearing his wig and the traditional dress of an Egyptian. He also had a different name. As they drew closer, he reasoned how to best deal with them.

They bowed low before him. His mind shot back to the dream he had so long ago. He remembered his brother's anger as he told them the dream. Now, here in front of his eyes were his brothers, bowing, just as the dream had predicted. He could still see the dream as if he had just dreamed it. He and his brothers were gathering grain, tying them into bundles, then his brothers' bundles of grain bowed before his bundle of grain. He also recalled their nickname for him, dreamer. His heart still hurt as he recalled the way they turned on him and wanted to kill him. Anger replaced remorse in Joseph's heart, too many hard years, too many sorrows.

He considered his best course of action. He used his interpreter to interrogate them. "Where are you from? Who is your father? Where is your younger brother?" Joseph's brothers grew more nervous with every question. Simeon started to lose his temper. Judah tried to intervene. They all did their best to explain.

Joseph spoke Egyptian. His interpreter was having difficulty keeping up with him. "You are spies!" he said in a low, menacing tone. "You have come into this land to see how vulnerable we are. You are here to spy out our weakness."

Jacob's sons were frantic. They began to all talk at once. "No, sir, we are a family. All of us have one father. There were twelve of us, but one son is gone, and our father would not allow the younger to come with us. He was afraid the youngest would be harmed." Joseph was insistent. "You are spies." Joseph watched his brothers squirm. They were sweating profusely. They still did not recognize him. He tried to look severe. "The only way I will believe you is if all of you except one stay here. One of you can return home. The only way I will release the others is if he brings the youngest son back with him." Joseph called to his guards. "You, take these men into custody." So he put them all into prison.

Joseph's wife, Asenath, had heard about Joseph's visitors. She had her own informants among the servants. Her handmaid was a close friend with the interpreter. She relayed the day's events to

Asenath with interest. "For some reason, Mistress, the master was certain these men were here to spy. They were taken into custody." Joseph's wife received the news with uncertainty. "You say they were from the land of Canaan?"

The young girl continued to serve Asenath as she spoke. "Yes, Mistress, I believe that is the country." She knew how much Joseph hated that prison. Alone at last, she was able to think. Why would he jail these men based on nothing more than suspicion? She was sure there was more to this.

Asenath kissed her husband hello. "You look tired." He removed the wig. Something he did first every time he came home. He hated the thing. She reached up and touched his face. "What is troubling you?"

Joseph took the hand she placed on his face in his, kissing it. He smiled. "I don't want to trouble you with my responsibilities." She smiled indulgently. "You know I love hearing about your work." At that moment, the boys came running in. They jumped on Joseph, and he was lost to her as he spent the rest of the evening playing with them. Joseph was so patient. He never complained about their demands on his time. He seemed to enjoy everything about them. She watched as he showed them his projects in the garden and patiently taught them the names of the plants. She was completely happy with this man. Sighing, she went to check on dinner for her husband. She had already spoken with the chef. He was preparing a special dinner Joseph was partial to. After their meal, the boys were scooped away by their teachers to finish lessons and eventually readied for bed.

She had not seen Joseph since dinner. He disappeared again into his study and was busy making plans for the upcoming weeks.

It seemed to Asenath her husband was needed by everyone in the world from the pharaoh to the farmer. Everyone looked to him to solve their problems. She watched him, admiring him, as he walked through the doors of the veranda. His long hair lay in curls. She, as her husband, much preferred him without his wig, but her reasons were very different.

Joseph seemed lost in his thoughts as he looked out over the city. The light breeze blew. The fragrant smells of garden flowers wafted toward them. She smiled to herself as she remembered how Joseph handpicked every flower in their garden, insisting on certain plants. He loved everything that bloomed and was passionate when he talked about his fruit trees. His handiwork was everywhere. She loved this man.

"Joseph." She moved to stand next to him, following his gaze. From here they could see the prison easily. She knew he often looked at it. But tonight his mood was somber. She moved her arm into the crook of his. "It's time for you to talk to me. News travels fast among the servants. I am sure I knew of the men you arrested before they arrived at the prison."

He exhaled. "I don't want to trouble you."

She listened then said, "I was given to you by the pharaoh. He told me at that time, 'This is a wise man. He will have many difficult decisions to make. Your job is to help him live with those decisions.' I think now you need my help." Joseph looked into the face of his beautiful wife. Dropping his head, he said, "My brothers came to me today. They looked older but the same. None of them recognized me. I kept my identity from them."

She watched Joseph. "So because of all they put you through, you put them in prison?"

Tears stung his eyes. "Yes." He looked conflicted. "No." Confusion swept his face. "I couldn't just let them go. I wanted to talk to them to find out about my father and Benjamin. It was all I could think of—to detain them."

She held her husband's gaze. "You are a good man. Any woman would be proud to have you as her husband. I know you. You will do what is right." She trusted him completely. She moved into his arms. Holding him, she said, "My love for you is greater than any love you have lost. I love you more than your father, mother, brothers, anyone." She raised her head and looked directly into his eyes. "I love you enough to make you forget the pain."

The sons of Jacob were introduced to the head jailer, who immediately put them in stocks. Reuben protested. "Sir, I assure you we do not need to be put in stocks. Where would we go? We aren't going to try to escape." He was flabbergasted. "We are honorable men."

"Are you now?" the robust man asked questioningly. "Well, I happen to know the prime minister very well. You wouldn't be here if he didn't have a very good reason." And with that, he slammed the cell door behind them.

The head jailer was quite entertained by the turn of events. He chuckled to himself as he considered the position Joseph had them in. Joseph had confided in him. He told him that his brothers had decided to sell him to the caravan of merchants. He smirked as he thought to himself, *Well now, the shoe's on the other foot.* He sent word back to Joseph by the guards who had delivered Joseph's brothers. "No problems, sir, the men are enjoying our personal accommodations and have been shackled to ensure they will not be trying to escape." He smiled once again as he thought of the day's menu. I'll have to speak to the cook and make sure they eat well while they are visiting. Walking toward the kitchen, he chuckled to himself. Joseph certainly had them where they deserved to be.

Right on the dot, they were served dinner. Judah looked at the meal as if he suspected it contained poison. "There is something wrong with that jailer. He seems to be as crazy as the prime minister." He sniffed his food then sat it down. "I'm not eating that." Levi looked at his brothers. "It's because of our sin. God has brought us here to destroy us. We were cruel and evil brothers to Joseph. We are paying. We will all die here."

"No." Judah shook his head and with conviction added, "We were wrong to harm Joseph. And we are, and have been, paying for it ever since we did that horrible crime. But even if God allows us to be punished, we are still the sons of Jacob. His promise to our father, Jacob, the promises he made to Isaac and Abraham, will come to pass. We will live, and God will fulfill his promises to those men through us. We will not die." Each brother listened and slowly agreed.

It had been three days since Joseph had imprisoned his brothers. He spent that time thinking of the best way to deal with them. He ordered them to be brought to him. Joseph was careful to speak to them through his interpreter. "I am a man who fears God. I have decided to test you and see how honorable you are. All of you may return home with provisions for your families, but one of you will remain here. When you return, you will bring your younger brother, or you will not see me. Guards, take this man into custody." He pointed at Simeon. "Tie him up, and take him to the prison."

Joseph's brothers were horrified. "This has happened to us because of what we did to Joseph. God is returning upon us our own sin." They broke down openly, discussing their sin against Joseph in front of him.

The interpreter watched his master. He knew Joseph understood his brothers perfectly. There was no evidence on Joseph's face. He sat there in front of his brothers as though he were stone. Nothing gave away his charade.

Reuben looked pale. "Didn't I beg you not to do this thing? Now this has happened to us because we are responsible for Joseph's murder!"

Joseph stood to his feet. He spoke to his interpreter in a very controlled tone. "Tell them I have something to attend to. I will return soon."

Joseph couldn't listen anymore. He quickly left the room. In his private rooms, he could allow himself to cry. He cried for all the wasted years, all the injustice, and finally, for all the pain their cruelty had brought to them. After a while, he was able to return and finish his conversation with them. He sent them away with a warning not to return without their brother. Joseph then ordered his men to fill their sacks with grain and return the money they brought to pay for the food. His brothers left the city. As they left, they had to walk pass the prison they had stayed in—the same prison Simeon was now in. They were filled with grief.

They traveled a long distance before deciding to rest. Gad reached into his sack and discovered the gold he had used to pay for his provisions was in his bag. They all checked their own sacks, and all of them still had the money they brought to pay for the grain. They were terrified. "What is going on? How can we explain this to that man? Our sins have come upon us!" they wailed.

When they arrived in Canaan, they explained to Jacob their trouble and how they had found the money in their sacks. Jacob was frightened as his sons explained, "We cannot go back unless we take Benjamin with us. The man told us he would not speak to us unless we brought back our youngest brother."

Jacob mourned. "Joseph is dead. Simeon is not here, and now you want me to let you take Benjamin! You cannot! He is all I have left of Rachel. I cannot let him go." The old man's lip trembled as he thought of his son.

Judah was adamant. "Father, we cannot go back without him." Benjamin listened to the frantic conversation of his father and brothers. "Father, we can't just starve to death. Think of all the others. Your grandchildren and their mothers are all counting on you, on all of us."

"No!" His father was determined. "You will not go!"

Time passed by, and provisions became scarce. The grandchildren were hungry. Jacob watched as they used the last of the grain. He turned to his son Judah. "You must go back to Egypt." Judah sighed deeply. "I will go. We will all go if Benjamin comes with us." Jacob instantly started shaking his head no. "Father," Judah continued, "that man is next to the pharaoh in authority. He was convinced we were spies. He will not see us unless Benjamin is with us. I give you my word, I will return with Benjamin. If I do not, you can hold me responsible forever."

Jacob was grieved. "Why did you tell him about Benjamin?"

Jacob's sons reasoned with their father. "He asked us. He specifically asked if you were still alive and if we had any other brothers. How could we know he would set this kind of condition?"

Benjamin looked at his brothers, then their father. "Father, I am not a child. I have allowed you to protect me. I've been content to stay with you and keep you happy, but I can't always be here. Someday I will have to be a man. You can't always protect me. Eventually, you will have to believe God is protecting me. You will have to trust Him to do His job."

Jacob acknowledged his sons comments, shaking his head. Softly he agreed. "If you are going to return, take this man a gift." Jacob made a list. "Here, take these balm, honey, spices, myrrh, pistachio nuts, and almonds. Also return the money you found in your sacks plus enough to pay for this purchase."

Jacob kissed his sons goodbye. Judah held his father close and whispered, "I will take care of him. I promise you. We will return." Jacob smiled at his son. "Thank you. God be with you, my son." Benjamin walked up to his father. "Father, God will take care of all of us. I am not Joseph. I will not die."

Jacob comforted himself with the words and promises of his sons.

Gad was concerned for his father. "Are you sure you will be all right here without us?"

"I will be all right. If something happens to Simeon or Benjamin, I will just have to accept it." The men left. Jacob went to his quiet place to pray.

The city of Pharaoh was alive with excitement. Benjamin watched with awe as they entered the city. There was a line that covered quite a distance. His brothers told him it was the line they needed to be in. They all took their places in the line and began to prepare for the long wait.

One of the guards who had imprisoned them approached them almost as soon as they entered the line. He looked at them questioningly then pointed to Benjamin. "Is this the brother you spoke of?"

Judah stepped between Benjamin and the guard. "Yes, sir, this is our youngest brother. We would appreciate an audience with your master."

The guard looked from man to man then nodded and left. They stepped out of line far enough to watch the man run directly up to the prime minister, whisper something, bow, and start back toward them. He returned. "Come, the master will see you now." Terrified, the men followed the soldier. Joseph looked all of them over. Then his eyes rested on Benjamin. He spoke Egyptian. He whispered to a man standing nearby. The man nodded his understanding, bowed to Joseph, and started motioning to them to follow him.

They walked along, apprehension overtaking them. "We are being singled out again because of the money we found in our sacks. This man is trying to set us up. He wants to pretend we stole it so he can keep us for slaves."

As they walked along, talking, they began to notice their destination. Looming in front of them was the palace. They wanted to turn and run. But from the looks of the guards posted all around the city, they knew they wouldn't get very far.

A man spoke to them in Hebrew. "Gentlemen, I am the prime minister's butler. He has invited all of you to dine with him for lunch. The master regrets that he is still occupied with business for a little while longer but suggested you might appreciate freshening up before your meal."

Levi spoke up. "Sir, we have been trying to talk to someone about a problem we have. You see we came here before and bought grain. But on our trip home, when we stopped for the night, we opened our sacks for the first time, and there was all the money we had brought with us. There has been an error. We never meant to keep the money. See we have brought it back as well as enough to buy more."

The man smiled at them and said, "Oh, don't worry about that. We collected your money. Your God must have placed gold in your sacks. Everything is fine."

They were introduced to another gentleman who explained he served the household and would be happy to show them to a place where they could rest. They followed the serious-looking man who kept watching them as if he suspected them to be thieves. Benjamin picked up an interesting vase. The man immediately grabbed it and set it down as though it were very valuable.

Reuben shot Benjamin a stern look. "Don't touch anything." Then he turned and noticed a beautiful Egyptian woman staring at him. He guessed her to be the lady of the house. She looked as though she knew who he was. The expression of disapproval on her lovely face made his skin crawl. Whoever she was, she didn't like him.

Asenath received news of her husband's guests from her butler. She studied them carefully from her balcony across the garden. One of the men noticed her watching them. The anger she felt toward these men waged war in her heart. She did not know how to think of them. These were the men who had betrayed Joseph, and yet they were his brothers. She wanted to trust them but couldn't. Joseph had made the decision to have lunch with them.

She would watch and see what Joseph did from here. One thing she knew, Joseph could not be unkind to anyone for long. He was too gentle. If he was ever to be completely happy, he would have to make peace with his brothers.

She sent in water to wash the men's feet and had them escorted to the dining room. Joseph was late. Their guests were arriving. They often had guests.

The door to the dining hall opened, and in walked Simeon. He was beaming from ear to ear. "I thought you would never return."

They greeted him warmly. "How have you been?" They were concerned for him.

He smiled as he said, "I am fine. The funny thing is the day after you left to return home to Canaan, I was given freedom in the prison. The guard completely changed his mind about me. He actually let me help him. I was allowed to come and go within the prison as I pleased. All things considered, they have been treating me very well. And now I understand we're invited to eat." He shook his head in disbelief as he realized his time of imprisonment was finally ending. "Thank God we are all together, and this whole thing has been sorted out."

At that moment Joseph entered the room. He looked at them as though he could read their minds. They shifted from side to side as he studied them each individually. He watched them squirm then abruptly turned and greeted his other guests one by one. Finally, Joseph turned back to speak to them. Through his interpreter, he asked them, "How have you been?"

They answered, "We have been well."

Joseph continued politely, "What of your father, the old man you told me about, is he still well?"

"Yes," they replied.

Reuben spoke up. "We have a gift for you." They handed him the gifts Jacob had sent. Each brother had something to present to him.

Joseph watched, knowing this was inspired by his father. He recalled another time when Jacob was in trouble with Esau. He also then prepared and sent gifts. His heart ached as they presented their gifts. But Joseph did not show the depth of emotion their gift had created in him. He was careful to control his voice and his expressions as he continued with polite conversation. He watched them with interest. "Is this your younger brother?"

"Yes, sir," they answered.

Joseph longed to embrace Benjamin. "May God be kind to you, my son." Joseph could take no more. He abruptly left the room. Alone in his chambers he cried. Then he washed his face and went back to the dinner hall.

There were three tables. Joseph sat at his own table. The Egyptians hated Hebrews, so they sat at another. Joseph's brothers also had their own. Joseph continued to speak to them through an interpreter directing all of them to be seated. They watched in amazement as he seated them according to their age. He motioned to Reuben to take the seat at the head of the table. One at a time he seated each brother. Benjamin was last. Joseph seated himself at his own table.

His brothers looked around at each other. "How does he know our ages?" they asked. The servants began to bring out the food. The feast was unbelievable. Their mouths flew open as they watched Benjamin being served. He was served five times as much food as his brothers!

Joseph raised his cup of wine then said something in Egyptian. Laughter rang out. "What did he say?" Reuben asked the interpreter.

The servant explained, "The master made a traditional toast." The brothers began to relax. They started to enjoy the food.

Joseph spoke to Benjamin through the interpreter. "How is your meat? Is the meal to your liking?"

Benjamin announced, "Sir, this is the best meal I've ever eaten." They all ate and drank freely, exchanging polite conversation with him.

Joseph watched Benjamin. He looked happy enough, but Joseph couldn't be sure. What if his brothers were treating Benjamin with the same contempt they had treated Joseph? He couldn't take the chance. He considered the options. *If I allow them to take him home, they may one day sell him to a caravan too or perhaps worse* . He smiled politely as he watched them, listening to their every word, straining to hear something that could assure him Benjamin was safe with them. The thoughts kept plaguing him. *What if Father dies? Will they allow Benjamin to live?* His mind ran wild as he replayed all the possible scenarios.

I must test them, he thought as he watched them laughing and drinking. They actually seemed fond of Benjamin. Joseph had to be sure.

The sons of Jacob left Egypt with joy. Their problems were finally over. They had plenty of food. The prime minister now believed them. They were at peace. Benjamin was a big hit with the prime minister. The man took Benjamin on a personal tour of the palace and the gardens. He spent the afternoon just talking to Benjamin. The interpreter had patiently interpreted everything either of them said. Benjamin was interested in everything the prime minister told him. The prime minister even introduced Benjamin to his wife and children. Benjamin was fascinated with the man and gave his brothers a blow-by-blow report of their conversation. Benjamin continued to speak, hardly taking a breath. "Did you know he is the one who planned this whole thing?"

His explosion of questions met a much-less-enthusiastic crowd of listeners. "Yes, we know, baby brother. However, he was not so kind the first time we were introduced." The brothers looked at each other as they listened to Benjamin carry on with the topic of the prime minister. "He must be the greatest man on earth. The pharaoh himself actually goes to him for advice. He told me he meets with the pharaoh every day. I asked him what Pharaoh was like. He said he found Pharaoh to be a good judge of character." Benjamin laughed as he remembered the prime minister joking with him.

Reuben was done. "Okay, little brother, we've heard enough about the magnificent prime minister. Can we please have some silence." But silence was not to come. At that moment, Reuben looked up, and topping a distant hill was a large group of armed soldiers. He suddenly became very sick. "What now?"

The others followed his gaze and also became sick. "Oh God!" They mourned as they watched the soldiers cover the distance between them.

Ruben spoke to the man who ran Joseph's house. "Sir, I don't understand why have you followed us. We thought everything was good between us and your master."

Joseph's servant walked up to him. "Why would you betray my master's kindness by stealing his cup?"

The men all began to deny the accusation. "No, sir, we did not steal from the prime minister. Search our supplies. If one of us has stolen from your master, he will die, and the rest of us will become your master's slaves."

"That seems fair," the servant answered. "Only no one will die. The one who has stolen, he is the one who will become the slave."

The sons of Israel unloaded their donkeys. Joseph's servant searched their possessions. He started with Reuben and worked his way down through the men according to age. Reuben and Judah looked at each other. They still did not understand how he knew who was oldest. It was unnerving. The cup was not found in any of their bags. Then he searched Benjamin's sack. There at the top of the bag was the shining, ornately designed cup.

Two soldiers grabbed Benjamin, one on each side. Benjamin looked at his brothers, terrified. He began to exclaim, "I didn't steal that! There's been a mistake! Sir, I did not take that cup!"

The sons of Israel tore their robes. "What is happening?" They had no choice. They loaded their donkeys and returned to the city.

Joseph watched his brothers enter the city from his balcony. His butler came to him and bowed, "Sir, we did as you instructed. The young man's brothers insisted on accompanying him back. They are all waiting to see you." It was still early morning. They did not see him, but Joseph had watched them leave from his vantage point on the veranda. He sat in the shadows, watching their exit from the city. The night before, he had instructed his men to place the cup in Benjamin's bag. It was the only thing he could think of to test his brothers. If they did not care enough to return, he would be able to keep Benjamin here with him. The boy would have everything a young man could desire: the finest education and all the opportunities of Joseph's position. If they returned, he would see their hearts. He would know for sure how much they loved Benjamin. Would they sell him out, or would they be true brothers to him? Joseph slowly dressed in his fine robes. His servant placed the wig on his head. Another servant put makeup on his eyes, drawing the perfect lines that so distinguished the Egyptians from other people of the region. Joseph took a deep breath. He was ready to face them. His servant announced his arrival.

Joseph seemed to be made of iron. His finger pointed at Benjamin. "This man has stolen my cup. Why didn't you realize I am able to discern such things?" Joseph's interpreter was at his side. Joseph watched as his brothers, with their garments torn, threw themselves in front of him. They bowed low on the beautiful floor. Their faces spoke without words their personal agony.

Judah spoke. "How can we defend ourselves? We have all returned to be your servants."

Joseph was adamant. "No, only the one who stole my cup will be my slave." The sons of Israel spoke openly to one another. "This is because of our sins."

Judah pleaded, "Sir, please listen to me. I know that just as Pharaoh could have me killed for speaking, so could you. Please be kind and listen to your servant. You asked us if we had a father and if he was alive. We told you yes. We also told you about our youngest brother. We told you that our father loves him. He is the only son left of his mother. We told you our father cannot live without the child. But you answered us by saying we would not see your face again unless we returned with the boy. When our father asked us to come here again and buy food, we explained that we could not return without the young man. I promised my father I would keep Benjamin safe or be held responsible forever. Please, let me stay here as your slave and allow the young man to go home. If he does not return our father will die from grief. How can I go home without him? I cannot bear to see my father's sorrow. I beg you keep me instead of the young man."

His plea was so sincere Joseph could no longer contain his emotions. He looked at his brothers. They were all bowing humbly. Reuben and Simeon were next to Benjamin as if somehow, even in their present predicament, they could protect him. Tears flowed freely down Joseph's face. They made their way to the front of his ornately decorated robe. The makeup so carefully applied was washing away as he began to sob uncontrollably. His servants reached out to aid him. They would do anything to stop or relieve his pain. Joseph would not allow them to come to his rescue. Holding up his hands, he stopped them from coming closer. "Leave me alone with them!" he demanded. His trusted servant bowed and quickly ushered the concerned servants out of the presence of their master.

Jacob's sons slowly lifted their heads. Their mouths flew open as they watched this tower of a man collapse in front of their very eyes.

Benjamin wanted to help. He carefully rose and slowly walked to the prime minister's side. "Sir," he said quietly, "may we help you?" His simple question left Joseph without defense. They had all slowly risen and were watching him as if he had two heads. Benjamin tried desperately to offer comfort. "I know a man in your position has many concerns."

Joseph finally gained enough composure to speak. "I am Joseph." His voice was barely audible. His brothers looked at him, trying to take in what they had just heard. He removed his wig. "I am your brother Joseph, the one you sold into slavery." They backed away as if their minds could not process the information. Joseph removed his lavish garments. Slowly he moved toward them. "I am Joseph."

They started to mourn. Terror replaced confusion. "We have sinned!" Their hearts broke as they faced their victim. Joseph reached out to embrace them. "Do not be angry with yourselves. God has brought me here. What you meant for evil, God has turned to good. Many people will survive because God placed me here for this time of famine. This is only the beginning. The famine will become very severe. God planned it so I would be here to feed people during these seven years of famine. "He watched them looking at him as if he were a ghost." I am Joseph. Is my father alive?" The cry of his heart pierced the room. His words penetrated their minds. Joseph began to weep uncontrollably. "Is my father alive?" His question rang throughout the palace. The grief of years exploded with those words. The emotion his heart so long denied was free. He collapsed into a heap as his brothers took in his words.

Benjamin was the first to speak. "Joseph?" The slight question in his voice was barely detectable. He cleared his throat and moved to embrace his brother. "Joseph!"

Then before he could release him, Judah grabbed Joseph and pulled him into his arms. "Brother." Tears ran freely down his face as he looked at Joseph. "I can't tell you how sorry I am." His words hung in the air, the pain still sharp in his voice.

Reuben looked at Joseph, his shame evident on his face. "Joseph, I tried to help you. I came back for you but I was too late. Forgive me." The words were wrenched from him.

His face mirrored his brothers. They all embraced Joseph, each offering his apology. Joseph tried to comfort them, but they continued to offer their words of regret.

"We love you!" Benjamin added at the end of the many apologies. Joseph looked into the tear-stained faces of the men who had so long ago betrayed him. They were all shaking their heads as they confirmed the words of Benjamin. "We were jealous of you. We were wrong. Please forgive us. We love you. Father has never gotten over your disappearance."

Joseph reached out to his brothers. "You must move here. I will take care of you. I will give you the best land in all of Egypt. This is just the first two years. There will be five more. Go home. Tell my father I am alive. Tell him I want to see him, and bring him here to me. Pharaoh will welcome all of you."

The servants of the palace were near the door. They waited to attend to Joseph's every need, hoping to offer him comfort. The crying was ending. They had heard the terrible wailing sobs of Joseph coming from the other side of the door. They looked around, concern marring their faces as they listened to the sounds of a wounded spirit. Finally, they could hear their master's grief was subsiding. Relief started to show in their expressions.

The butler had sent for his mistress. She came down the palace steps quickly, her long, flowing robes billowing behind her. "How is he?" she asked alarmed.

The butler moved to block her entrance. "He wanted to speak to them alone, Mistress. I just thought he might need you. I wanted you here if he did."

She nodded her understanding. "Thank you," she whispered. She realized she was holding her breath in anticipation.

"It is quiet now," the servant added, trying to comfort her. "I believe he is all right." He smiled, and they all waited for Joseph to call for them. Suddenly it happened. Joseph was summoning them.

His wife walked boldly into the room and over to Joseph. She was fully prepared to protect her husband in any way she thought necessary. She slipped her arm through his, and he wrapped his opposite hand around hers.

"My dear," he said, smiling, "I would like you to meet my brothers. We have talked things over, and they will be coming to Egypt with my father to live." Her expression of surprise quickly turned to one of graciousness. She turned on the charm and offered her best smile. "You are welcome," she said with as much sincerity as she could muster. "Please, my husband, introduce me."

Joseph was beaming. She could not recall him looking happier. He looked ten years younger. His normal worried expression was replaced with one of peace. He swept his arm out and introduced her to each of his brothers. As he did, he explained who their mothers were and gave her some interesting little facts about each one of them, from the oldest to the youngest.

She could see for herself Joseph was finally at peace. As she watched her husband, she offered up thanks to God, who had given him this gift of reconciliation. Tears moistened her eyes as she thought, *Joseph is right. He really is a God who cares for each of us. He longs to show us His love and make us happy.* Her smile, genuine now, radiated from her soul. She wanted to know this God who loves all of mankind. She recalled Joseph telling her once, "God forgives men if they will only ask. His desire is to be reconciled with men. His love for mankind is so great! It is vast like the stars that rule in the heavens! There is no end to His love for mankind!" She had listened in awe. Now, here, at this moment, as she watched her husband, she knew it. God is love!

17

JOSEPH LIVES

And Israel said, It is enough; Joseph my son is yet alive: I will go and see him before I die. (Gen. 45:28, KJV)

"Joseph's brothers have been here, sire." The servant bowed humbly before Pharaoh.

Pharaoh was intrigued. "Did he accuse them of being spies and imprison them again?" he asked with the humor of a young man enjoying a good joke.

The servant's lips turned up slightly as he continued to repeat the palace gossip, "This time they brought his younger brother. You know, the young man, Benjamin, his mother's son."

Pharaoh recalled his friend's stories of his younger brother. "Oh yes, I remember. Is the young man in good health?"

"Yes, sire, he is. This time the prime minister invited them to eat with him. It was quite an expedition. They had lunch, a wonderful time, and the prime minister acted as if everything was fine. All the while, he was making plans to trick them." He moved in confidentially. "I understand he actually had his servants place his cup in the top of Benjamin's possessions. Then when they had completely left and were on their way home, he sent the palace guards after them. Joseph instructed them to make a big to-do about how they had stolen from him and the man who had the cup would be his slave."

Pharaoh was amused. He threw back his head and laughed. "Ha! That is Joseph for you. He always has a plan." Pharaoh urged his servant. "Well, what happened?"

His servant was enjoying the story as much as the pharaoh. "Well, they all came back, fell down, and begged him to let them serve him instead of Benjamin. They said it would kill their father if the young man did not return. They actually confessed it was their sin that brought this trouble upon them."

Pharaoh was surprised. "They did? What did Joseph do?" The servant shook his head and looked a little concerned. "The prime minister took it hard. He broke down right there in front of everyone. Then he demanded that all his servants leave while he spoke with them personally." Pharaoh took in the words of his faithful servant. "How is he?" Concern etched Pharaoh's face, "Did they harm him?"

'No, sire, he is fine. They have reconciled. His brothers all confessed their sin and asked Joseph to forgive them. He did, of course. He forgave them. Then he invited them to come and live here in Egypt with him."

Pharaoh absorbed the information. "So then they will be coming here to Egypt to live near Joseph?"

"Yes, sire, the prime minister was very happy!" Pharaoh's servant finished the story with great enthusiasm.

Pharaoh paced the floor. This was his opportunity to show Joseph his thanks. "We will help him rejoice! Bring in my party planners. We'll throw a celebration for Joseph to celebrate his reunion with his family. And when his father and brothers return, we will give them anything they want." His magnanimous proclamation rang out through the halls of the palace. Pharaoh was on a mission to be a blessing to Joseph and his family.

Pharaoh stood and walked across the room, his arm sweeping the air as he instructed his servant, "Send for Joseph. I want to speak to him immediately."

"Yes, sire," the man began to bow as he exited the room. He walked over to one of his young messengers. "Pharaoh is asking for Joseph."

The young man nodded, turned, and was gone. He quickly made his way to Joseph's rooms. He approached the butler. "Pharaoh has sent for the prime minister."

Joseph was quick to respond. He immediately made his way to the pharaoh's main hall. Pharaoh watched his friend approach. Joseph's walk was different. The look of peace on his face was profound. Even if he did not know what had recently happened between Joseph and his brothers, Pharaoh would have noticed the look on Joseph's face. He rose from his throne—something Pharaoh did for very few people—and approached his friend with joy.

He reached out to Joseph and embraced him. "Let's walk in the gardens," he suggested—something they often did when they were together. "Joseph, I am very happy for you!" His smile echoed his words.

Joseph was still very moved with emotion when he thought about it. He nodded his head and looked down as tears started to burn his eyes. "Thank you, sire," he choked.

Pharaoh continued his quest to bless Joseph. "I insist you command your brothers to load their beasts with provisions. Also send with them carts and wagons to make their move. Tell them not to worry themselves with their things. When they arrive here, all the land is at their disposal."

Joseph was overwhelmed. He shook his head affirmatively, "Thank you, sire." He looked into the face of the most powerful man in the world and smiled. "Thank you," he repeated.

Pharaoh looked at his friend with great respect. "You are one of the few people I trust. You are like a father to me. I welcome your family with open arms."

Joseph knew Pharaoh had often been very lonely. He was plagued with the knowledge that many of his closest friends and even family would do away with him just for the opportunity to be more powerful themselves. He had learned the hard way not to trust people. When he found someone he did trust, he trusted them completely.

Joseph did as Pharaoh commanded. He sent the wagons and the beasts laden down with provisions for Israel and his relatives.

"We will return as soon as we can," his brothers promised. Joseph gave them all gifts of clothing, but to Benjamin, he gave silver and five times as many garments. Joseph was determined to make up for all the years he had lost with Benjamin. He wanted to spoil the young man completely.

They embraced as Benjamin prepared to leave with the others. "It is better if I go with them. Father may not believe them if he can't see for himself that I am fine." Joseph smiled at his wise young brother. "You are so like him," he whispered. I cannot believe how much you have grown up to look like father." Benjamin smiled. He liked it when people told him he looked like Israel.

"I will be back soon. We will spend the rest of our lives making up for the lost time." Benjamin promised with tears running down his face.

Jacob sat stone-still as he listened to the words of his sons. His mouth was wide open with surprise as he sought to comprehend the news. He watched as a large caravan of wagons moved slowly toward his settlement. The wagons, ornately trimmed, bearing a distinctively Egyptian design, now stood in front of his tents.

Surprise mixed with enlightenment washed over his face. "My son Joseph is alive?" He observed his sons search for words to explain their despicable behavior. He ignored their mumbling and asked, "He is the prime minister of Egypt? The man you said was hostile toward you?"

"Father, we are sorry for all the pain we have caused you and Joseph. We will spend our lives trying to make amends for the wrong we have done."

Jacob was becoming lightheaded. The next thing he knew, they were trying to bring him back to consciousness. He repeated himself. "My son Joseph is alive!" This time he believed them. Strength entered his spirit. "I will go and see my son before I die." His eyes filled with tears of joy. His sons once again began to apologize. He waved their apologies aside. "Who am I that you should apologize to me? After talking my brother into selling his birthright for a bowl of stew, I deceived my father and stole my brother's blessing. Esau was angry enough to kill me. But he didn't. He forgave me. I learned a lot from Esau that day. Forgiveness is a gift we give ourselves. Joseph has forgiven you." He looked over at his sons and took in their dejected faces. He finally understood their pain. I am the one who should ask you to forgive me. I didn't understand how much I was hurting all of you. You must ask God's forgiveness, then forgive yourselves and move on." He threw his hand up in the air as if to wave away their grief, and with those words, Israel was done discussing the pain. "I must make plans. I am going to see my son Joseph."

"There is no God like Jehovah!" The words of the precious old man rang out loud as he walked away from his sons. He turned his back on their guilt. His only concern was praising God. The words wafted through the air and hung like a sweet fragrance as he continued, "Who is like our God?" His aged frame disappeared as he spoke to the only one he cared to converse with. "My God is an awesome God. His throne is in the heavens, and the earth is just His footstool." The words rang out as he continued to walk to his quiet place where he could speak intimately with God. From a distance, the sons of Israel listened to the familiar sounds of their father worshipping God. There in the distance in the shadow of his favorite tree he knelt. The moonlight high-lighted his frame. The man of God was no longer concerned with the sorrows of life. God had returned to him his son. The grief of many years was quickly forgotten as he worshipped and praised God. There in his place of peace, Jacob sought and blessed God with all his being.

18

JACOB AND JOSEPH REUNITED

And Joseph brought in Jacob his father, and set
him before Pharaoh: and Jacob blessed Pharaoh.
(Gen. 47:7, KJV)

The day dawned bright for Israel as he prepared for his journey
to Egypt. His heart was restored as he thought of his son. God
had truly visited his people. The little camp was buzzing with
the news of Joseph. Jacob as patriarch walked out of his tent. The
family and friends were watching as he moved with the aid of his
staff. His sons tended to him as though they thought he might
break. All the years of suffering had left Jacob weak, a shadow of
his former self. The young men still in their prime reached out
to help Jacob. Today he was different. The man who had for so
long lived with grief was in good spirits. He spoke to his family.
"Prepare yourselves. We will go to Egypt and visit my son Joseph.
God has done a wonderful thing and sent Joseph there ahead
of us. He is now the prime minister of Egypt. He has promised
to provide for us during this time of famine. There will be five
more years. It is his desire that we settle there with him until God
brings us out of that land."

There was a great shout as the family of Jacob began to rejoice. "Joseph is alive!"

"Benjamin," one of his nephews called out to him. "Benjamin, what is Joseph like? Does he look like an Egyptian?"

Some of the other young men joined him, asking, "Did you really have lunch at the palace?" Benjamin watched as they all began to swarm him. He was just the little brother to their fathers, but to his nephews, he was a hero. He laughed and began to entertain them with his vast world travels. "Wait till you see it," he exclaimed. "It is magnificent! The floors are made of precious stones. The rooms are enormous. You should see the gardens. They have flowers you have never seen from all over the world and trees for fruit as well as their beauty." As he spoke, he took in their expressions and laughed to himself as they watched him, in wide-eyed wonder, describe the beauty of the city.

They were all properly impressed. They fingered the ornately decorated wheels of the wagons. "The pharaoh sent these for us to ride in?"

Benjamin watched the younger boys as they looked over each wagon. "Yes," was all he could say before his father called to him. He left them and ran to join Jacob.

Jacob rode in a beautiful wagon the pharaoh had sent for him. His heart pounded as he thought about his son Joseph.

"Father," he heard the voice of Reuben, "Father, we will be nearing Beersheba soon. I will tell the others we are to make camp."

Israel watched his sons as they prepared to stop. They were all weary from the day's events. Jacob had insisted he would not leave Canaan without offering a sacrifice to the Lord. He chose a lamb, perfect, without blemish. Jacob addressed the family. "The Lord God spoke to my Grandfather Abraham when he brought him out of the land of Ur of the Chaldeans. He promised to make of him a great nation. He led him into this land of Canaan. God promised him this land for his children's inheritance. He promised to make him famous and a blessing in the earth. And the Lord will surely do all He has promised to do. He is God over all the earth. His kingdom is without end. He sets up kings and takes them down. He is able to bring us again into this land He has promised to Abraham and Isaac." He blessed the Lord and offered the lamb as a sacrifice.

> And God spake unto Israel in the visions of the night, and said, Jacob, Jacob. And he said, Here am I. And he said, I am God, the God of thy father: fear not to go down into Egypt; for I will there make of thee a great nation: I will go down with thee into Egypt; and I will also surely bring thee up again: and Joseph shall put his hand upon thine eyes. (Gen. 46:2–4, KJV)

So Jacob, his sons, daughters, grandsons, and granddaughters all traveled to Egypt in the wagons Pharaoh had provided for them. They brought their herds and all their things.

"Judah," his father called to him.

Judah went to his father's side. "Yes, Father."

Jacob motioned ahead of them. "Ride ahead to Joseph. Ask him where we should go. I don't want to go into town or even close to the city with the little ones and the herds."

Judah agreed with his father. "I will go."

"Joseph!" There was a messenger running toward him. "Your brother Judah is here. He is asking where he should take your family. They have their herds, and your father is with him. He sends his greetings!"

Joseph dismissed the many people who were waiting to speak to him. "Bring my chariot. I will go meet them and escort them into the land of Goshen."

Judah was waiting. They greeted each other warmly. "Where is Father?" he asked.

"He is waiting for instructions from you." Judah's carefree smile reflected the youth he had once been. "He is so happy, Joseph!"

They rushed out the side door of the palace to the waiting chariot. "Here." Joseph motioned for Judah to ride with him.

Many of the palace guards were also ready. They galloped in front, alongside and behind the prime minister.

In the distance Jacob saw them coming. The long procession stirred the dust as they rode at a gallop toward him. He noticed the golden chariot with armed guards flanking all sides of it. Even from the distance, he could see the man coming was dressed in the finest of robes. The Egyptian wig and makeup could not hide the face of Rachel. He would have known Joseph anywhere. Tears of joy ran down his face as Joseph and Judah arrived.

"Father!" Joseph cried as he ran to the man he had so desperately missed. "You are really here!" Joseph looked at Israel. The years he had been away from his father showed. The man he once thought could fight a lion stood in front of him, aged but still the same. "Father." He spoke the word with the emotion of a lost son who now was found.

Jacob reached out to the man in front of him. "Joseph my son!" Tears streamed down his face as they embraced. The years of sorrow were washed away by the joy of their reunion. Joseph held his father and wept onto his shoulder.

Jacob embraced the man as though he were just a youth, patting his head. He said softly, "It is all over now, my son. Only death will ever part us again." Gently he eased the pain of the young man as only a father could.

Joseph finally lifted his head from Jacob's shoulder. "Who are these people?" And with that, introductions were made. One by one the many who had accompanied Jacob faced Joseph. Joseph looked with wonder on his family. The young boys who had questioned Benjamin looked into the eyes of their new hero. He smiled back at them, the face of Rachel reflected in his features.

"My son." Jacob reached out to touch his face. "I would have known you anywhere. Your face is the face of your mother."

Benjamin looked in wonder at Joseph. "He looks like mother?" The question rang quietly from his lips.

"Yes," Jacob said. "She was so very beautiful. Joseph looks just like her."

Joseph showed them the land of Goshen. It was best for their herds and cattle. The Egyptians hated herdsmen. They would not want them to live nearby.

Joseph was insistent. He wanted his brothers to speak to Pharaoh wisely. "If Pharaoh asks you what your occupation is, tell him you are cattlemen. He will let you stay in Goshen."

Joseph took five of his brothers and introduced them to Pharaoh. "Your Majesty," he said with the dignity of his many years of service. "I have brought five of my brothers to meet with you. The others are still with the little ones settling in."

Pharaoh looked questioningly at the men in front of him. "You are welcome," he offered graciously. "Joseph is my most trusted friend. What is your occupation?"

Judah spoke first. "We are herdsmen, sire. We have tended flocks and herds since we were children."

Ruben added, "Sire, our fathers for many generations before us were herdsmen. We continue to follow in their footsteps."

Pharaoh tried not to look too repulsed. "Yes, I see. You will lead your herds to Goshen. The land is at your disposal. You are welcome to the best of it." The sons of Jacob were speechless.

Joseph promised them they could stay and told them how to answer Pharaoh, but they still found it hard to believe they were so blessed. Relief flooded their faces. "Thank you, sire! You are very kind!"

They watched as Pharaoh smiled warmly back at them. He was relieved his plan to bless them was well received. "Joseph, give them the best of the land, and if any of them are especially talented, place them over my livestock as well."

Joseph responded, "Yes, sire." His smile warmed the heart of the king. Pharaoh looked up and saw an older gentleman. "Is this your father?"

"Yes, sire." Joseph motioned his father forward. "Sire, this is my father Jacob, also called Israel by God Almighty."

"How old are you, sir?" Pharaoh asked.

"I am 130 years old. My life has been hard. I still have not lived as long as my fathers." Pharaoh listened to Jacob as he told him the stories of his generations. Jacob blessed Pharaoh. "The Lord has spoken to my father, his father, and also to me, reaffirming His promise to bless those who bless us and curse any man who curses us. The Blessing of Abraham, Isaac, and Jacob rest upon you. The Lord bless you and keep you. The Lord make His face to shine upon you and give you peace."

Pharaoh was deeply moved by the kindness of this dear man. He marveled to himself, "There is no wonder Joseph is such an inspiring person. His father is a man like no one I have ever met." As he watched his friend Joseph and these men leave the throne room where he was king, Pharaoh thought, *These men are princes on earth following the great God of their fathers.* Something deep inside of him stirred in recognition of royalty.

Jacob walked slowly from the great hall of the pharaoh. His stature, once young and strong, was old and frail. The eyes that once beheld the beauty of Rachel took comfort in the faces of her sons. His heart, once full of love for his wife, was now full of love for his God. The boys he once rocked stood strong in his place. He leaned heavily on his staff as he crossed the great hall. His hip injury still plagued him, making his limp pronounced. Pharaoh followed his exit, never taking his eyes off Jacob. Even at this age, he was one of the most fascinating men Pharaoh had ever encountered.

He looked over at Joseph as Joseph slowed his step to match his father's. Joseph looked up at Pharaoh. Their eyes locked for a second. They knew without speaking they shared an understanding. They had just spent time with a man whose mantle was one unseen but nonetheless real. Jacob was clothed supernaturally with the anointed mantle of God, something his age only seemed to enhance.

—◦◦◦◦—◦—◦◦◦—

Joseph settled his family in the land of Goshen. Jacob lived another seventeen years. He called for Joseph. "My son, please promise me you will not bury me here. Promise me you will bury me with my fathers."

Joseph looked at his father. Tears ran down his face as he knelt next to Jacob's bed. "I promise, Father."

Time passed by, and Jacob became very ill. They told Joseph of Jacob's illness. He went with his sons to see his father. When Jacob learned Joseph was coming to see him, he raised himself up and made himself ready to welcome Joseph.

"Joseph, I am glad you have come to me." His eyes were weak, but he was sharp. His countenance was almost youthful. "God visited me in Canaan. He said to me, 'From you will come many nations. I will give this land of Canaan to you and your children as your possession forever.' I am adopting your two sons. They will inherit with my own sons." Jacob was almost blind. The years had taken their toll on the eyesight of Israel. He strained to see them. "Bring them closer."

"Yes, Father," Joseph said.

Israel embraced and kissed the young men. Jacob said, "I never expected to see you again. But God has allowed me to see your sons." Then he blessed them. The younger, Ephraim, received the greater blessing (see Gen. 48).

Ephraim and Manasseh watched the old man they had come to love. He was like their father but different. They were both wise men. They didn't just do anything. When they moved, there was a purpose behind their decision.

Ephraim left his grandfather's room. His father would never have done that! Joseph would have blessed the oldest son. He would have done it by the book. This was like some of the stories his father had told them of Jacob when they were younger. His heart was racing, and his thoughts were going a million miles an hour. He cautiously looked at his brother then their father. They were thoughtful. He thought it best not to mention the blessing thing just yet.

Jacob called for his sons to come to him for their blessing. He blessed them each, telling them of their future. He reminded them of the cave Abraham had purchased for a burying place. After he was finished, he lay back and died.

"Father." Joseph was beside himself with grief. He threw himself over the body of Jacob and cried. Then he ordered them to embalm Jacob. Joseph asked for permission from Pharaoh to bury his father. He explained he had promised to return his father to the family burying place. Pharaoh was very kind. He sent Joseph to bury his father with many of his highest-ranking officials to accompany him. They mourned for Jacob the appropriate number of days. Then they returned to Egypt.

Joseph lived to the age of 110. He called for his brothers to come and visit him on his death bed.

> And Joseph said unto his brethren, I die: and God will surely visit you, and bring you out of this land unto the land which he sware to Abraham, to Isaac, and to Jacob. And Joseph took an oath of the children of Israel, saying, God will surely visit you, and ye shall carry up my bones from hence. So Joseph died, being an hundred and ten years old: and they embalmed him, and he was put in a coffin in Egypt. (Gen. 50:24–26, KJV)

19

MOSES

> Now there arose up a new king over Egypt, which
> knew not Joseph. (Exod. 1:8, KJV)

Moses's mother was beside herself with fear. She had hidden the child for three months. She knew if she didn't act soon, someone would discover the child and perhaps report her. The Egyptians would use the child as an opportunity to abuse her family. The night before, while praying, she made a decision. She held her child, suckling and shushing him. He giggled sweetly in her arms. Softly, she cried out to God, "I can't do this by myself." She whispered into the silent darkness, "You have to help me, oh God!" She wept.

The cry of a broken heart rose to the throne room of heaven. Father God listened to the soft, gentle pleading of a mother. He was touched by her sorrow. He raised His scepter and pointed it toward the humble dwelling of a slave. "Go," he said softly. "She will need help." The words hung in the air as God hovered over the prayer of a slave mother.

In her time of great struggle, she pleaded with God to spare the child. The next morning she rose early. She took a basket she had waterproofed and placed her precious little boy in it. She looked at Moses.

Tears rolled down her face as her heart tore apart. She reached out and kissed the tiny little hand and prayed, "Oh God, Jehovah, there is no one like You. You are able to protect my son from the enemy. I place him in Your hands. Guide him as You guided Abraham, Isaac, and Jacob. Care for him as only You can."

As she spoke, the angel of the Lord stood beside her. His smile reflected the beauty of heaven. He walked ahead of her into the water, watching her closely. He spread his wings to shield his little charge from evil.

She stepped into the Nile River. The water was cold. She used it for cover as she sank deep into its shelter. She watched in all directions as she swam close to the shore. She trembled with fear as she moved along into the reeds. No one had seen them. If she were caught, the child would be killed in front of her. That thought was unbearable.

Pharaoh had enslaved the children of Israel. God fulfilled his promise to Abraham, Isaac, and Jacob. He made a great nation out of their children. The people of Israel populated the land of Egypt. Pharaoh was afraid they would rise up with his enemies and fight against him. He thought if they were slaves, they could be controlled. That did not happen as planned. They continued to multiply. Recently Pharaoh had decreed that any male child should be thrown into the Nile River and drowned. She could not do this evil thing. She had chosen to hide her son. Now she gave him to God to protect. She watched as the river carried his little makeshift boat along with the current through the reeds. Before she stepped into the water, she posted her daughter Miriam in the brush with instructions to follow the ark from land. She had to know what happened to the baby.

Miriam slipped through the brush undetected. She had many times sneaked away from the Egyptians by hiding herself in the brush. She had learned to be very quiet. She watched as the little basket came to a stop in the reeds near where Pharaoh's daughter was wading.

The daughter of Pharaoh had become bored. She went outside to watch the river. She loved the water. Reaching down, she moved the water with her hand. Her attendants helped her as she prepared to bathe. She was enjoying her daily swim. Her servant walked along the bank of the river.

The princess looked out toward the reeds and noticed something bobbing in the water. She called to her servant. "What is that floating among the reeds?" she asked.

The servant girl peered around to get a better look. "It is a basket, Princess."

The princess was curious. "Bring it to me."

The girl stepped into the water. The water rose to her waist as she reached for the object. She pulled it toward her and guided it as it floated toward the princess. The princess reached down and opened it. There in this beautifully fashioned basket was a child. He began to cry. His tiny hands and arms reached out to her.

She picked him up. "No, little one," she coed at the child. "Don't cry." She touched his soft cheeks with her finger, letting it slide along his chin. Her heart sank as she realized the desperate act of a mother to save her son. Deep emotion moved her as compassion overwhelmed her heart.

"This must be one of the Hebrew children," she said. She cuddled the child. His cry started to worry her. She had no way of feeding this baby.

"How shall I nurse this child?" she asked her servant.

Out of the bushes emerged a young girl. The little girl was lovely. "Princess."

The princess looked toward the sound of a child. The little girl was bright eyed. Her hair was dark. The cascade of curls fell haphazard around her face and down her back. She smiled at the princess. Then with great courage, she asked, "Would you like for me to get a woman to nurse the child for you?"

The princess smiled with sincere relief, amused by the child. She almost laughed. "Do you know of such a woman?" she asked as if unaware of the connection.

The child rushed forward, anxious to please. "Yes, Princess, I do!"

The princess moved gracefully toward the young girl. She bent down to accommodate the child's level.

"Then please, by all means, bring her to me. Also tell her I will pay her wages to nurse the child."

"Yes, Princess." Miriam's heart skipped a beat as she heard the words of the daughter of Pharaoh. "I will go right now." She turned and ran to her mother. "Mother, Mother, come quickly, the princess is asking for you!"

"The princess?" Miriam's mother was confused.

"I'll explain on the way." She took her mother's hand and pulled her along. Miriam talked without taking a breath as she made her report. "The basket came to a stop right in front of the palace. Mother, the princess was wading in the Nile when she saw it. One of her servants fetched it for her. She loves him, Mother. She was really happy to find him. She wants you to nurse him for her, and she said she will pay you!"

The young mother could not believe her ears. "Praise God!" she exclaimed with all the depth only a mother who had just had her child raised from the dead could understand. "Praise God!" She stopped running long enough to catch her breath. She was still crying, but now her tears were tears of joy. "There's no God like Jehovah!" she exclaimed as she started to run again.

The princess watched as the woman and the girl ran toward her. "Oh, you're here. Thank you for coming so quickly. I believe the child is hungry."

Moses's mother looked at her beloved son. "Of course, Princess." The young woman addressed her with a small curtsy.

The princess handed Moses to his mother. A knowing look passed between the two women. "You will take him home with you until he is weaned. Then bring him to me. I will raise him as my son. He is a gift from the gods. I drew him from the water. His name is Moses."

"Yes, Princess." The Hebrew woman bowed before her. Without thinking, she took the hand of the princess and kissed it. "Thank you, Princess." She looked up as she spoke the words, tears filling her eyes.

"You are welcome," the princess replied, compassion evident on her face. "I will pay you well for caring for my son."

The Hebrew mother left with her daughter and her baby. Everyone was fine. Her heart pounded out the words: "Moses will live!"

That night there was a celebration in the home of a family of slaves. "Praise Jehovah!" The words rose and filled the room of the little home.

Moses's father couldn't help believing God had saved his son for a purpose. Wonder replaced sorrow as his wife and daughter told him and his son Aaron their story.

Moses's mother was glowing. Her eyes filled with tears of joy as she shared her happiness with her husband. She reached out to hold both of his hands in hers. "God has seen our affliction. He has delivered our son from certain death. Just as He brought Joseph before Pharaoh, He has arranged for our son to be raised in Pharaoh's house. Isn't this God's mighty work?" she asked her family, still awed herself as she wondered what this meant. Joy overwhelmed the family as they watched their gift from the Lord kick and smile his funny little baby smile.

The slave who was the mother of Moses held her son often. She never wanted to let go of her son. She comforted herself with the knowledge that God's divine purpose was evident in her son's life.

The day arrived, and true to her word, she packed up her little angel and walked the long path to the palace. She was met by the guards at the door who refused her entrance. One became hostile as she declared, "The princess will want to see me."

He snarled. "See you?" He seemed to think she had lost her mind. "Why would she want to speak with a Hebrew slave?"

She lowered her gaze. "Please tell the princess I have brought her son to her."

The guard looked confused. He stepped back slightly as he announced to the palace butler, "There is a Hebrew woman to see the princess."

The butler seemed to think it was quite normal. "Show the woman in." He looked at the slave and asked, "Is this the child?"

"Yes, sir," she answered with a little catch in her throat.

He nodded his understanding. "Come with me."

She followed him down a long hall. She was overwhelmed with the beauty of the palace. She had only heard stories. Seeing it now took her breath away. She watched as they made each turn, taking in the surroundings, trying to memorize each corridor, each place of interest. She wanted to always remember this place. She would imagine Moses playing here.

She was introduced to a somber-looking lady who after a word with the butler told her to wait in the room to the right.

"Why is she here?" She heard the hateful sound of a female voice. The butler was explaining something to the woman. She heard him demand that the woman get the princess. Then she could hear the sound of footsteps trail away as the woman went to obey.

The doors flew open. "Where is he?" the princess asked as she entered the room.

Moses's mother held him tightly in her arms. She had been thankful for the last few moments alone with him.

The princess was thrilled. "Oh, he is beautiful, isn't he?" She smiled as she made her proclamation. The princess reached out, taking the baby into her arms.

Moses's mother responded, "I think so, Princess."

They looked into each other's eyes. The princess watched the woman who had cared for her son with pity. "I will give him a good home. He will want for nothing." She started to cry. "I have been very unhappy. A woman should be a mother, don't you think?" she asked the slave.

Moses's mother smiled sweetly, her voice barely audible. "Yes, Princess. I wish you and your son every happiness. God has smiled on you. He is a wonderful boy. Any woman would be proud to call him son." Her heart nearly broke as she looked away.

The princess reached out to comfort her, if possible. "I love him. I needed a son. He is the answer to all my prayers. I have prayed very hard for him." Moses's mother looked into the eyes of the only woman on earth who could have spared her son. And with strength she did not know she had, she smiled her most gracious smile. "Then you are very blessed, Princess. Your joy brings me great delight." With those words, she curtsied, turned, and walked away from her beloved son.

The princess smiled as she watched the Hebrew slave leave. She had known great women, women of extreme beauty and poise. As she watched the mother of her son disappear, she thought, *She is the most magnificent woman I have ever seen.* She watched as the shabbily dressed figure walked down the hall. Her head was held high. Her regal gait denied with every step that she was anything less than royalty.

20

MOSES IN THE PALACE

> And it came to pass in those days, when Moses
> was grown, that he went out unto his brethren,
> and looked on their burdens: and he spied an
> Egyptian smiting an Hebrew, one of his brethren.
> (Exod. 2:11, KJV)

"The boy is incorrigible." Pharaoh paced the floor with long impatient strides. "Can't you control him?" he asked his daughter.

The princess sighed. "Father, he is curious. It is only natural. Boys should be curious. He is very intelligent."

Pharaoh sniffed at her statement. "If he is so intelligent, why does he stutter?"

The princess was annoyed by her father's question. She hardly thought before she answered, "Because you yell at him. He is a good boy. He tries hard to please you, but you continue to pressure him to do better. He is a little boy. He wants you to love him as you love Rameses."

Moses stood dejected listening to the dialogue between his mother and grandfather. His mother moved protectively toward him. "Tell Pharaoh you are sorry, Moses."

The boy moved to bow to his grandfather. "I am sasasa-sorry, Grandfather, I will tatatatry to do bababa-better." But the words did not come out the way he wanted them to. His speech was labored as he stuttered his way through the apology. His face blushed with shame as he worked to speak.

Pharaoh's demeanor changed as the little boy apologized. "You will pay more attention next time?" he asked.

Moses nodded his answer.

Pharaoh was perplexed. He was raising boys to rule in his palace. He couldn't have them running around carelessly. He looked over at his daughter. Her eyes were pleading with him to show the boy compassion. "Well then," he said. "If you promise to try harder, it is settled. You and I will start fresh."

"Yes. sir." The boy's face became one of great beauty as he smiled with relief.

"You see, Moses," Pharaoh continued," I don't wish to make life harder for you. It's just that I know how much responsibility I am leaving to you and Rameses. I desire only the best for both of you. You are a son to me. You have a great deal to learn. I only have a few years to teach you."

Moses shifted slightly. "I know sir," Moses said, his love for this man showing in his expression. "I will make you papapa-proud," he promised.

Rameses waited for Moses in the hall. His smile turned to laughter as they quickly ran down the hall away from nosy ears. "Father was really mad that time, Moses," he said.

"I know." Moses was not quite as happy as his playmate. His shoulders slumped as he acknowledged, "I have to do better for him. I can't keep disappointing him all the time."

Rameses looked at Moses questioningly. "I don't understand why you only stutter around Father. You aren't stuttering at all now." Moses shrugged. "You're different. I can tell you anything. It's just that when I talk to other people, I can't get my tongue to move."

Rameses studied his brother and friend. "I know. I will help you. We'll work together until you stop being so nervous."

Moses appreciated his brother's help. "Do you think I can learn to stop stuttering?" he asked, his boyish innocence showing as he imagined not having that problem.

"Sure you can," Rameses assured him. "You only stutter when you're unhappy or nervous. You just have to learn to not be nervous. That's all."

Moses sat back against the palace wall, his heart sinking as he thought of not feeling nervous. "What if I can't stop the nervousness?" he asked, clearly in pain.

"You can," was all Rameses had to say about it. "Let's go swimming." A couple of minutes of seriousness was all Rameses could stand. He had too many happy things to think of to worry about the serious stuff.

Pharaoh's daughter kissed her father and left. Alone he could think. It wasn't as if he didn't love the boy. The truth was he did. Moses was one of the most beautiful babies. His heart had melted as quickly as his daughter's when she presented Moses to him. She was so happy. Pharaoh didn't care where she had gotten the boy; he made her happy. That was really all that mattered.

But Pharaoh had noticed several problems with the child. He did not have the charm of Rameses. It was impossible for the boy to speak, let alone run a country. Moses was often angered. Pharaoh thought the boy became flustered easily, causing him to get angry. This could be a problem. He knew firsthand. He himself was easily angered. He wanted better for his son and Moses. He would petition the gods to help him better guide the boys. He rose from his throne and walked down the hall. He was tired. He decided to rest. He would sleep on it. Perhaps things would look better tomorrow.

The princess slept fitfully. She had become concerned for Moses. Her father continued to pressure the child. He constantly compared

Moses with Rameses. She was always trying to comfort her son. As he grew, he was more discontent. He could not understand why the Hebrews were slaves.

She offered her opinion. "You will be a great leader one day. If you desire to change such things, you can. But for now you must be patient."

He had grown up overnight. His handsome face reflected the concern of a young man disturbed by injustice. He watched as young Hebrew men were insulted, worked, and often beaten. Still trying to sleep, she turned over.

She thought of his most recent conversation with her. He was angry. She watched as he grew more unhappy and angrier almost daily. She could no longer kiss his scrapes and make the pain go away. This was pain that struck him so deeply it scared her.

"I have given you everything," she told him. "I have denied you nothing. I would die for you. I don't care if you are the child of a Hebrew woman. You are my son, Moses. I drew you from the Nile. You were a gift from the gods. I have made you an heir to all of Egypt. You can help the Hebrew people because you are my son. All of Egypt is at your feet. You are a man of destiny. It does not matter who gave birth to you, you are my son." Her heart reached out to the angry young man before her. He did not listen to her. He turned and walked away. He went back to his people. As she waited for him, unable to sleep, she felt a dread that was earthshaking. She was sure something terrible will happen.

She reached out to the God of the Hebrews. "I have denied You. I claimed I received Moses from my gods, but I know You gave him to me to fulfill Your desires for the Hebrews. I ask You to take care of my son. He is all that matters to me. Please watch over him as You lead him toward Your purpose." Her heart reached out to the one true God, the God of the people of Israel, the God of her son Moses. "Whatever Your plan for him, protect him." Tears burned a trail down her face as she sought comfort from this foreign God.

Moses sneaked quietly past the guards and down the corridor of the palace. His hands hurt from the battle he had fought. That day he witnessed an Egyptian beating a Hebrew. His temper shot out of control. He looked from side to side. No one was there. He took the knife from his belt and attacked the Egyptian from behind. His hands trembled as he realized it had been easy for him to kill the man.

The Hebrew slave was barely alive. He quickly buried the Egyptian, working fast to cover his sin. The slave threw his arms up to shield himself. "Please don't kill me," he begged as Moses approached the man to help him.

"I am not going to kill you," Moses assured him. He picked the slave up, carrying him to his home. Moses set the man outside the door. In the dark he said, "You can't tell anyone I helped you. I will be executed if anyone finds out I killed that man. Do you understand?" he asked. The slave agreed, and Moses left.

Now back in the palace, his heart was beating a hundred miles an hour. He was a murderer. Moses sat alone in the dark, thinking about it. Sleep did not come that night. He was not sorry for what he had done. The Egyptian deserved to die. Moses was tired of living a lie. He was the son of slaves, no matter what his mother said. The blood of Hebrew slaves ran through his veins. He was not Egyptian. Pharaoh never let him forget that fact. He was never good enough, no matter what he did to try to please his grandfather.

Rameses, his childhood friend, had grown up to be a spoiled, arrogant man. He still loved Moses, but they both knew things had changed between them. His mother was the one bright spot in his world. She had truly done everything she could, giving him every advantage, but the rage that rose inside of him was more than she could understand. He tried to explain to her. He could not pretend to be what he wasn't.

Now in the solace of his room, he talked to the God of the Hebrews. "Today I killed a man. I am not sorry. Someone has to help these people. You haven't. They say You will deliver them, but where are You? If You truly exist, how can You stand by while they are abused, raped, beaten, and hated? Can't You hear their cries? What kind of a God allows His people to suffer?"

His anger still raging, Moses thought about his advantages. His mother was right. He would pretend just a little longer. He would put his anger aside and play the game. He could help his people from the palace more effectively than from the position of a slave. The night passed as he planned his ascension. If he could please his grandfather enough to be given authority over the Hebrew slaves, he could make a difference in their lives. His mother's influence over the pharaoh would be very useful. She had groomed him for just such a position. Reason replaced his hotheaded anger. He would start today. *I must mingle with the Hebrews and research their circumstances. If I can formulate a plan to make them more productive and gain Pharaoh's confidence, I can move into position as liaison between Grandfather and the Hebrews. If I work quickly, Grandfather might appoint me immediately.* His heart lightened as he planned for his mission.

He walked the streets of Goshen. His step was one of youthful exuberance.

He loved these people. He was finally on the right track. Hadn't his mother tried to explain this to him time and time again? Now he understood. For the greater good of the people, leaders must set aside their own desires and rule. Yesterday he had not been able to see clearly for the rage. Today he was ready to learn from yesterday's events. He breathed a sigh of relief as he walked the streets near where he had killed the Egyptian. The Hebrews watched him with guarded eyes. That was normal when any of the pharaoh's family came here. He thought nothing of it. He took a minute to check on the man he had helped. *That's odd*, he thought. *No one answered the door.* He was sure the man would be in. His injuries would have kept him in bed. He walked a little further. He could hear the sounds of men fighting in an alleyway.

He walked down the alley toward the men. "Brothers," he called out to them. He moved in to stop them. "Why are you fighting?" He looked at the man who was in the wrong. "Why did you hit this man?"

The Hebrew slave responded, "Who appointed you a prince and judge over us? Are you going to kill me the way you did the Egyptian?"

Moses was suddenly struck with the realization that the murder had not remained hidden. He stumbled backward. Why couldn't they realize he was there to help them? He turned and ran away from them.

"There he is!" A guard pointed a long menacing finger in the direction of Moses. He panicked and ran the opposite way.

The guards ran after him. "Moses!" they called. "Come back here. Pharaoh wants to speak to you."

He ignored their cries. His heart pounded. He was trapped. He could feel the sweat beading at the back of his neck. His princely robe, ornately decorated, was too obvious. He hid himself behind a pile of brush. He was near the water. The reeds once used to hide his Hebrew mother now shielded him from the growing number of palace guards chasing him. He would stay hidden until he could escape under the cover of night. He watched as each soldier ran past him. For the first time since he had killed the Egyptian, he found himself truly sorry.

Once the soldiers were out of sight, he slowly worked his way through the maze of reeds, continuing to use them to hide. He was still trying to understand why the Hebrew slave had told on him. Hadn't he saved that slave's life? The only answer was for money, or perhaps a better living or working situation. But the slave seemed sincere when he promised. He thought about the incident. After thinking it over, he was convinced someone other than the slave he helped had talked. There must have been someone watching him. He looked around suspiciously. Someone could be watching him now. His eyes scanned the distance. He checked the nearby brush.

One thing was clear: what had started out as a day of hope for his people was now a day of trouble. He could not help them. Not now. He slipped away from the city. He would have to make a run for it. Pharaoh may have been willing to cater to his daughter by allowing her to raise a Hebrew for a son, but he would never forgive a Hebrew killing an Egyptian. He couldn't. If the Hebrew slaves saw that he had gotten away with it, they might become more aggressive. Pharaoh would have to squash any insurrection immediately. Moses felt sick. In his haste to save one slave, he had lost the opportunity to help an entire nation of slaves. Finally, the darkness fell. He slipped away into oblivion, alone and dejected. His shoulders slumped as he realized he was no more than a fugitive. His future, just yesterday one of promise and pleasure, was nothing more than that of a vagabond. Moses was alone, without hope.

The princess panicked. "Father, you can't be serious. Moses would never kill anyone. I don't care what this slave has told you. It is a lie!" Her voice rose to a shriek as she fought to stay calm, while a voice inside of her confirmed the report. Hadn't she known in the night when she woke to such fear? Her beautiful features contorted with pain. "Father, please, I beg of you. It's Moses. I know you love him. You can't put him to death." She pleaded with Pharaoh through a river of tears.

"Yes," Pharaoh sighed sadly. "It is Moses, my own son. He has risen up against me to commit this unspeakable crime. He knew when he made this decision. I would have no choice but to render swift judgment."

The princess wilted as she heard her father's words. The heart of a mother with a child gone wrong sank to depths of unbearable pain. The pain of a thousand arrows sank into her heart as she realized she would never see her son again.

The pharaoh ordered the servants to remove the princess. "Take her to her chambers and care for her." The words of a heart breaking screamed an earthshaking moan: "My son, my son, my son!"

Pharaoh watched as his daughter was carried from his presence, his pain rivaling that of the princess. What had he done wrong? Why had Moses grown up to doubt his love? His own pain great, he took control. Once again the ruler had to lead. Setting aside his own feelings, he did what was best for his people. With a face and voice of stone, he ordered his men: "Find him."

Moses's Hebrew family was rushed upon by armed guards. "Where is he?" One of the guards pushed past Miriam. Entering the house, he made a complete search. "Take her!" he ordered the other men. He turned to her. "Where is your brother?"

Miriam was terrified. "He is with Father, working."

"Why aren't you working? What are you doing home?"

She fought tears as she stated, "I was sent home to fetch something I have been making for my mistress."

The guard looked suspicious. "Why would anyone give you such freedoms?"

"I am a slave for a lady. She is good to me. The princess appointed me to attend to her."

His face became hard. "Oh, did she? Well, we'll just see about that." He pulled her along as he barked more questions at her.

She finally started to understand. Moses had killed someone. They wanted to know if she knew anything. Her parents and brother were lined up before Pharaoh. "But sire, we know nothing," Aaron was speaking. "We are loyal servants of the king. My mother did nurse the child after my own brother died, but she returned him to the princess years ago."

Pharaoh looked at the family before him. He believed they did not know where Moses was. He knew Moses would never endanger his family by going to them, just as he knew without asking his daughter had not and would not see Moses. He was suddenly weary. "If you do hear from him or if you discover his whereabouts, you will report back to me?"

"Yes, Pharaoh." The young man standing before him was the mirror image of Moses.

Something in Pharaoh broke. "You're dismissed. Leave me," he cried.

Back in the sanctuary of the little home, the family of slaves who had once celebrated the miracle of God choosing their Moses began to pray. Moses's father's baritone voice resonated through the humble shelter as he sought the God of Abraham, Isaac, and Jacob. "This is a hard thing, oh God. But we remember your favor. Joseph was sold into slavery. He was sentenced unfairly and imprisoned, until the day of your great appointed time. What man meant for evil, God used for good. We will believe the Lord. Save him from destruction. Guide his steps, oh God, as he searches for You. Lead him in the path of Jehovah." The prayers of a slave, the prayers of two mothers, the desire of a king, and the call of his God pressed a broken, lonely man on into the desert.

THE CALL IN THE DESERT

And the angel of the Lord appeared unto him in
a flame of fire out of the midst of a bush: and he
looked, and, behold, the bush burned with fire,
and the bush was not consumed. (Exod. 3:2, KJV)

The cold night air cut into the fugitive prince. His beautiful robe
so well suited for a warm desert day was ill suited for a cold desert
night. Moses pressed on not knowing where he was going. He
only knew he could not go back. He had to go forward. All night
he walked. The grains of sand rubbed his sandaled feet raw. Still
he pressed on.

He managed to steal a container of water before leaving the
city. He was fearful of running out, so he guarded it carefully,
counting the sips. He saved the precious fluid for the desert day.
He walked on, looking for a shelter he could use to hide and rest
during the heat of the day. He planned to rest by day and walk
by night. Pharaoh would send his guards after him. Finally, he
came to a suitable spot. He was exhausted. He did not sleep the
night before. He was to the point of collapse. There in the most
unlikely place was a little cluster of rocks. He burrowed into the

side of the rocks, hiding himself like a wild animal. Alone and exhausted, Moses saw the irony of his predicament. From the slave who would be king to the murderer who would be a deliver to the fugitive in need of a deliverer. Moses thought on the mess he had made of his life as sleep finally took him to a place of rest.

He woke up, his conscience troubling him. Deep inside he felt he deserved this exile. He had taken a life; no matter what his reason, it was wrong. He could have stopped the man from beating the slave with a few well-chosen words. He was, after all, a prince in Egypt. The truth was that he wanted to kill the Egyptian. He wanted the same kind of brutal judgment placed on him that was daily placed on the Hebrews. His stomach ached not from hunger as much as from knowing he had turned into the kind of man he himself claimed to abhor. He was no better than the man he killed.

On he walked through the night. He stumbled along, his feet refusing to work. Finally, he fell facedown into the sand, too exhausted to go any further. He wasn't sure how long he had slept. When he awoke, it was still dark. He knew enough to follow the stars. He had used them to guide him away from Pharaoh. He pulled himself up and walked on.

Day was beginning to break. He looked out over the country. Pharaoh's soldiers had not followed him this far. He began to breathe a little easier. He had to find food and water. He pressed on even though the night was gone. He noticed a change in the desert. It was no longer desolate. In the distance, he saw a mountain. Something drew him toward it. As he drew closer, he could see, even at a distance, vegetation. He walked faster, spurred on by the hope of finding water and food. For the first time since his escape, he felt relief.

He saw a well; he ran to it. He reached out. Cupping his hand, he pressed it into the water. He was at last able to drink his fill. He watched carefully, looking all around as he brought the water to his lips. His eyes searched the distance as he continued to drink. He was too tired to eat. He found a place hidden from view and slept.

In the distance, he could hear the sound of bleating. He set up watching the distant scene. He remained still. Seven young ladies topped a small knoll with their flock. He watched, interested, as they prepared to water their animals. They worked hard. When they were about half-done, a group of shepherds approached. The girls seemed upset as they watched the men coming. Moses's interest turned to concern as the men moved closer. They were aggressive and rude. They ordered the girls away from the well. The young women stood their ground. One girl moved to the front of the others. She was tall and slender, with long, dark hair that wrestled its way out from the bottom of her scarf. One of the shepherds shoved her aside. He and his men began to move their own herd in where the young ladies had been working, filling the troughs for their flock. These men intended to let their herd drink.

Moses stepped out of the shadows. Without thinking, he swept through the men, grabbing them and shoving them. He threw them down hard. His blind rage made him a force to be reckoned with. The men were not prepared to actually have to fight a man for the well. They backed off. Moses ordered them with the authority of a king: "Move your flocks back. These ladies were here before you!" He stood tall, holding a staff he had taken from one of the men. He held his ground, ready to fight anyone who defied him. The men backed away. He watched them as though they were vipers until they had left. He began to fill the watering troughs once again for the young ladies. He was sure the men would be back the moment he left, so he didn't leave.

"Water your sheep." His voice was kind.

Quickly they worked, finishing the task they had started. They thanked Moses and left.

Moses backed off when the ladies left. He watched cautiously as the men took their turn watering their flock. He was still close enough to see the well. He did not intend to leave just yet. He needed to rest for a while. He moved out of sight, hiding himself. He had a good view of the land. From here he would know if someone were still pursuing him. His body ached from the long nights of escape. Hunger started to get the best of him.

The men finished watering their sheep and left. This was what he had been waiting for. He slipped back down to the well to drink and fill his container before moving on. In the distance he noticed the young ladies he had defended coming toward him. They were waving and smiling.

The older one began to speak. "Sir, our father has sent us back to invite you to eat. My name is Zipporah. We would consider it an honor if you would come home with us. Allow us to return your kindness. We told father how you helped us. He was displeased with us for not inviting you to come home with us immediately." Her smile and deep, wide eyes were enchanting.

Moses was starving. "I can't stay long," he said. "I would appreciate something to eat."

She smiled. "Good. Father will be delighted." They walked along, talking comfortably.

Her sisters giggled and asked questions Moses was not ready to answer: "Where are you from, Moses? Why haven't we seen you before?" They continued, steadily grilling him.

He answered cautiously. After a while, they ran on ahead, playing. Anxious to change the subject, Moses studied the mountain. "What is this mountain called?" he asked her. A strange feeling came over him as he watched it. She answered, "It is Sinai. It is holy. God lives on the mountain."

His mind went back to his perception of God. A strange taste came up in his throat. He did not like to think of a God who could not hear the cries of His people. He thought once again of his charges against God. The familiar feelings of anger and dissatisfaction came flooding back. She continued to talk, not noticing his discomfort. Moses tried to listen. He did not want to go down that path of anger. Finally, her beauty and the constant chatter of her conversation captured his attention.

Jethro, the priest of Midian, greeted his guest with enthusiasm. "Welcome!" he exclaimed as Moses was introduced to him. Moses instantly liked the man. "Sit, sit, eat," Jethro commanded.

The food was simple but delicious. Moses consumed the food like a man who had not eaten in days. He looked at his host. Jethro was watching Moses. Moses apologized. "Excuse me," he said with his mouth still full.

Jethro seemed quite satisfied as he said, "On the contrary, your enthusiasm is wonderful. We are pleased you are enjoying the food." Moses smiled for the first time in days. He was truly content. Jethro looked at his young friend. "Where are you going?" he asked.

Moses shrugged. "It doesn't matter. I haven't really thought about it."

Jethro invited, "Why not stay here, at least for a few days? You can always move on later."

Moses considered the invitation. Here he had shelter, food, water, and good company. What did it matter if he stayed? "I would want to work in exchange for your hospitality," he said.

"Of course," his friend replied. "You can tend my flocks. My daughters are beautiful, but I don't have a son to protect them." Moses glanced at Zipporah. Jethro followed his eyes. "Zipporah could help you. She is the oldest. She has had to bear the burden of not having a brother, acting as a mother and a protector to her sisters."

Moses was convinced, nodding his head affirmatively. "I will stay."

Jethro smiled. He was happy to have a helper, but more than that, he felt Moses needed him too.

That night, for the first time in several days, Moses rested peacefully.

Moses was a dependable shepherd. Zipporah taught him many things about tending to sheep. He began to see her as the most amazing woman he had ever known. She was not like the women of the palace. They were soft and beautiful but seemed to lack purpose. He often became bored with them. Zipporah was nothing like them. She had the courage of a lioness. Her eyes blazed when she was angry and seemed totally peaceful when she was not. She was not dressed in the finery of the palace women. Her garments were suitable for work. She did everything without complaint. Her skin, already dark, was darkened more from the hours in the sun. Moses thought she is completely lovely.

Jethro sat in the shade of his tent, watching Moses. To him the young man was a mystery. Moses had no real skill for common labor. His hands were not the hands of a shepherd. He had heard rumors of a prince who had escaped Egypt after murdering a man. He was sure this was Moses. He did not care. He loved Moses like a son. He just could not figure out why he did not ask for Zipporah's hand. Jethro needed a son-in-law, a man to care for his daughters should something happen to him. Zipporah was well past marrying age and very beautiful. As Jethro reasoned it out, he decided to speak to Moses.

"She is a beautiful woman, Moses." Jethro watched the younger man with interest. "She would make you a good wife."

"Yes," Moses answered, "and I would be honored to be her husband. But there are things about me you don't know. I am not in a position to marry."

Jethro leaned back. "You might be surprised what I know," he stated, looking directly into Moses's eyes.

"And what is that?" Moses asked.

The older man said, "I have heard of an Egyptian prince who killed a man. I was asked if I have seen this man. I, of course, said no. Maybe you should tell me what really happened. I know you, Moses. You must have had a very good reason for doing it. You are like a son to me. I trust you. You can make a life here. Zipporah would ease your pain."

Moses sighed. "I killed a man. He was beating a slave. I killed him, and I didn't regret it. I am a murderer. Is that the kind of man you want to marry your daughter?" Moses said the words with the bitter sorrow of a man who was lost.

Jethro spoke carefully. "I know a man who placed his life in danger, rescued my daughters, and has worked hard caring for my flocks. I don't know this murderer you speak of. Whoever you were then, that is not who you have to be now. It is not by accident you came here to us. God sent you to my home. He has a purpose for your life."

Moses took in the words of his friend. "There are those who would agree with you, but I can't see it. I once thought God placed me in the palace to help my people. But how can I help them when I can't help myself?"

Jethro wanted to know more. "I'm sorry, Moses. I am afraid I don't understand. How did God place you in the palace? You have told us you are a Hebrew. But when you came here, you did not know how to work. Your hands showed no sign of having been a slave, and you were wearing the robe of a prince. How is it you were placed by God in the palace?"

Moses was relieved to finally tell the story without omitting parts of the truth. "I am the son of Hebrew slaves. The man who raised me as his son was the pharaoh of Egypt.

"Before I was born, Pharaoh became concerned that the Hebrew population of slaves would revolt against our Egyptian hosts. He feared them killing and eventually taking the land for themselves. Pharaoh took drastic measures by ordering all the male Hebrew babies to be put to death. The girls were considered more docile than boys. So he decreed that all boys be thrown into the Nile River to drown.

"He also ordered midwives who tended the slaves to kill the babies at birth. However, these women feared God and would not obey the king. They claimed the Hebrew women were stronger than the Egyptian women and gave birth without their help. The interesting thing is that it is reported among the Hebrew people that God rewarded them for their faithfulness and gave them homes. Grandfather believed the women but then ordered the parents to kill their own children.

"That's when I was born. My Hebrew mother and father feared God and would not kill me. So my mother wove a basket, waterproofed it, and placed it into the Nile. My sister hid in the brush to see what would become of me. The daughter of Pharaoh found me and adopted me as her own son. She used to say I would someday be a great leader. She would tell me I was sent to her by the gods."

Jethro added, "To be adopted by the daughter of Pharaoh is not a small thing. God would have to have guided the basket."

Moses nodded. "Yes, she is the only mother I really know, and I have broken her heart. I couldn't help the Hebrews. Instead, now I am a fugitive. I have failed everyone I love miserably. I always knew I was different. Grandfather never quite accepted me. He did try, but I think I was too much for him. After I was older, I learned the truth. It was my friend who told me, Pharaoh's son. He was raised with me as my brother. For him it was different. He was wanted. I asked my mother if it was true. She could not deny it. She claimed she drew me from the water. She said I could help the Hebrew people best by using my position.

"At first I just wanted to know more about them. I went to my birth mother. She was very helpful. The princess hired her to nurse me while I was young. I will never forget how happy she was to see me. She said God, Jehovah, had saved me. My Hebrew family seemed to think I could deliver them from the tyranny of Pharaoh. I didn't know how to tell her I was just a second-class prince to Pharaoh. After a while, I decided perhaps they were right. In time I would gain the trust of Pharaoh and be placed in a position that could ease their pain. But before I could formulate a real plan, I killed an Egyptian for beating a slave. I became so angry I wanted that man dead. I thought I could hide my crime. I tried, but it was well known by the very next day. I knew I had to run. Pharaoh could not let me live. If he is merciful to me, others will rise up in rebellion. Egypt will become a battleground."

Jethro absorbed the story. "So, you came here to hide." Moses dropped his head ashamed of himself. Jethro continued, "I am more convinced than ever God has brought you here. You can run from a pharaoh, but you cannot run from God. You think God has forsaken you. That is why you came here. You believe God has turned His back on His people and now you have failed Him, so there is nothing left for God to do but forget the whole thing. You think He needs you to deliver His people. You are wrong. He never did need you. God is peculiar. He does not think like men. He does not need men to fulfill His plans, but He uses men to fulfill His plans. You are a pawn in His hand. It was not an accident your Hebrew mother risked her life saving yours. It was not an accident you floated up to the palace, and it is not an accident you are here.

"Pharaoh made it hard for you. Did you ever consider he too felt the call that God has placed on your life? Have you considered perhaps he fears you? You think you are insignificant. In the palace you learned many things about leading and governing a nation. You were educated, but you know nothing about God. It is now time for you to learn how to follow. Following is much more difficult than leading. It requires that you submit yourself to someone or something else. That is hard for men to do. You must follow God to lead His people. Only a man who learns to follow God well can lead that great nation to freedom."

Moses sat listening. His face was frozen from shock. Even after his confession, his friend thought he could help the Hebrews. "Who am I that God would use me? Didn't I just tell you how miserably I failed Him?"

Jethro laughed at his friend. "You failed because you were the one doing it. You see, Moses, you grew up thinking Pharaoh was god on earth. Pharaoh is not god. He is only a man. It will take God, the one true God, to deliver your people. You must listen to His voice. When He is ready, He will call you, and you will go!" Moses was overwhelmed by the completely uncomplicated conviction of Jethro. "You have given me a lot to think about." Jethro went back to his original subject, his daughter. "So do you want to marry my daughter? She is a good woman. She would be a good wife for a man who is called to such a destiny." Moses smiled. Laughing, he said, "She would. I would be happy with her."

"Good," Jethro responded. "We will celebrate."

Zipporah was a little perplexed with her father and Moses. She knew Moses would be a good husband, but she would have enjoyed being asked. Women were not considered in matters such as marriage. Their fathers simply chose a man, and that was that. She had thought Moses would speak to her first, but he didn't. And when she asked him why he hadn't mentioned it to her, he told her it was her father's idea. Well, that was special. Her blood boiled. She wasn't sure she wanted to marry a man who had to be talked into the idea.

Moses was concerned by Zipporah's recent hostility. She was always so kind and giving. He watched as she served her father and him. She gave him the evil eye. She said nothing rude. It was just the way she looked at him with those eyes.

Later that evening, he found her under the stars. "Zipporah, I want to know why you are angry with me. Don't you want to marry me?"

The expression on her face was not at all one of a good, submissive wife. She tilted her chin up just a little higher than usual as she reminded him, "You had to have my father ask you to marry me. You didn't want me enough to ask for me yourself." She was clearly insulted.

Moses began to laugh. "Is that what's bothering you?"

She could not believe him. "Why are you laughing?"

His expression changed to one of seriousness. "It's not that I don't want to marry you. If I didn't want you, I would not marry you. It's just that I have come here hiding for my life. If Pharaoh finds me, there could be danger. I couldn't bear knowing you were hurt because of me."

She seemed to soften as she added, "My father told me all about your situation. He said I was to marry you and teach you to follow God. He said someday God would call you back to Egypt." Moses asked her, "Is that why you are unhappy? If you don't want to marry me, I will tell your father I've changed my mind." She started to cry. "It's just that you had to be asked to marry me. I thought you cared for me."

He moved closer, trying to assure her. "I do care for you, that is why I am marrying you. I love you. Since the first day I saw you, I knew I could be happy here with you forever. Your father saw that. He knew how much I wanted you for my wife. He had to talk me into believing I was good enough for you. When I came here, I thought my life was over. Anything other than that of a fugitive was impossible for me. You and your father have taught me I can still have a life worth living. I don't know if God will call me back to Egypt. Your father thinks He will. I believe Jethro understands things the rest of us don't. I only know that I love you. If all I do is live to be your husband, then my life will be more than I have a right to ask for. But if your father is right, if God calls me to Egypt, I will go. If there is anything I can do to help my people, I must try."

She tilted her head, trying to look him in the eyes. "You go, Moses. I will wait for you. Whatever you have to do I will understand."

The wedding was lovely. Moses and his bride marveled at the joy of being in love. They were blessed when she gave birth to their first son. Moses named the baby Gershom: "I have been a stranger in a strange place."

Moses kept the flocks of his father-in-law, Jethro. Just as Jethro had promised, Zipporah was a wonderful wife. She made their life together one of meaning. He lived to be a better man for her. She continued to amaze him with her ability to do everything.

Time flew by. He had been a fugitive from Egypt for forty years. It seemed to him he would never leave this place of refuge.

> And it came to pass in process of time, that the king of Egypt died: and the children of Israel sighed by reason of the bondage, and they cried, and their cry came up unto God by reason of the bondage. And God heard their groaning, and God remembered his covenant with Abraham, with Isaac, and with Jacob. And God looked upon the children of Israel, and God had respect unto them. (Exod. 2:23–25, KJV)

One day while he was tending the sheep, Moses moved his flocks near the mountain called Sinai. He looked up and saw a bush burning. He noticed it did not burn up. He decided to investigate. *Why doesn't the bush burn?* He was captivated by it.

God spoke to him out of the bush. "Moses! Moses!"

Moses answered, "I am here."

The voice continued to speak. "I am the God of your ancestors, the God of Abraham, Isaac, and Jacob. Do not come closer. Remove your shoes. The place where you are standing is holy ground." Panic filled Moses. He covered his face, afraid to see the face of God!

The Lord said, "I have seen the persecution of my people. I have heard their cries. I have come to deliver them from their bonds. I will lead them into the land of their fathers, a land that flows with milk and honey."

Moses felt smaller than ever before in his life. Why was God speaking to him? Now face-to-face with God, he understood the evil of man in the presence of this Holy God. His entire body trembled as he remembered his sins. He was not worthy to be in the presence of this great God! His heart raced as he tried to think. He had to escape!

The Lord said, "Go to Egypt. I send you to Pharaoh. You will lead my people out of slavery. Go, and I will be with you."

Now faced with the actual command to go, Moses had second thoughts. Hadn't he killed a man? He didn't have the ability to speak with the king of Egypt. Pharaoh wanted him dead!

Moses asked, "Who am I to speak to Pharaoh? How can you expect me to lead the Israelites out of Egypt?"

Moses was certain no one would listen to him. All he had been for forty years was a shepherd. He was no one. Pharaoh would laugh him out of the room. "The Hebrews won't believe me. They don't know who I am. If I tell them the God of your fathers has sent me, they won't even know who I am talking about. They will ask for your name. What should I tell them?"

> And God said unto Moses, I am that I am: and he said, Thus shalt thou say unto the children of Israel, I am hath sent me unto you. And God said moreover unto Moses, Thus shalt thou say unto the children of Israel, The Lord God of your fathers, the God of Abraham, the God of Isaac, and the God of Jacob, hath sent me unto you: this is my name for ever, and this is my memorial unto all generations. (Exod. 3:14–15, KJV)

God did not take no for an answer. He continued to tell Moses to call together all the leaders. "Gather together the elders of Israel. Tell them I have spoken with you and I have come to deliver them from their oppressors. I will lead them out of bondage into a land of milk and honey. Then you must go and petition Pharaoh. Tell him to allow you to go three days' journey into the desert to sacrifice to your God. He will not do it. He will not allow the people to go. I will do many miracles in Egypt. Then he will let the people go. The Egyptians will want you to go. They will give you gifts and send you away."

Moses had to make the Lord understand. "They won't believe me. They will say, 'God didn't appear to him.'" Moses remembered well the feelings of rejection first from the Egyptians then from his own people.

God asked him, "What do you have in your hand?"

Moses looked down at the staff he carried. "It is just a shepherd's staff."

"Throw it down," the Lord commanded.

Moses threw the staff on the ground. It immediately turned into a poisonous snake. Moses jumped and ran from it.

God said, "Pick it up by the tail."

Trembling, Moses reached out for the snake. He knew if it bit him, he would die. Quickly he grabbed it by the tail. Instantly it was a staff again. He began to see the power of God.

God told him to put his hand inside his coat. He did. When he took it out, it was completely covered in leprosy. He gasped at the sight.

The Lord instructed him, "Put it back in the coat."

Moses obeyed again. As he removed it, he marveled that his hand was perfectly healed. He held up his other hand and compared the two.

God said, "They will believe you if you show them these signs. But if they don't, take water from the Nile River. When you pour it on the ground, the water will turn to blood."

Moses thought of his speech impediment. "But Lord, I am a terrible speaker. I can barely get the words out."

The Lord asked him, "Who gives people the ability to speak or not speak, to hear or not hear, see or not see? Isn't it me? I will help you speak well, and I will tell you what to say."

Moses was pleading. "Please, Lord, send someone else."

The Lord became angry with Moses. "All right. What about Aaron, your brother? I know he speaks well. He is already on his way to meet you. Show him the signs I have shown you, and tell him what I have said. He will be your spokesperson. You will tell him what to say, and I will help both of you."

Moses could no longer argue with the Lord. He knew the calling that had always followed him had finally caught up with him. Jethro was right He could run from a man, but he could not run from God. He was moved in a way he could not describe. He was convinced this was what he had waited for all his life. He just couldn't understand why he was so apprehensive. Excitement started to well up inside of him. He was going home. He was going with the God of Abraham, Isaac, and Jacob. Deep inside he knew he was finally going to fulfill his destiny.

Moses went directly to Jethro and asked for permission to return to Egypt. "I want to know if my mother is still alive. I want to see my family."

Jethro watched Moses. He knew Moses well. He saw the square of his shoulders, the look of determination on his face. Jethro knew God had spoken to him. Nodding to his son-in-law, he said, "Go, you have my permission."

Moses packed up his wife and sons put them on a donkey and went back to Egypt. God spoke to him before he left, telling him not to be afraid; the people who wanted him were dead. Moses started his journey, carrying the staff the Lord had used to show His wonders. For the first time in a long time, Moses had a purpose. He walked with his head held high as determination began to replace fear. Something deep inside of him had been awakened. He had long ago set aside the sorrows of the slaves in order to settle down in Midian. Now, after hearing from God, the place in his heart he had denied existed came flooding back with a sense of being in the exact will of God for his life at that moment. Moses had found God.

LET MY PEOPLE GO

> And afterward Moses and Aaron went in, and
> told Pharaoh, Thus saith the Lord God of Israel,
> Let my people go, that they may hold a feast unto
> me in the wilderness. (Exod. 5:1, KJV)

The children of Israel gathered to hear the news. The slaves of
Egypt stood in awe as they listened to the words of the prophet of
the Lord. Moses said, "The God of your fathers, Abraham, Isaac,
and Jacob, has sent me to you."

Their hearts lifted as they thought of God's mercy. His words
of deliverance rang out like the blast of a heavenly trumpet. Moses
dropped his staff on the ground. It twisted and turned, then faced
him, hissing. It was no longer a staff. Now it watched them. It was
a poisonous viper. It lunged toward him. He grabbed it by the tail;
the snake became a staff again. He showed them the signs God
had given him to increase their faith. They remembered God led
Abraham, Isaac, and Jacob through the land of Canaan. He told
them that God would give them the land. He promised to their
forefathers so long ago. The long siege of slavery was ending; 430
years of serving a people who hated them was finally over.

Their hearts were humbled by the words of I am's messenger. All the nation of Israel bowed their heads in unison and worshipped their God. "He has heard our cries for deliverance!"

Worship, such as they had never before felt, poured out of their slaveravaged hearts. God, the God of Abraham, Isaac, and Jacob, visited them. He was not only going to deliver them from their oppressors but He also promised to give them a land flowing with milk and honey. Tears of gratitude washed the faces of a people who had learned to expect nothing while the reality of a loving God, who could do everything, overtook them. There the city of slavery became a sanctuary of praise for an entire nation of people, God's people!

Moses and Aaron bowed before the awesome presence of the Lord. They were humbled by the call they could not deny. Watching the children of Israel worship set the hearts of Moses and Aaron on fire. God was sending them. They could think of no greater call.

Moses and Aaron walked purposefully toward the palace of the pharaoh. Moses had often entered its walls. As he approached the familiar doors, he felt that his life had finally come full circle. He was here to do God's bidding.

"Tell Pharaoh Moses is here to speak with him." Moses held his shepherd's staff in his hand. The robe he wore now was far different from the one he had worn so long ago. Aaron stood beside him. The shepherd and the slave, their faces set like stone, waited to be given access to the most powerful king on earth.

The servant of Pharaoh approached him, slightly discomfited. "Pharaoh, Moses is here, and he requests audience with you."

Rameses looked out through the crowd of people who had gathered. Moses was standing in the doorway of the throne room. His hair and beard were long and flowing. His robe was sturdy and plain. Even from here, Pharaoh could see he was no longer the intimidated young man he had been. Moses stood tall with his head held high.

Pharaoh was curious. "Show him in." He watched as Moses walked boldly toward him, waiting for some of the old friend he had once known to emerge.

Moses was all business. "The Lord of the Hebrews has visited His people. He says to Pharaoh, 'Let My people go that they may hold a feast for Me in the wilderness!'"

Pharaoh answered them arrogantly. "Who is this God? I don't know Him. I will not let the people go."

Moses and Aaron stood their ground. "Let us go into the desert, three days' journey, so we can make an important sacrifice to the Lord to prevent Him from becoming angry with us and coming against us with disease or with the sword."

Pharaoh was annoyed. "Moses, you should be dead. After all this time, you come to see me just to make demands of me." His face turned a shade of red as he blustered, "The people are lazy! They take advantage of the hospitality of Egypt then complain. They are soft. You're keeping them from working. They can make bricks without straw. That will keep them busy. Tell them to produce the same number of bricks. The count must not diminish. I have spoken."

Pharaoh watched his old friend leave. Moses was still the same self-righteous, condescending, sappyacting underachiever he had always been. He smiled to himself and settled back more comfortably on his throne. Let Moses's so-called people work without straw. They will soon throw Moses away, just like Moses threw Egypt and the throne away. He placed his hands together, thinking he liked this new game of cat and mouse. He was going to enjoy letting his little mouse have just enough room to get trapped. His thoughts became less playful. As for the children of Israel, they needed something to put them in place! They had recently become lazy and disrespectful to their masters, the Egyptians.

⸺ ∘∘◦▌◉▐◦∘∘ ⸺

The children of Israel mourned. Their workload was already heavy. It became unbearable. They scoured the countryside, looking everywhere for any form of stubble to use to make brick. The number of brick they produced was simply not enough. They were exhausted from working all day as well as most of the night, when they had to look for straw to make bricks.

The Egyptians noticed that they had not kept up their required number of bricks. The Hebrew officers were responsible for the production of brick. Therefore, since the children of Israel could not keep up, the slave drivers beat them.

Moses was miserable. He cried out to the Lord, "Why, Lord, have You brought me here? Since I spoke with Pharaoh, it has been harder on the Hebrews."

Then the Lord said, "Go before Pharaoh and speak to him again. Tell him this is what the Lord says: 'Let My people go.' But," the Lord explained, "Pharaoh will not listen. He will not let My people go. I will bring the children of Israel out of the land of Egypt with a strong hand and with mighty works."

Moses was breathless as he walked into the great hall. He knew God was going to perform miraculously. His heart raced in anticipation.

"So you have returned, Moses," Pharaoh said with a smirk.

Moses ignored him, refusing to be bated. "This is what the Lord says, 'Let My people go so they can worship Me in the desert.'" Aaron watched Moses. The brothers locked eyes as Moses nodded to Aaron. He added, "Throw down your walking stick." Aaron threw his stick down onto the floor. It became a deadly serpent.

Pharaoh was not impressed. He called in his own magicians; they also threw down their rods, which also became snakes. The magicians, witches, and such were quite proud of themselves.

They began to explain to nearby people. "Oh, it's really simple." Modestly, they passed their amazing achievements off as insignificant. "Yes, I did study for years. But it's not nearly as complicated as one would think."

Moses watched a squatty and somewhat shifty individual give his explanation. He looked over at Moses as if he knew Moses for nothing more than a fake. "Really anyone who has studied under one of the masters can do the same." His accusation of Moses being nothing more than a magician was short-lived. At that moment Aaron's snake began to eat all the other snakes.

Of course, the man was not concerned; he simply had never seen such a thing. He would have to search his records to discover how this nut, Moses, had arranged that.

Pharaoh's wife saw the serpent of Moses and Aaron eating the ones their magicians and witches had conjured up and was disturbed. She reached out to Pharaoh. "Husband!"

He noticed her trembling. "Moses, this is nothing more than a cheap magician's trick. Doesn't your God have more impressive miracles than this?" His comment caused a roar of laughter to hit the great hall. The men and women present began to make fun of Moses, Aaron, and this foreign God.

Pharaoh threw his head back, laughing at Moses. He held his wife's hand, comforting her. "Do not worry, my dear." He kissed it reassuringly. She smiled. He studied Moses, daring Moses to do something else to entertain him. Moses did.

The next day the Lord told Moses to go meet Pharaoh. "He is at the river."

Moses went out, and in front of Pharaoh, he pronounced a curse on the water, saying to Aaron, "Stretch out your staff." Aaron lifted the staff over the water.

"Look!" One of the servants pointed to the water. The river, along with all the tributary waters, turned into blood. Soon the fish all died. Egypt smelled from the blood and dead fish. The people could not drink the water. Great thirst filled the land.

The magicians and witches were called in. Once again they did their incantations. They actually caused water to become blood. Again Pharaoh was not impressed. He became angry, refusing to let the children of Israel go. The Egyptians dug all around the river. That was the only water they had. The Lord left the water as blood for one week.

But in the land of Goshen, where the children of Israel were, there was no blood.

Then the Lord sent Moses to see Pharaoh again, saying, "Let My people go that they may serve Me in the desert. If you won't let them go, then, out of the river and all the water will come frogs. They will be in everything—in your beds, in your food, in your ovens. They will cover you, your family, your officials, and your people." Pharaoh did not let the children of Israel go.

Pharaoh was angry. What had started out as a game had turned into a nightmare. After Moses told him of the plague, frogs started to come up out of the river, canals, and marshes. The land of Egypt was covered with them. They were in all the houses of Egypt. Moses and his God were hateful! He could not understand this irrational God, who actually thought he, Pharaoh, god on earth, would just let these people go! He paced the floor, kicking at frogs, as he wondered how long this would last.

Pharaoh called upon his magicians. They were happy to be challenged. They used their craft to produce frogs. They just couldn't make Moses's go away. His servants and soothsayers watched with concern as he barked out new commands. Pharaoh was in no mood to be approached. Still, they had to speak out. "Sire, it has been days, and still these frogs plague us."

Pharaoh was appalled by their whining. He was tired of these foul creatures. His wife was whimpering something about her hair. "Enough!" he screamed. "Call for Moses and his slave of a brother!"

Moses and Aaron were ushered into the throne room. As soon as they appeared at the palace, the sorcerers were summoned. They stood close by. They watched Moses with suspicion. Moses was not in the mood to notice them. He swept past them as though they were not worth his valuable time.

"You called for me, Rameses?" His use of Pharaoh's name caught the attention of onlookers.

Moses watched as Pharaoh tried to maintain his dignity while frogs covered the room of his great hall. To Moses's amazement, frogs also covered the expensive draperies. He looked around briefly. As he did, he noticed the frogs hanging from the garments of the sorcerers. They were trying unsuccessfully to look unconcerned. He also noticed the frogs on the chandelier and candelabras.

Two servants were positioned to constantly remove the frogs from Pharaoh's throne. They were working to keep them back from His Majesty when one of them noticed a frog leaping onto the royal leg. Pharaoh jumped, scaring the frog, which also jumped, landing on His Grace's royal shoulder. Pharaoh grabbed for it as his two servants reached to retrieve the creature, forgetting their assignment to keep Pharaoh's throne clean. It seemed to Moses at that moment that the frogs had all plotted their attack. They were moving in on the throne and starting to cover both Pharaoh and his servants. Pharaoh was not amused. The guards moved in to help. With some effort, they were able to eliminate the creatures from Pharaoh's person.

He was blustering, "You incompetent fools! Moses, I am tired of these detestable creatures. Please, speak to the Lord for me and beg him to deliver us from this plague. Tell the Lord his people may go for three days' journey and make their sacrifice."

Moses watched with great interest as Pharaoh's dignity once again began to falter. He reached into his robe, catching and removing one of the frogs by the leg. Pharaoh looked positively desperate. "When shall I pray to the Lord for you, your household, your officials, and your people?"

Pharaoh responded, "Tomorrow."

Moses was satisfied. "It's agreed then. I will pray for you and your people tomorrow. You will know the power of God when you see Him do it."

The next day, true to his word, Moses prayed to the Lord. Then the Lord caused all the frogs to die. The dead frogs were everywhere. They gathered them all into large piles. The land of Egypt stunk. The foul odor of the dead frogs covered the land… The magicians and soothsayers, along with Pharaoh's officials, were nauseated. The smell of those creatures was so pungent they could barely breathe. Pharaoh looked over at his entourage. His blood began to boil. Their puny incompetence sickened him. His face snarled as he watched them just stand around complaining, their noses covered with clothes.

But just as there were no frogs in the homes of the Hebrew slaves, there was no smell in the land of Goshen, where the children of Israel lived.

Pharaoh was annoyed beyond reason. "You mean to tell me there were no frogs in Goshen, and there is absolutely no smell there?"

His servant swallowed hard. "Yes, Pharaoh."

Pharaoh smoldered as he considered the nerve of this God who tried to force his hand. "I will not let the Hebrews go! Their God has had His fun. Now I will have mine."

His officials rushed to caution him. He would not listen. Moses said to Aaron, "Hold out your staff and hit the dust of the land. It will become lice through all the land of Egypt." Aaron did as he was told. The dust began to move. There was life in each little particle. The dust blew in the air. Lice covered the land of Egypt.

Pharaoh was not happy! Immediately after he refused to let the children of Israel go, the dust in the air and on the royal floor became lice. His wife frantically pleaded, "Husband, do something—anything—to stop this horrible plague." She jumped up from her royal seat and ran from the great hall, proclaiming she was going to take a bath.

Pharaoh looked at his magicians and witches. "Can you cause lice to appear from dust?"

They were horrified. "Well, Pharaoh, we have never tried. I have heard there are incantations. We will get right on it." They worked for hours but could not produce lice from dust. Finally, they confessed the obvious, their faces red from worry. Sweat beaded up and rolled down their backs as they tried to account for their incompetence. "No, sire, it isn't possible. We have tried everything. This is the finger of God." Exasperated, they added, "He has won. There are lice on all of us, even the animals. How can we go on with this terrible plague? Sire, you must let these people go. Their God is too powerful for us!"

Pharaoh watched them through his long, dark lashes. "What did you just say to me? Did I hear you correctly? This is the finger of God? I know you realize that I am god on earth. As such, I am sure you realize also that no God is going to tell me what I have to do!" The pulse in Pharaoh's forehead beat quickly as he rose from his throne to shove the soothsayers from his presence. "Don't come back either, not unless you are called for, or I'll have you all killed!" His voice could be easily heard throughout a large section of the palace.

His wife refused to listen to his blustering. She was taking a nice bath with oil and herbs. She lowered herself into the water, trying to rid her hair of the pests. The only place safe was in water. *How long could I stay here?* she wondered as she thought of trying to make it through the night with those things all over her bed and clothing. The idea made her itch intensely! "I need more water," she said as her servants, themselves itching unbearably, tried to ease her suffering.

Pharaoh lowered himself into a bath. The lice from his body floated in the water. He dipped his head into the bath. Lice floated away from him. He began to plot his next move. "How can I get even?" he asked himself. All at once he remembered the children of Israel. "Guard, send some men into Goshen. I want to know if they also have lice!" He received the news that the only lice in Goshen were on those guards who had gone there. Pharaoh had to admit, at least to himself, he had not encountered anything like this Hebrew God! His heart pounded out the message: their God is God! He leaned back. It seemed to him that their God was testing him. He was not happy, not at all. He itched everywhere, and his skin was sore from scratching. Pharaoh, god here on earth, decided to have a fit!

His servants, tormented by the lice they could not get rid of, rushed to his side, begging him to calm himself. "Your Majesty, you need to quiet yourself. How can you rule your beloved people if you are ill?" his servants reasoned.

Pharaoh slept fitfully, trying his best not to notice the creepy things crawling on his bed. A couple of hours into the night, he gave up. He slipped into his son's room. The child was whimpering as he slept. His tiny face and hands flinched as lice crawled on him. Pharaoh reached out to swish them away. The lice moved, quickly avoiding his hand. He grew angrier by the moment. He looked over at his wife. She was also sleeping. He noticed lice swarming her sheets.

He walked out into the hall and summoned his servants. "Why has the queen and my son been left alone, with no one to keep the lice out of their beds?" His fury was barely contained.

His trusted servant bowed respectfully, saying, "Her majesty was concerned, sire. She knows how little we have been sleeping due to all the torments brought on us by Moses. She asked us to all retire and try to get a good night's rest. She assured us that she and the child would be fine."

"Well, they're not fine," Pharaoh said through gritted teeth. "I want someone watching and caring for them around the clock. You can all sleep when this is over."

"Yes, sire," the servant said, bowing respectfully. "I will see to it at once."

Pharaoh passed the night in torment. He thought of how difficult it would be for him and his people to do without the Hebrew slaves. He wondered how much more they could all take. Maybe this God will become tired of this game. Daybreak came slowly.

———∘∘∘❈∘∘∘———

Moses awakened, refreshed from a wonderful night's sleep. He marveled how easy it was to rest. He had slept very well since returning to Egypt. He looked out over the land of Goshen; the sun was beginning to make its move. Before falling asleep last night, he had spent time with the Lord. He had come to look forward to any moment he could use to slip away and speak to God. While he was walking and talking with God, the Lord told him to "Get up early and go down to the water to meet Pharaoh."

———∘∘∘❈∘∘∘———

Moses walked confidently up to Pharaoh. The servants of Pharaoh parted as he walked toward them. They eyed him carefully, keeping a distance from the man of God. They did not want to upset him in any way. Pharaoh looked over at the man he once called brother, his heart sinking as he thought on the words he knew he would be hearing again.

Moses spoke with authority. "This is what the Lord says, 'Let My people go! They must go into the desert to worship Me. If you don't let the people go, I will send flies that will plague you and all your people and your land. But I will separate the land of Egypt from Goshen. You will have swarms of flies, but there will be no flies in the land of Goshen, where My people live.'"

The next day the swarms of flies started. They rose from out of nowhere. Pharaoh and his officials watched from the veranda as the swarms of flies descended on the land of Egypt. They were in everything. The animals began to act mad as they tried desperately to rid themselves of these pests.

The magicians and soothsayers stood by helplessly. They had been on call since the plague had been announced. They looked at each other speechless. How could they be expected to duplicate this plague? Their eyes widened in surprise as they watched the swarms moving toward the palace at an unbelievable rate of speed.

"Quick, inside," someone said. They all ran for cover, trying to close the doors as quickly as possible. The palace windows had been closed for hours in an effort to ward off the attack. The place, usually well ventilated, was already beginning to feel warm. The day promised to be unusually hot.

They did not know how it was possible for the flies to enter the palace with it closed off. But to their dismay, the swarms soon found their way in. Pharaoh was suddenly inundated with a swarm that seemed only interested in him! In fact, it seemed to everyone present that there was a swarm assigned to each of them!

"Please, sire, think of your beloved people. How can they endure this misery?"

Pharaoh had to agree. He swatted at the flies to keep them from landing on his face. Glancing over at the others, he noticed them working furiously trying to kill the pests. There were too many for them to kill. His son came in running up to his father, who immediately took him in his arms. He held his son, placing him under the covering of his robe. Pharaoh swished the flies away from the child's face.

"Nurse, come over here. Take care of my son now!" he demanded. He looked over at a woman who had obviously succumbed to the onslaught. Then he bellowed, "Help her!"

Guards rushed to the nurse, waving at the flies. They worked frantically to help the woman. She regained her composure and took the child from Pharaoh.

Pharaoh turned to the guards. "Bring Moses to me!"

Moses and Aaron looked out at the land of Egypt. Everything was going wrong. The animals and people were so tormented they couldn't do their work. They walked into the palace unannounced, the guards ushering them immediately into Pharaoh's presence.

"All right, you go ahead and make your sacrifice to your God. But don't leave Egypt."

He swatted flies as he spoke. One of the flies landed on his face just below his nose. He slapped at it, but it did not move. He tried to kill it, but it just flew in a circle around his head. Aaron watched the scene feeling just a little glee as it landed on the Pharaoh's head, buzzing around his ear.

"That is not good enough," Moses said firmly. "The Egyptians will see us killing the animals, and they will be angry with us. They will turn on us to murder us. We cannot sacrifice to the Lord in front of the Egyptians."

Pharaoh became grumpy as the fly on his ear walked down his neck. He swatted at it but couldn't see where it was. The flies seemed to congregate right around the throne. He was very depressed. Exasperated, he sighed heavily, "All right then, go into the wilderness. But don't go very far. Hurry and pray for me." Moses felt some sympathy for the child he had once loved. Aaron felt none.

Moses said, "I will pray to the Lord for you. But beware, do not change your mind again."

Moses walked out of the palace. He raised his hands toward heaven and prayed. "Lord God, deliver Egypt from this torment. Show your great power to all the people of the land." The flies disappeared as quickly as they had appeared.

Pharaoh watched from his veranda. He could see from here the entire scene. He thought of the children of Israel. There they were relaxing comfortably, while he and his people suffered this unspeakable oppression. The familiar feeling of his heart beginning to harden started. His anger, never far away, rose like the tide in the ocean. He considered letting the Hebrews go. If their God thought He could mock him, He was wrong. This God of Moses had another thing coming. He would not let the people go!

The soothsayers trembled. The very thought of the Hebrews not leaving Egypt was unfathomable. They pleaded. "Sire, we beg you. This God of the Hebrews is too mighty. All of Egypt will be destroyed."

Pharaoh turned on them. "It is your fault! You are all incompetent. If you were any good at your job, you would be able to conjure up these flies with no problems. But no, you snivel and squirm, trying to convince me that the God of mere slaves is mightier than me or any of our gods! I've had it with your excuses. Either you find out the secret to these tricks of Moses, or I will have your heads! Now, out! All of you! Out of my presence! Now!" His face was crimson. The little pulse that beat on his forehead pounded out his annoyance.

The magicians and soothsayers fled from the presence of Pharaoh. They would need to find a way to conjure up flies, or they were all dead men! They searched their scrolls for incantations that might save their lives. Their eyes hurt from reading. The squatty one began to complain of a migraine. His head was pounding. He started to panic. "We're all finished!" He mourned, too distraught to care what anyone thought of him. He began to cry. "The king is asking the impossible. How can we compete with a God?" The others looked at each other. They were all feeling the pressure, but he always seemed to be a little more melodramatic.

"One thing is certain, we won't find an answer if we don't try." This statement was issued from one of the more assertive types in the crowd; he was always acting like he knew everything.

The squatty one continued, "I tell you, I have been through those scrolls. There is nothing there. We are done for!" A hopeless whimper escaped the lips of a man who looked at his future with dread!

The Lord spoke to Moses. "Return to Pharaoh. Tell him to let My people go so they can sacrifice to Me. If he will not, I will send a deadly plague on Egypt's livestock—all their horses, donkeys, camels, cattle, and sheep. But I will make a difference between the Hebrews animals and the animals of the Egyptians. Not one Hebrew animal will die! This plague will happen tomorrow!"

The next day the livestock of the Egyptians began to die. The people cried out to Pharaoh. He lost most of his livestock by the middle of the day. He could see them fall over dead from his veranda! His mind reeled as he tried to think of a way to stop this thing. "What do the veterinarians say about this plague?" He was hopeful they would have some answers. "Can they cure the animals?"

The aid who offered his report had spent the morning with those who worked with livestock. "They are puzzled, sire. They have no idea what has hit the herds. They say this is something they have never seen."

At that moment one of his spies was announced. "Well, is it true?" Pharaoh held his breath as he made the inquiry.

"Yes, sire. The Hebrews are experiencing no problems with their livestock. They are completely healthy." The spy looked concerned, shaking his head as he answered the king.

Pharaoh was not willing to let the children of Israel go, especially since they now had the healthiest livestock. He needed them to work the fields. He intended to have the Hebrew livestock rounded up and brought to him!

Moses and Aaron went back to see Pharaoh. They had been instructed to gather soot from a furnace. Moses tossed the soot into the air in front of Pharaoh. Pharaoh watched as boils began to rise on his body. He jumped, certain that it was a deadly disease. The pain was excruciating. The bottoms of his feet began to swell. Everyone around him started to cry out in pain. Boils were on everyone except Moses and Aaron. He shook his finger at Moses. "You go too far, brother!"

The magicians who had been summoned the moment Moses and Aaron were noticed walking toward the palace began to whine; they were being pushed to the point of breaking. They could not stay. The pain was unbearable. "Sire, we beg of you. Do not anger this God of the Hebrew's any further. Let these people go into the desert to make their sacrifice before Egypt is destroyed!"

Then a messenger arrived to tell Pharaoh that the livestock that were still alive were also suffering with these boils. Pharaoh, god on earth, shook with anger. Then he noticed an uncomfortable feeling on his royal person. A roar came out of him that shook his servants in their shoes. "I will not let these people go!" Moses and Aaron left.

The next day the Lord told Moses to return to Pharaoh.

Pharaoh looked over at Moses. Misery was written on his face. He had spent the worse night of his life suffering with these boils. Moses could still see the spark of fire that came from Pharaoh's eyes as he approached. "The God of the Hebrews says, 'You let My people go so they can worship Me. If you don't, I will send a plague that will prove to you that there is no other God like Me in all the earth. I could have destroyed all of you by now. I could have sent a plague to wipe you and your people off the earth. But you are alive for this reason. You are My witnesses. You will tell everyone of Me, and all the people of the earth will know of My power. But you still refuse to let My people go. So tomorrow I will send a hailstorm that will destroy Egypt. Now you must act quickly and bring your servants and livestock out of the fields, or they will die.'"

The people who respected the word of the Lord brought their servants and livestock in from the fields. There were those who did not respect the word of the Lord; they left their servants and livestock out in the open.

The next day the Lord spoke to Moses. "Lift your staff toward heaven so there will be hail in Egypt." Moses lifted his hand toward heaven, and the hail started. Fire also ran along on the ground where the hail struck. The servants and animals that were left in the fields died. There was hail in all of Egypt.Crops were destroyed along with anyone or anything in the field. But in the area of Goshen, there was no hail.

"Send for Moses!" Pharaoh cried out. He did not like thunder. Ever since he was a child, he found it terrifying. Of course, he did not admit that to anyone.

Pharaoh looked pleadingly at Moses. "Moses, I and my people were wrong. The Lord is right. You may go and sacrifice. Only pray to God that He will stop this thunder and hail."

"I will pray to the Lord that He stop the thunder and hail. But I know you and your officials still do not fear the Lord as you should."

Moses went out of the city and prayed to the Lord. The Lord took the thunder and hail from Egypt. The hail had destroyed the flax and barley crops; the barley was ripe, and the flax was in bloom. But the wheat had survived. Pharaoh did not let the children of Israel go.

Then the Lord told Moses, "Go back to Pharaoh and tell him to let the children of Israel go. If he does not, beware! God will send locusts that will be so many they will cover the ground. They will eat everything the hail and fire did not destroy. They will devour the trees and any crop still in the field. They will be in your palaces and all the homes of Egypt." Moses did as the Lord commanded. Then he walked out of the presence of Pharaoh.

Pharaoh's officials were frantic. They appealed to Pharaoh, "Egypt is in ruins. Let these people go."

Pharaoh weakened. "Bring Moses back."

Moses stood before Pharaoh. Pharaoh said, "You may go and serve your God, but who is going?"

Moses replied, "We will all go—young, old, sheep and goats— we will all go to serve the Lord. We must do it as a congregation." Pharaoh was furious. "I know what you're up to. You will not take your children. Only the men will go to sacrifice to the Lord. Now, go sacrifice to your God. Get out of my presence!" Moses and Aaron were thrown out of the palace.

Then the Lord said to Moses, "Stretch out your staff over the Land of Egypt." Moses did, and a wind from the east started to blow. It blew all night long.

The palace walls were made of stone, but the sound of the wind was still heard. The cold was bone chilling as the eerie sound continued to shake the windows. Egypt waited in horror for the next plague.

The next morning there was a strange humming noise. Pharaoh jumped out of bed and ran to his window. He looked out over Egypt. The ground was dark. *They are here!*

"Sire"—his servant rushed in to speak with Pharaoh—"the land is covered with locusts."

"Send for Moses and Aaron!" Pharaoh looked out at his beautiful veranda. The plants were eaten to the earth. The locusts covered the patio. It was also dark. He noticed, with horror, they were coming into the palace through the corners of the windows, through little holes he didn't even know were there! They were like a mighty army. They advanced forward.

Moses and Aaron walked along, scrunching the locusts under their feet. They were awed by the destruction of Egypt. The land was no longer recognizable. God had used all the land to show His power. They would have many stories to tell their children and grandchildren about how God brought them out of the land of Egypt with great power and a mighty stretched-out arm. These miracles would be talked about everywhere. God was getting the attention of the whole world!

Pharaoh was relieved to see them. "I have sinned against you and the Lord. Please pray to the Lord and beg Him to forgive me this one time. Ask Him to remove this terrible plague."

Moses prayed. The Lord sent a wind from the west. Then there wasn't even one locust left in Egypt.

Pharaoh walked out on his veranda. From here he could see Egypt. The devastation sickened him. Hadn't his people been there when these Hebrews had first come begging Joseph for food? Hadn't Pharaoh, in his mercy, extended the best land of Egypt to these people? Now, because of them, Egypt lay desolate. The Hebrews weren't touched. Their cattle and flocks, everything they had, were fine. Now Egypt needed them, but all they could think of was sacrificing to their God. The least they could do was help Egypt replant! How dare they leave now when Egypt needs them so much?

The fire in his heart would not allow him to let the people go. They would stay and rebuild Egypt! He would make sure of that, if it was the last thing he did! His mind was sick with power. His heart was sick with the greed of a people who would not let go of slavery!

Then the Lord spoke to Moses. "Extend your hand toward heaven. There will be darkness over the land of Egypt, even darkness that can be felt."

Moses extended his hand over Egypt, and a thick darkness covered the land for three days. The Egyptians barely moved. They could not see each other.

Pharaoh's servants tried to light the room. They lit the lamps, only to see nothing. There was a flame, but the darkness was so deep it did not help. They chose to be very still. Pharaoh, the queen, and their son stayed close to each other. The darkness frightened the boy. He cried often. Only the sound of his mother's voice comforted him. They placed him in the bed between them. The queen sang every song she knew. Thankfully, he slept.

Pharaoh was deep in thought; he did not sleep. His wife spoke to him out of the darkness. "How long will you force us all to endure this agony? Don't you understand, Egypt has fallen before this God? It is hopeless to antagonize Him. He is the one true God. He has shown us His power. Is there any other god who can do as He has done?"

Pharaoh had lost his will to argue with her. She had been talking since the first plague had hit. Now in this darkness, he just listened. Tears began to roll down his face. He was conquered, conquered by a God of slaves with no army. His nation was devoured by plagues, containing insects that obeyed the Lord. God brought thunder and hail with fire and water that turned to blood. His mind turned as he rehearsed every encounter and every word spoken by Moses for his God. Pharaoh lay in the darkness longing for light that did not come.

Then Pharaoh sent for Moses. "Go worship your God. Only don't take your livestock."

Moses was adamant. "No, we must take our livestock. We don't know what the Lord will ask us to offer to Him. We must take all our animals to sacrifice to our God."

Pharaoh listened as Moses told him he would not leave the livestock. He knew what their God was doing. They would never return. Egypt would be left in ruins with no livestock or slaves. He could not contain himself. "Leave my presence! If I see you again, you will die!"

The Lord told Moses to have the children of Israel speak to the Egyptians. They were to ask for the jewels and wealth of the Egyptian people. The people of Egypt handed over everything they had of value. They just wanted the Hebrews to leave Egypt. They begged the people to remember they had been kind to them.

Moses stood one last time before Pharaoh. "Here is what the Lord says. I will pass through Egypt. All the firstborn sons will die in every family in Egypt, from Pharaoh's son to the oldest son of his lowliest slave. Also the firstborn of the animals will die. A loud cry will be heard in Egypt. But among the Israelites, it will be so peaceful that not even a dog will bark. Then you will know that the Lord has chosen the Israelites."

The Lord instructed Moses and Aaron to celebrate this occasion as the first month of the year. "Tell everyone to choose a lamb or a goat, one that has no imperfection. Take special care of this lamb until the fourteenth day of the month. Then kill it. Place some of the blood on the top and sides of the door of the house. Roast the lamb and serve it with bitter herbs and bread made without yeast. If they are a small family, they should join with another to help them eat the dinner. They were to eat this dinner with their shoes and traveling clothes on, holding their walking sticks in their hands.

The land of Egypt was quiet as the people waited for the angel of the Lord. Many hid their oldest children in an effort to keep the Lord from finding them. Pharaoh sat quietly with his son. He too was hiding his child. "We shall play a game. Now be very still and very quiet. We don't want the servants to find us." He looked over at his wife, who was holding her son, her eyes wide with fear.

"Mommy, why are you shaking?" The prince whispered his question into the night.

"Mommy is just cold, darling. Stay close to Mommy so I can get warm."

At exactly midnight, a presence filled the land of Egypt. Screams started in the east and began to draw closer to the palace. There were screams in the streets and in the households of Egypt. Pharaoh listened as his people cried out. The most bloodcurdling sounds filled the land. He felt the presence fill the palace. Then screams came from the halls, from other rooms and hidden passages. His son took a sharp breath and then stopped breathing altogether. Pharaoh, god on earth, was out of answers. He looked at the child lying limp in his wife's arms. She screamed a cry that seemed to come from the depths of her soul. He reached over and grabbed the child. Laying him on the floor, he began to lift his son's arms up and down. He checked his mouth for any obstruction. He rolled the child over and pounded on his back. He tried all the things he had seen his healers do. Nothing worked. His wife continued to scream. He grabbed her and shook her until she stopped. She fell into his arms, her body limp. Her face was wet with tears. He looked into the eyes of his wife. She seemed to have gone to some distant place. He pleaded with her not to go away. She trembled uncontrollably. He held her tight, rubbing her arms and legs.

He said, "Please, darling, you must not leave me."

She looked at him. Recognition came into her face. He held her tight, fighting the shock that had overtaken her. Slowly she began to come out of the shock. Her horror-filled eyes stared up at him. She clung to him. "You must let the Israelites leave Egypt, or we will all die!"

Pharaoh did not wait till morning. "Guard, bring Moses to me now!" The guard bowed and left.

Moses entered the palace. The golden glow of the lights lit his path down the hall and right up to Pharaoh. Moses could see Pharaoh had been crying. The queen sat stone-still next to him. "You have won, Moses. You and your God have won. I cannot fight the Lord any longer. He has taken everything from me. All that is left is our lives. Leave us. Take your cattle, flocks, children, men, and women, and get out of Egypt! Do not waste time. Be gone from us!" The man once so powerful was beaten. His throne, which once represented a kingdom, lay in shambles.

Moses nodded. "We will go." He left.

The children of Israel had been spared the plagues of Egypt. They had not felt the sting of the death of a loved one. The lamb of God had saved them. There on their doorposts smeared for all to see was the blood of the lamb, the tender-eyed, beautiful, innocent lamb. They were spared because of the sacrifice.

The New Testament tells us that John saw Jesus coming toward him. He spoke to his disciples, telling them, "Look, there is the lamb of God."

The Lord used the lamb's blood on the doorposts of Goshen to show His own Son's destiny. He was foretelling even then the sacrifice of Jesus. Jesus was the Lamb of God slain for anyone who would believe.

> For God so loved the world, that he gave his only begotten Son, that whosoever believeth in him should not perish, but have everlasting life. For God sent not his son into the world to condemn the world; but that the world through him might be saved. (John 3:16–17, KJV)

The children of Israel received word. They were free to leave Egypt. They packed their bags quickly. Young, old, all of them were free! The day of deliverance had finally come. It has been 430 years since they arrived in Egypt to the day they left. The Egyptians were thrilled to see them go. They gave them gifts of gold and silver willingly. They plundered Egypt as though they were a mighty army. They left with the spoils of the land. The slaves who had worked for nothing more than food and a place to stay journeyed from the land of Egypt as wealthy people. Six hundred thousand men plus women and children walked into the desert following their God. A magnificent army of freed slaves marched out of Egypt!

The Lord led his people into the wilderness. He did not take them through the region of the Philistines. He said, "If they come face to face with an army they might become afraid and return to Egypt." He led them instead toward the Red Sea. He led them with a cloud by day and a pillar of fire by night.

Joseph made the children of Israel promise him they would carry his bones back to Canaan when they left Egypt. He knew God would one day lead them out of Egypt and to their homeland. They honored the promise of their fathers. They would bury his bones in Canaan.

Pharaoh watched as the sun beat down on Egypt. His eyes surveyed the damage that covered his vast territory. He took in the wasteland that lay before him. The day before, they buried his son. The whole land of Egypt mourned. There was not one home in Egypt that had not buried someone.

Pharaoh fell defeated onto his throne. He was beaten by the God of slaves. His servant arrived with word, "Sire, our spies report that the children of Israel make no move to return in three days. In fact they were seen moving further away from Egypt." The servant took a deep breath. "Sire, they have escaped!"

Pharaoh grew angrier with every word of the report. "Moses and his God have lied! They never intended to return. It is just as I suspected. The sacrifice to their God is a hoax. These slaves think they can leave and I will not follow them." His blood boiled. "Does Moses think Egypt will just give up her slaves? Egypt needs them. How can I rebuild Egypt without slave labor?" He looked out across the barren ruins of Egypt. "I will kill every last one of them!"

He called together his military force. He looked out over his troops. Many of his men had lost family members. Many had lost sons. All of them had lost someone. He stood in front of his men. His head held high. He addressed them, "I, as many of you, watched the children of Israel leave Egypt. I was anxious to rid our land of them." His voice lowered an octave. "But I am not prepared to let them live! They are gone from Egypt. My family is now rid of them. Egypt is safe from their God. But I cannot let their God ravage Egypt, kill my son, the heir to my throne, and just let them live! If I do nothing, I cannot face his mother. I cannot face myself. I cannot face my people! I will go into the desert after them. When I catch up with them, I will kill them. I will kill all of them, until there is no one left alive. Then their God who has brought all of this evil on Egypt will have no one to worship Him. I will not let them go! They will all die!"

Cheers rang out. Pharaoh asked, "Who will go with me!"

The crowd waved and chanted, "Ramses! Ramses!" He smiled as his mighty men prepared to go to battle with him.

Pharaoh's army approached the children of Israel. They rode hard and fast. There were times when they felt like turning back, but they did not. From a distance, they could see them. The children of Israel were camped alongside the Red Sea. They were trapped! Pharaoh and his army watched them at a distance. They were not going to allow them to escape. The wilderness was on one side and the Red Sea was on the other! At last Pharaoh and his men would have their revenge! They praised their gods, "No one lives! No one escapes!"

The children of Israel could see the army of the Egyptians behind them. They began to pray for God to deliver them. Then they became angry with Moses, "Didn't we tell you to leave us alone? At least as slaves we could have lived." Their faith was quickly replaced by pending doom.

Moses answered them, "You will not see them again after today. Stand where you are and watch the Lord rescue you! The Lord will fight for you." Then the Lord moved a cloud behind the children of Israel, between the Egyptian army and the Israelites. The Egyptians could no longer see the Israelites. At night the cloud became a wall of fire. It became a light, lighting the whole area. God spoke to Moses telling him to lift up his staff and hold it out over the Red Sea. Moses extended his staff over the water. A wind from the east began to blow. The people watched gasping as the water parted leaving a path through the sea. The water stood up and formed walls on both sides of the path. The wind blew all night. The path became dry. Early in the morning, the children of Israel walked through the Red Sea on dry land!

Pharaoh and his army waited. The night was eerie as they were unable to see the children of Israel. The sound of wind sent shivers down their spines and chilled them to the bone. The spies who tried to sneak up on the children of Israel soon hit a wall. They could not see nor could they get close to them. Now they watched as the last of the children of Israel crossed the Red Sea. "We will pursue them." The orders were given; the army of Egypt advanced. They entered the dry Red Sea in hot pursuit. The rocks were a problem. They tried to navigate their chariots.

> And it came to pass, that in the morning watch the Lord looked unto the host of the Egyptians through the pillar of fire and of the cloud, and troubled the host of the Egyptians, And took off their chariot wheels, that they drave them heavily: so that the Egyptians said, Let us flee from the face of Israel; for the Lord fighteth for them against the Egyptians. And the Lord said unto Moses, Stretch out thine hand over the sea, that the waters may come again upon the Egyptians,

> upon their chariots, and upon their horsemen.
> And Moses stretched forth his hand over the
> sea, and the sea returned to his strength when
> the morning appeared; and the Egyptians fled
> against it; and the Lord overthrew the Egyptians
> in the midst of the sea. And the waters returned,
> and covered the chariots, and the horsemen, and
> all the host of Pharaoh that came into the sea after
> them; there remained not so much as one of them.
> (Exodus 14: 24–28, KJV)

The children of Israel watched from the shore. The army of Pharaoh screamed as the walls of water came crashing down on them. Their chariots, their horses, and all their mighty men destroyed with the brush of God's mighty hand! God had already done so many awesome miracles for His people! Now, once again, He destroyed their enemies right in front of them. The Israelites bowed their heads struck by the wonder of their God who had saved them!

> And Israel saw that great work which the Lord
> did upon the Egyptians: and the people feared
> the Lord, and believed the Lord, and his servant
> Moses. (Exodus 14:31, KJV)

The nation of slaves freed by their God, whose power could not be measured, worshipped Him! His hand reaches into the heavens! He controls the world and all the solar system! He was there to save them! He brought them out of Egypt with a strong arm! He had heard the cries of His people and delivered them, Himself, from their oppressors! There, on the banks of the Red Sea in a great worship service, Moses and the people of Israel worshipped God.

THE WILDERNESS EXPERIENCE

> And it came to pass, when Pharaoh had let the people go, that God led them not through the way of the land of the Philistines, although that was near; for God said, Lest peradventure the people repent when they see war, and they return to Egypt. (Exod. 13:17, KJV)

Joshua watched as the children of Israel moved laboriously through the desert. They had gone without water for two days. Moses had assured them God would provide, but the people were weary. His heart went out to a child stumbling along in front of him. He had very little water left in his own container, but he could not allow this child to go on thirsting as he was.

He caught up with the boy. "What is your name, son?"

The child whispered, "Reuben, sir."

"That's a fine name." Joshua smiled back at the child. He looked up at the sky then said, "It sure is hot. I need a sip of water. Would you like some?"

The child looked at Joshua anxiously. "Yes, sir." His little face reflected his appreciation. "We ran out this morning."

"Well, it's a good thing I came along then. Here you go." He handed the boy his water container.

Reuben took a careful sip. He handed the life-sustaining fluid back. "Thanks, I'll be all right now." His tiny features toughened as he spoke.

Joshua admired the boy. He would be fine. Joshua moved on ahead in and out of the people. They were all hurting from thirst.

A woman in front of him fainted. He reached out as she was starting to fall and caught her in his arms. She was beautiful. He was very content to keep walking as he carried her, but he noticed a rather large gruff-looking man who was frowning fiercely at him. He spoke up, trying to avoid an encounter. "She fainted. I was just trying to help her."

The man's expression softened. "She is exhausted. We have to find water soon." He called ahead to a young man. "Bring your sister some water." The young man ran back to them. Slowly he poured the water onto a rag then wiped her face with it. Stopping, he began to squeeze some onto her lips.

She began to revive. She was completely humiliated. She raised herself up. "Thank you," she said as she made a valiant effort to go on.

Joshua was somewhat disappointed with her attitude. He would have liked to talk to her. He was forty years old. He had not married. Many years ago he had been engaged to a wonderful young woman, but she had been abused by her master and died in childbirth. He had chosen not to marry after that. The idea of one of the Egyptians being able to just take his family away was too much for him to consider. But he was no longer a slave. He watched her sashay away from him, her head held high, walking quickly away in a slave's garment as though she were far too good for someone like him. He was shaken from his thoughts by a disagreement going on in the crowd. Some of the people were beginning to complain about Moses. He could not believe his ears.

"Why are you complaining? Moses is God's man!" He could feel his temper beginning to flair. Next to him was the brother of the young girl. The young man moved in closer to hear the many opinions being thrown around. Joshua could see the color beginning to drain from the young man's face. He was sure, by the look of him, he was the type to start hitting and ask questions later. Joshua moved between him and the rather loudmouthed fellow, placing his hands on the chest of the young man.

He said to the girl's brother, "Listen, buddy, that guy isn't worth it. We are all really tired and thirsty. What do you say we just let him talk? You and I will go to Moses. He should know something by now. Maybe we are close to water. Let's go ask. By the way, I'm Joshua."

The young man relaxed slightly as he considered Joshua's words. "Okay, let's go see Moses. Do you know him? I've heard he's really strange. I hear he talks to God and all."

"No, I don't know him. But I'm sure if he talks to God, he's someone I'd like to know." Joshua took in the mere size of his new friend. The man's shoulders were enormous. He looked like he could replace two men easily as he worked.

"By the way, I'm Caleb. Thanks for stopping me back there. That little man should learn to keep his mouth shut before someone shuts it for him."

Joshua smiled to himself as he considered the sight of this giant jumping onto that overbearing big mouth. "It wouldn't have been much of a fight. You would have clobbered him. Anyway, he's more my size. If he gets too far out of line, I'll take him on." Both men laughed as they thought of shutting that big mouth up.

They were able to go right up to Moses. Joshua was surprised there was no one protecting Moses from the many people who would demand his attention. He cringed as he imagined one of Pharaoh's spies penetrating the encampment to find Moses unattended. He mentioned it to Moses. "Sir, shouldn't you have guards posted around you? What if an enemy found you unprotected?"

"No, I think I am quite safe. The Lord will protect me." Moses seemed preoccupied.

"We were just wondering, sir. Do you know when we will reach water?"

Moses nodded. "We should be there soon. We are almost to Marah. I understand there is water there."

When they arrived at Marah, the water was undrinkable. The people, already exhausted and thirsty, couldn't go any further. "Why have you brought us here?" The people began to mourn. They quickly turned into a mob, demanding answers. "What are we going to drink?"

Joshua and Caleb moved between the crowd and Moses. "Why are you coming after him? He is the prophet of the Lord. He is the man God used to bring this great deliverance. God will not forget us. He will give us water. Leave and let Moses talk to God. The Lord will tell him what to do." They stood their ground as Moses moved toward the water to think and pray. Some of the young men who were concerned for Moses's well-being stepped up beside Joshua and Caleb.

Moses walked along the bank of the water. He noticed a branch nearby. He took the branch and threw it into the water. The water became fresh. He bent down, his long beard nearly touching the ground. He cupped his hand, scooping some of the delicious water into it. He drank. "Look, the water is good." The people began to rejoice. They quickly crowded in to drink themselves. They were at last refreshed.

Joshua watched as the people rushed to the water. They were polite, but this placed Moses in an unprotected position. He did not like leaving Moses without a guard. He spoke to the men near him. "We can't leave him unprotected. The people are still too easily angered. They don't always think before they speak. What if they rush him? Even if no one means to hurt him, the way people just rush up to him, they could cause him to lose his balance. Something could happen to him. We have to protect him."

The young men listening were also concerned. He was their hero, and he was far too valuable to lose. Joshua watched this wonderful man with fire in his eyes and purpose in his step. At that moment, he knew he would gladly die for Moses! The young men teamed up, forming a guard to watch their most important leader.

Caleb and Joshua took the first shift. They spent the day making sure Moses was not harassed. They handled as many of the people's needs as possible, trying to relieve Moses of any undue stress. They made a point of checking on him periodically to see if he had any needs. Then quietly they watched him, trying to stay in the background.

Caleb slapped the shoulder of his newfound friend. "You are coming with me. My mom and sister are the two best cooks in the camp. How do you think I grew so big?"

Joshua was thrilled with the invitation. He did not have a family to go home to. A home-cooked meal sounded wonderful.

Caleb asked just enough questions during the day to know Joshua's story. His mother and father were poorly treated by their masters. His father died from the enormous load placed on him. He had been expected to work too many long, hard hours. During construction of a city, he had slipped and was crushed. Joshua's mother had died from being expected to work sick. She did not recover and passed away in her sleep. Joshua was left to raise his siblings. Each of them now had families of their own. Caleb was not able to find out why Joshua had not married. He only said, "After the death of my parents, my brothers and sisters had taken my time."

They walked toward Caleb's family, talking about the best places to station sentries around the camp. Caleb explained to Joshua his wife had been ill before their release, but since leaving Egypt, she was in perfect health. However, his mother and sister still would not allow her to cook and do the chores. They were still worried she might become sick again.

"But I'm not worried," the big man said. "I know God has healed her."

Joshua enjoyed the easy way the family interacted. Caleb's wife turned out to be a joy. She was working alongside her mother and sister-in-law. Caleb smiled as they insisted she rest while they finished the dinner. Caleb's mother stood firmly, her hands on her hips. "Go and talk to your husband. You have done enough."

Caleb's sister smiled often and joked with the family. She was even more beautiful when she wasn't suffering from a lack of water. Joshua watched her. His friend spoke confidentially when she was out of earshot, "She is widowed. Her husband died working in the fields a few years back. She came home then. She has been taking care of my mom and dad. He would have loved all this. He was a good man. He would have been with us today."

Joshua watched his new friends, happy for their company. There was a hint of sadness in Caleb's sister. Now Joshua knew why. "Any children?" he asked.

Caleb shook his head no. "Just her. She was pregnant a couple of times but couldn't carry them. We don't know why. It's a pity, really. She was such a good wife. A man would be fortunate to have her by his side. She'd be a wonderful mom."

Surprised by Caleb's comments, Joshua looked at his friend. Caleb looked him square in the face. "You could do worse."

"She is beautiful," was all Joshua could say. He watched her move out of sight. After a while, he excused himself and left.

Joshua was up early. He wanted to check on Moses. He passed the tent of Aaron. The tent of Aaron was quiet. He went on toward Moses's tent. He was amused to find the two older men there, laughing and teasing their sister Miriam as she was preparing breakfast for them.

Joshua stood back, watching the tent of Moses. He wanted to be close if Moses needed anything. Joshua had waited on his master in much the same way; he now intended to wait on Moses.

He was the steward for an officer in the Egyptian army. He often watched and listened closely to his master planning strategic maneuvers. His master was a military genius. Unlike many of the Egyptians who had treated their slaves badly, Joshua's master was good to Joshua. He formed a friendship with the older man much like one of a father. They often trained together. He taught Joshua several of his techniques in hand-to-hand combat. Joshua had a natural aptitude. His interest and ability had caused him to flourish under his master's tutelage. The man had been proud of his protégé. He also taught Joshua to read and write, stating no officer should have to do without a schooled assistant. Joshua suspected it was an excuse his master gave in order to have him schooled, but he still appreciated the education. His master died in battle when Joshua was still a young man. After that, Joshua was treated like any other slave. As he prepared to assist Moses, he was thankful for all the things he had learned under his teacher. He knew he would need them to be of any real help.

Moses spoke to the people. "If you listen to the Lord and do what is right, obeying His commandments, He will place none of the diseases of Egypt on you. The Lord says, 'I am the Lord who heals you.'"

The Lord who heals you! The words sunk deep into Caleb's heart. He looked over at his wife. Tears rolled down her cheeks. She looked up at him. He smiled and tenderly wiped the tears away. She was healed. She no longer had to suffer. The God who had delivered her had also healed her. She dropped her head. Under her breath, she thanked the God whose name is I am.

Joshua watched the touching scene. He noticed his big friend tenderly touching his fragile wife. Something in the scene moved him deeply. For a long time, the possibility of love had been a forgotten dream. But watching Caleb and his beautiful bride caused him to glance at Rachel, beautiful Rachel. He watched her as she too wept. Why? He wondered. Was she crying for her late husband? Did she miss him? He decided to ask her some time.

He wanted to know if she still loved the man. For some ridiculous reason, that thought troubled him.

Moses was entertained by his new guards. These young men just showed up and started guarding him. Joshua was the one he was most intrigued by. The young man was educated. He was trained in warfare and, for some reason, was certain Moses needed his services. He told the young man daily he did not have to wait on him, but Joshua insisted it was his duty. He was spouting something about "After tending to the needs of someone who could buy or sell him, it was an honor to tend to the man who had changed all that." As Moses thought on it, he did understand. He tried to tell the young man he owed him nothing, but Joshua insisted he owed him everything. He, of course, acknowledged the Lord's mighty hand of deliverance but insisted the only way he could thank the Lord properly was by offering himself as a servant to the Lord's prophet. After a while, it was easier to allow the young man to have his way.

Joshua had become a right arm to Moses. He was certain he would not be able to function nearly as effectively without him. He watched as Joshua, always somewhere nearby, posted guards. Joshua was a natural leader. The men just did whatever he suggested. Joshua would plot out their day's or week's activities, and they would fall right into step. As time went by, Moses handed much of the military duties over to Joshua. This left him more time to deal with the unending demands of the people.

Aaron was also dependant on Joshua, but Aaron had sons who were always at his side, seeing to any need he had. After the first few encounters with Pharaoh, Moses sent his wife and sons home to his father-in-law. Moses had been afraid of Pharaoh using them to stop him. He could not take the chance of them being harmed. Now he was alone much of the time. But there was Joshua, often the first person he saw at the beginning of the day. Joshua would not leave until Moses was tucked safely into bed. Of course, Joshua never left without a guard posted nearby. He was a servant who did so willingly. Tears came into Moses's eyes as he considered the honor of being loved by someone that much!

The children of Israel continued to journey through the wilderness. When difficulties arose, they blamed Moses and Aaron. God heard their complaints. The Lord started to cause manna from heaven to be on the ground each day. Manna appeared with the frost. When the sun dried up the ground, they could gather it and make cakes out of it. The people looked at it and were confused by it. They had never seen it before, so they asked, "What is it?" On the sixth day, they gathered twice as much. The seventh day was a day of rest. God fed them with manna for forty years while they wandered in the wilderness.

Joshua eventually approached Rachel, asking her why she cried the day the Lord spoke. She told him, "If God heals us, perhaps I will someday have children. My husband wanted a son. I was never able to give him a child."

"You should have many children," he said to her softly. "I am sure you would be a wonderful mother."

Joshua's job was more difficult all the time. Moses had not realized the people would be so hostile at each new challenge. Joshua knew he could never fight off the people if they actually attacked Moses or Aaron. But he also knew God would deal with the people accordingly. All he had to do was care for the older gentlemen. When Aaron was with Moses, they were both his charges. But when Moses was alone, Joshua stayed where Moses was. He was Joshua's primary concern.

Rachel grew tired of waiting for Joshua. She walked up to him and asked, "Are you going to ask me to marry you or not?"

Joshua was surprised by her directness.

"You know very well. I thought you would ask me to marry you by now. Why have you waited? Are you just not interested in me?"

He studied her. "I spend all my time with Moses. He needs me. What kind of a life is that for a woman?"

She was insulted. "Do you think I am so shallow I am unable to understand how important your job is? Moses needs you. I would be happy to serve a man like that with you." The look in her eyes challenged him to say anything else.

"You could live like that? I mean, you wouldn't resent Moses or me?"

"I was a slave. My husband and I saw each other only when our masters were not in need of us. I would be honored to serve Moses by being a wife who is there when you are free to come to me. You serve God by serving Moses. I would serve God by serving you. A man of destiny needs a strong woman to care for him."

The children of Israel began to complain. They complained about everything. Lately they were speaking against Moses and Aaron. They said, "Why have you brought us here? We have not had any meat. All we ever eat is this manna." They were so upset by their diet they actually wished they were back in Egypt. They missed Egypt! They wanted the unhappiness of slavery over the uncertainty of freedom. They remembered the foods they had eaten there.

Their complaints reached the throne of God. He had brought them out of Egypt just weeks before by giving amazing signs and wonders! But they were stuck in their thinking. They could not see past the moment. They were not willing to trust the Lord.

The Lord led the children of Israel by day with a cloud. The cloud provided shade. They could see it move; they knew the Lord was in it. God was leading them. He moved them on to Rephidim. There was no water. The children of Israel became thirsty.

Joshua walked through the camp. The people were suffering from thirst. Their cattle were at the brink of death. The children of Israel were complaining. There was talk of electing leaders and returning to Egypt. The children of Israel were to the breaking point.

Joshua activated every man he trusted. It was never a good sign when the people were angry. He arrived at Moses's side. The people were threatening Moses. They all had rocks in their hands.

Joshua looked at his guards. They seemed to be terrified. "Hold your position," he stated to his men. He stood in front of Moses, ready to kill anyone who tried to pass. Caleb was positioned in front of Aaron.

The people were quickly turning into a mob. They shouted, "Moses brought us here to kill us! He tricked us into leaving the safety of Egypt! We are all going to die! How long can our cattle live without water?"

A woman in the front threw a rock. Joshua stepped in front of his hero. It struck his body. He looked at her with murder in his eyes. He pointed his weapon at her. I will kill anyone who tries that again. Moses is not our enemy!" His men crowded in next to him, forming a barrier between Moses and Aaron and the crowd. Moses questioned, "Why do you try the patience of the Lord?"

Moses went to the Lord. "Lord what can I do? The people are thirsty. They are ready to stone me."

The Lord answered him, "Bring your shepherd's staff and some of the elders. I will meet you at the rock near Mount Sinai. You will hit the rock with your staff, and water will come out of the rock."

So Moses went to the rock. He hit it with his staff, and water poured out of it. The leaders watched as the Lord did this great miracle. The children of Israel had all the water they could use.

War came to the people. The armies of the Amalekites surrounded the people of Israel. They intended to wipe the nation of Israel off the earth.

God told Moses to send Joshua with his military force to fight the Amalekites. Moses gave Joshua the plan. "You will lead the men into battle. I will be at the top of the hill with my staff raised to God."

The next day the battle was on. The men of Israel knew not only their lives but the lives of their wives and children were at stake. They fought with all their might.

Moses was at the top of the hill. Aaron and Hur were with him. Three of God's spiritual giants watched the scene below. Moses raised his staff to the Lord. "Great and mighty are You, oh Lord. You are our strong deliverer!" His companions joined him. They knelt and prayed fervently for the soldiers fighting below them. His arms were held up in worship toward the living God! Praise rang forth as he watched the army of Joshua grow stronger than their enemies. His arms became tired. He lowered his arms just a little. Immediately the children of Israel started to lose. He raised them quickly. The army of Israel began to succeed.

Aaron and Hur became concerned. "How long can he do this?" They saw a rock. They worked hard and moved it where he could see the battle and sit on it. Then they helped him by holding his arms up for him. Moses watched the mighty act of the Lord. Tears rolled down his cheeks and down his beard. "Our God is an awesome God!" The three men of God fought the most important battle of all. They understood the real enemy was not made of flesh and blood. "For we wrestle not against flesh and blood, but against principalities, against powers, against the rulers of the darkness of this world, against spiritual wickedness in high places (Eph. 6:12, KJV).

Joshua and his men could see Moses. They knew the Lord was fighting for them. They fought through the day. By sunset the men of Israel had won the battle!

The Lord instructed Moses to make a permanent record against the Amalekites, stating the Lord would destroy them from the earth forever. He also told Moses to speak to Joshua, telling him God would destroy the Amalekites.

Moses built an altar to the Lord in that place. He spoke to the people. "The Lord has done a mighty thing for us. Once again the

Almighty has heard our prayers of deliverance and has brought us out of trouble. This altar is a reminder of God's deliverance. We will call it, 'The Lord Is My Banner!'"

Joshua's men were tired. Many of them were injured, but they were all grateful! They raised their hands in praise to the Lord!

CONSEQUENCES IN THE DESERT

> I am the Lord thy God, which have brought
> thee out of the land of Egypt, out of the house of
> bondage. (Exod. 20:2, KJV)

Jethro, Moses's father-in-law, heard news of the amazing
miracles the Lord had done for Israel. He also heard that they
were journeying through the desert and were camped near Sinai.
Zipporah, Moses's wife, and his sons had been living with Jethro.
She urged her father daily to take her to her husband. He decided
it was time.

Jethro arrived at the camp of Israel just before dusk. He spent
the last several minutes trying to explain to the very intense young
man standing before him he was not a spy. "I've told you my name
is Jethro. I am the priest of Midian. I am Moses's father-in-law.
This is his wife, Zipporah, and his sons. Please tell Moses we are
here to see him."

The guard watched Jethro as if he very much doubted Moses
could have a father-in-law. He sent word on ahead with a young
man. Then Eli ran through the camp. He was on a mission.
"Moses!" Eli stopped, trying to catch his breath. "Moses, there

is a man who says he is the priest of Midian. He says he is your father-in-law."

Moses looked up from his business. "Jethro is here?"

"Yes, sir." Eli nodded. His dark eyes danced as he watched Moses's expression turn to one of joy.

Moses smiled from ear to ear. "Aaron, my father-in-law is here. That means he has brought my wife and sons." He hurried through the camp, back through the path that Eli had taken, to greet Jethro personally.

"Father, I am so glad you have come." Moses bowed to his father-in-law. They embraced then he greeted his wife and sons. "Zipporah, you have arrived at just the perfect time."

He turned to his father-in-law. "You must stay with us for a while. I have to tell you everything God is doing for us." Moses was excited. He looked into the faces of those he loved most in the world. At last they were with him.

The campfire warmed them as the light from the pillar of fire lit the entire camp. Moses explained, "The Lord sent me to speak to Pharaoh, but Pharaoh would not let the people go. The Lord wanted to use Pharaoh to show the world he is God." He continued, barely taking a breath.

Jethro noticed many new things about Moses, one of which was when he spoke of God's miracles, he did not stutter. His whole demeanor changed as he spoke of each event. His face was different too. He actually glowed. His whole countenance was changed by his encounters with God.

When Moses was through telling everything that the Lord had done for Israel, Jethro, his father-in-law, praised God. He offered to the Lord a burnt sacrifice. Jethro spoke. "Oh Lord, we praise you. You are God. Among the gods there is no one like you! All praise and honor are yours." Tears of joy rolled down the faces of those who watched this gentleman worship the Lord Most High.

The next day people came to Moses to settle their disputes. They were there all day long, waiting for Moses to hear their individual cases. Jethro was concerned for Moses and the people. "Moses, why do the people come to you with all their problems?"

Moses answered, "I help them by telling them what God would have them to do."

Jethro listened to his son-in-law and then said, "You are doing this wrong. You will tire yourself and the people out. Choose men you trust and teach them the laws of God. They can hear all the simpler cases. This will give you an opportunity to deal with the difficult problems."

Moses chose men whom he knew cared about the Lord. He trusted them. He encouraged them and prayed over them. "God, anoint these men to lead your people."

The Israelites traveled for two months. They moved slowly. The journey was long and often difficult, but the Lord was with them. God was teaching them. Every day He showed them more of Himself. They arrived at Mount Sinai.

"Stay here." Moses moved on without the people. His heart was set. He had been dreaming of this day, how much he wanted to return and speak with the Lord. He smiled as he climbed. The terrain was rugged, but Moses's heart was light. He was filled with expectation.

> And Moses went up unto God, and the Lord called unto him out of the mountain, saying, Thus shalt thou say to the house of Jacob, and tell the children of Israel; Ye have seen what I did unto the Egyptians, and how I bare you on eagles' wings, and brought you unto myself. Now therefore, if ye will obey my voice indeed, and keep my covenant, then ye shall be a peculiar treasure unto me above all people: for all the earth is mine: And ye shall be unto me a kingdom of priests, and an holy nation. These are the words

which thou shalt speak unto the children of Israel.
(Exod. 19:3–6, kjv)

Moses was thrilled. He longed to share the word of the Lord with the children of Israel. He walked down the mountain. The rocks under his feet moved as he navigated the difficult terrain. Joshua waited for him at the bottom of the mountain. He glanced at his hero. Moses was full of the light of God. His face radiated the beauty of the Lord.

"We will do all the Lord asks." The words of the Lord were welcome. The hearts of the slaves now free softened because of God's love for them. Out of respect they cleaned themselves and put on their best clothing. They were instructed not to go beyond a certain area.

"Expect the Lord to visit you. He will do a great thing in three days."

Lightning flashed, thunders roared, the people began to tremble. A thick cloud descended on the mountain. The people heard the sound of a ram's horn coming from the mountain. They were terrified. Out of the cloud the Lord called, "Moses!" in a voice like thunder. All the nation of Israel could hear the Lord as he called to Moses. "Moses, come up here." Moses arrived at the top of the mountain.

"Go back down and warn the people not to come up the mountain, or I will punish them. Bring Aaron back with you."

Moses descended Mount Sinai. "The Lord has sent me back to warn you. You must not go up the mountain. The Lord will punish anyone who disobeys. Aaron, the Lord has called for you." The two elderly gentlemen hiked up the mountain to meet with the God of all creation. He is holy. His throne extends into the heaven. At that time only certain prophets and priests could stand in His presence.

And God spake all these words, saying, I am the
Lord thy God, which have brought thee out of

the land of Egypt, out of the house of bondage. Thou shalt have no other gods before me. Thou shalt not make unto thee any graven image, or any likeness of any thing that is in heaven above, or that is in the earth beneath, or that is in the water under the earth: Thou shalt not bow down thyself to them, nor serve them: for I the Lord thy God am a jealous God, visiting the iniquity of the fathers upon the children unto the third and fourth generation of them that hate me; And shewing mercy unto thousands of them that love me, and keep my commandments. Thou shalt not take the name of the Lord thy God in vain; for the Lord will not hold him guiltless that taketh his name in vain. Remember the sabbath day, to keep it holy. Six days shalt thou labour, and do all thy work: But the seventh day is the sabbath of the Lord thy God: in it thou shalt not do any work, thou, nor thy son, nor thy daughter, thy manservant, nor thy maidservant, nor thy cattle, nor thy stranger that is within thy gates: For in six days the Lord made heaven and earth, the sea, and all that in them is, and rested the seventh day: wherefore the Lord blessed the sabbath day, and hallowed it. Honour thy father and thy mother: that thy days may be long upon the land which the Lord thy God giveth thee. Thou shalt not kill. Thou shalt not commit adultery. Thou shalt not steal. Thou shalt not bear false witness against thy neighbour. Thou shalt not covet thy neighbour's house, thou shalt not covet thy neighbour's wife, nor his manservant, nor his maidservant, nor his ox, nor his ass, nor any thing that is thy neighbour's. (Exod. 20:1–17, KJV)

Lightning flashed; smoke rose from the mountain. The people fell down on their knees trembling. They were terrified. The sound of the horn was deafening. They listened as the Lord spoke to Moses. The smoke continued to rise from the mountain.

Moses came down to talk to the people. "Don't be afraid. The Lord is showing you His awesome, mighty power. Remember this, and don't sin against Him."

"Moses, you speak to the Lord. We will do whatever you tell us. But if we stand before Him, we will all die!" The people watched as Moses went back to speak to the Lord.

The Lord continued to give Moses instructions for the people. They were instructed how to offer a sacrifice, how to treat their slaves, what to do in case of personal injury. There was nothing of importance that God did not explain to Moses. He gave complete instructions on how all things should be dealt with.

God was merciful. He took the time to give people His direction. He made a covenant with the children of Israel. He gave them the law.

Aaron did not go back to speak with the Lord. He stayed with the people as Moses went back up the mountain.

The people sinned. Moses was gone for forty days and nights. The people told Aaron to make a golden calf that they could worship. Aaron instructed them to bring him their gold—the gold the Lord had given them as the spoils of Egypt. They designed a golden calf and began to worship it. "These are your gods that brought you out of Egypt." Quickly they turned from the Lord.

Moses was with God for forty days and nights. During this time, he did not eat or drink. His mind and heart were completely on the Lord. The Lord had written the Ten Commandments Himself on tablets of stone. The finger of God carved every word into the priceless tablets.

The Lord spoke to Moses. "Go down to the people, for they have sinned."

Moses made his way down the mountain. The tablets of stone were in his hands.

Joshua met him. "Moses, there is war in the camp. The people are crying out."

Angrily Moses replied, "It is not the sound of war that we hear. The people are partying."

When Moses saw the people, he raged at them. "No! No! Do not sin against the Lord. What have you done?" He threw the stone tablets with the words of God down and broke them in the presence of the people.

The people stared at their leader who had been gone for over a month. The man of God's voice carried over the crowd. Moses looked at Aaron. "What did they do to you to cause you to go along with them?" His voice was loud enough to be heard by the multitude. The people began to tremble as Aaron made excuses.

Aaron trembled uncontrollably. The look on Moses's face was something he had never seen. Moses's eyes pierced him as though he could see right through to Aaron's heart. "The people are stubborn. You didn't come back. So they gave me their gold. He lied. I threw it into the fire and it came out a calf."

Fire blazed in the eyes of Moses. "Who is on the Lord's side?" The sons of Levi stepped forward. "This is what the Lord says, 'Take your sword and go through the camp, killing every man and his friend.'" The sons of Levi obeyed the Lord. About three thousand men were killed that day for worshipping the golden calf.

Moses's heart was broken. He spoke to the people. "I will go back again and speak to the Lord on your behalf. Maybe He will forgive you." Moses walked that long trail back up the mountain. His heart ached as he spoke to the Lord. "Oh Lord, they have committed a terrible sin by worshipping the golden calf. Please forgive them. If you will not forgive them, then remove my name from your book of life."

The Lord answered, "The one who has sinned is the one who will be punished. Go lead these people. I will send an angel. He will go before you. I will not go with the people myself. If they sin again, I will destroy them all."

Moses returned to the people. He told them the Lord would send an angel before them, but the Lord would no longer be among them. The people mourned when they heard the words of Moses. Then the Lord sent a plague as punishment for the sin of idol worship.

Moses continued to serve the Lord. He would go to the temple and meet with God. Moses wanted to see the Lord. The Lord said, "No one can look upon my glory and live." But the Lord agreed to let Moses see part of Him. The Lord said, "Moses, stand on this rock, and when I pass by, I will hide you in a crack of the rock and shield you from total exposure. When I pass by, you will witness the glory of the Lord. I will let you see my back side."

Moses had broken the two stones the Lord had made. The Lord told him to carve out of rock two more stones. "I will carve the words into them again for you." Once again God delivered to mankind the Ten Commandments. Lightning flashed as the Lord God moved. Moses stood upon the rock.

> And the LORD passed by before him, and proclaimed, The LORD, The LORD God, merciful and gracious, longsuffering, and abundant in goodness and truth, Keeping mercy for thousands, forgiving iniquity and transgression and sin, and that will by no means clear the guilty; visiting the iniquity of the fathers upon the children, and upon the children's children, unto the third and to the fourth generation. And Moses made haste, and bowed his head toward the earth, and worshipped. And he said, If now I have found grace in thy sight, O Lord, let my Lord, I pray thee, go among us; for it is a stiffnecked people; and pardon our iniquity and our sin, and take us for thine inheritance. (Exod. 34:6–9, KJV)

Moses loved the Lord. He spent hours worshipping God. He was lost in the magnificence of the eternal, unchangeable, undeniable, most excellent Lord God Almighty!

Finally, Moses raised himself up off the ground. He was changed. He was changed from the inside out. He had encountered a God of not only physical deliverance but also spiritual salvation. God, the forgiving and merciful, is the deliverer of mankind.

Slowly he walked down the path to the camp of the children of Israel. He carried the two tablets of stone; written on them were the most important words ever given to mankind. They were the words of God. As he walked, he thought of none of the petty life-consuming things men get caught up in. All he thought of was the God of everlasting promise. He was not aware of the outer transformation. He had walked into the very presence of God. His skin took on the appearance of the heavens. His eyes were sharp; they held the fire of God in his expression. His smile was one of an angel. He had encountered a life-changing God, whose presence reflected in the very appearance of Moses. Moses did not realize until the people saw him that he glowed from his encounter with God. The people were unable to look at him, so he covered his face with a veil as he talked with them. When he went into the tabernacle of the Lord, he removed the veil. There he spoke with God face-to-face.

Moses sent spies into Canaan to spy out the land. Joshua and Caleb were among the men who went through the land. When they returned, they were exhilarated. The land was a good land full of milk and honey, just as the Lord had said. But the other spies came back with a different report.

"There are giants!" The men spoke the words as though they were a death sentence. Caleb could not believe his ears. A red flush ran up his face. His big hands flexed into fists as he grew angrier. Joshua looked at his friend as they listened to the reports.

One by one, with exception of Joshua and Caleb, the spies all said the same thing: "The people of the land are too strong for us!" Joshua spoke up. "They're wrong." He looked around, his eyes searching the crowd. "It's true the people of the land are strong, but God is stronger!"

One of the spies stood up in defiance of the Lord. His wide-set eyes opened a little wider. A look of panic crossed his face as he began to elaborate. "They are huge. We were the size of grasshoppers next to them. What does it matter if the land is flowing with milk and honey? There is no way we can fight these people! They are too strong!" The other spies shook their heads, agreeing with him.

The words hit their targets. The people began to mourn. They were unable to believe the Lord. Disheartened, they all began to speak evil against the Lord. They quickly forgot His favor He had shown them. "The Lord has brought us out of Egypt to kill us! Our children will die in this land."

"No!" Joshua and Caleb cried. Grief replaced the joy they had felt as they searched the land. Joshua and Caleb tore their robes. "The land is good! We can take the land with the Lord's help. Don't listen to these men. The Lord delivered us from the Egyptians. He can help us defeat the people of the land."

The people had spoken against God. Their very accusations were filled with poison. God had already done so much for them, but still they could not believe. The Lord spoke to the children of Israel, telling them they would not go into the Promised Land. "You will all die in this desert. Your children will go in and take the land in your place. You will wander in this desert forty years, until all of you who have complained have died. Only Joshua and Caleb will enter my land of promise." The hearts of the people broke. They were doomed to never leave the desert alive.

The Lord spoke to Moses and told him to anoint Joshua to lead the people in his place. All the complaining the people had done became a stumbling block to Moses. The Lord told Moses, "You will not go into the Promised Land because you disobeyed me in front of the people when you struck the rock."

Moses had sinned. He had become angry with the people. Once again they were thirsty, and once again they had complained.

Before, when the people were thirsty, God told him to strike a rock the Lord had pointed out to him. This time was different. God told him to speak to the rock and water would come out of it for the people. But Moses was angry. He hit the rock, saying, "Do God and I have to draw water for you?"

The Lord was displeased. "You will not enter into the Holy Land. You will die as the others on this side of the Promised Land." The Lord had wanted to use the illustration of the rock as an example of Christ. Jesus is the rock. He was struck once at Calvary. That finished it. Since that time throughout eternity, mankind need only speak to Him. He is there to save us.

Moses prepared to die. He was old. He had led the children of Israel for forty years. During that time, he had delivered the commandments of God as well as all of the Lord's instructions to the people. He wrote Genesis. The Lord explained what had happened from the beginning, and Moses recorded it for mankind. He wrote Exodus, in which he gave the testimony of the events that had taken place, leading up to and including the deliverance of Israel from Egypt. The Lord delivered the law to him. He recorded it in Leviticus, named for the children of Levi, the priests of the people. He went on to write Numbers, giving the number of men who were ready to go to war. This included their family's genealogy. He recorded Deuteronomy. There he reminded the people of the laws of God. He appointed Joshua as his replacement and charged the people before the Lord.

Moses was heartsick. He pleaded with the Lord to let him see the Promised Land. The Lord spoke to Moses. "I will show you the land, but you cannot enter in. Go up to the top of the Mountain of Nebo near Jericho. You can see the land from there."

> And Moses went up from the plains of Moab unto
> the mountain of Nebo, to the top of Pisgah, that is
> over against Jericho. And the Lord shewed him all
> the land of Gilead, unto Dan, And all Naphtali,
> and the land of Ephraim, and Manasseh, and all

the land of Judah, unto the utmost sea, And the
south, and the plain of the valley of Jericho, the
city of palm trees, unto Zoar. And the Lord said
unto him, This is the land which I sware unto
Abraham, unto Isaac, and unto Jacob, saying, I
will give it unto thy seed: I have caused thee to
see it with thine eyes, but thou shalt not go over
thither. (Deut. 34:1–4, KJV)

Moses died at the age of 120 years old. His eyesight was clear, and
he was as strong as when he started out. The children of Israel
mourned his death for thirty days, as was their custom.

And there arose not a prophet since in Israel like
unto Moses, whom the Lord knew face to face,
In all the signs and the wonders, which the Lord
sent him to do in the land of Egypt to Pharaoh,
and to all his servants, and to all his land, And in
all that mighty hand, and in all the great terror
which Moses shewed in the sight of all Israel.
(Deut. 34:10–12, KJV)

PRAISE THE LORD!

Today God is still delivering His people. The children of Israel
were to the world a literal example of God's amazing power and
His willingness to deliver His own.

The hand of a loving God is ready to swoop down and deliver
us from the oppression of an enemy we cannot see and very often
do not acknowledge is there. We, as the children of Israel, are
stuck in the degradation of the familiar. Just as they were afraid
to go forward, we look back at our former lives and desire to
turn away from God rather than face the fears of the unknown.
Moses led the nation of Israel out of Egypt. There was no war.
That mighty man of God, God's prophet, followed God into the

very lair of the oppressor and demanded their release. Then, by God's mighty hand, an entire nation walked out of the hands of their captors.

Just as they were held captive, many of us are also captives. We need to ask God for deliverance. His son, Jesus, has walked into the lair of the enemy of our souls and demanded our release! He fought for us! He gave his life at Calvary, looking ahead to us! Just as the blood of the lamb applied to the doorpost and above the doorway of the believers was a sign to the Lord not to take the lives of the firstborn of the children of Israel, the blood of Jesus, the perfect lamb of God spilled on the cross is a sign to God that we are His people. We are covered by the blood of the Lamb of God. We are saved from death by simply asking Jesus to come into our hearts and change us from one of those condemned to death to one of His! We can ask Him for life!

Just as the children of Israel, we walk through a desert. They became stuck in their place of wondering. They were God's own people, but they never entered the Promised Land. It wasn't until the next generation rose up, believing God's promise was for them, that the people moved into their inheritance. We can be as the men and women who were slaves. We can allow our slave mentality to hold us back, to stop us from claiming what is rightfully ours because of the blood of Jesus. The same God who delivered His people from the power of the enemy then is able and will deliver us from the strongholds of Satan today. That menace to the souls of man cannot hold us back from receiving our rightful inheritance, unless we fail to realize the delivering power of Almighty God.

He created the universe. He breathes out life with every breath of His nostrils. There is nothing that is too hard for God! He is able! He is able to create in us a new heart, a new attitude, and a new mind. We don't have to wander around in a desert. We don't have to go back to Egypt. We just have to follow Him, knowing the enemy is out there. We must keep our hearts and minds ready for battle. And the same all-powerful God, who delivered over a million plus slaves from their slave owners, can deliver us from the tormentors of our souls. Our lives can be redeemed. We can expect to walk into the very gates of heaven, having fought a good fight. We are the children of God Himself!

JOSHUA

> Moses my servant is dead; now therefore arise, go over this Jordan, thou, and all this people, unto the land which I do give to them, even to the children of Israel. (Josh. 1:2, KJV)

Joshua sat alone. Loneliness invaded his soul. How could he do all that God had called him to do? He searched the law, his heart pounding for answers. "Oh God, give me strength." He looked out toward the Jordan. The people of God were camped behind him. The unknown lay ahead of him. While Moses was alive, he had not doubted. He knew God controlled and worked through Moses. But he was not Moses. No one knew better than Joshua the sacrifices Moses had made to lead the people. Oh, they had been rebellious; often they tempted the Lord, and they paid for it. He wasn't sure he was ready. How could he do this thing? Doubt plagued him. Grief of Moses's death shook his soul. "Lord, he was like a father to me." All night he prayed; time had ceased to exist for him. He needed God. "Only You, Lord, can teach me how to lead the people." How long had he prayed? He no longer knew; night turned into day, day into night again. Time continued. With all his heart he sought the Lord. The answer was with God. He must seek the Lord's word.

Suddenly, from out of nowhere, great peace began to fill his soul. He sensed the presence of the Lord.

> Moses my servant is dead; now therefore arise, go over this Jordan, thou, and all this people, unto the land which I do give to them, even to the children of Israel. Every place that the sole of your foot shall tread upon, that have I given unto you, as I said unto Moses. From the wilderness and this Lebanon even unto the great river, the river Euphrates, all the land of the Hittites, and unto the great sea toward the going down of the sun, shall be your coast. There shall not any man be able to stand before thee all the days of thy life: as I was with Moses, so I will be with thee: I will not fail thee, nor forsake thee. Be strong and of a good courage: for unto this people shalt thou divide for an inheritance the land, which I sware unto their fathers to give them. Only be thou strong and very courageous, that thou mayest observe to do according to all the law, which Moses my servant commanded thee: turn not from it to the right hand or to the left, that thou mayest prosper withersoever thou goest. This book of the law shall not depart out of thy mouth; but thou shalt meditate therein day and night, that thou mayest observe to do according to all that is written therein: for then thou shalt make thy way prosperous, and then thou shalt have good success. Have not I commanded thee? Be strong and of a good courage; be not afraid, neither be thou dismayed: for the Lord thy God is with thee withersoever thou goest. (Josh. 1:2–9, KJV)

Lightning shot through Joshua. The spirit of the Lord moved upon him. His soul was renewed. God had spoken to him! Filled with strength and joy from the Lord, he felt energized. His eyes glowed as he thought of the words of God: "As I was with Moses, so I will be with you." He knew God would not fail him. God had renewed the promise he had made to their fathers. They would inherit the land!

A stirring had started in the camp. Caleb was anxiously awaiting Joshua's return. He knew his friend; Joshua would not act until he had heard from God. As he thought of their lives in the desert, he heard the people starting to say one to another, "Joshua is back."

Now Caleb saw for himself that Joshua had been with God. The fire in his eyes was bright. He recognized the spring in Joshua's step. He was ready to fight the biggest giant. Joshua was at peace with God.

Listening, he heard Joshua commanding the officers: "Go through the camp and tell the people to prepare food. In three days we will go over Jordan into the Promised Land." Joshua remembered the words of Moses. He had been there when the tribes of Reuben, Gad, and the half tribe of Manasseh had promised to go before the rest of the children of Israel with their men of war armed for battle and ready to fight. God gave them the land on this side of Jordan because it was good for cattle. Moses made them promise they would not stop fighting until all the children of Israel had their land, as God had promised the people.

These men were mighty men. All of Israel had fought to take the land their cattle now grazed on. The time had come for them to fight for the rest of the people. Joshua stood in the middle of these men. "Do you remember your promise to Moses?" he said. "Your wives, your children, and your cattle will stay here until the Lord has given rest to your brothers. Then you can return to your homes."

The men answered Joshua, "Everything that you command us we will do. Where you send us we will go. Only God be with you as he was with Moses. As we obeyed Moses, we will obey you. Any man who does not listen to you or follow your command will be put to death. Be strong and courageous."

Joshua gave them three days to prepare. They would have to act fast. They talked for a while and then turned for home. There were still many men to talk to; the word had to be spread. Some of the men went on ahead to tell the rest of the people, "We will go before our brothers into the land of promise."

Aaron felt a strange stirring. He had inherited, as the Lord had said, on this side of Jordan. Now he would go with his friends into the land of Canaan. His brothers would also have a place of inheritance. Excitement grew as he thought on God's promise for all his people.

There was joy mixed with sadness. He knew his mother would worry. He had been preparing for this day. He had not talked to her about it; but they both knew, eventually, he would be called to go, and he would answer the call. He had built stalls and fences; anything he could do while he was waiting for the word to go, he did. His mother was a desert baby. She was born shortly after they left Egypt. All her life Israel had wandered. This was her first real home. She had put down roots and would do fine while he was away. The only one he really worried about was Rachel, his wife.

She was pregnant with their first child. He had been praying for a son, so to leave her now would be almost impossible. He was torn between his beautiful wife and his promise to God. He had to go; there was really no choice. God would care for her in his absence. It was strange how he could be so full of expectation for his people and yet apprehensive for his wife and unborn child. "Father God, I place them in Your care." He prayed for many hours that God would be with his family. His heart longed after his child. "Lord, You will have to be his father while I am away." There he sat, his soul making intercession for his family, himself, his friends, and his people. "Oh God, guide the hand of Joshua, and give me the courage I will need in battle."

Rachel was watching the horizon for her husband. She had heard. Everyone had heard. Where was he? Worry mingled with aggravation. Then she saw him. All thoughts of anger were gone. She loved everything about him. The sight of him coming to her now was enough.

A knowing look passed over his face as he drew near to her. "You were worried," he said, smiling.

"Yes," she replied. Tears threatened her as she realized their time together would be short. A moment later, she was in his arms. Nothing mattered as long as he held her.

Down the road, a similar scene was unfolding. Reuben looked at his son. "You are the man now. You will have to take care of your mother, brothers, and sisters."

The young man looked pleadingly into his father's face. "I want to go with you." His steady gaze showed his father how close he was to manhood.

"No, my son, you are needed here. I am depending on you to care for your mother and the others. Be sure to check on our neighbors also. Rachel will be giving birth soon. They will need help around the place. I will get word to you if I possibly can. You can best help us fight by staying here." Somehow the young man did not think it was the same, but he knew his father was counting on him.

"Yes, Father," was all he could say.

Rebecca walked up on her husband and son, embracing them. Smiling, she asked, "When will you leave?"

"Daylight," was the answer.

Her smile was radiant. "I thought you would say that. I have packed you something to eat on the journey."

Reuben smiled. This meant he would be able to feed himself and several friends for quite some time. "Elishama and Daniel, his son, will meet me here with some of the others. Daniel told me his father is anxious to be going. We want to be there long before Joshua needs us."

Rebecca looked at her husband with fire in her eyes. She was proud of this man. Both of their fathers had died in the desert because of the unbelief of their generation. She and Reuben had spent many evenings saying goodbye, preparing for this day. God willing, they would not make the same mistake as their fathers.

Morning came too soon. *Goodbye* was a word that could not say what was in their hearts. "I will pray for you," they both promised. Before leaving, Reuben bowed his head and worshipped God. His family was in the hands of God; what better place could he leave them? He kissed his children and, finally, his wife. Then he turned and joined his friends.

Aaron cradled Rachel in his arms. "I will return," he cooed softly, confidently into her hair. "God will fight for me. He will bring me home to you." Slowly the sobs began to subside. He held her close, not quite willing to let her go. Praying softly, he continued to comfort her. "You will see, I will come home."

She smiled slightly as she said, "Yes, God will protect you." He looked around and saw his friends coming in the distance.

His mother reached out and embraced him. "I will take care of her and the child. Don't worry, we will be fine."

He said one last goodbye. His mother also had packed enough food for a small army. He looked at his friends and started down the path to join them.

All over the land of Reuben, Gad, and the half tribe of Manasseh, the men of war said goodbye to those they loved. They had a mission to fulfill. So, faithfully they left those most important to them and joined their brothers, the children of Israel. They came armed for war. They marched past the women and children, past the herds and flocks, on toward the front, past the others who would also fight. They were to be a wall between the enemy and Israel. They were the first to inherit; if need be, they would be the first to die.

THE SPIES

And the king of Jericho sent unto Rahab, saying,
Bring forth the men that are come to thee, which
are entered into thine house: for they be come to
search out all the country. And the woman took
the two men, and hid them, and said thus, There
came men unto me, but I wist not whence they
were. (Josh. 2:3–4, KJV)

Out of the shadows crept two men. Quickly they made their
way through the city. Early that day they followed a caravan of
traders right into the heart of Jericho, no one suspecting them.
They spent the day looking over the city, memorizing the way it
was laid out. They knew where it was weakest. Crossing to the
other side of the street, they moved quickly into the shadows.
Something was wrong. Their hearts pounded fiercely within
them. They breathed short, shallow breaths. Adrenalin filled
them with renewed strength. They watched as soldiers ran down
the street past them as though they were invisible.

Their clothing was unusual. People had started to notice
them. They knew now they were not going to be able to hide long.

They made their way to the wall. They both knew they would not be able to go out the gate. They would have to go over the wall. Slipping up the steps, they ran to an open breezeway.

"Up there!" someone called.

Quickly they slipped through the door. Their gaze landed on a woman. She looked startled. One of the men put his finger to his lips, signaling her to be silent. Her eyes were wide, her breath short as she looked at the men. Outside she could hear the soldiers questioning her neighbors.

In a split second, she made a decision: "Come." She motioned to the men. They followed her to the roof of her house. "Quickly," she whispered as she started taking up the stalks of flax.

They could see her intention; silently they helped her. She quickly replaced the flax, her hands shaking slightly as she realized what she was doing. *Calm down,* she thought and drew a deep breath. Calmly now, she walked back down the stairs.

Bang! Bang! There was a heavy, intrusive pounding on her front door. She jumped and rushed forward. *Slow down,* she thought as she moved to open it.

"What took you so long?"

The gruff voice was one she knew well. Actually, she knew many voices well. "I'm sorry." She smiled her most beguiling smile. She moved closely to the man speaking. His eyes sparkled as he looked at her.

"Rahab!" the other man snorted. "We are here on business. The king himself has sent us to tell you to send the strangers out." She looked at him, a question on her face.

Gentler now, the gruff-voiced soldier began to speak. "We know they were with you. We want to question them. They are spies."

Shock etched her face. "Spies, here in my house? Are you sure? What do they look like?" she asked. She looked positively terrified, giving them her most helpless expression.

"They are strangers to the city. Their clothes are different. We believe they arrived with a caravan. Have you seen them?"

"Yes, I have." The two men immediately came to attention. "They were here, but they have gone. I don't know where. If you follow them, you can catch them."

The soldiers looked confused. "You're sure they're gone?"

She confirmed, "Yes, of course."

The soldiers turned to their companions. "They've gone." With that, they left.

When they were completely out of sight, she closed the door. Quickly she grabbed a red rope. She ran to the roof. She spoke quietly. "The men of the city are terrified of you. I know the Lord has given you the land, and all men fear you. They faint because of you. We heard that the Lord parted the Red Sea for you. We know of your victories when you fought the two kings of the Amorites, Sihon and Og, whom you destroyed.

"When we heard these things, our hearts melted. There was no courage left in any man because of you. Your God, He is God in heaven above and on earth beneath. Now, I beg you, swear to me by the Lord, since I have shown you kindness, that you will show kindness to my father's house. Will you promise that you will save the lives of my father, my mother, my brothers and sisters, all that they have, and deliver our lives from death?"

The men looked at each other. "Our lives for yours," one of them said. "And when the Lord has given us the land, we will deal kindly and honestly with you."

Tying the rope securely, she dropped it out the window. The darkness was their cover.

Out of the shadows she heard one of them speak. "Two things you must do. We will not be responsible for any of your lives if you fail. Bring your family here and stay within these walls. Also tie this cord in the window of this house. If anyone leaves this place, we will be blameless. If you repeat any of this to anyone"— there was an air of menace in his voice—"we will be released from our promise to you."

Fearfully she responded, "I will do as you say. Go to the mountains and hide for three days. By then the men will stop looking for you, and you can return to where you came from."

One at a time they shimmied down the rope, a wave goodbye, and she watched them disappear into the darkness.

She pulled the cord up and held it in her hands. Her eyes searched the darkness for a witness of her action. Now she was a traitor. She would be in danger until the men returned. Tears welled up and slipped unbidden down her face. She was betraying all her neighbors, the whole city. Only God knew if these men would keep their word. Bitterness reared its ugly head. *Why should I care about any of these people?* she thought. *The women hate and laugh at me, and the men, they are worse.* Her thoughts reflected on her beautiful face as her eyes darkened from the sorrow.

The thoughts that haunted her were painful. How many times had they called her worthless? Despair beat at her heart. She could not go on like this. Her life was a mess. She longed for love. *Will anyone ever love me? No, probably not.* In her mind she saw children playing happily on her floor. Someone stood smiling, staring at her with pride in his eyes. "I'm a silly fool," she chided herself. "No one will want a prostitute for a wife." She moved slowly across the room. The tears dried. She once again hardened her heart to the pain. "No one cares for me. Why should I care for them? I must make some plans."

Systematically, now she began. First, she tied the rope in the window. She refused to listen to her heart, the soft rhythm beating quietly. *What about the children? No, I can't think of them. I cannot save them all.* "Oh, God of Israel, help me to be strong, if you take thought of someone like me." The cord was in the window. The prayer slipped unconsciously out of her lips. She sank to the floor for no particular reason, and yet for every reason in the world, she cried. The long, hard sobs brought up and out all the junk in her life. She thought of everything and wept in a way she had not wept before. There was a peace that slowly replaced the pain. Somehow she knew He had heard her, and He cared for her. A stirring of hope began to rise up within her. She understood now. She was not just placing her life and the lives of her family in the hands of these men; she was placing their lives in the hands of God. Somehow she knew she could trust Him. She tilted her head questioningly as she wondered at the thought. *Trust, how long has it been since I trusted anyone other than family?* She would not wait; she would go to her family tonight.

She raised herself up off the floor. There was lightheartedness about her she could not explain. For the first time in a long time, she had hope.

The streets were quiet. The excitement of this evening was winding down. She slipped down the street, unseen by others. She reached her destination and knocked then walked in. "Mother, Father," she called. They looked at her and smiled. "How are you, Father?"

He smiled. "I'm better today." He patted her hand as she bent to kiss him. His pale color and shortness of breath told her of his lie, but she pretended not to notice.

"Rahab." Her mother spoke her name. "Did you hear there were spies in the city today?" Her mother's eyes showed the worry she did not speak.

"Yes, Mother, that's why I'm here. I think it would be best if all you stayed with me for a while. We should be together if the city is attacked." She weighed their expressions and saw that they were looking for the kindest way to say no. "Please," she pleaded. "They were at my house today, and I'm afraid they will return. If we are together, we will have a better chance of escaping."

Her mother looked frightened. "They were with you?"

She answered, "Yes, but they left. I told the soldiers to follow them. I don't know if they caught them."

Her father watched his wife and daughter. Rahab was keeping something back. His sharp eyes took in her appearance. He knew his daughter was up to something.

Rahab spoke quickly, reassuring her mother she was unharmed. "Really, Mother, I'm fine."

The sharpeyed man said, "You want us to move in with you because you are afraid?"

"Yes, Father." She couldn't quite meet his gaze, so she looked at her mother. Her smile trembled slightly as she tried to pretend fear was her only reason before the hawk eyes of her father.

"What did you talk about?" he asked.

Rahab flushed. "Father, you know I don't like discussing these things with you."

He persisted. "Were they friendly?"

She looked directly into his eyes. "Yes, I suppose." She dropped her head and stared at her hands.

"Rahab, what have you done?" His question was spoken softly and to the point.

Her eyes met his steady gaze. "I can't say."

He watched her. "All right." He shook his head affirmatively. "We will come with you."

The two spies made their way into the mountains. They stayed there in a cave for three days, as Rahab instructed them. She was right. The men of Jericho quickly became tired of searching for them, and after only three days, they gave up. From their vantage point, they could see the valley below. There was no sign of the enemy.

Joshua was satisfied. He looked out from his perch over all the people of Israel. Everything was going well. The people were ready. The time had finally come. They would cross the Jordan and go into the Promised Land. Praise be to God!

His spies had returned last evening with word of Jericho. *God had given the city to Israel. It was just a matter of taking it. What was her name, Rahab? Yes, that was it. Even Rahab, the harlot, had told the spies how God had placed fear in the hearts of the men of Jericho. God was once again showing his power to save and deliver Israel. He had given his promise.* Smiling, he said out loud, "God, He will fight for us."

THE ROCK PILE

And the priests that bare the ark of the covenant
of the Lord stood firm on dry ground in the midst
of Jordan, and all the Israelites passed over on dry
ground, until all the people were passed clean over
Jordan. (Josh. 3:17, KJV)

The people began to set up camp. They stopped at the banks of Jordan. Three days passed before they received word from the officers to make way for the ark of the Lord and leave a space between the people and the ark. They were to follow at a distance. Also, Joshua had commanded them to purify themselves.

The young warrior Aaron watched with interest; the people seemed ready. There was an attitude of business everywhere. He observed different men and women go before the priest with their offerings to God. People were somber, yet there was joy. There was something else too. They were resolved to follow God. He had not seen such dedication in his lifetime. He had heard how, at times, the people followed God, but this was different. God was moving just for their generation, and they were ready to follow. Excitement bubbled everywhere.

He slipped off to a place of solace. He needed to prepare himself before God. "Father." The word came out with his breath. "Oh God, Jehovah, I am so inadequate to go with your people to war, but I place my life in Your hands. I ask that my strength, such as it is, be enough. You are my strength, my shield, and my buckler. I pray for your anointing on my life. Rule over my heart as my only King. I will follow you to my last breath." He spoke to God as though God was his own father, a habit he picked up not long after his father's death.

How long he was there with God, he did not know. He had slipped into that special place with Father God, which only a child could understand. His soul hungered for refreshing, and his Heavenly Father filled that longing perfectly. He felt the moving of God, the tender stirring. Armed with weaponry not of this earth, he stood to his feet, picked up his sword and shield, and walked back to camp. God had prepared him. He was ready for the unknown.

Reuben saw his young friend coming. He had begun to worry. It was almost their watch. "Talking to your father again, Aaron?" he asked with laughter in his eyes. Reaching up, he playfully ruffled Aaron's hair and pulled the young man close to him in a half hug. "I, too, have spent some time with Him. I have waited so long for this day. We will see God deliver the land into the hands of our brothers together! Praise be to God!"

Joshua had waited on the Lord; the last three days he spent in prayer. Now, with his face before the Lord, he continued his prayer for guidance. In his eyes was the depth of his dependence on God. As he raised his face to God, he began to worship. Praise rose from deep inside of him. God had already done so much. He recounted the deliverance of the Lord from Egypt and wept like a child as he remembered the Passover lamb. With every fiber of his being, he reached out in praise. "Oh God, thank You for Your saving power! I remember Your mighty works while we were slaves in Egypt, how You brought us out with the power of Your strength and delivered all these people from the hands of their oppressor. I remember how You parted the Red Sea, and all of Israel walked over on dry land. You, oh God, delivered Your law to Moses and led us through the desert in a cloud by day and a pillar of fire by night. You fed us in a barren country and gave us drink when we were thirsty. You healed Your people and punished their disobedience. Who is like You, oh Lord, in all the earth?" He ended his prayer with strength only God can give. His face was wet with tears. His hands reached up to wipe away the tears that had ran down his face, onto his mustache, and wet his beard. God had given him peace. Tomorrow the Lord would give him direction.

Off in the distance, a guard walked to and fro, watching, listening, ever vigilant in his duties. All around the camp they watched, and out in the horizon a fire blazed ahead of them. Their God was watching also.

The morning dawned brightly. The river Jordan rolled by them at a constant pace. The people began to sing all over the camp. They sang songs of victory their mothers and fathers had taught them. Joy bubbled over and was heard in the chatter as well as the music. They were going home! The day was breathtaking. Joshua watched as the people readied themselves.

The Lord spoke to Joshua, saying, "Today I will magnify you in the sight of all the people. They will know that as I was with Moses, I also am with you. Speak to the priests and tell them to step into the river in front of all the people."

Joshua spoke to the children of Israel and said, "Come here and hear the word of the Lord. This is the way God will show you He is with you, and He will help you to be victorious over all your enemies. He will give you the land He has promised."

Joshua chose out twelve men, each man representing a tribe of Israel. "You will all pick up a rock from the middle of the Jordan, which you will take to your tents tonight. Tomorrow you will place the stones in a large pile, as a memorial to the Lord, on the other side of this river. When your children will ask you, 'Why are these stones here?' You will tell them it is because the Lord dried up the Jordan, and the children of Israel crossed over on dry land."

Then he chose twelve other men, each representing a tribe. "You will choose a stone and place it where the priests, who carried the ark, stood. Place the rocks in a pile as a reminder that Israel walked across this Jordan on dry land."

Now he was ready. Joshua called out to the priests, who carried the ark, to go ahead of the children of Israel. The priests, arrayed in their finest robes, lifted the ark of the covenant of the Lord. The familiar weight rested on the shoulders of the four priests. Each priest carried an end of the pole. There were two poles, which ran through rings on the ark. They lifted the ark and proceeded to walk into the river. The Lord was there and did a great thing in the sight of all the people. As they walked out into the Jordan River, the river dried up on both sides and stood up, away from its natural course. It was no longer flowing but backed up to the city, Adam; even the waters that ran into the Salt Sea were stopped. During harvest, the Jordan normally flooded. Now, where the people walked, it was dried up completely. The people crossed the Jordan, into the Promised Land, on dry ground. Joshua called out to the twelve men chosen to place the stones in the Jordan. "Go, each of you. Place your stone where the priests, who carry the ark, are standing." They obediently did as he said. Then he said to the priests, "Go on over to the other side of this river." They did; and as they stepped out of the Jordan River, the river began to flow again. However, now there was a place in the middle of the water, where the priests had stood with the ark, that rippled, as a memorial to the Lord.

JERICHO

> Now Jericho was straitly shut up because of the children of Israel: none went out, and none came in. And the Lord said unto Joshua, See, I have given into thine hand Jericho, and the king thereof, and the mighty men of valour. (Josh. 6:1–2, KJV)

The stones the second group of twelve men was to carry and to keep in their tents overnight were used to build a memorial to the Lord on land. This was to remind the generations to come what the Lord had done for Israel. Each man was careful to select his stone. They chose stones that were beautiful. Reuben asked Aaron to help him carry his stone. It was large. The two men hoisted it with considerable effort. The children laughed and played, teasing them as they heaved it onto the bank.

Aaron looked at his friend. "Do you think it's big enough?" Laughter rang as they each dared the other one to carry it to the camp and place it in Reuben's tent.

Because the Lord had dried up the river Jordan for them, there was joy in the camp. The women worked quickly, preparing dinner for their families. They sang and laughed as they busied themselves. The children of Israel were overwhelmed with gratitude. The Lord God of their fathers had not failed to be with them all the time they were wandering in the desert. Now He was preparing them to receive the promise of the Holy Land. They looked out at the land their forefathers had journeyed in and blessed the God of heaven and earth.

The next day the camp became somber as the last stones were set up for a memorial to the Lord. Joshua spoke with conviction to the people. "When your children will ask you what are these stones for, you will tell them this is a reminder of God's faithfulness. He dried up the river Jordan for the children of Israel to cross over, just as He dried up the Red Sea! He is the same God today as He was yesterday." Joshua's eyes blazed with excitement. "God has promised, and He will do all He has said He would do."

Aaron listened to Joshua's words. His eyes filled with unshed tears. Joshua worshipped the Lord, as did many others. He hazarded a glance at Reuben. Reuben, the strong, the mighty, the fearless, sank to the ground like a child before the Lord. At that moment Aaron thought Reuben was the strongest man he knew. He was so moved by the outward affection of the people for the Lord. He could only stand there, shaken by the vastness of God's power and might. Never in his life had he felt so small. Standing there, he was moved to a faith in God he had never known. Oh, he knew what God had done to the Egyptians. He believed. But somehow it meant so much more, knowing God was moving for his generation. It was no longer stories; it was for him.

He bowed his head and joined the crowd of those who were too awed to speak, too humbled to move. Worship such as he had never known filled him. This is the Lord God's doing, and it is marvelous in our eyes!

There was an unsettling atmosphere all over the land of Canaan. Men and women had watched for days as the children of Israel camped on the other side of Jordan. People were filled with fear at the very thought of what the God of those people had done to the great land of Egypt. Never before had they seen such a thing where a God fought with such power and might on behalf of His people.

They knew their own gods would be powerless before Him. Fear increased while the people of Canaan waited to see what the God who moved in a cloud by day and a pillar of fire by night would do.

The king of Jericho himself was plagued with nightmares of this God. He had not slept for three days. His mind whirled with various notions of how this God would bring him down. Now, what he heard took his breath and robbed him of what little fight he had left. His spies had just reported that the God of Israel had dried up the Jordan, just as he had the Red Sea, allowing his people to walk across on dry land. The king's heart melted within him. His face was pale. His eyes filled with horror. He spoke softly, almost to himself. "Who can stand against them?" His house of beauty, his robes of finery, his crown of gold, his army…"What good were they before the God of these people?"

The soothsayers, enchanters, and priests of the temple stood waiting to offer comfort to the king. But he did not call them. They were of no use to him now.

Word spread throughout Canaan. All the kings had heard of the God of Israel. They listened to the stories their spies told about the Jordan drying up. Reports continued to filter in all over the land; people had witnessed it. The reports were true. Fear such as they had never known overtook them. They were as dead men before the God of Israel.

Rahab paced the floor. She too had heard. She looked out her window; the people of Israel covered the land.

The camp was busy with activity. The people were setting up camp and preparing to stay the night. Joshua walked through the camp. He noticed familiar sights and sounds. There was a fuss over a child who had slipped away from the camp. A mother reached out lovingly as her child was returned safely to her arms.

The princes of the tribes made their way toward Joshua. Caleb smiled his familiar smile. They were happy. God had blessed them. "Joshua," Caleb said. "How long before we storm the city?" "The Lord has determined we stay here a few days," replied Joshua. "While we wandered in the desert, we did not circumcise our men. Now we must renew our covenant with God."

As he spoke the men nodded. "Yes, yes, this is good. We will obey the Lord." So Joshua made knives and circumcised the children of Israel. And the Lord said to Joshua, "This day I have taken away the reproach of Egypt from you." And the children of Israel camped in Gilgal and kept the Passover on the fourteenth day of the month, at even, in the plains of Jericho.

And they ate the old corn of the land on the day after the Passover, unleavened cakes and parched corn on the same day.

And the manna stopped on the day after they had eaten of the old corn of the land. They did not have manna anymore, but they ate of the fruit of the land of Canaan that year.

It happened that Joshua was near Jericho. He looked up and saw a man ready for battle. This man had His sword drawn and was ready to fight. Joshua went to Him and asked Him, "Have You come to help us, or are You against us?"

He answered, "I am here as the captain of the Lord's army."

Joshua fell on his face to the earth and worshipped and said to Him, "What instructions do You have for me?"

And the captain of the Lord's host said to Joshua, "Take your shoes off your feet, for the place where you're standing is holy." And Joshua did as he was instructed. There, in that holy place, God spoke to this mighty man of war. His general, His pastor, the one God had called to lead His people to victory and promise, was now reassured and guaranteed success.

Time passed slowly for the people of Jericho. Their king watched in horrified wonder as the land to the east of his city filled with people. Just outside the walls of Jericho, the people camped. His spies brought constant reports of their activities, but he could not tell what was going to happen next. From what he understood, they were ready for battle. There was an army of several hundred thousand men, who stayed in front of the people at all times. Guards were always on the alert, and it seemed there had been a time of religious observance. He did not understand.

Word went throughout Canaan that no one would be permitted to enter Jericho. However, with the nation of Israel camped right outside the wall, no one was stupid enough to try to enter. The king of Jericho was mystified. What were these people doing? If it had been anyone else, he might have felt safe behind the walls of Jericho. It was a virtual fortress. However, how could he think he could fight against an army whose God seemed to be capable of anything? His mind whirled. There were reports of his own soldiers wanting to work out a truce. The people were panicked. Frantically, he offered his gifts to his gods. Perhaps with so many gods, he could change his position; after all, the children of Israel only had one.

Rahab could see the people camped below her window, the same window she had used to allow the spies to escape. Absentmindedly she fingered the tassels of the red cord she had used for a rope. Her father watched her. He had given up asking, but she knew he was watching. She noticed the looks pass from her mother to her father. They knew her so well. Also, they had been quick to comply with her rule, that no one leave her house. They watched her panic as her little sister returned with water that day. She had let down her guard when the child was gone. "You must promise me not to leave here!" She was so emphatic the poor child started to cry. Her mother asked her, with a guarded tone, if they were to be prisoners. She did her best to reassure her that was not the case, but her mother's eyes did not reflect confidence. "I will go, Momma," she said. "It is dangerous for the children, and you are busy caring for Father." Slowly her mother accepted her answer. *I must be careful*, she thought, but could not shake the feeling of apprehension.

She had stopped taking gentlemen callers. She was sick of the way she felt when they touched her. It was easy to dismiss the advances by simply explaining she had company. She could not face the looks her parents would give her if she were to continue business. Anyway, there wasn't a lot of interest with the city under siege; everything was changing. She knew her life was going in a direction she had no control over ever since she had asked the God of heaven and earth to help her. She was different. She had made such a mess out of her life without Him. It was comforting to know He was in charge. She continued to pray to Him every day. After all, He was the only one she could really talk to and trust.

Moving away from the window, she sensed His nearness, even now. How could this God of goodness care for her? But something inside her told her He did. So alone in her room, once again, she spoke to the only one who really understood.

The day dawned brightly as Joshua prepared to address the camp. He had heard from the Lord. All the men of war were to go around the city once each day for six consecutive days. He also instructed seven priests to carry, before the ark of the covenant, trumpets of rams' horns. "The seventh day you will circle the city seven times. Then the priests will blow the trumpets. When you hear the trumpets, everyone will shout as loud as possible. Then the walls of Jericho will fall down flat. Then go take the city. Remember, no one is to speak or make any sound until it's time for you to shout on the seventh day.

Rahab was astonished. There outside her window, on the other side of the wall, this great army marched. In the front was a great company of soldiers, armed, prepared for battle; behind them seven men clothed in priestly robes sounding a steady sound of rams' horns. Behind them walked more priests carrying a large gold box. *What were they doing?* They did not look at the wall. They simply circled the city once and went back to camp.

The king felt faint. "Oh, how long must they blast those horns?" He leaned back on his throne, feeling very close to a royal tantrum. His servants worked frantically to please him.

They tried a damp cloth for his headache then various herbs for his upset stomach.

"Please, Your Majesty, try to relax," they pleaded.

"How can I rest with that incessant noise!" he exclaimed. His head hurt. His stomach was upset, and he was quite sure these people were trying to drive him insane! All at once the noise ended. "What are they doing now?" Jumping up, he ran over to the balcony.

"It appears, Your Majesty, they are leaving."

"What?" Looking, he could see for himself. They were leaving. They were all marching back to their camps. "Well"—he almost laughed—"they seem to actually be retreating." His joy was short-lived, as the general of this mass of people looked back. He could swear he was looking at him.

"Sire, I'm certain they are through for now," one of his counselors confirmed as he watched them retreat.

"Why? Why would they do this?" He suddenly remembered his headache. "What were these peculiar people with this unseen, unknown God up to?" Walking back to his place of resting, he lay down. His thoughts, however, were far too troublesome for him to sleep.

Joshua stood watching the palace wall. The Lord had told him no one but Rahab and her house would be saved. He made a mental note of the balcony that the man with a crown stood on. He would make sure there would be no escapes!

The attitude of the camp was serious. The people knew God was making Himself known to all the surrounding nations. They were determined not to fail Him this time.

The king was now fit to be tied. Early this morning that unspeakable noise had started again. "What do these fools think they are doing? For three days now they have marched around the walls blasting their horns. This is ridiculous! Shoot them, I say."

"Sire, we can't. We have tried."

"What do you mean you've tried?" The king was beside himself. "We've used our best archers, but they are out of reach. We can't seem to hit them no matter what. We fire on them. They just keep marching, looking straight ahead. They say nothing. They just march."

Rahab watched from her perch in the window. From here, she could not tell one from the other. But she looked anyway, trying to catch a glimpse of her allies. She knew now who the leader was. She recognized him even from here. He was the one in the front. He carried himself with confidence that left little doubt of his identity. The day's events seemed to be winding down. They were heading back. They started here and ended here. She was in the perfect location to watch.

Guards had come and searched her house for any sign of the enemy and decided there was nothing here. That was a couple of days ago. They hadn't bothered her since. As she watched the army disband, she became lost in her thoughts about what had led her to this place. The priests said, "She was chosen to be used by the gods." Only the most beautiful young girls were chosen for such things. She remembered the fear she felt when she was taken from her home to serve in the temple. She had been so young. Even with everyone telling her how fortunate she was, to be honored by the gods this way, she had not felt lucky. But with time, she'd learned to use her position to her benefit. She had supported her family and maintained this house all from the generous gifts the men had given her. Lost in her memories, she started to feel sick. She hated her past. Slowly she allowed herself to fantasize once again. She could see a curly haired child smiling, with his huge brown eyes, laughing as he played near her. In her arms she held a newborn, soft and full of innocence. Somewhere close was a man who would not turn on her. He would never hurt her. The warmth of his love would cause the past to melt away.

Joshua spoke to the people. "Today God will fight for us. We will march around the walls seven times. The priests will blow the trumpets. They, as before, will go ahead of the ark of the covenant. When you hear the sound of the trumpets, you will shout. God has given us the city. At the sound of the trumpets and the shout, the walls will fall down. Every one of you will go and take it. Remember, everyone must die except Rahab and her house. She is to be spared because she hid the spies I sent in. Everything in this place is cursed. The men, women, children, ox, and sheep—all will die. We will take none of the spoil. It is cursed. The silver, gold, and vessels of brass and iron will be given to the Lord, and only Rahab and her house will be saved."

Around and around they marched. The king was consumed with fear. "Why haven't they stopped today? Tell the people to arm themselves. We must be ready for anything." He had not slept well all week. His headache had persisted even when the trumpets were not sounding. Panic rose in his heart.

He heard a long blast of the trumpets. People were screaming. He glanced out of his window and saw the army of the Lord of hosts standing in front of the wall of Jericho, shouting at the top of their voices. The trumpets blasted, the people shouted, panic was everywhere. There was another sound too. Suddenly the floor beneath him began to shake furiously. "Guards!" he shouted. There was rumbling under his feet. Timbers cracked; something split and gave way. Looking up, he saw a wall falling toward him...

The two spies ran quickly for Rahab's house; Joshua had instructed them to protect her and her family. They were careful to situate themselves close to her home. The walls were falling all around them. The area Rahab lived in stood firm. They quickly climbed the crumbling stairs. She opened the door.

"Let's go!" they shouted.

"My father is ill. He is slow."

"We will carry him. Quickly." One of the young men bent down and picked up her father.

"Come, Mother!" She screamed as her mother hesitated with fear. She called out to her brothers and sisters. She took the hand of her little sister, while the second spy guided them out and around a corner of the wall that lay in pieces beside them. They heard the sounds of the city—the cries of the people dying behind them. Her house was giving to the strain of the power that had destroyed the rest of the city. Behind them lay the ruins of the house they had just stood in.

"Over here!" The men continued to lead them away from the battle toward the camp. "You'll be safe here. Don't move. We'll come back for you."

She watched as the men ran back toward the city. From here they could hear the screams of the people in battle. Fire was everywhere. They could feel the heat. They all cried, overwhelmed by the sight of the city. They watched in a dazed shock.

It was over. She looked up as the army emerged from the city. Her two young friends were coming toward her. They were safe.

"Rahab!" One of them called to her as he waved her over to them.

She moved toward him, her family following cautiously behind her. One of the young spies reached down, picked up, and once again carried her father.

"Sir, this is Rahab and her family." She looked into the face of Joshua for the first time. Would he spare them as his young men had promised?

He looked tired, but his eyes held an alertness she did not miss. "You are welcome," he said. "We will honor the promise my men made to you. You placed your life in danger for them. We will not forget that. Thank you." His eyes of steel pierced her as though he were able to read her heart. The trembling she had grown used to began again. Joshua smiled at her then, looking at the two men, said, "You will see to them. Make sure they are comfortable, and introduce them around."

The young men graciously agreed. They were different in front of this Joshua. They respected him. The love the spies showed the older gentleman spoke volumes to Rahab. She noted to herself *they would die for this man*. She did not realize she was holding her breath until she released it.

> And Joshua adjured them at that time, saying, Cursed be the man before the Lord, that riseth up and buildeth this city Jericho: he shall lay the foundation thereof in his firstborn, and in his youngest son shall he set up the gates of it. So the Lord was with Joshua; and his fame was noised throughout all the country. (Josh. 6:26–27, KJV)

Sin in the Camp

> But the children of Israel committed a trespass in
> the accursed thing: for Achan, the son of Carmi,
> the son of Zabdi, the son of Zerah, of the tribe of
> Judah, took of the accursed thing: and the anger
> of the Lord was kindled against the children of
> Israel. (Josh. 7:1, KJV)

Word spread throughout Canaan. Spies delivered news of the
end of Jericho. Their kings waited in suspense, unsure of their
own future.

Joshua too had spies. He sent men from Jericho to Ai. These
men were to spy out the land. They returned with a favorable
report. Joshua stood listening.

"There is no need for all the people to go out against Ai.
The people of Ai are few in number. We only need about three
thousand men."

Joshua was pleased with the news. Looking around, he chose
Reuben. "You take three thousand men with you. Go up to Ai
and take it."

Reuben lifted up his eyes; he saw his friends. They were coming already to volunteer. He looked into the face of his friend Aaron. His smile was young and innocent. Reuben took a deep breath and exhaled slowly. Something was wrong.

Aaron was saying, "We will go up and take Ai for the Lord." His confidence never faltered, but Reuben sensed something.

"Aaron," he said. "I feel the men with families should stay."

Aaron's smile faded slightly. "You don't want me to go with you?" He looked hurt.

Reuben floundered, searching his mind for something to say. He sought to reassure his young friend. "I can't explain it. I felt this way when I heard the report the men brought back. Something is wrong. I sense it from the Lord. Do you trust me enough to stay here this time?"

Aaron shifted, a little embarrassed. "I don't understand," he said.

"I know, but if you will stay here and continue to guard the people, I would feel more at ease."

Aaron nodded. "All right." His boyish charm returned with his quick smile.

Reuben turned to the crowd that was gathering. Quietly to himself, he asked the Lord for wisdom. He chose carefully from the men of his tribe. The sense of forbearing dictated his decision to choose the men without families.

They looked out over Ai. Reuben was certain now; his premonition was not his imagination. He had followed the spies into the heart of Ai. He saw little threat to the men with him. But there was still that undeniable sense of something being wrong. He had prayed, but had not found comfort. He and his men listened carefully to the plans the spies had made for attack.

The battle did not go well! The two spies were dead. Reuben fought with all his might to stay alive. He called a retreat, but the men of Ai pursued them relentlessly. His body ached. He was more tired than he had ever been. Another one of his men fell dead beside him. Again he cried out, "Retreat! Retreat!" He and his men ran for their lives. "Oh God, save us!" He prayed as another friend fell dead beside him. For a moment he stopped, cradling the body in his arms. He searched for any sign of life. He was gone. Looking around, he saw a place of escape and, with renewed strength, guided the men toward it. Mercifully night fell. Under cover of darkness, the men of Israel made their way to camp.

Joshua looked up in the distance. He saw his men. The light from the pillar of fire burned bright. "No!" he cried. Even from here, he could see they had met with disaster. His men were bleeding and looked as though they were going to collapse from exhaustion.

In the early hours of the morning, Joshua listened to the earth-shattering news. His men had fallen before Ai! Thirty-six men were dead. The wounded were everywhere. His heart sank. Throughout camp the people were mourning. Wherever he looked, there seemed to be suffering.

In anguish he ripped his clothes and fell on his face to the earth before the ark of the Lord. The elders of the people joined him. Their sorrow was too deep for words. They put dust on their heads and cried out to the Lord, all day long, until evening. Joshua lay on the ground. His heart ached within him. Why did they fall before Ai? Why had God left them? Remorse overwhelmed Joshua. "O Lord, what shall I say, when Israel turneth their backs before their enemies (Josh. 7:8, KJV)! The people of the country will hear about this. They will surround us and wipe out our name from the earth. What then will You do for Your own great name?"

The Lord said to Joshua, "Stand up! What are you doing down on your face? Israel has sinned. They have violated my covenant, which I commanded them to keep. They have taken some of the devoted things. They have stolen, they have lied, they have put them with their own possessions. That is why the Israelites could not stand against their enemies. They turned their backs and ran from their enemies in defeat because now Israel has been set apart for destruction. I will not be with you unless you destroy those things that you have taken."

> Up, sanctify the people, and say, Sanctify yourselves against tomorrow: for thus saith the Lord God of Israel, There is an accursed thing in the midst of thee, O Israel: thou canst not stand before thine enemies, until ye take away the accursed thing from among you. In the morning therefore ye shall be brought according to your tribes: and it shall be, that the tribe which the Lord taketh shall come according to the families thereof; and the family which the Lord shall take shall come by households; and the household which the Lord shall take shall come man by man. And it shall be, that he that is taken with the accursed thing shall be burnt with fire, he and all that he hath: because he hath transgressed the covenant of the Lord, and because he hath wrought folly in Israel. (Josh. 7: 13–15, KJV)

Standing, Joshua wiped the tears from his face. The sun now setting painted orange, gold, and rose patterns in the sky behind him. Praise poured out of him like water.

> God be merciful unto us, and bless us; and cause his face to shine upon us; Selah. That thy way may be known upon earth, thy saving health among all nations. Let the people praise thee, O God; let all the people praise thee. O let the nations be glad and sing for joy: for thou shalt judge the people righteously, and govern the nations upon earth. Selah. Let the people praise thee, O God; let all the people praise thee. Then shall the earth yield her increase; and God, even our own God, shall

bless us. God shall bless us; and all the ends of the
earth shall fear him. (Ps. 67:1–7, KJV)

There, in the presence of Almighty God, he prayed for hours.
He remembered the faithfulness of God. God's mercy endures
forever.

Turning, Joshua walked back toward the children of God.
The majesty of the sunset was all around him. All he saw was the
beauty of an awesome God, whose loving grace and presence far
surpassed the beauty of mere creation.

There was a new attitude in the camp. The children of Israel
knew God had spoken to their beloved Joshua. God intended to
clean house. The serious nature of the crime against the Almighty
had been demonstrated at Ai. There would be judgment today.

They were instructed by Joshua to set themselves aside
before the Lord for this day. The early morning brought many to
alertness. The night had passed slowly. Prayer had brought great
comfort to the men of Israel, all, that is, except one.

He and his sons stood toward the back of his tribe, their dark
eyes wide with apprehension.

He recalled the words of his sons: "How can we do this thing?"

He had foolishly dismissed them. "No one saw me," he said.
"Who will know if we keep just a few things? You were there. You
saw the place. There was wealth beyond our wildest imagination,
and everyone there was burning it!"

His son's eyes had fallen on the beautiful robes, the gold, and
the silver. "Well, if you're sure no one saw you."

He had smiled then, confident he had been undetected. "Help
me," he said as he happily dug a place under his tent to hide his
treasures.

Things were different now. The joy was replaced by fear. His
heart pounded furiously as he watched Joshua bringing the heads
of the clans forward. Sweat beaded his brow as the tribe of Judah
was chosen. One by one the families of Judah came forward. The
clan of the Zarhites was called forward. His mouth fell open, and

he swallowed hard. They were chosen. Family by family presented themselves before the Lord. The family of Zabdi was chosen.

Now he was calling for each man of the family of Zabdi. Achan moistened his lips. His mouth felt dry. He trembled uncontrollably as slowly, inevitably, he was being brought before the judgment of God. *Run*, he thought, but he could not. His feet were drawn unbidden to the judgment seat. The sound of his heartbeat was so loud in his ears they hurt. Panicked, he asked himself, *Why didn't I know God saw me?*

Joshua was speaking to him. He heard him as though he were calling to him from a tunnel. The words came slowly. Achan was found out. God had seen him. "Confess now, my son." The words of Joshua filtered through his confused thoughts. "Give God glory, and tell us what you have done."

He had no desire to lie. The peace of God rested on this man of war, who now confronted him. His guilt-ridden conscience confessed his crime. "It is true! I have sinned against the Lord, the God of Israel. This is what I did. When I saw in the plunder a beautiful robe from Babylon, two hundred shekels of silver, and a wedge of gold weighing fifty shekels, I coveted them. They are hidden in the ground inside my tent with the silver underneath."

Joshua glanced up at two men near him. "Go find them, and bring them to me."

Soon the men returned with the things. Joshua had a sick feeling in the pit of his stomach. Righteous indignation welled up inside of him. His eyes were bright with determination. The cursed things lay on the ground before the Lord.

Joshua and all of Israel took Achan, his sons and his daughters, his oxen, and his tent and all that he had and brought them to the valley of Achor.

"Why have you brought trouble on us? The Lord will judge you today." All the people of Israel stoned them. Then Joshua gave the order, and they burned them. They also placed a large mound of stones on the graves. So the Lord turned from his anger.

Meanwhile the kings of the land had heard the good news. The men of Israel had fallen before the men of Ai! Oh, this was wonderful! For the first time in several weeks there was cause for celebration. Jabin, king of Hazor, was beside himself with relief. He utterly roared with laughter as the runner, one of his own spies, described the fear of these unwanted pests.

"They actually ran in defeat!"

"Yes, sire," replied the spy. "The men of Ai have run them completely out of the area."

Throwing his head back, Jabin laughed uncontrollably. His fear of the past weeks had been unnecessary. Why, Ai was a small, almost insignificant place. If the handful of men in Ai could put this army on the run, his would obliterate them.

"Quickly," he said. "Summon my counselors. We must make plans to wipe these people off the earth." Rising from his throne, his kingly robe tossed in a careless fashion, he walked toward his courtyard. He instructed his servants, "Send word to King Jobab and the others. Tell them what you've told me. Oh, and be sure to bring gifts for all of them. We have much to celebrate. I want to make my personal congratulations to the king of Ai, along with my thanks to the men of Ai who have won this great victory." While the kings of Canaan rejoiced, the Lord was speaking with his servant Joshua.

30

AMBUSH

And the Lord said unto Joshua, Fear not, neither
be thou dismayed: take all the people of war with
thee, and arise, go up to Ai: see, I have given into
thy hand the king of Ai, and his people, and his
city, and his land: And thou shalt do to Ai and her
king as thou didst unto Jericho and her king: only
the spoil thereof, and the cattle thereof, shall ye
take for a prey unto yourselves: lay thee an ambush
for the city behind it. (Josh. 8:1–2, KJV)

After hours of prayer, this precious man of God, who had received
his instructions, gave praise to his Commander and Chief and
reverently bowed his head and worshipped. "Oh Lord God, who
is like You in all the earth?" The sunset traced its patterns of gold,
orange, and red lights across the sky as the soldier prayed on.

Early the next day, Caleb paced the tent of his camp. He too
had slept very little, choosing to pass much of the night in prayer.
Ever since the men had returned with the news of their defeat,
he had felt helpless. He should have been there with them. His

thoughts ran wild as he remembered the senselessness of their deaths.

This business with Achan was hard to take. But he knew now, God would be with them again. He paced on as he considered what one man's greed had cost the whole nation. God had refused to bless them because of the sin in the camp. Now that Achan had been dealt with, they could move on under God's covering. Caleb was certain— it was only a matter of time before the Lord would instruct Joshua to act. This time he would not stay behind. He intended to win every inch of land their fathers had failed to take forty years ago.

He and Joshua were the only ones left of the original army.

He had witnessed many times as the Lord spoke through Moses and told them they would possess the land. He remembered well that God told Moses he would inherit the land he had spied out. This was a setback, but definitely not the end. He couldn't wait any longer; he had to speak to Joshua. He stepped out of his tent and, with determination, made his way to where Joshua would be.

Aaron watched Caleb. His stride was long and easy. His steps were that of a young man. In truth, Caleb amazed Aaron. The big man seemed an endless source of energy. His face, browned by the sun, was ageless. Caleb seemed to be capable of doing anything he set his mind to. Aaron had watched the older man when they were in battle and was convinced he was a champion's champion. His wide shoulders rippled with muscles earned from hard work. His health seemed unending. He often spent time with Joshua. Caleb was one of those people everyone followed. He was an excellent friend for Joshua.

Aaron thought of the difference between the two men and realized how their friendship balanced each other. There was something restless and ready for action in Caleb, whereas Joshua never seemed to be in a hurry. He was patient and practical, always thinking through each step. They were both tremendous men of faith, and that faith had brought them to this place.

Joshua smiled pleasantly at Caleb. "Yes," he said. "We will go to Ai. This time all of us will go. I want you to lead an ambush against the city. We'll discuss this later after I choose the rest of your men. God has promised us victory, just as at Jericho. Only this time, we can keep the treasure."

The two men spoke freely with the comfort of lifelong friends. Their smiles radiated their joy. After only minutes of business, they lapsed back in time, recalling all the mighty deeds of God. They had watched His power at work, and neither of them could forget how awesome He was. Every recollection brought back their own personal account of what they had seen. Soon they were doing what they both enjoyed the most—they were giving God the glory. The little tent shook with the low resonating sounds of the two men who had gone from slavery to freedom all because of a loving God. Praise ascended and was heard on high. God the Father was being glorified!

Caleb, the fox, lay in wait for Joshua's signal. He was sent ahead with thirty thousand of Israel's finest fighting men. He was instructed to move in behind the city of Ai and wait for the signal. Joshua and the rest of the army would attack, drawing the men of Ai out. Then Joshua would retreat, drawing them away from the city. Caleb and his men would go in and take the city, burning it. No one was to survive. The Lord had promised Israel the livestock and wealth of the city. Joshua had been careful to instruct them in the ambush, and they were ready. As he smiled to himself, Caleb thought of the beauty of the plan. God had taken their defeat and instructed Joshua to use it to trick Ai.

Early the next day, Joshua called together his army. They marched up to Ai. Then they camped in front of the city, with the valley between them. Joshua had also chosen out five thousand men to set an ambush to the west of Ai.

The king of Ai was pleased with himself. He had received many gifts and congratulations from the neighboring kings. Looking out now at Joshua, he was convinced the man was beside himself. Speaking directly to his steward, he exclaimed, "The man is a lunatic! Didn't we just run his army out of this place?" Now, with a sigh of resignation, he went on. "Well, I suppose these people are determined to let their pride get the best of them. We will just have to teach them a lesson, once and for all. Prepare my troops. Every man is to go to battle. We will make them sorry they ever looked our direction." He was quite satisfied with his decision. So turning, he walked leisurely back toward his room. Stopping himself, he decided to offer a special gift to his gods, just in case.

Joshua was not disappointed; his ploy last night had worked. He could see the king of Ai, with his chariots and men of war, coming out to meet him. The sun was beginning to show itself, and so was Ai.

The men stood their ground with Joshua, allowing the men of Ai to come completely out. The men of Ai were ready for battle. Running quickly, they pounced on the army of Israel.

Israel pretended to try to maintain their position. They allowed the men of Ai to overwhelm them. Feigning themselves fearful, the army of Israel began to run from Ai. Ai pursued hard after Israel, but something was wrong; Joshua and the men of Israel stopped running!

> And the Lord said unto Joshua, Stretch out the spear that is in thy hand toward Ai; for I will give it into thine hand. And Joshua stretched out the spear that he had in his hand toward the city. (Josh. 8:18, KJV)

Trapped, the men of Ai frantically sought to escape. Behind them there was the smoke of the city; in front of them stood Joshua and his massive army. They were doomed!

Joshua and his men pursued the people of Ai in the fields. They hunted them down and killed them in the desert. They killed all the army of Ai. Then they returned to the city and killed the people who were left there. They obeyed the Lord. They also plundered the city and took the livestock.

He also hung the king of Ai. That evening he instructed his men to take the body down. They placed rocks on the grave at the entrance of the city.

Joshua built the Lord an altar on the mountain of Ebal. They built it according to the instructions God had given Moses. They used stones that had not been cut. There they gave an offering to the Lord. The entire nation of Israel and all the foreign people living among them stood for the reading of the word. They were divided into two groups. One group was at the bottom of Mount Gerizim. The other group stood at the bottom of Mount Ebal. The priests who carried the ark of the Lord's covenant stood between them. Joshua read the word of the law that was given to Moses to all the people. He read to them of all the blessings and the curses. These depended on the behavior of the people. God promised to bless them as long as they followed Him. He also warned them they would be cursed if they disobeyed His law.

As the children of the Lord, we can safely rest under His protection. When we willingly walk away from His guidance, we walk out from under that protection. We are like anyone else who chooses to sin. It is not His nature to hate or destroy mankind. He warns us of the consequences. We have the right to choose; and with that right comes responsibility for our actions. When we disobey Him, we can find ourselves living with the consequences of our unwise choices.

The day was long. Rahab stood mesmerized, as many others, unable to move. The words of the Lord poured out like rain on a dry place. She stood there overwhelmed by the holiness of God. As she listened, her eyes moistened, and tears ran down a face filled with shame. She clutched her veil tighter over her face as Joshua continued to read the words of the law: Thou shalt not commit adultery. Thou shalt not covet. Thou shalt not bear false witness. The list went on. She had done so much. Guilty, her heart cried out to every charge. She dropped her head, unable to bear the reproach. Then there were words of atonement. Something inside of her responded to the promise. An offering could be made for her sin; she could be cleansed.

She listened as the rules were given concerning issues such as washing your hands and preventing disease. The list went on, covering so many things; she found it difficult to remember them all.

She had wondered, since Jericho, why the children of Israel killed everyone. Now she understood. She cringed as she recalled the screams of men, women, and children. Here, at last, was the answer. God warned them not to leave the people alive because they would become like them. He said they would marry and raise their children to be unfaithful to God like the nations that lived in Canaan. He reminded them of how some nations burned their children to Molech, sacrificing them to the pagan god of the land. God said, "You will not worship other gods." God said they would become like them and follow their ways and destroy the land He was giving them. He said, "You will not kill." God did not want them perverting their relationship with Him by sacrificing their young to Him or any other god!

She became physically ill as she thought of the human sacrifices she personally witnessed. She had her answer. God was a just God; He could not stand by idly watching people sacrifice their children and not become angry. She knew in her heart if they left the children alive, the children would grow up and go back to the practices of their parents. He once destroyed the earth with a flood because of sin. He promised never to flood the earth again; but He is still just.

As evening fell, she came to several truths. The first, she knew she was a sinner. Second, she knew there was forgiveness. This mighty, awesome, holy God provided cleansing from her sins. She was now convinced God cared for mankind. She had just stood for hours listening to a book, God's laws, containing instructions to cleanse from sin and protect from disease. He had provided answers with such detail; she knew only a God who cared for His creation would do this. Her mind reeled as she considered the gods of wood and stone; they had eyes but did not see, they had ears but did not hear. They were dead. They weren't really gods at all. This God, who demanded that men serve only Him, was a God she could not see; but she knew, beyond a doubt, He saw her. His throne ascends into heaven, and the earth is no more than His footstool.

She stayed near the altar long after the others had left to go back to their tents. She remembered now how she knew, even without being told, He heard her. So once again, she prayed. She poured out all her sins to this great God, who is too holy to behold the sins of man, and promised Him she would offer a sacrifice for her own sins as soon as she could.

Joshua saw the young woman lingering. "Rahab, is there something I can do for you?"

Rahab smiled. Joshua was so busy, and yet he was offering to help her.

"You've been so kind already." He watched her, waiting for her to finish. "It's just that I understand now. I have been so wicked. I don't know what to do."

He looked into her eyes with compassion and said, "All that is behind you now. You are no worse than any of us. If God chose to reward us for our sins, we would all be dead. But He shows us mercy, and we are forgiven our sins. You are now under the shadow of the Almighty. You have placed your life in His care, and He is full of compassion and mercy."

As he spoke, they walked slowly back to camp. With each step, he explained the sacrifice for sin offering. He also spoke of a savior who would come. His words were life, filled with the wisdom of hours spent studying the book he expounded to her.

Joshua left Rahab at her tent. He had much to think about. Rahab was still a very beautiful young woman. She was now, here, under his protection. He needed to know what God's direction was for her. He decided he would pray for wisdom. He had a few problems since she'd come here. Her beauty had not escaped the eyes of some of his young men; and already, they were asking her father if he would consider them for marriage to her. Her father had approached him for advice concerning the young suitors.

He smiled as he recalled the look on Salmon's face when he first met Rahab. He was a good man. Joshua liked him. Rahab, however, would have nothing to do with any of her would-be suitors. It seemed to Joshua she was weary, even at such a young age, with the idea of men. Whoever won her hand would certainly have to work for it. Rahab had already proved herself useful to the people. Joshua had done as much as he could, personally, to make her feel at ease. She was industrious and was already taking in laundry and sewing to maintain her independence. She was helpful to everyone around her. She had made many friends. Joshua was most impressed by her commitment to serve God. He knew her heart was hungry for the truth.

Rahab turned away from watching Joshua. His shadow disappeared into the night. She looked at their temporary housing. It was not the shelter of a stone house built upon a wall, but she felt safer here than she had ever felt before. Her family was sleeping. The place was small, but sufficient. She had never known such peace. Her thoughts roamed once again to the words Joshua had read. Looking at her parents sleeping peacefully in each other's arms, she said a prayer of thanks to the only true God, who had delivered them all from certain death. As she prayed, she also considered gratefully the way her father's health was improving every day. It was true; there were no sick or feeble among God's people, and now even her own father improved daily. "Thank you, God," she whispered as she kissed the sweet face of her little sister sleeping on the floor. The soft tendrils of hair fell over her rosy cheeks. She watched the little ones as they lay innocently resting. "I can never thank you enough," she whispered to the one who always hears.

PLANS FOR WAR

> And it came to pass, when all the kings which were on this side Jordan, in the hills, and in the valleys, and in all the coasts of the great sea over against Lebanon, the Hittite, and the Amorite, the Canaanite, the Perizzite, the Hivite, and the Jebusite, heard thereof; That they gathered themselves together, to fight with Joshua and with Israel, with one accord. (Josh. 9:1–2, KJV)

The kings of the land were in turmoil. They had been so happy over the triumph of Ai; but now, there was anguish.

"I tell you, we must destroy these people!" The king of the Hittites was insistent.

"We cannot stand before them. We will be destroyed," replied the king of Canaan.

The Hittite king's face was livid with anger. "We can if we do it together." The king of the Hittites let his words sink into the ears of his listeners. Quietly, with the control of a man who had meticulously considered the options, he continued, "The Israelites have taken and utterly destroyed every nation that has stood in their path, from Egypt all the way to Ai. My spies have informed me that their God has promised to give them our lands. We have no choice but to fight these people. But we have many things on our side. First of all, we know the land. They have never before been here. Second, we are few if apart, but many if we join forces. And as for their God, who is He against all our gods? Sure, He was strong against the people before us; but if we are together, we will triumph, with the help of our gods, over Him."

Reluctantly all the kings had to admit they would be forced to fight. "This is a good plan." The king of the Amorites cast his vote. Soon they were all in agreement. "We will fight together. We will win together!"

News of the forthcoming battle reached the men of Gibeon. The kings of the Hittites, Amorites, Canaanites, Perizzites, Hivites, and Jebusites had decided—they would fight against the people of Israel. The men of Gibeon were expected to align with them since they were also Hivites. People were joining themselves to these kings from all over the land of Canaan.

The men of Gibeon, however, were not so happy. "We cannot go out against these people." The voice was one of wisdom. Everyone listened to the speaker very closely. He often counseled them. His words were wise and always true. "We will fall before their God. I am old. I will not have to go to battle, but my grandsons will, and they will die. I remember what happened to Egypt. Many of us remember. My son was only a boy, but he remembers also. Their God is mighty. He has proved Himself. He is the only true God. We will not stand before His power. I have seen and heard of His deeds myself. I know very well how He destroyed Sihon, king of Heshbon, and Og, king of Bashan. They too thought they could win, but they died, and their land was given to some of these people. I beg of you, listen to the words of an old man. We cannot win if we fight them. But I have an idea. I believe we can trick them." Murmurs went through the crowd of listeners.

"How, how can we do this? They will find us out and kill us for sure."

"No, no, listen!" The old man raised his hands to quiet the crowd. "It is true. It will be very dangerous, but if we fight them, we will die for sure. However, if we trick them and convince them to swear before their God, we may escape death. I will accompany a group of volunteers. We will go right into their camp, dressed as travelers from a far country." They listened as he explained, in detail, his plan.

Joshua and the people were camped at Gilgal. There had been a short time of rest since Ai. The men had divided up the spoil. The sun beat down on him as he went about his daily routine. It was still hours before sunset. Joshua was just about to take comfort in the shade of his tent when he saw it. There was a caravan of men riding toward camp. The sentry watched cautiously as the caravan drew closer. Joshua waited to see what the strangers wanted. They came quickly toward him. Smiling, they bowed humbly and began to introduce themselves.

Joshua watched them carefully, rising to look them over. He noticed their ragged clothing. The man speaking had holes in both of his shoes. Bringing his mind back to the speaker, he heard him say, "So, you see, sir, we have heard much about your people. We know your God has driven out all your enemies before you. We are here to congratulate you on your amazing victories. We represent our people. We have traveled a great distance. We desire peace. We are here to form an alliance with you."

Joshua stared in disbelief. "How do we know you aren't from around here? You may live near us, and if so, we can't possibly be allies."

The older man of the group began to speak. "Sir, just look at the way we are dressed. Our garments were new when we left our land, and now, look, they are old. Look at our shoes. They too were new." The gentleman walked over to his camel and took something from the pack. Holding it out, he showed Joshua and the elders some molded bread. "This was fresh when we started our journey. We have looked for you for some time."

In unison, the men of Gibeon spoke up: "We are from a far country."

"See sir"—he turned as he spoke, displaying once again his ruined food—"we have traveled far to find you."

Joshua was embarrassed. He felt somewhat awkward as he realized he had forced this kindly old gentleman to reveal his useless provisions.

"I am sorry." Joshua walked forward, taking the old man's arm to assist him. He said, "We have been so long in the desert I have forgotten my manners." Motioning to his servant, Joshua said, "Bring these gentlemen water to wash their feet." To the women nearby, he said, "Please set a table for our guests. We will eat and then talk business."

The face of the old man was transformed. He beamed as a smile warmed his face. Joshua did not know how happy his visitor really was. "You are too kind," he said as he leaned heavily on the arm of his new friend Joshua.

The evening progressed with dancing, singing, and all the food they could eat. Their guests looked at each other with a good deal of pleasure in their faces.

"You see, sirs,"—the gentleman was speaking to all the heads of the tribes, as well as Joshua—"we are a peaceable people. We have much respect for your God. Our fathers have all told us of His power in Egypt. This is a great day for all of us. We desire to be your friends. We are willing to even be your servants. We desire peace between you and us."

Joshua looked at the men. The spokesman was the old man's son. He was eloquent and looked very much like his father. One thing he had noticed was the respect all the men showed this older gentleman. Joshua liked that.

"Friends." Joshua spoke the words softly. "You must understand we have been commanded by our God to take all the land in front of us."

"Yes, yes, that's true," Othniel said. Othniel was a young prince of Judah. Joshua liked him very much. He showed great leadership and was a warrior of renown. Othniel continued, "But we don't have to fight these men. They have come in peace. I say we form an alliance with them."

Joshua listened as the other princes of Israel cast their votes in favor of the treaty.

Slowly he started to agree. "All right, we will be allies." Joshua laughed at the looks of relief he saw on the faces of his new friends. "We will have peace between your people and ours. We will not kill you. We will let you live." With this, all the princes of Israel agreed, swearing an oath. It was done. They had agreed before God. They would not go to war with the men of Gibeon. Even as they finalized their agreement, they did not think to ask guidance from the Lord. It was a few days before Joshua and the leaders of Israel received word they had been tricked.

"It can't be true!" Caleb paced back and forth, his long robes swaying with each long stride. Joshua sat listening, not ready to speak.

"It is true, sir. We saw it for ourselves." The two young men had just returned from spying out the land ahead. "They are our neighbors." Joshua took the news as though he had received a bad-tasting medicine. The words of his spies caused his mouth to pucker and his nose to curl.

Caleb was livid. "We should have known!" he said to Joshua.

"Yes!" Joshua answered at last. "We should have asked counsel of the Lord before ever giving our word."

The crowd was beginning to gather. Joshua raised his hands to quiet the questions. "I am afraid it is true. We have sworn to live in peace with some of the very same people the Lord commanded us to destroy."

Many of the people persisted. "What will we do?"

Joshua exhaled slowly. "Tonight we will sleep. Tomorrow we will go and see them." He dismissed the crowd. "Go home."

Caleb turned to his old friend. "What have we done?" The question stood there between them, neither knowing how to account for their mistake in judgment.

Three days later, Joshua came to the cities he had made peace with: Gibeon, Kephira, Beeroth, and Kiriath Jearim. The whole congregation of the Israelites were angry. Joshua did not attack. "We have sworn an oath to let them live. We cannot kill them." Joshua turned to Reuben. "Assemble some men. Go into Gibeon and bring me back the men we spoke with."

"Yes, sir." Reuben stepped back, signaled some others, and left. The Gibeonites bowed to Joshua and the leaders of the people. "Why did you lie to us?' Joshua looked at them in disgust. "You have cursed yourselves. You will always be servants in Israel." "Sirs," the old man started to speak. "We were told how your God had commanded his servant Moses to give you all the land and wipe out all the people of this country. We feared for our lives. That is why we did what we did. We are in your hands. Do whatever seems right to you."

Joshua looked at the men in front of him. "We have sworn an oath, and we cannot break it. But you will never be anything more than woodcutters and water carriers among us."

The men of Gibeon bowed again to Joshua. "We are your servants." That is when they became servants in Israel.

THE GIBEONITES

And the men of Gibeon sent unto Joshua to the camp to Gilgal, saying, Slack not thy hand from thy servants; come up to us quickly, and save us, and help us: for all the kings of the Amorites that dwell in the mountains are gathered together against us. (Josh. 10:6, KJV)

"Traitors, they are all traitors!" Adonizedek, king of Jerusalem, rose from his throne in anger. "The people of Gibeon will pay for this."

His servants watched him carefully. He was a man of temper, and no one wanted to face his brutal hand today. The spy who had just brought him the report watched nervously as Adonizedek began blasting orders. Anger gave way to fear as he realized the full impact of Gibeon's betrayal.

Speaking now to his counselors, he trembled at the thought. "If other people from nearby cities find out they have betrayed us this way, we are finished. No one will fight against this God of the Hebrews."

The servant trembled also. "Yes, sire, and everyone knows that the men of Gibeon are great warriors."

The king continued, "This city is critical to our success in defeating the people of Israel. Gibeon is one of the royal cities. If they are afraid to stand against Joshua and his men, we are doomed!"

Adonizedek lowered his voice, speaking to himself as if his servants were not there. "They must be punished." A sly wicked smile began to move over his face as he considered his options. "Call all the kings together." Laughing, he continued, "They betrayed us by refusing to fight these people who cover Canaan as locusts. But they will fight us. We will obliterate them. We will wipe them off the face of the earth!" Throwing his head back, he began to laugh in a loud, cold way that caused the hair on the back of the necks of the onlookers to stand up. "Well, what are you waiting for?" he bellowed. Quickly, the servants backed out of his presence. Alone now, he could plan the attack on Gibeon more efficiently.

Adonizedek, king of Jerusalem, sat shaded from the desert sun by a shelter his servants had quickly built for him. Hoham, king of Hebron, had arrived earlier that day. Five kings had formed an alliance. They waited now as the king of Jarmuth, the king of Lachish, and the king of Eglon gathered themselves together to go to war against Gibeon.

Panic struck Gibeon. The men of war lined the wall of the city, "What will we do?" The people pleaded with their wisest men for counsel. "We should not have made a league with Joshua!" One of the young men spoke the words everyone was thinking.

Rising to his feet, the wise old man, who seemed to always know what should be done, quieted the people. "My friends, you are wise to be concerned, but I beg of you do not let this frighten you. We have already sent several of our best runners after Joshua and his army. You must have patience. Joshua will not leave us here alone and defenseless to be murdered by these kings."

"How can you be sure?" The woman who had just asked the question looked beside herself with worry. "You yourself said Joshua was angry with us for tricking him. What's to stop him from letting this army do to us what he couldn't because of the treaty?"

He smiled patiently. The crowd, echoing their agreement, quieted enough to hear his answer: "Their God will stop them. They did not just say they would not kill us. They agreed we would be allies. They swore before their God. He will not allow them to forsake us. They are men of honor. When they give their word, they keep it. They will come." He was suddenly very tired. "My friends, be patient and offer prayers to this great God who rules all men. He will not forsake those who trust in Him. Joshua will come." Turning, he leaned heavily on his staff and slowly made his way home.

Joshua received the news of the Amorite's attack against Gibeon with stride. Since early morning runners from Gibeon, apparently sent out sporadically, had been arriving with news of the war. The word was the same: "Come quickly! Do not waste time! Save us! Help us! Your servants are under attack! All the kings of the Amorites have come to fight against us!"

Caleb was furious. "We are fools." His low, bass voice spoke with feeling.

Joshua looked at his friend. "Yes," he said. "We are fools. We failed to take counsel with the Lord concerning them, and now we are obligated to care for them as if they were our children." Fastening his sword into its sheath, he stopped and said, "I need time with God."

Caleb knew that look on Joshua's face. Sighing deeply, he said, "Of course, excuse me. I will go prepare the men."

Alone with God, Joshua spoke his heart. He poured out his soul in prayer for the safety of Gibeon and his own men. Guilt plagued him as he realized the position in which his arrogance had placed his men. "Holy God, forgive me for my failure to seek your guidance before making a league with these people." The peace he had sought filled him. Joshua, the man of war, was ready.

Joshua went up from Gilgal with his entire company of warriors. He brought all the men with him. No one stayed behind. They marched all night and came upon the enemy quickly.

> And the Lord said unto Joshua, Fear them not: for I have delivered them into thine hand; there shall not a man of them stand before thee. (Josh. 10:8, KJV)

The five kings of the Amorites sat comfortably, relaxing as they planned their attack on Gibeon. Adonizedek said, laughing with his friends, "We will attack tomorrow. They aren't going anywhere tonight." They said their good nights, and they all turned in. They would need to be fresh in the morning.

Joshua appeared from out of nowhere. There was confusion in the camp. One by one the kings were awakened to the sounds of disturbances outside their tents. As Adonizedek lifted his eyes toward the horizon, panic gripped him. "Who is this army?" he cried in disbelief.

"It is the army of Joshua," his commander answered.

There was little time to collect his thoughts as he saw his own troops thrust upon by this massive army of strangers.

The battle was hot. The kings were not prepared for this. Their men fought valiantly as they tried to stay alive. There was no escape. The men of Israel were too mighty for them.

Confused and frightened, the kings watched in horror as their men fell before Joshua. "We must escape!" they cried. Their army's began to retreat. They made their way toward Bethhoron.

The kings cried out in fear as the weather changed. "It's hailing!" The hail stones were so large they were killing their men.

Adonizedek gasped as the hail fell all around him. The storm was unlike anything he had ever seen.

Hoham, the king of Hebron, looked at his friends; fear and anguish were etched in their faces. He watched as men fell dead all around him, not from the sword of Joshua or his men. They were dying from the hailstones. He watched in horrified wonder as man after man dropped over, beaten to death by the enormous stones. "It is their God!" he shouted in agony of spirit. "We are doomed! We are doomed!"

Joshua was exhilarated. He knew God was fighting for Israel. More enemies were dying from the hailstones than the hands of his men. "We must not stop!" he shouted. "We have to pursue them till they are destroyed!" Looking up, he saw it was obvious; they would have to give up at nightfall. They could not pursue an enemy they could not see.

He remembered the words of the Lord. The Lord had promised victory! "We will not stop!" His heart pounded hard in his chest. His determination did not falter.

Joshua cried out to the Lord in the presence of all the people. "Oh sun, stand still over Gibeon. Oh moon, stand over the valley of Ajalon." So the sun stood still and the moon stopped until Israel had revenge against their enemies. That day the Lord listened to a man. The sun did not set, and the moon did not move. The Lord held them in place for about a day. That was one of the most unique days ever recorded.

The cave was a place of refuge for the kings. They were out of the storm and hidden from Joshua. Perhaps they would live through this battle. Adonizedek sat stone-still, worry marring his face. He could still hear the screams of his men as the hailstones struck them. He could not help noticing that not one stone had struck the army of Joshua. "Their God was God of all!"

"Someone's coming, hide!" King Hoham warned the others. The kings retreated farther into the cave, hiding behind some large rocks. The two men who looked around seemed satisfied, turned, and left. "They didn't see us." King Hoham watched their retreat.

As they watched them leave, all the kings breathed a sigh of relief. "We are safe for now." They could still hear the sounds of war in the distance.

The men of Israel fought the armies of the Amorites. They continued to pursue them till they had killed all the men, except a very few.

Aaron lowered his sword for the first time in hours. Sweat poured off his face. "Never have I seen such a thing." Looking up, he saw the sun begin to go down. He wiped his face with his sleeve. Everywhere he looked men were dead. He could not remember how many he had killed. He looked down at his sword. His hand ached from holding it. He massaged his arm, hoping his hand would relax. He placed his sword into its sheath. The muscles in his hand seemed frozen to it. He was more tired than he had ever been in his life. He had lived through several battles. This one was the worst. Joshua and the men took a moment to regroup. Joshua spoke clearly. "God has given us a great victory today. He fought with us and sent the hail. He extended the length of the day. He has given us our enemies, which he commanded us to destroy."

They were all tired but found the strength to return to their camp at Gilgal.

Joshua received word from two of his men: "The five kings of the Amorites have fled to a cave and are hiding there."

Joshua ordered, "Go to the cave. Seal it with some large rocks. I want guards posted outside the cave."

The battle had ended. The kings had peeked out of the cave long enough to watch as the army of Israel slowly left. Alone, they finally began to warm. The storm had left them cold and damp. Fear of being discovered kept them from lighting a fire. Now, at last, they sat, warming themselves by the fire. "Joshua is gone. Tomorrow we will leave before he returns." Finally, exhaustion overcame them, and they slept fitfully.

"What was that?" Hoham awoke to the sound of men. The others were also aware of the intruders. Piram, king of Jarmuth, sneaked slowly back farther into the cave. Suddenly they knew what was happening. The cave was being sealed up with them inside!

"It is our tomb!" The king of Eglon said as he ran to the opening of the cave, but it was sealed.

They looked at each other. "There is no way out!"

After Joshua was finished, he commanded his men to open the mouth of the cave and bring out the five kings. Joshua told the mighty men of war, "Do not be afraid. Come place your foot on the necks of these kings." So the men did as he told them, and they placed their feet on the necks of the kings. Joshua said, "This is what God will do to all your enemies you fight." Then he killed them and hung them. At the end of the day, he had their bodies taken down, thrown into the cave, and the cave sealed up. Later Joshua and his army pursued the people of the land and destroyed them and their cities, taking the country, as the Lord had promised.

The people of Gibeon stood dumbfounded. They had watched the most spectacular battle. The men of Joshua had shown up just in time. They could not believe the sight as boulders of hail fell from the sky, pounding their enemies. Even though it was cold from the storm, beads of sweat had formed and worked its way down the face of the guards as they recognized God was fighting for Joshua and the Israelites. There on their perch from the walls of the city. They had frontrow seats to the whole scene. Their hearts pounded as they watched the army of Joshua destroy the army of the kings. Trembling with disbelief, they were frozen in horrified amazement as the sun stood still. They recognized the wisdom of the old man as they watched Joshua and his men pursue this army relentlessly. This scene before them would have been their own fate. They were very happy they had made friends with Joshua and his men.

The old man lay peacefully on his bed, hearing the sound of the not-so-distant war. Joshua was there to fight for them. He smiled to himself. All those he loved were safe. It had been an unusually difficult few days. Tired but comforted by the presence of his friend, he fell asleep.

33

VICTORY

And these are the countries which the children of Israel inherited in the land of Canaan, which Eleazar the priest, and Joshua the son of Nun, and the heads of the fathers of the tribes of the children of Israel, distributed for inheritance to them. (Josh. 14:1, KJV)

Jabin, the king of Hazor, sat breathless as he listened to the report of the battle between the five kings of the Amorites and the children of Israel. "These people are a plague upon the land! Everywhere they go leads to destruction! They destroyed Egypt. Now they have come into Canaan to destroy us!"

His spies continued their report. "Their God is like no other. He fights for them. He sent hailstones to beat the soldiers to death. We have several eyewitness accounts from those who escaped. They tell us that the general spoke to his God, asking his God to not let the sun go down. "Sire"—the gentleman speaking cleared his throat—"these people say the sun did not go down."

King Jabin exclaimed, "What? Are you as crazy as these fools who come running to me for my protection? Do you honestly believe their God has the power to make the sun stand still? Who is this God? I do not know Him. Where did He come from?"

Fear griped the hearts of his servants. "Sire, their God is very powerful. He literally destroyed Egypt with one plague after another. He turned the water into blood, even the great Nile. He also rained down hail at that time, destroying the crops and devastating Egypt!"

Jabin, the king, leaned back, thinking. "Okay, so we must find a way to fight these people and their God. Call my soothsayers and enchanters. Bring in all my counselors. I will enlist the aid of all our neighbors. Let's see what Joshua and his men can do against an army that covers the land like sand on the seashore." His laugh was low and harsh, the anger he felt far outweighing his fear. "The kings of the Amorites underestimated Joshua. I will not make the same mistake. Send my best runners with this message to all the kings of the surrounding territory.

> Greetings, my friends,
>
> It is with great sorrow and deep concern I come to you today. I have just received word that the military efforts of our dear friends and neighbors did not go well. As you well know, they were valiant men alone, and together they were a massive military presence. However, my spies tell me they were devastated by this army from the wilderness. They cover the land and are moving toward us like locusts. Alone I fear the worst, but together we are an insurmountable force. Let us come together as friends to fight these people and destroy them from off the earth. I believe our very existence is at stake!
>
> Sincere regards,
> King Jabin

Jabin looked out across the land at the army marching toward them. Something had been bothering him. King Jobab, the king of Madon, and the others were not as certain of their victory as he was. In fact, king Jobab was quite sure they would all die. Jobab continued with his list of all the great deeds of this God these people worshipped. He reminded everyone there of what this God did to Egypt and how he knew for a fact this God had parted the Red Sea and also the Jordan.

"So," Jabin exclaimed. "You speak as if we have already lost this battle! I believe if we fight these men with all our might, we will conquer these people once and for all."

The other kings started to argue. "They have completely destroyed mighty kings."

King Jabin continued, "Don't you understand. This is for our very existence as a people. They are determined to wipe us off the earth. They kill everyone—man, woman, and child—in their path. They will not take my land without a fight!" Jabin was crazed with determination.

"Yes," all the kings agreed. "They will have to take our land with the blood of their own men. We will not give it to them."

Jobab agreed. He would fight. However, he already knew the outcome—they would lose.

Rahab was waiting for news of Joshua and the army. She understood they were standing against the whole land of Canaan in this battle. It seemed as though every king in the world was fighting Israel. She prayed for her newfound people.

She was also concerned with the welfare of one soldier in particular, Salmon. He had become very important to her in a short period of time. After the battle of Achor, she tended his wounds. He had no family. Joshua asked her to care for him until he was better. At first she just obeyed Joshua. But as time went by, she found herself going to look after him just because she wanted to see him. He asked Joshua if she could marry him. He was

Joshua's first choice for her out of all her suitors. Joshua told her he thought Salmon would be a good husband. All she knew was, for the first time in her life, she loved a man, and he loved her.

Joshua came upon the kings and their army quickly. Jabin and the others were surprised by the speed of this army. Joshua encouraged the men before battle. The Lord spoke to him and told him, "don't be afraid. Tomorrow they will be dead. Cripple their horses. Then burn their chariots."

The battle did not go well for the kings. King Jabin screamed and started to flee. "Run for your lives!" King Jabin ran. "Retreat, everyone, retreat!" Fear swallowed him up. His eyes searched wildly for some answer. What had he said about this God? His heart melted. "I must hide!" He whipped his chariot horses as hard as he could. He ran toward safety.

Two men stood together, fighting. They had fought so many battles side by side. They worked as one, anticipating each other's needs, guarding each other. Back to back, side to side, Aaron and Reuben used their swords on the enemies of the Lord. Then they saw him, the coward, running for his life. Quickly they jumped on two nearby horses. They chased down the king.

King Jabin realized, too late, he was in trouble. He shifted to toss his javelin at Aaron. He never saw the sword of Reuben.

Joshua captured Hazor and killed its king. The Israelites destroyed all life in the city. Then Joshua burned the city. So Joshua took control of the entire land just as the Lord had instructed Moses. He gave it to the people of Israel as their special possession, dividing the land among the tribes. So the land finally had rest from war.

Rahab married Salmon. They were blessed with their son Boaz. He was the great-grandfather of King David.

Joshua divided up the land and gave it to the children of Israel just as the Lord God had promised them, just as He had promised their fathers before them. He fulfilled His covenant with Abraham.

The nation of Israel was born. God fulfilled His promise. The Lord spoke to Israel through Joshua and reminded them of His faithfulness to them. God asked only that they serve Him and put away their false gods. Joshua stood and made one of the greatest proclamations of all time. He announced in the presence of all of Israel this statement:

> And if it seem evil unto you to serve the Lord, choose you this day whom ye will serve; whether the gods which your fathers served that were on the other side of the flood, or the gods of the Amorites, in whose land ye dwell: but as for me and my house, we will serve the Lord. And the people answered and said, God forbid that we should forsake the Lord, to serve other gods. (Josh. 24:15–16, KJV)

In the generations that followed, Israel became a super-power—the richest, most influential nation on earth at that time. King David rose to the throne as God had promised him. This beloved leader followed God and led his nation to great victories, leaving behind a legacy of peace for Solomon, his son.

King Solomon, the wisest man of all time, ruled and governed his nation during the best of times. He built the temple of the Lord, leaving behind his great legacy of wisdom for all of mankind to study in the books of Proverbs, Song of Solomon, and Ecclesiastes.

Israel has contributed to the world the greatest gift of all—Jesus Christ— the son of God, as well as the Bible. This precious Word of God was maintained for the benefit of all mankind by the people of Israel.

The Lord promised Abraham three things: (1) that his children would be as the sands of the sea or the stars of heaven in number, (2) that God would give Abraham's children the land of Canaan for their inheritance always, and (3) that through

Abraham's seed all the nations of the earth would be blessed. As was foretold by the prophets, out of the descendants of Abraham came Jesus Christ the Messiah.

I praise God that He gave us His Son, as it says in John 3:16, KJV:

> For God so loved the world, that he gave his only begotten Son, that whosoever believeth in him should not perish, but HAVE EVERLASTING LIFE.